Annabel Lomas

Stephanie Johnson is the author of several collections of poetry and of short stories, and many fine novels. *The New Zealand Listener* commented that 'Stephanie Johnson is a writer of talent and distinction. Over the course of an award-winning career — during which she has written plays, poetry, short stories and novels — she has become a significant presence in the New Zealand literary landscape, a presence cemented and enhanced by her roles as critic and creative writing teacher.' *The Shag Incident* won the Montana Medal for Fiction in 2002, and *Belief* was shortlisted for the same award. Stephanie has also won the Bruce Mason Playwrights Award and Katherine Mansfield Fellowship. Some of her novels have been published in Australia, America and the United Kingdom. She co-founded the Auckland Writers' Festival with Peter Wells in 1999.

THE WRITERS' FESTIVAL

Happy Birthday
Claire

STEPHANIE JOHNSON

... and from the Wanaka Writers
with lots of love X

VINTAGE

UK | USA | Canada | Ireland | Australia
India | New Zealand | South Africa | China

Vintage is an imprint of the Penguin Random House group of companies,
whose addresses can be found at global.penguinrandomhouse.com.

Penguin
Random House
New Zealand

First published by Penguin Random House New Zealand, 2015

1 3 5 7 9 10 8 6 4 2

Cover and text design by Carla Sy © Penguin Random House
New Zealand

Cover photograph by Peopleimages.com/gettyimages

Author photograph by Annabel Lomas

Printed and bound in Australia by Griffin Press,
an Accredited ISO AS/NZS 14001 Environmental
Management Systems Printer

A catalogue record for this book is available from the
National Library of New Zealand.

ISBN 978 1 77553 798 4
eISBN 978 1 77553 799 1

ARTS COUNCIL OF NEW ZEALAND TOI AOTEAROA

The assistance of Creative New Zealand towards the
production of this book is gratefully acknowledged by
the author and the publisher.

penguinrandomhouse.co.nz

For A.S.J., with love

'I know not any thing more pleasant, or more instructive, than to compare experience with expectation, or to register from time to time the difference between the idea and reality.'

SAMUEL JOHNSON
FROM *THE LIFE OF SAMUEL JOHNSON, LL.D*, BY JAMES BOSWELL

'There is only one correct and accurate interpretation of history, and only one explanation that is closest to the truth. There is a pool of clear water, and there's no need to stir up this water. Doing so can only cause disturbance in people's minds.'

XIA CHUNTAO
FROM *THE PARTY FOREVER: INSIDE CHINA'S MODERN COMMUNIST ELITE*, BY ROWAN CALLICK

JANUARY

A writer

In January he gets on a flight and they let him go. There is no sudden boarding of the plane while it sits still on Chinese soil, no dragging down long corridors to beatings in closed rooms; there will be no gang of thugs to meet him in Taiwan or Hong Kong to administer the punishment he has endured so many times.

He's free. He knows it as he's never let himself know it before. He is as free as the rest of the world will allow him to be. He has received invitations already to speak at literary festivals in the West, in America, in Europe, in Oceania, at those extraordinary occasions when the world's writers in all combinations meet and mingle and talk to enormous audiences, sometimes numbering in their thousands. Where writers take to the stage singly or in groups and are politely questioned about their work. When challenges and queries rise from the floor and are met with good humour from the stage, without fear. One invitation is from a country he has heard very little about, a country so far away that he has never before entertained any notion of it. It is the last country, he understands, ever to be added to the map of the world. The very last. And even there they have writers' festivals.

There were people in that country, a few, who wrote letters and raised money to save him, but mostly salvation came from Europe. He is leaving now because of his German friends and admirers, who put pressure on their own government to get involved. Is he being watched? Someone behind him, or on the other side of the aisle, could be watching his reflection in the double-paned sleet-flecked window. Read the story it tells you, he thinks. Read my fiction written on the glassy page: I'm leaving without a backward glance, and Germany has been forever my favoured exile.

But his heart is aching, burning under his ribs, trembling with the vibration of the warming engines. When the plane begins to taxi he thinks only that he is leaving his elderly mother, that he will never again visit his young wife's grave or the resting places of his daughter, his brother. He will soon be the only one living, and now he goes to live somewhere else.

The life he would have had if they'd left him alone passes before him in a flash, as they say real life does when you're dying. The now impossible imagined life. He sees how he would have stayed on in his tiny Beijing flat, doing what he had always done, living as frugally as possible while he recorded the ordinary existences around him, giving them a simple dignity, a reality, sating an appetite in the West for true tales of China. He would have travelled again, as he had so many times this past decade, and he feels himself lift out across this vast ancient land spreading around this tiny reverberating plane speeding across the frozen tarmac. He would have travelled even more inside China than before, into Tibet and Mongolia, collecting lives and writing about them, giving them possible eternity in prose or verse.

And he would have been arrested yet again, and this time possibly killed. Shot. Left to starve.

They're letting him go. This time. Even though he is an enemy of the state and lucky to have all his fingers and toes and his eyesight still functioning, though failing now in middle age. He has no swollen knuckles or missing nails, or electrode burns or bruises or fractured bones.

They're letting him go. He's free.

The director

Freedom is something Rae thinks a lot about these days, as she goes from one address to another, *boing boing, boing boing*, five days a week, from one type of chaos to another. In each place there is an unholy mess, one confined to a desk and small space in an open-plan office, the other filling an entire house. Both seem, at this moment, on this midsummer Friday morning, insurmountable.

Boing boing, boing boing, she goes, from one address to another, repeatedly, five days a week. Where is the freedom in that?

What if, now that she has dropped off the children at Holiday Care, what if she were to turn her wheels towards the motorway and join the million or so others on their crowded commute, but to go the other way — *against the traffic*, as they say, though the traffic goes every which way, up and down, round and round. She would go against some of it. From an overbridge she sees the gridlock glinting below, most cars with a solo occupant grinding and halting their way from distant faubourgs to newly built satellite business districts, from central towerblock apartments to far-flung industrial estates. A million commutes longer and more stressful than hers, which is only across two leafy gentrified suburbs to join an arterial road, and two blocks east from there. Twenty minutes. Three sets of traffic lights. Half an hour if the traffic is heavy.

Half an hour to listen to the news, an unnecessary outmoded habit since she mainlines it all day, a hundred Google alerts to bring to her notice any literary matters stirring in the wider world. Several times a day she finds herself reading also accounts of murder and mayhem, global unrest and freak weather until she turns away from the computer to pick up one of the hundreds of books sent by publishers and literary agents, which is generally calming, no matter the subject. It's as if the deep concentration the writer needed to write the book somehow passes from the pages through her hands and into her body, stilling her anxieties.

Boing, boing. Back and forth, office, home, office, home, office, home, office as if she's caught in a giant rubber band, or one of Nellie's pink fluffy hair elastics. The weekends widen to a trip to the supermarket, to deadly hours at the cricket pitch while Ned's team loses another game — little inner-city softies, paler and thinner than less privileged teams bent on winning. And on Saturday nights, drinks with friends.

Yay! Drinks with friends, most like her, with young families and demanding jobs. Yay for drinks! Too many drinks, mostly.

Regular oblivion. A problem.

The wide streets, the stirring shops, the emptying houses, the sunburned gardens, the bus stops full of school kids, the franchised cafés open since six, the foreign-owned supermarket open all night, the Asian two-dollar shops, dog walkers, the city workers, the suicidal cyclists, the heat, the traffic, the traffic, the traffic, the heat.

What if she were to hit the road south of the city, leaving it all far behind? She would drive until the lake of her childhood holidays opened up before her, the mountains behind summer-gaunt and grey as they would be at this time of year, the winter snows months away yet. The lake would be at its best in the autumn. The waters chill and deep. Morning mists and leaf fall. See you in the fall, an American writer had said once, a few years ago, when she'd finally got hold of him by telephone, since he didn't respond to emails. Didn't do them at all. Was famous for it. Then. Surely you've succumbed by now, John Freeman. At the first set of lights she rummages in her handbag and digs out a neglected notebook, finds the words copied from his *The Tyranny of Email*: '. . . by its sheer volume we are forced to talk in short bursts, we are slowly eroding our ability to explain — in a careful, complex way — why it is so wrong for us and to complain, resist, or redesign our workdays so that they are manageable.'

Some of us, she thinks, will welcome the microchip implant to save time finger-tapping. How lucky he was to have thrown it off all those years ago. Freeman was trans-Atlantic, dividing his time between London and New York, and would make frequent flights back and forth, reading and sleeping, watching movies, eating, drinking, perhaps composing a letter or two on his laptop to print out later and post. It occurs to Rae, as she continues on her way to work, that he could enjoy on a plane the kind of peace people used to find in a church, sitting in rows, all facing forward, intent on the same destination. Would he remember her from New York? Perhaps she could invite him to her festival, if he'd like to come this far, if he'd relish the minimum two-day flight.

But his book is dated now. Pre-Facebook. Pre-social networking. Pre-relentless connection. His protest is quaint, antiquated. The world spins by so fast.

Slow down!

More traffic lights. Columns of traffic turning towards a major onramp. In the car next to her, an elderly woman white-knuckles the steering wheel, and Rae thinks of her mother, who rang last night. Has rung nearly every night since Dad died, the sound of the landline phone pealing through the house just as they've sat down to dinner. Almost her own private phone, these days, the only person they know who still uses it. Even the kids ignore it; it is as outmoded as Rae's grandmother's cast-iron mincer, as the set of Arthur Mee's *Encyclopaedia for Children* they'd found at Aunty Merle's.

'Hello Mum,' Rae always says, as soon as she picks it up.

Last night she told her, 'I'm never alone, I'm never not *communicating* with someone. I'm going crazy!' Moaned on. About how she texted people from the toilet seat, how she took phone calls in the shower, how she now had a voice-activated virtual assistant app so she could make phone calls while she was driving, how at this stage of the festival she could in a single day send a hundred emails. Literally a hundred. She moaned to her mother who has few friends left alive, who could be the last person on earth to have only a landline phone and a wooden letterbox.

Her mother had said, 'That's daft.'

Oh, for Godsake get a grip.

And she does. Drives on through the streets of this particular part of the free world until she reaches the old industrial building — a one-time wool store — that has been reincarnated to hold a dozen arts organisations. Arm out the window of her battered Toyota, the parking card swiped, she turns into the basement, parks the car, hurries towards the lift, up to the second floor and first in to the office. Lights on, across the polished concrete floor to the corner, flick the screen to life, and wish for a takeaway coffee. Hot and airless. Midsummer.

Oh, to be at the beach.

In the chair, heavily, and open an email from the Chinese writer, or from the man who helps him communicate in English. At long last! A slight lift in Rae's endorphins, which lately have not been as robust as they ought to be.

```
Dear Rae McKay,

Thank you for your invitation to speak
at the Oceania Writers' Festival in
June. Liu Wah would be delighted to
attend. Please forward all future
communications to this address.

Mr Liu arrived in Berlin a week ago
and is starting to settle in. He sends
you his best wishes and would like you
to know he is very grateful for your
invitation.

Best regards,
Gert Richter
PEN International
```

Another piece of the puzzle filled. Race a reply across the screen, enthusiastic and grateful. Send. Open up the document that holds the list of acceptances so far to add Liu Wah, reading first through the names luminary and obscure, the two columns, and with them comes the potent mix of dread and anticipation. How will it all come together? Will it work? It's like planning a vast and expensive dinner party. Who should talk to whom? Who is likely to get along, or not? How can she predict, anyway? It's not as if any of the writers will be reading a common script to show the punters how much fun they're having.

The first name belongs to a British woman crime writer, this one as good as they come — ex-Army Command, tough, Thatcherish in appearance, with pearls and bleached hair, and sales figures around eleven million. She is head judge of this year's Opus Book Prize, and the festival is hosting the awards ceremony.

And the South American magic realist, one of the last surviving of the old guard, who had stood shoulder to shoulder with Gabriel García Márquez and Mario Vargas Llosa. Elderly now, but still stealing hearts around the world with his meltsome eyes, flowing moustache and mellifluous voice — or apparently so, there was something about a publicist in Sydney. And someone in Vancouver. And a publisher's assistant in Bali. He is a legendary lover.

Then there's the mid-forties Australian memoirist and novelist, balding, charming, fast-talking and back on track with his first book in over a decade, a sexy rural saga. Father of six and recently married for the fifth time to a startlingly talented young poetess, or so he impressed upon Rae in his early correspondence, and so she invited her along as well, to be sporting.

Next the latest marvellous magic to come out of India — but actually a local, since Adarsh Z. Kar grew up here, having left Fiji as a baby a year after the coup. The young writer's first novel, out last year to enormous acclaim, a gay Hindu love story, a break-through.

And thinking of Adarsh, one of Merle's old students, makes Rae remember that she had said she'd visit Merle after work on Friday, which is today, with the kids, and maybe have takeaways for tea. Aunty Merle's, where there is a new tree hut in the grapefruit tree and a slithery, licky puppy to replace the old stinker that finally died. Why'd she arrange that? She is getting in too deep with her, and she really doesn't have the time. First cousins once removed are not so close a relationship that you have to have any sense of duty. Bugger Mum, who told Merle that having her grandchildren every day after school *knocked the stuffing out of her*. And of course Mum's cousin Merle had offered to look after Nellie and Ned so they didn't have to go into paid after-school care, and had done since then quite a bit, being clucky for grandchildren of her own and the only likely source still single and living abroad. Did the kids know about the arrangement for tonight? Had she told them? If she hadn't, then perhaps she could wriggle out of it and go home and collapse with a bottle of wine.

And thinking of Merle brings the other ex-student to mind — two in one year, even though Merle had told her it was a long time between drinks — Tosh Hendrix, which is surely a pseudonym. His novel in verse, *Mother Fucker*, was on everyone's lips a few months ago, broken through the barriers. 'White Mother Fucker, White Mother Fucker.' A character on the favourite prime-time soap had recited the famous stanza and the All Blacks had taken an inoffensive line for their promotions. His book had come out last year, and he had debuted at the festival. This year he would be back, with new material as yet unpublished, and supported by the brothers who are also writing rap novels. A whole new genre! Not many festival artistic directors could boast of that.

Then there was the most recent Booker Prize winner, from Ghana, a man who had once worked for the UN; and a lesbian poet/comedian/film-maker from Canada, and an economist from Taiwan, a mythic epic poet from Norway, a religious historian from Istanbul, a political scientist from Croatia, a marine biologist from Japan, and twenty other names she sweeps her eye over. Just as soon as the shortlist for the Opus is announced, then those writers will be invited too, as well as the international judges. There is a huge buzz that goes with hosting the Opus — all kinds of associated parties flying in.

She's quietly, privately, mighty proud. It's fantastic. What a feast! At the last board meeting she was roundly congratulated — and she feels delighted, she truly does, very pleased with herself, sitting here now at her desk. Only her second year in the job — only her second back in her hometown, for Godsake, since she and Cameron returned from five years in America. One thing had led to the other. If her father hadn't fallen ill and if she hadn't at the same time realised just how much harder life in New York was going to be with two children rather than one, it wouldn't have happened. If she had stopped with Ned and not had Nellie, then they could still be there — Rae working for New York Book Week and Cameron a big whale cryptographing for PRISM. His new job developing programs for the local branch of Serco, as he never ceases to remind her, is a step down. How could it not be a slide, a cataclysmic fall from designing global security systems to screwing prison administration costs down to the bottom line? He reassures himself that by replacing human prison warders with complex computer systems the job will be better done, and there is the other advantage to the company of assembling and collecting data from one of the biggest per capita prison populations on the planet.

Rae's job, though modestly paid, is most definitely a promotion.

'Don't you miss New York?' friends still ask her, and she will say, 'It's better here for the children,' or 'Cameron misses it more than me,' or 'My mother is very glad we've come home.'

On occasion, during the first year, depending on her hormones, or how drunk she was, or whether or not Cameron was ever interested in sex, which he mostly wasn't even though he knew it kept her sane and on the level and that he should oblige more often, to stop her straying yet again, she would wail, 'Ye-e-es!' And there would follow a moment of deep embarrassment, or more usually a too-intimate conversation with someone she barely knew, or else with a friend who was having worse problems and so almost cancelled out her own, because a sense of dislocation on homecoming is piss-nothing. The friend could be failing on an impossible mortgage, or could have a kid with cancer, or be in the midst of a divorce, or long-term unemployed, and there you are whinging on like a baby-boomer who doesn't know how good she's got it.

Google the Ghanaian and search for an image to go with his publicity pack. He's certainly very handsome. Fabulous jaw. Kind, clever eyes.

At least there are fewer opportunities for wickedness here than there were in New York. People — the people she knows here —

behave themselves, pretty much. Life is duller, but less stressful and healthier, and all because of two contemporary cultural phenomena that shape this very positive turn in her life. The first is that despite predictions of the death of the book for about thirty years — almost her entire lifetime so far — the world is aglitter with book festivals. People queue to hear writers speak, to buy the written word, to luxuriate in fine minds. To taste the work of many writers and then decide whose work they will read, whose work will claim those hours of their lives.

The second phenomenon is antipodean cultural cringe, still alive and kicking nearly two hundred years into the postcolonial period, which makes her the girl for the job, no matter how many others applied with CVs loaded with local experience. And there had been a few, a couple of them women friends of Merle's, all much older than Rae. Women who'd been stalwarts of various other arts organisations, off and on the government payroll local and national, or some with their own business or history in the publishing industry. One of them, Ripeka, had taken the consolation prize of becoming the director of the Fringe, and for Rae's first year in the job had slandered her around the town, which was small enough for some of it to come to Rae's ear. 'What were they thinking?' asked Ripeka of anyone who'd listen. 'An administrative assistant for New York Book Week! What does she know about the local scene? She's only in her thirties! She tells people she's a *ferocious reader*!'

But Rae was definitely in line for a promotion. The references were glowing.

'You only got it on your connections,' Cameron had said by way of congratulations the day after she'd had the phone call. 'I hope you don't disappoint them.'

Remembering this, as she often does when overwhelmed — she still has writers to finalise and about a hundred chairpeople to find, and she still has to write copy for almost the entire programme — chills her heart, leaves her unforgiving but also tougher, able to cope with anything. When you truly love someone, don't you go out into the world with him in spirit, and imagine his day, who he talks to and how his hours unfold? Don't you have a curiosity about how life is for him? She hardly thinks about Cameron and is pretty sure the psychic abandonment is mutual.

'They don't pay you enough,' he likes to say, and 'Do you know what time it is?' when she's talking to an agent or writer or publisher on the other side of the world, 'When are you going to turn that thing off?' when she puts in the last screen-glowing hours at night, and 'How can you bear to work for such a stripped-down organisation?'

Certainly it's stripped down today, with Martin Marketing and Sponsorship at a meeting with a patron or media outlet, and Orla Festival Director probably gone along too because, as she cheerfully confesses, she's a Type A personality and never knows when to butt out. The fact she's not here is a blessing, because the moment she is she'll want to talk about ballooning expenditure on internationals' airfares, go on and on in that annoying Irish-smirish voice, behave as if the festival is short of cash and up against the wall. Which, just now, it isn't.

'You can't put the cart before the horse, young Rae.'

Rae is older than she is, by five years. Orla has just turned thirty.

There's a courier at the Festival Office door with a box of books for Gareth Heap, the only local judge for the Opus Prize.

'A mistake,' she tells the guy, and has him wait while she finds the correct address. 'Don't know why it's come here. This is where you'll find him.'

After he's gone, Rae makes herself a coffee, makes lists for the next three days, and starts on the budget spreadsheet, her own version, which she will take to the next board meeting for general comparison. They've got to find the money for three more writers who all want to fly business class and bring their spouses. A spreadsheet with written analysis will contain the facts, and Orla will just have to deal with it.

A writer

Why on earth has he agreed to be a shortlist judge for the Opus Prize? As he takes delivery of another carton of books, Gareth is suddenly terrified. With shaking hand he signs the electronic doodad, while the courier leans against the doorjamb with his mouth open, gasping. A fat bloke about his age, forty-something, would have lugged it up two flights of stairs, and Gareth should offer him a glass of water, and he would, but he finds himself isolated from his fellow man by a tsunami of reading and assessment. An international book prize. More of a terrifying climb than teaching writing; a steeper, lengthier continuum of constant evaluation than straight marking ever is. He won't be able to read the novels in the way he likes to read for pleasure — that is, to let the words wash over him, to carry him away, to send his critical faculties into outer space, to read only for sensation, to allow the writer to conjure him into another world. To forgive any sin, any clunky imprecision, any unbelievable character as long as it's minor, as long as the writer gets him there.

Although he can't be completely indiscriminate — he could never read those pulp writers who make millions, the droning Dan Browns and Bryce Courtenays and Di Morrisseys.

Only if they were the last books left on earth. Even then.

Never read shit.

Is this shit? The other extreme? Literary squirty shit? Pretty hefty for a batch of only five or six books, and until the last Booker he had thought the fashion for fat novels was passing. His own forthcoming is just shy of ninety thousand words and every genial page a marvel of sparse and lyrical prose. Here's hoping.

In the kitchen he dumps the box on the table and takes his Swiss army knife to the slippery plastic tape wrapped around and around — and then he's nicked his finger and has to go in search of a Band-Aid, a search he gives up immediately he spies a tea towel. A fat summer fly rises from it as he grabs it up off the bench, and noisily circles above his head. Horsefly? Where are the identifying white specks, the intricate details he should be able to see at a distance, though anything close blurs? Glasses. Good ones. He can afford them now. He should buy some. He narrows his eyes.

No white specks. You used to see horseflies until the hosts themselves got further and further away as the city spread out, pushing away the paddocks and pony clubs and horse shit. Maybe it's a native fly, thinks Gareth. Sometimes the females of that species forget to oviposit in time, and will explode mid-air in a mass of tiny wriggling maggots as they're buzzing over food. He wishes this one would explode. He's never seen it happen. It must be gross. Maybe it's not even true, one of those useless pieces of information that is so useless you doubt its veracity.

The fly helicopters unbursting towards the window and strikes against it, a soft audible bump. In the corner, the spider Gareth encourages as insect control shifts in her web. Jacinta, mid-summer fat.

Tea towel in a nifty knot, he wields the knife again, and eventually the box is agape. Six volumes swim in toxic squashy white foam beads. Lots of men: good, a welcome relief. Hopefully not all of them angry or whinging tub-thumpers for some cause or other. One or two look more like aspirants to his own tribe, some of the writers he was compared to with his first novel, and others he's always worshipped, the likes of Jonathan Franzen, Richard Ford, Tim Winton, David Malouf, Ian McEwan. Julian Barnes, at a pinch. Colum McCann. Cormac McCarthy. Margaret Atwood. Percival Everett. You've got to be representative.

Will they surprise him? Oh, for the startling depravity of Michel Houellebecq or Charles Bukowski, or early Will Self and Irvine Welsh! Or even the quietly intricate unfolding of Richard Powers. Will there be any like that? Pushing whatever shaky boundaries remain? How blissful it would be to just pick a couple at random and climb out the kitchen window to the fire escape rusting three feet above the reflective roof of the next-door warehouse, climb out with a coffee, and read the way he likes to. 'And if I be a man of some reading, yet I am a man of no remembering,' said de Montaigne. To remember only what really struck him, to sit out there above the roasting shiny roof, half steamed alive, a human dim sum, sweaty and porky, especially if he's been into the takeaways. Spice and garlic exuding through his skin. He could sit out there now in the January oven and heat up. At this time of year it would be hot. Sizzling. He weighs a thick hardback, cool and shiny. A good read. Coffee. His sunhat. Escape.

Immm. Delicious . . .

But the human Jacinta is due at any second to collect the last of her things and he would only be interrupted, which he does not like. Interruptions make him bad tempered, which he must not be, because it would demonstrate that he is engaging with her, that he is seeking and receiving an emotional response, which he must not do. At all. His counsellor has made him write the resolve down to make it *incontrovertible*.

I will not engage with Jacinta on an emotional level.

'Just in and out, a few things,' she'd said.

He supposes, as he gazes out the window at a plume of white steam lifting from an air-conditioning duct on the drycleaner's roof, that she could be so insensitive as to bring the twins with her, since she most often has the care of both of them now her ex-husband has returned from Europe. A sensible person would leave them behind with a sensible person to look after them. But Jacinta is not sensible.

What could he have been thinking to get involved with her in the first place, two years ago? He must have been insane. Insane with the delight of being able to write again after a long block, a heady delirium that turned him inside out and upside down and flung him into the arms of a beautiful, selfish and vain woman who could have destroyed him. At its giddy peak he even chucked in his job teaching creative writing, and at his departure the department had seen fit to restructure. It was a progression common to many creative writing departments around the free world. CW reached a critical mass, so got divorced from the dying English Department and became attached to a thriving new department called Creative Theory. A PhD was imported from UCLA, a humourless, virtually unpublished postmodernist who decided against renewing the contracts of teaching staff without qualifications in CW.

Poor old Merle, put out to grass for lack of letters after her name. The theorist versus the practitioner. A struggle unto death.

He hadn't meant to have such an effect on other people's lives. He really hadn't meant to. He should get in touch with his old colleague, but the impulse is quashed, as usual, by the worry that she will hold him somehow responsible for the loss of her position. Her income. Oh God, the guilt, but he had to. Get out of the job. And then out of the relationship. The other day he'd remarked to his half-brother how he could see why they'd made the rule you shouldn't fuck your students, since a teacher has a long distance to fall, being at least partly mythologised in the lover's mind as a wise man. A man worth of Respect. Almost as bad as a doctor fucking his patient.

His half-brother had said, 'Get over yourself.'

A rowdy helicopter, a real one, arrives to hover a block or two away, visible between two multi-storeyed buildings on the near horizon. Perspective makes it only marginally bigger than the fly, the rotor spinning silver in the bright sun, before it speeds away into the blue, towards the harbour. Police or tourists, crimebusters or sightseers? I should do that too, thinks Gareth. A helicopter ride. Glasses, dentist, and some of the money on a helicopter ride. A high, darting flight above this city I've spent my entire dreary fucking life in.

High in the window the fly bumps perilously close to the web.

Ten minutes till the ex-love of his life appears, or more precisely the love of six months of it. Six months of love and laughter and more sex than he could shake a stick at, so much sex that he had stinging friction speed stripes on either side of his dick. Then there was the eleven months of trying to get her to move out, until she went, quite suddenly, one afternoon, another place all organised and she hadn't breathed a word. He would have moved out himself but for a handy, easy inheritance that had come at the right time, just when he was removed enough from Jacinta not to tell her about it. He even gave up drinking for a while so that he wouldn't blab.

If she'd known, she would never have moved out, he realises, which makes him feel guilty. Why should he feel guilty?

But he does, just now. So guilty that he finds himself paralysed and staring at the blank smeary wall above the stove. He should have moved out, not her. He had money, not her, and he didn't even care that his father died. His father who had left the family when Gareth was five and whom he'd seen perhaps a dozen times since. Hadn't even known he was ill. It was the kind of endowment that happened in Victorian novels, grief-free and serendipitous. He hadn't known the man. Didn't need to. It was enough to have a genial, elderly stepfather. All he needed. His stepfather and his half-brother — and he could have had in addition a beautiful wife and two cute stepdaughters.

To hell with it. It all worked out. Seated now on the only kitchen chair, a step-up ladder positioned by the window with the lofty view of two Countdown supermarkets separated only by a Caltex and a real-estate agent, he contemplates yet again the prospect of buying property. Too far away from up here to see any detail in the photographs in the real-estate window — just a blaze of colour and overpriced land. He could do it now. Get into the market. Get on the ladder. There's enough for a deposit on an apartment, or a small house in an outer suburb. He should do it, he should. Glasses, dentist, helicopter, house.

Or should he do what he's always wanted to do, and that is to go to London or New York? Just go, do it, now, at long last, while he's got the money, while he's still young enough, only in his forties, and time it perfectly with the publication of his second novel, which is currently with Curtis Brown and could very well result in more money. The agents are delighted to have him, Gareth Heap, past winner of the Opus Prize, and predict the book will go to auction.

Marvellous, said his agent. Risky, brave, honest, rousing, sexy, true.

The breath catches in his chest like it used to, before the shortlist cartons started to arrive at the end of last month. Then his own excitement lessened, got slowly drowned, ebbed away. It's nice to feel it again, the breathless throb. It will be exciting again, sometime in the future, but for now the reading and reading and thinking and judging and more reading.

It's an honour to be asked, he thinks. He supposes it is. It can only help to raise his profile. An honour.

Stop sighing all the time! Like an old man!

Not old. Still young in all the ways that matter. He pulls out another book. It has an Indian look about it and approaches the dimensions of Vikram Seth's *An Unsuitable Boy*.

Stop sighing all the time.

If Jacinta sees the box she'll want to know all about it, but he's not allowed to talk. He signed a confidentiality agreement. He puts the box on the floor and kicks it under the table where it skids on a long-forgotten pizza wedge, smearing a thin veneer of cheese and browned tomato paste in its wake. At first the knotted tea towel proves ineffectual but he scrubs hard enough to remove some of the muck at least, bent double, his back killing him, and reminds himself that, going well, he won't have to live like this much longer. A high velocity surges in his intestines, more ecstatic than good ecstasy, warmer than the best single malt, and ameliorates the crick in his back. He'll get a cleaner!

Do the dishes, put the milk away. Find a fucking sticking-plaster. Jacinta. Any minute now.

He'd imagined, when he'd moved in with her, that she'd be as intent on writing as he was, that the domestic realm would be insignificant in their lives. But he hadn't thought it through. First there was the kid that had to be fed and kept clean, a twin separated from her sister by thousands of miles and inevitably suffering some kind of trauma. Second there was the fact that Jacinta had always had a cleaner, always, since she was little, even when they didn't have a bean. Gareth had suggested it was perhaps the cleaner who didn't have a bean, since she was the one cleaning houses. They'd had a furious row and he'd ended by feeling sorry for her, how distressed and anxious she was about mess and dishes and the woman's role in the house.

'Haven't we come full circle?' he had liked to ask in the early days, when he could be bothered. 'Most women just accept it now, post-feminism, post-GFC, post-Western domination. If women have been driven back into the kitchen, then the world's a better place for it, divorce statistics have steadied, society is more stable.'

Only half-joking. If he was to be Jacinta's third husband, then he wanted it to work. He would have mowed the lawns, if they'd had any. Set the mousetraps. Changed the light bulbs.

A key in the lock, two sets of footsteps down the hall, or is it three?

'Oh. Didn't know you were home.'

When he was a kid, Gareth's mother had lived for a while in Australia, and he had kept a bluetongue lizard. It never looked directly at him in the year he had kept it alive and he became convinced that it couldn't see him, that it only looked intently at the space around him. He was less a presence than an absence, a hollow in its primitive perception where the expected world was not. He tries to inhabit that lizard brain now, to see Jacinta only as a Jacinta-shaped gap at the kitchen door, and beside her two smaller hollows that match the twins.

But he catches the eye of the one that had accompanied Herman to England for a year and a half and then back again a few months ago. Lila. Holding tight to her mother's hand and still smaller than the other one. The bigger, more confident girl, the one he knows, Venice, must have got hold of some scissors — great chunks of Lila's hair are missing, the scalp showing gleaming bald in places white as porcelain.

Jacinta sees him staring and says, 'Venice did it. They were playing hairdressers. I can't wait for them to go to school.'

A pulse of resentment at this shared domestic information. Their separation is compromised by it. It's almost offensive! What does he care? And anyway, the poor no-necks spend most of their lives in the holding pen. Going to school won't make an iota of difference. Jacinta already spends most of her life alone, supposedly writing her novel. The other day on Facebook, something about how she'd been given a new computer by a patron — *a patron, for Godsake* — since her other one blew up, and was hoping to finish the second draft soon.

Puke.

Two things. Get the key back, and tell her they should mutually, at the same time, Unfriend. It isn't right that they can still spy on one another, get presented with details of one another's lives they have no business knowing and that are mostly irksome. He knows, for instance, that she and the twins have moved into a two-bedroom divided bungalow in a heritage suburb and that Herman lives elsewhere, close by.

'Cool story,' he says instead, a deliciously rude and childish rejoinder he picked up from a group of teenage boys in the library.

'Is it your birthday? Did you get a present?' Venice scoots under the table and tugs out the box. The pizza wedge comes with it — Jacinta makes exaggerated gagging noises.

'You are so gross.'

The child thrusts a book into her hands. 'Look Mum — it's got an elephant on the cover!'

'*Gay Times with Ganesha*,' reads Jacinta, aloud, 'by Adarsh Z. Kar. Ha! You won't be able to do it!'

'What?'

'Judge the competition! Conflict of interest. You'll have to pull out — he was one of your students.'

'Merle's.'

'You mentored him.'

'She examined him.'

'But he was on the course!' Jacinta is delighted, a happy malicious grin spreading from newly exposed ear to newly exposed ear. Her hair is shorter, blonder, a new cut. Kind of dykie. Or mumsie. And has she put on weight?

She zeroes in on him, narrows her sights. Those brilliant, unfaded blue eyes.

'You didn't know! You didn't recognise his name on the list! Hopeless! God, what a joke. Tra-agic. There's truly nobody home with you, Gareth. Ever so dim.'

That knife-edged English accent.

Oh fuck. Oh fucking Jesus. What an idiot.

She gives the book back to Venice and walks past him into the bedroom, or what was their bedroom when they were together.

Gareth remains marooned, a phrase lifting in his mind, a phrase he's read a thousand times. *He was rocked by the news*. He was. He is. He feels his guts rock back and forth as if he'd just stepped off a sideshow ride.

'Where's the —' Jacinta is returned and standing too close '— duvet? It's mine. I need it.'

Adarsh. Fine-boned, not very tall, literally lived in a dairy, earnest, smart. Oh fuck fuck fuck. He'll look a complete dickhead. He'll have to email the Opus people and explain that not only does he know Adarsh, but he could also be seen to be responsible in some way for the young man's success. Or not? Do they happen all the time, these vague alliances? They must do. Look at the *London Review of Books*. All those blokes up each other's arses despite a female editorial panel. Is it even a problem?

He could say nothing, make sure Adarsh says nothing. He could help Adarsh to win. Nepotism. That's how the world goes round.

No. Too many people would be worried by the close connection. He'll have to resign his position as local judge. Or he could just declare a conflict of interest.

Venice seems to have picked up on his meditative state and is staring intently at the cover, holding the book in her sticky fists.

Black fingernails, her hair dull and dirty. Why does he notice these things?

'It's not a very good elephant,' she announces. 'It's got a person's tummy.'

'Here.' He clicks his fingers for the book.

The other twin trailing behind, Jacinta's heading for the sleeping room. A sleeping room, not a bedroom — it has no bed in it since she took it away, only a mattress and nest of bedding. No bedside lamp. Strictly sleeping. A monk's life. The celibate cell. Write! Write! Only write! If he stuck to that, he wouldn't get into any trouble.

'Here. Hurry up. Book. Give it here.'

The child, when he first met her, had a serene, guileless face. Now there is a shadow over it, a pugilistic set to the jaw, a more calculating light in the eyes, as if she had learned already by age five, or whatever she is now, that to survive you have to fight from your corner.

Tra-agic, Jacinta.

'Come on. I'll give you a lolly.'

The book is swiftly in his hands, and on the desk in the other room is a packet of barley sugars — she follows him through while Adarsh's author photograph pulses at him from the jacket. He might never have twigged, and no wonder. Adarsh Z. Kar is unrecognisable. A new worldliness in his pretty eyes, maybe a sadness, and he's grown a beard which, though he can't yet be thirty, already has silver threads.

Risky, brave, true, said the *Guardian, not since Salman Rushdie . . . the lovechild of Edmund White and Arundhati Roy . . . colourful and spicy . . . more heat than dust . . . ground-breaking . . . a work of love and courage . . .*

And in the author note it says only that Kar was born in Fiji and makes no mention of the country he grew up in further south. An easy mistake. Anyone could have made it. Maybe Adarsh Kar is a common Indian name. Maybe Gareth should keep quiet and hope nobody takes umbrage. Hope nobody notices the connection or draws attention to it. Fingers crossed all the other judges eliminate Kar so he doesn't have to. That would solve the problem.

'Where are you?'

Jacinta locates them. The duvet, dragged off his mattress and mounded in her arms, is speckled with mildew. Does she really want it back?

'He gave me a lolly,' announces Venice, who has finally succeeded in getting the wrapper off. She gives it to her sister, simultaneously holding out her other hand for another one.

There aren't many left. For old times' sake — because couldn't he have been the kind, indulgent stepfather if everything had worked out? — he gives her the rest of the packet, and the act of generosity fires oxytocin through his brain and nervous system. A moment of genuine happiness, intensified by Jacinta's scowl.

'They're not allowed sugar. It makes them hyperactive.'

'We all like our drugs,' he says mildly.

A flock of seagulls has come into land on the hot roof below the window. They take off again almost immediately, squawking loudly, as if their feet have been scalded by the warehouse roof. Jacinta's profile is caught in the reflective glass of the window, the late-morning sun slanting in from the high north-east, the soft burnish of her glistening cheek. New, soft lines mark her high brow. Her eyes full of life. Beautiful. So beautiful. Great tits, even though she's had twins. Couldn't breastfeed, she'd said, maybe that's why. Who was it who first noticed that women in their thirties are at their most beautiful? Full-blown roses, late summer, the exquisite sadness of fading beauty. It would have been fabulous if she wasn't such a crazy bitch.

Look away.

'Look at Adarsh.' He shows her the cover, and Jacinta takes the book from him, letting the duvet draggle to the dusty floor. 'Would you have recognised him?'

'He looks exactly the same except for his beard. I never liked him. So up himself. Wanker.'

'I can hardly remember him.' He remembers him perfectly well. 'Well. Obviously.'

'Didn't even know he was a shirtlifter.' Of course he did.

He doesn't think he's ever seen Jacinta's lip curl so excessively. Almost a snarl.

'Just as well. Since you're such a homophobe. And a misanthropist.' Oh dear.

'A woman-hater,' she adds.

'I think you mean misogynist.' He can barely pronounce the tired, over-used, dreary word with so many tedious associations in life and literature, drummed into him since his eighties adolescence. 'Misanthropy is the hatred of people generally.'

Too late he remembers his resolve. Do not argue. Do not engage. She is showing her teeth.

Classy. Clean. Expensive. He'd always liked her teeth. They made him feel relaxed, cushioned by her family money. And there they are again, exposed as high as the little pink thing, whatever it's called, the tiny triangular membrane above the two front incisors. An exploratory tongue finds his own snagglers and roams around, furry and stale. Should have had a brush-up to keep her sweet, but since he didn't, perhaps he could tell her that he's started a new book, a third novel, which is very distracting from the general business of life and that's why things are a bit of a mess — not that it's any of her businesses any more, really.

Sweets bulging their cheeks, the twins are gazing at their mother and mimicking her fierce expression, the upturned corner of her lip — some kind of primal response, like little chimps. It's cute enough to make him laugh. Glaring at him, 'What's funny?', Jacinta is gathering up her ancient duvet and marching into the kitchen, and the twins are hurrying after her. One of them, Lila, trips over the trailing edge and howls so loudly that his skull plates move in time with her wails — horrendous, deeply disturbing, thank God he never had kids — and then suddenly cuts off, like a switch, on an in-breath. She's clutching at her throat and struggling for breath.

The barley sugar is stuck in her windpipe.

'Get a glass of water!' shouts Jacinta. 'What are you? Fucking useless!' She is banging on the kid's back and the kid is going purple.

Everything goes into slow motion, a phenomenon he's noticed before in the company of children, and he wonders always if it's because the adult sense of time passing is so different from theirs. Children have faster heartbeats, they're quicker on their feet, have faster responses, but time for them actually passes more slowly. A week as long as an adult year. I remember that, he thinks, I remember how time passed when I was a kid. He would write the thought in his notebook but it's in the other room.

Venice beats him to the sink by miles, turns the tap on hard and catches most of it in a polystyrene potnoodle container, which she duly delivers to her mother. Jacinta glares at it — a flash of worry about the toxins and bacterial populations that she is introducing to her daughter, and then she's coaxing her to drink, calming, murmuring, on her knees in front of the child, who turns her face away from the proffered cup and gives a last heaving convulsion, puking the sweet into her mother's hand.

Jacinta biffs it violently away towards the kitchen sink, where it sticks to the wall among the summer's flyspecks before landing with a clatter. In one fluid movement she's standing with Lila in her arms and the kid's head drooping on to her shoulder, eyes closed, lids so translucent they show blue through the quivering skin. On the other side, Venice draws close, hooking an arm around her mother's thigh.

'Fucking useless,' she says clearly, looking at him.

'Hush, child.' Jacinta rocks Lila in her arms.

'Is she um . . . breathing?' asks Gareth.

Jacinta nods towards the pizza crust. 'Can't you pick that up, you pig?'

Obedient — he really wants her to go — he picks it up and drops it into the sink with the lolly.

'"I wanted to have been married forever to one person, my ex-husband or my present one. You couldn't exhaust either man's qualities or get under the rock of his reasons in one short life." Who wrote that?'

Gareth shrugs.

'Grace Paley. Have you ever read her? One of the greatest writers of the twentieth century?'

He shakes his head. 'Not that I can remember.'

'Any women on the list?'

'Not so far. You've got the Orange Prize.'

'So?'

'Imagine if there was a man-only prize. Maybe I'll invent one. The Gareth Heap Award—'

'For the Most Repressed Emotionless Shit Ever.'

'—for Men's Fiction. Or For Fiction by Men. What do you think? When I'm rich and famous. My legacy to the world.'

With her one free hand Jacinta starts taking his half-dozen wine glasses out of the cupboard and lining them up on the bench.

'Aren't those ours? I mean, didn't we get those together? Shouldn't we negotiate?'

'They were a loyalty prize from the supermarket. I saved the coupons. You wouldn't've had a clue. You wouldn't stoop so low.'

'Fucking useless!' says Venice again, in a closer imitation of her mother than she managed before.

'What else are you going to take?'

'The table. A knife, a fork, a bottle and a cork, that's the way you spell New York.'

'Co-caine,' finishes Venus. 'Running around my brain.'

'Nice nursery rhyme,' says Gareth. 'What else?'

'Whatever I can fit in the van I hired.'

'Oh for Chrissake, Jacinta. Have some pity.'

He'll be left with nothing except his books and step-up ladder, a few ragged towels, a few cheap pots and pans with carcinogenic coating peeling into his food. His computer and desk. His desk! His old one had finally given up the ghost and Jacinta had had one handy. He'll have to go shopping.

He hates shopping. Even though he's rich.

'You should go and empty it out. Your desk. The girls can do their homework on it, when they start school.'

'Where are they going?' He shouldn't have asked. Why would he want to know? His curiosity dries immediately she tells him. Of course. It would have to be private. Herman is to pay the fees.

'And um . . . when are they going?'

'March. Early March.'

'Are you going to come to our party, Gareth?' asks Venice. Very carefully, her back to her mother and shoulders hunched to hide her busy hands, she is silently unwrapping one of the barley sugars from the packet with admirable concentration and technique. 'Can he come to my party, Mum?'

'I don't think so.' Jacinta sorts cutlery with one hand, the child still heavy in her arms. He admires her technique too. And her strength. Mother's arms. She used to hold him tight enough to squeeze the breath from him.

'I want you to come to my party, Gareth,' the child continues, two sweets in her mouth at once. 'After all, you are a sinnifigant present in my life.'

Gareth laughs. She's adorable.

'Run and get one of the cartons we carried up, Venny.' Venice obliges while Jacinta looks around for somewhere to put Lila down. 'Here. Be a chair.'

Lila, incontrovertibly asleep, is ladled into his arms. He wishes he was asleep too. And she's heavy. Heavier than two cartons of books at once.

'Who's your patron?'

'Pardon? Patron?'

'On Facebook the other day. I saw you had a patron.'

Jacinta has blushed. He remembers her telling him proudly one night, after too much wine, that she's a born liar and ipso facto a born writer. But he doesn't think she is much good at either. Born liars don't blush.

'Isn't it true?'

'I meant it ironically.'

'An ironic patron?'

'She's not a real patron. She just gave me a computer.'

Venice is back. She shoves the carton at her mother, though she should have given it to him. It could be a cradle, it's big enough to hold the smaller twin like Jesus in the manger. Then he could go out for a walk and come back when she's gone. Let her take it. Whatever she wants. Who cares? It's only stuff.

The glasses are being wrapped in newspaper — yesterday's, which he hadn't read but intended to. Jacinta is rolling and tucking, packing the box. Silence but for rustling paper, the slightly snotty breathing of the sleeping child in his arms. After a moment, Venice comes over to her sister, leaning on Gareth's legs to peer into her face.

'Who did?' He wants to know. 'Who gave you a computer?'

Jacinta is uncomfortable. He can tell even from the back view of her head.

'What's the big secret?'

'No big secret. It's none of your business, actually, dickhead.'

The child is heavy in his arms.

Venice pipes up. 'Merle. Merle gave her a pooter.'

'Oh do shut up, Venice!'

'A new one?'

'No, just one she had lying about. It's old, but goes okay. I just use it as, you know, a glorified typewriter.'

'Merle, eh? Thought you didn't think much of her.'

'Oh!' Exasperated, facing him with her hands on her hips. 'I just met up with her on the beach and I was having a bad day — everything seemed hopeless and dark and loveless — and I was so upset and I cried and cried all over her and she wanted to help me and so I told her I couldn't even write any more because my computer had broken and so she offered and I said yes. End of story.'

The twin in his arms has woken up and is staring warily at her mother. You and me both, kid. Are we going to get a re-enactment?

Jacinta is welling, but he can't help it. 'Did you go round there? To her place?'

'Why're you so interested? Give me a hand with the table. Put Lila down.'

She pulls herself together and he follows her instructions, setting drowsy Lila on the dangerous stepladder and taking up one end of the table.

'You stay here with your sister,' Jacinta tells Venice, and he helps her lug the table down the two flights of stairs to the hot street, where a parking official is tapping out a ticket for the hired van. Three hundred dollars for parking on the footpath.

Jacinta goes to plead with him, leaving Gareth to shove the table in. A fairly new table, but made of old native timber — recycled floorboards — and he puts it in upside down, pushing hard — a graunch of metal slicing wood. Twin curls of varnish form on the van's metal rim, like antennae. Two deep scratches run parallel into the gloom.

He won't tell her. Why open the door to more misery?

From the corner of the van he watches her, animated, waving

her arms about, hears how she tries to dull her English accent to improve her case. But the parking warden isn't moved. He presses a button in his device and a ticket spews out.

'Fuck you,' Jacinta says to Gareth after the man has moved on. 'Couldn't you have talked to him bloke to bloke?'

The fresh air has revived him, renewed his earlier resolve not to argue. He turns away, leading her upstairs to fetch the twins, who hold his hands down the stairs and are willingly strapped in across the bench seat. Duvet and wine glasses stowed between the upturned table legs, Jacinta drives off — he hopes for the last time.

Bless.

———

Upstairs again, Gareth takes Adarsh's book from the box and leafs through it. Who should he email? Whom, that is?

Or phone.

Sometimes it's worth just picking up the phone.

Rae McKay. Pronounced McKai? Or McKee? McKae? Ask for advice, since the Writers' Festival is hosting the awards night. Yes. She'd know, since she'd organised it all. Organised the do, the literary lords and ladies of these latitudes and longitudes and trade lanes gathering at a glittering dinner, along with sponsors, judges, arts bureaucrats, publishers, agents, patrons, the curious, the students, the aspiring writers, the readers, the winners. The losers. Rae McKay would know how to play it.

Still time to bow out gracefully, to say he hadn't realised even though he'd seen the list a dozen times before the books were delivered. Twenty-one names was quite a lot. Wasn't it? Surely he could be forgiven. And whatever traction he'd get from the competition he'd had already anyway — there had been some publicity about his appointment as the local judge, a radio interview, some Sunday paper guff.

Ask Rae's advice. Find the number.

The director

Coming up the front steps of Merle's place, Ned and Nell holding on to either hand — though Ned is seven and really doesn't need to, she should encourage him to run ahead — Rae hears excited children playing in the garden and the puppy barking ecstatically.

She really isn't in the mood. Enough. Enough already. The end of the week, though she is likely to work some of tomorrow and possibly Sunday, and there is a New York agent to ring tonight. It would have been good just to sit with Merle on her own. She feels as indignant as Ned, who is rapping on the door, sharply as a bailiff in a Victorian novel, while Nellie is jumping up and down, 'Yay, some friends!' Five years old, and every new face a potential mate.

'Someone is playing with Merle's puppy!' says Ned, outraged.

Do not let Brendan talk you into a glass of wine.

The door swings open and there he is, Merle's husband, her first-cousin-once-removed-in-law, beer belly in tattered tee-shirt and sulu, bare feet pattering on the grass mat as he leads them down the hall. It's the scruffiest house on a street where properties fetch well over a million, and hasn't changed since it was a student flat. Original features. Dust, dog hair, incipient dirt. Skirting boards, plaster arches and posters peeling from the wall. Merle and Brendan moved here thirty years ago and haven't shifted. There's something altogether arrested about them, something quaintly mid-twentieth century in their old-fashioned leftie politics and world view, the fact they've been together for so long, in the same place, with the same posters, the same ornaments gathering dust on the shelves.

Merle is sitting on the back deck with a visitor, and there are two little girls playing with the puppy in the garden, and four glasses set around a wine bottle — one for her. Brendan is pouring out and Merle is doing the introductions and Rae feels herself zone out. Too many names, too many to remember — writers, publishers, agents, publicists, the characters and identities in the writers' books, the endless reading — she misses the young woman's name.

A new arrival, by the look of her. White skin, unfaded lips. Not enough summers under the baking South Pacific sun. Short-cropped hair, no make-up, a shapeless grey silk top Rae remembers from Karen Walker's shop window. Expensive, unobtrusively tailored. New Doc Martens with shiny kick-ass toes. Money, then.

The little girls are called up from the garden, one of them dragging along the puppy, SPCA special with giant feet. He wriggles and squirms, his baby belly still mottled and bald. He's yellow, muscled, with emerging big shoulders, pale eyes and pink gums, white teeth and matching tuft of white hair round his little penis, a whippy rat tail. Ghastly. Not the kind of dog to have around small children, and too much for Merle to exercise and discipline. Insane. Classic empty-nester viper-in-the-nest syndrome. The puppy barks wildly, writhing, a snapping jaw coming close to the face of the bigger girl, who is carrying it. Non-identical twins, or born very close together.

'Ned and Nell. Meet Venice and Lila.' Merle takes the puppy away from them and puts him on the ground.

The children stare at one another. The smaller twin is paler, with rough chunks cut out of her hair, and looks as if she's been crying or just woken up.

'Hi!' says Nellie, and Rae hears the last vestige of her New York accent, the twang she picked up from nursery school. It's almost gone.

'They're girls,' says Ned scornfully, looking up at his mother. His accent is stronger, more enduring. Girrls.

'Girls are cool, don't you think?' says the twins' mother. 'I think they are!'

'Venice and Lila are the same age as you, Nell,' Merle says, and she fetches them a bag of crisps and some mandarins to have a picnic in the tree house. A soft grey pashmina is wrapped around her shoulders even though the evening is warm, and Rae detects a tiredness. A slump. Osteoporosis maybe. Or maybe it's just because it's Friday, though every day must be the same for them since neither of them works. Not really. Not like Rae does. Both of them are writers.

'Come on then. Come down to the garden and we'll find Parry's ball,' says Merle, leading the children down to the garden. The puppy lies on his back, Brendan rubbing his big brown toe on the bare pink tummy. What is he writing, again? Rae knows she's asked him and can't again, not that he ever asks her how the festival is going. She takes a sip, tries to remember — Merle has finally finished her sixth novel and Brendan is writing . . . something with very limited appeal. Another sip and she remembers: an examination of a hundred years' pronunciation of native placenames, some of the phonetics more than a century old. Light-hearted and funny, he tells her, not so much what it's about, but what it acknowledges — a century of post-colonialism — and whenever he talks about it he gives her that look she is coming to recognise from other writers. *When it's published, put me in the festival. My book is very important.*

'Any more of that wine, Bendonbra?' asks the twins' mother.

Brendan refills her glass and offers Rae another. Her glass is empty already. Just as he holds the bottle out, the puppy hurtles from the far end of the veranda and smacks into his legs. Red wine sloshes over her cream linen jacket and, because he's a bit pissed, she supposes, Brendan laughs.

'Fuckin' munter! Isn't he an idiot? Come here, Parry — you didn't mean to, did you boy? Say sorry to Stingray.'

He's the only member of the family who still uses her childhood nickname, and she wishes he wouldn't.

Parry laps up the fallen wine and Rae takes off her jacket and heads towards the kitchen, Merle hurrying after her — 'Oh no, Rae — I'm so sorry — what a shit, what a bugger, I'm so sorry love' — and they find the salt and pour a stream over the stain, while Merle offers to pay for drycleaning.

'It doesn't matter, Merle.'

Merle peers at her. 'You all right? You look like you're about to burst into tears.'

Her favourite! The first time she'd had anything that colour for over seven years, since before Ned.

'Are you okay?' Merle takes the pashmina from her own shoulders and wraps it around Rae's, though she doesn't need it. She feels very hot and flustered.

'You're really pale.'

'Um. Overwhelmed.'

'How's it all going?'

Careful. There's so much she'd like to tell her but should probably keep to herself. It's a bit murky, Merle's attitude to her little cousin getting the festival job fresh from New York. One of her best cronies applied for the position, so Rae had heard, a woman in her fifties with years of local arts administration experience. One of many applicants, of course. Hundreds, perhaps. Merle's friend had consoled herself with taking up the direction of the Fringe. But the festival board chose pizazz. They chose New York. They chose Rae. They chose serendipity! Fresh air for the kids and a festival to direct. A new start. An attempt to revive the marriage after her last affair. If you could call it an affair. It was kind of desultory. One night with a Texan writer, an armageddonist with erectile failure who fully embraced the end of the world. And only three other men in ten years. It wasn't too bad. Was it?

The cream jacket will never be the same. The salt crystals absorb the wine, turn pink and red. Blood in the snow.

'You know Gareth, don't you?' Rae asks. 'I had a phone call from him just before I left work.'

'Oh, Adarsh, yes. I wondered if that would be a problem when I saw that Gareth was one of the judges,' says Merle absently, laying the jacket aside on a pile of newspapers and picking up an ancient, grimy dishcloth. She wipes a milky substance on the bench and clicks the lid shut on a container of melting ice cream. Beside it sit two bowls, sticky and smeary, mostly licked clean.

'Oh! Would Ned and Nellie like some Hokey Pokey?'

Merle removes the lid again and doles ice cream into the bowls, which must have belonged to the twins, who could be incubating colds or measles or Ebola or the latest disease to cross the species barrier but look healthy enough, tearing around the garden with Ned and Nellie. Ned is climbing the ladder to the new tree house, a haphazard creation of Brendan's. She hadn't realised how haphazard — there's a closer view of it from the kitchen window. She can see nails sticking out. So much danger. Would the twins be vaccinated? Who knew these days? Their mother looks like the sort who wouldn't believe in it.

Clean spoons at least.

Rae helps herself, lays them in the bowls, and tells Merle about her phone call from Gareth. She would be interested, since she worked for many years alongside him.

'Can you believe it? A conflict of interest. The only locally appointed judge, and he lets the side down. How come he didn't know? Does he go around with his eyes shut?'

Merle shrugs. 'He mustn't have realised. It mightn't matter that much.'

'But it will! He helped Adarsh write that novel. It's too close. He'll have to pull out.'

'No, that won't be necessary.' Merle is flicking the salt off already — if Rae was doing it, she'd leave it for longer. 'He'll have to abstain from voting for Adarsh, which will lessen his chances. Otherwise there could be accusations of favouritism.'

'It's not very fair.'

'Happens a lot, I think. If the book's that good, the other judges will shortlist it. Gareth's only one of four.'

'Do you think so? Will it be all right? I don't think it's fair. Doesn't matter who wrote the book — it's not their fault a judge is compromised.'

'Don't make too much of it, Rae. It'll sort itself out.' Merle has spread the jacket out, is applying more salt.

Rae heaves a sigh — she can't possibly let it sort itself out, she'll have to get in touch with the Opus people and tell them. It's the honest thing to do. They mightn't know of the connection since it's all so far away in New Zealand and who cares what happens there. Merle doesn't understand. Strange how there's a tolerance of corruption on the left wing, when it's a common accusation they make of the right.

'He might have had his mind on other things. He's started his third novel, according to Jacinta,' says Merle.

'Who?'

'Gareth.'

'Oh. Yeah. I read one of his once.'

'Submerged in it.'

Submerged. That can't be a good thing. Rae twirls her empty wine glass. How lovely it would be just to get pissed. But there's that 11 p.m. phone call to an agent about the South American magic realist and the Canadian comic poet.

Stay sober.

'Who's Jacinta?'

'A young writer. She's—'

'Man, how those three words make me tired,' interrupts Rae, as Merle's gaze comes to rest at a spot above Rae's shoulder. The twins' mother is there with a new bottle of wine, refilling their glasses, having got bored with Brendan, who is alone out on the veranda, smiling, watching the children risk life and limb in his crooked, nail-spiked tree house.

The tide turns in Rae's glass, and with it comes a rosy vision of herself and Cameron happy, much happier than they've ever been, living in this vast, rambling house. Her and Cameron buying into this pretty, old, quiet central suburb, with parks and cafés and ten minutes across the bridge to swim in the reasonably clean ocean. Her house. First she'd gut the whole place. Ditch the ugly ranchsliders that frame her view of the tree house and the garden and Brendan in the foreground grinning at the children like a dingbat.

A delighted grin. Almost dozy. Clucky. Maybe men shouldn't have babies until they are at least fifty. Better father second time around. Everyone said that. Maybe that would happen to Cameron, since he wasn't interested in this batch of kids, though he maintained he was. 'I answer every need, don't I?' Since the iPads came, there had been even fewer demands for attention, a thought that always makes her skin prickle with guilt. Hours and hours staring into their screens, and neither she nor Cameron doing enough to police it. Their worst fights were always about perceived faults in one another's equally neglectful parenting.

Merle is saying something about a computer, and her friend is saying how wonderful it is to have it and how grateful she is, and how as soon as she saw how completely fucked her duvet was she knew just the place for it and how she'd come straight round here to deliver it. She points to the dog's basket, billowing with a grubby cream cotton duvet and an old brown dressing-gown that apparently Brendan once lived in for about four years.

'Who's Jacinta?' Rae asks again. 'This person who told you about Gareth's third novel?'

After talking to Gareth on the phone she'd wondered how such a wooden, stiffly spoken and socially uncomfortable man could write such *effortless, burning prose*. She had read *Root* from the distance of New York — or was it London — his *cri de coeur* for the non-indigenous of this country, and she had applauded nearly every word. Tour de force. Incendiary. Shocking. Comforting. Everything they'd said about it was true.

'Is she Gareth's girlfriend?'

Merle looks sharply at the wine-bearer and back to Rae again, and the wine-bearer is smiling, pointing at herself.

'I'm Jacinta! Does he talk about me?' She leans closer, and Rae realises Merle's friend is straight, or was. Straight enough to sleep with Gareth, which probably isn't very.

But multiple birth, short hair, boots and no make-up equals gay, doesn't it? And Jacinta is beautiful, but then so are lots of lesbians.

Merle comes to her rescue. 'No, no, Jass. We were talking about something else.'

'Adarsh! I bet you were talking about him. The great white hope, not counting Tosh.' She says this bitterly, as if his success is a personal affront.

'Isn't Adarsh Indian?' asks Rae.

'Oh, you know. Just an expression.'

Merle sighs, hands Jacinta the bowls of ice cream, says, 'Wrong mother', then takes them back and departs for the garden.

Rae is left in the kitchen with Jacinta — inquisitorial, bright-eyed, leaning forward at the waist.

'Last weekend Merle gave me a laptop to finish my novel.'

'Generous.'

'It's very old. Early 2000s. I'll have to get a new one, but this saves me from having to think about it until I've finished the book.'

'Oh.'

'I was one of her students. The most promising she'd ever had, she told me.'

It doesn't ring true. Rae can't imagine Merle saying that to any of her students — but maybe she's short-changing her. Jacinta might be brilliant. Brilliant, but spoilt and English and a bit ditzy. We write what we are not, someone once said. The rule of the mental mirror image.

Maybe she's a genius.

Out in the garden Merle is carrying the ice cream towards the children. Brown summer limbs protrude from the window of the tree hut, Ned's and Nell's. The twin girls, one of them halfway up the ladder and the other standing below, are almost as pale as their mother. Perhaps they don't get taken to the beach or the park much; maybe they're always in hats and long sleeves, or slathered in toxic sunscreen.

'And I will fulfil that promise.' Jacinta holds the wine aloft, pours again, an emotional wobble in her voice. 'I'll make her proud. It shouldn't only be the male writers who get all the attention.'

'Right.'

Rae turns to the sink and uses a knife to scrape off the red salt. It lands in sodden, crystalline heaps. Does Merle think she and Jacinta could be friends? Is that why she invited them around together? Or did Jacinta say she just arrived out of the blue? They're about the same age; so are the kids, who play together okay. They could be friends. But my friends list is full, she thinks, panicked; Merle's about six months too late. I can barely service the friends I've got.

That too is strange, since the first year back was lonely, lonely, lonely, until she made an effort and found old schoolmates, had some dinner parties, reached out. Jacinta could be a Facebook friend only perhaps, one of her 800.

'What do you do?' comes that English voice from behind her. 'I've filled you up. It's just behind you. What do you do for a job?'

'I . . . um . . . run the—' Rae begins, but is saved from answering by an ear-splitting yell. Ned has grabbed Nellie's Hokey Pokey and is shovelling it in at a rapid rate, leaning out the tree-house window, holding the bowl out of Nell's reach. In the gloom of the hut's interior Rae can just see the gleam of her daughter's open howling mouth.

Jacket over her arm, she goes out to Merle who is trying but failing to adjudicate. Brendan joins them in the garden, laughing, 'He's such a boy, isn't he? He's your perfect bloody boy! It's what you'd expect', and Rae wonders if he's on some kind of psychotropic that causes inappropriate hilarity.

Mum, that font of all family information, says that nobody likes him, that he gives too much of their little money away to worthy causes, that he and Merle live on the smell of an oily rag, on money Merle mostly earns, or used to. That he had a breakdown some years ago, pulled himself together with a live-in shrink, and then he wrote a book, creative non-fiction, about memory. No, more specific than that, the memory of books. What it is we remember about them. What lasting images we take away from our reading, visual memories prompted only by print. Rae hasn't read it — she can't be expected to read everything — but the book has done reasonably well. Apparently. At least, it sold into the Northern Hemisphere.

'When our boy was little,' he's saying now, loudly, excitedly, over Nellie's howling, 'there was an insane idea that you could raise boys with no reference to gender. Give them dolls and shit! But this guy — he's a real boy! On you, matie!'

'Because he's greedy?' Rae snaps. 'Because he steals his sister's ice cream? Get down, Ned, we're going home.'

'Has he got toy guns?' asks Brendan. 'It's all right, you know. Less harmful than half the games they play online.'

In the car, Rae reflects on how Merle offered no protest at the evening being called short. She didn't say, 'Don't go yet, Rae. Sit down for a bit. How are things with Cameron?'

Perhaps Jacinta has replaced her in Merle's affections. Who cares? It really doesn't matter. But maybe if they'd been alone Rae could have sounded her out on the problem with Liu Wah. Gareth's phone call hadn't been the last of the day. There had been another, more disturbing one, just as she was flicking off the lights, making her way out of the office. It was Malcolm Murchison, from the university, who wanted to call a meeting about the Chinese writer's involvement in the festival. It's a problem for them, as stakeholders. The Chinese Consulate has been in touch. What, Rae wonders, would Merle think of that? A major university responding to editorial control from the Chinese Embassy? Sometimes old lefties can be good to talk to, to give you the historical perspective, the utopian ideal. They fire you up on the big picture.

From the back seat Ned whines steadily and Nellie asks one

question over and over, quietly: 'Are we still going to have fish and chips? Are we having fish and chips? Mum? Are we?' As the car moves along Nellie is making a swiping movement with one finger on the window as if it's the screen of her iPad, one swipe for each repetition of the question.

'Stop that,' says Rae, more from alarm than irritation. Does she think the passing streets aren't real?

At their local strip Rae trails into the takeaway and makes a weary request. Sometimes it really comes down to being able to put one foot in front of the other and that's about it. She sits on a bench seat to wait, hopes the kids aren't fighting in the car. The last time she'd come here she was with her mother, and Mum had announced loudly in a crowded Friday night shop: 'They're all Asians now, aren't they, dear? Poms in my day, Poms and the working class running the dairies and fish and chip shops. Working every hour God gave them. Poor devils. Just like this lot.'

Thank God she'd said nothing to Merle. She could have sounded as blinkered as her mother. For all she knew, Merle could see China as some kind of communist ideal and agree with the university. Keep the peace. Would she?

I'm so tired, thinks Rae, and swivels to check through the window on Ned and Nellie sitting in the car. They look peaceful enough, so far. Ned's whining shut off as she'd got out, but he'd had that look on his face.

That particular look.

'You tease her, I scrag you,' she'd told him. She could have expounded to Brendan what she'd learned about raising boys since they made smacking illegal. You have to keep one step ahead. Scragging proves an effective method of halting him mid-tease by grabbing the back of his neck, not too hard but firmly enough to make him giggle and writhe, and sometimes hard enough to pinch so that it turns into a rough-housing kind of game, but with an edge to it, i.e. don't step out of line, little chimp, or Mama will hang you upside down by your feet. It was the silverback's job really, but he's never home to do it.

And he's not home now, she sees, as she parks in the empty double garage in the basement of their inner-west 1960s brick-and-tile that neither of them really likes but was what they could afford. Ned runs ahead up the interior staircase, doing his gorilla walk, bounding on bent legs, his shoulders slumped, hooting at the prospect of fish and fat and salt, and Rae wonders how would it be to see the world through primatologists' eyes. There's one coming to the festival — a leading primatologist with a recent book. Frans de Waal and his *The Bonobo and the Atheist*. Humanity at the smallest remove. Good for the soul. Rae's mother is a geriatric ape who survives so long only because she lives in captivity with food delivered to the door of her suburban home and bills on automatic payment. Jacinta's a jostling young female chimp, and Merle a fading skinny red-haired orang-utan on the brink of old age. And Nellie the wide-eyed infant macaque returned from washing her hands to regard the prodigious heap of food.

Cameron's monkey-id can't be summoned. Far too sophisticated in his dark suit and boring striped shirt and Servilles haircut. On a Friday night he often drinks at a bar in town or goes out for a meal with friends. Or maybe he's having an affair, this very minute with his pants off in a hotel room, having one of his subdued orgasms with someone from work. Tit for tat. Fair dibs. But she'd be surprised that a woman, any woman, could find him interesting.

Why don't you leave him? she asks herself, yet again. When they shifted from New York would have been the chance to do it, to have separated once and for all. He could have happily stayed there but didn't, he says, because of the kids, and now he resents them for being the reason he's stuck at the bottom of the world, which he doesn't say. But it's true. He's punishing them for existing. Just for being here.

Think about something else that doesn't do your head in.

She lets the kids turn the television on, tops up her glass and goes into a singles chatroom.

FEBRUARY

A writer

In the last six months he's hardly been home, but he is now, bursting in the sweating, shitty door with his cabin luggage and laptop, all he ever travels with. Fellow travellers, women mostly, like to exclaim, 'Is that all you've got? How long are you away for?' and Adarsh will smile enigmatically, enjoying the shared notion that it is nothing less than extraordinary that he always looks so neat and clean, considering how little he carries!

'Every writer needs an address even if it is more than one,' said Bashevis Singer, and this is his, for now. In Delhi. He is home.

Clothes unpacked and added to his small, scuffed chest of drawers only double the permanent collection. The fine pale-green cashmere sweater joins a pink one of the same manufacture, dark woollen slacks lie with a previous incarnation, the spare drip-dry shirt and two pairs of underwear most recently laundered in a hotel room in Berlin fold neatly into the top drawer. He returns his toilet bag to the cupboard-sized bathroom and notes that the dripping tap has spawned lush green moss in the cracked sink. On investigation it proves to be more slime than moss, and slips down the plughole easily enough with a twist of the tap — which is a relief, because he's reluctant to touch it. Who would have thought it, that Delhi water could grow anything that colour? At first glance it had looked almost edible, the same shade of phosphate green as the cropping grass in the fields of the country he grew up in. Fresh and lush. Islands surrounded by sea thousands of miles away on the other side of the world. Water, water, water everywhere, and gallons of it to drink, deep lakes and wild rivers and dams. Free, safe water to slake your thirst. They think it's dirty but it isn't. They don't know real dirt.

He's thirsty and forgot to buy water on his way in. There's half a bottle in his day bag in the only other room in the third-floor conversion — he returns to it and stretches out on his charpoy and thinks of his family at home, how he would like to be there now, filling a big glass from the kitchen tap and slugging it down. He's so thirsty.

A full glass of water and his father sitting behind him at the table, reading, his glasses perched on the end of nose, sucking his teeth in that annoying way he has, sighing over the newspapers, his sisters teasing and laughing. The roar of traffic on the arterial road beyond the shop door, the night passing by. The usual drunks and human trade that made up his shift, before he could slip out into that beloved South Pacific city. Three hours till closing time. His father reading aloud some piece of lunacy and chuckling over it. The peace, especially since his mother died.

He misses his father and his sisters and his double life. Who could have thought he would ever miss that?

It's because he's been writing about it. Living in the past. One is not supposed to. One is supposed live forward, to revel in one's freedom, to experience opportunities the world offers, not long for Daddy who was mostly disapproving. An irony. The first of many. Irony upon irony. You could count them up.

The second irony is the latest deposit from his American agent. It was more than he could compute. He'd read the number three times and sounded it out slowly, like a word in a foreign language, aloud in his Toronto hotel room. Thinking of it now, he is half-panicked by a gut-wrenching anxiety — so much money and what to do with it? He has to save it, eke it out, hold onto it. This moment in the sun may not last. How rich is Rohinton Mistry these days? Or Vikram Seth? Or even Salman Rushdie, who must have spent truckloads on lawyers?

If he is to stay here in Delhi, in the most expensive city in India, he needs to be parsimonious. He's comforted by this thought. Parsimony comes naturally to him. He'll never be one of those flashy roosters loaded with gold neck-chains in the clubs and bars, the diamond rings, the shiny cars. The family mansion in Vasant Vihar, the multiple servants, possibly murderous. There are daily accounts in the papers of murderous servants. Yes, staff are to be avoided at all costs. Anyone. He turns them away. Does it all himself.

An uncluttered mind. Parsimony, detachment and impermanency. He thinks of his writing tutor on the other side of the world and the visit, two years ago, to the shoebox eyrie Gareth shared with a Taiwanese student, a convenient flatmate who rarely came out of her bedroom except to go to university. Apparently. The tutor had made a joke about the 'greasicles' hanging from the spice shelf above the stove, slowly dripping depositories of solidified fat — an installation of theatrical filth. Adarsh had almost gagged at the sight, even though the strong pervading scent of male effluvia that rose off the plump white man, of sweat and garlic and spice, had shamefully, secretly, half-turned him on. Soon after, the poor bastard had moved in with that terrifying English student Jacinta. Adarsh supposes he doesn't live like that now, since the Englishwoman had money. Strong teeth, flawless skin and ex-husband a doctor.

Parsimony is not filth, though; Gareth got that wrong. Adarsh's little flat is as clean as a whistle, or as clean as he can keep it, given the grey dust that settles over everything. He looks around, takes in the layer on the narrow sill, on the top of the whirring air-conditioning unit and the old chest of drawers, dust accumulated in the three weeks he's been away. A fine layer shifts gritty on the pillow under his cheek.

The irony of parsimony in the face of wealth.

Third irony: the book he has written, the book that has his name in lights and a shortlisting in the Opus Prize, that has approximately eighty characters and all of them part of various tightly knit but intersecting families and communities, is full of love and forgiveness and companionship. Readers assume it is in some way autobiographical, that he came to Delhi as a Mumbai native supported by legions of sisters, aunties and uncles, proud liberal parents, all accepting of his sexuality. A fantasy world. Sometimes he manages to stutter out that the novel is not autobiographical, and once acerbically to an elderly lady professor in a sari that his hero dies in the last paragraph and here he is alive and well. Emphasis on the *well*. And alone. Alone in an agglomerate of twenty-three million.

He could do something about that. He could go into town, take a careful route to the underground gay club he's been to before. It was the main reason he'd chosen Delhi — apart from the fact that his original publisher is here — that it is the least dangerous city for a man like him. More dangerous since the law change.

There's always tomorrow, he tells himself in the deepening gloom of his tiny apartment. A face could loom from the crowd and Adarsh would know the moment he saw him that he was It. Or he could meet him at the post-merger publishers' party in Vasant Vihar, diaried for tomorrow afternoon. A mere waiter. A publishing assistant. A diplomat. Someone's husband. Or another writer, a man as dedicated to his craft as Adarsh, with a vocation strong enough to sweep him along in the wake and get him started on his second novel.

A hundred pages. That's all he has so far. Printed out, mostly, in a clearfile on his desk iced with fine dust, a sheen of it in the dying sun. He knows from conversations with other writers — from his long-ago writing course! — that a hundred pages for some people is quite a lot. A whole novel already! But he remembers the first stages of *Gay Times with Ganesha*, how at a hundred pages he was barely getting started, how he was just warming his engines, listening to the play of piston and carburettor, spinning his wheels in preparation for the long road ahead. Second time around he has drawn close to the nub too fast — it's because he's hurrying, never left alone for long enough, scurrying away from the threat of company. He's raced through the love story and out the other side to stare disillusionment in the face. He doesn't want that, to have to dissect the failure of the human heart, to go along those well-worn grooves of loneliness and isolation. A quote of Merle's comes dimly to mind — something from Janet Malcolm, about the tired, predictable quality of too-oft-told tales.

Quick. Think of something cheerful. It comes immediately.

Startling, said a reviewer of the first book. *Adarsh Z. Kar is the literary lovechild of Alan Hollinghurst and Arundhati Roy.*

Adarsh wishes that the lovechild would close his eyes and go to sleep, because he really is exhausted and hungry and thirsty, but not as lonely as before, because he remembers one night in Canada surrounded by writers and their various entourages and longing for the peace and solitude of his Delhi flat, third floor in Jangapura.

No, not peace. There isn't much of that. His row of houses flanked on one side by a congested, busy street and on the other three by rising towers, where the builders, labourers and day-wagers put in as many long hours as his poor mother had in the superette. A psychiatric nurse had told him once, a friend of a friend who hadn't known Adarsh's genesis, 'The maddest people I've ever met are the wives of Indian dairy owners. They do nothing but work.'

By the nurse's lights the whole of India would be insane, sleep-deprived, overworked, even the millions with no definable job other than the struggle to stay alive. Working, working, just to keep breathing. He feels the seething megacity spread around him for hundreds of miles — 700 square kilometres, a statistic he would marvel at yet again, if he wasn't so tired. He closes his eyes, drifts to sleep, floating on his good fortune.

7 a.m. and at his desk, confronting the dusty pages, ignoring his growling stomach. In the next four hours he rises only twice, once to use the bathroom and locate his earplugs, once to make some weak black tea. He finds his concentration unwavering, a shining silver stream of words flowing from his brain to his arm to the pen to the words appearing on the page. It was one of Merle's cautions — to write away from the sticky web, either by hand or on an internet-incapable machine. It could have been the best piece of advice she gave, he thinks, though the jar of bright, inkless husks on his desk is chocka and will only add to the plastic crust slowly choking the oceans.

At eleven o'clock he counts his words the old-fashioned way, the number of lines multiplied by an average count of words per line, and calculates 5000. Enough.

More than enough. His heartbroken boy discovers life after love, his heartbreaker encounters karma in the form of a nasty as yet undiagnosed new disease, and it seems a previously minor character is going to draw to the fore and carry the story on, which could mean as much as a complete change in voice. It's a worry this far into the novel, but if he's careful it could work. It will mean going backwards, inserting more about this character, meeting him earlier.

He makes some notes, possible directions for his next writing session — though he knows he will likely ignore them — and goes out, walking the streets in the heat of the day. The *unseasonable heat*, it hardly bears remarking. He considers himself acclimatised to it, whatever it is, original climate or new, the relative stability of the seasons after the changeable islands of his youth. Here on the streets it's a sunny winter Delhi day, crowded, dirty, dusty, insane development, a building site on every block, beggars, touts, traffic, noise, foul smells, human suffering, shit.

None of it leaves a scratch on him. Sustained by the morning's work, he's unmolested, buoyed along on helium wings for an hour and a half, revelling in the blur, until he finds himself in Old Delhi, eating chaat at a proper restaurant. It's one favoured by tourists, perhaps because it's directly over the road from a McDonald's and so they notice it from the window, and see other tourists going in and out and no evidence of sudden gastric disturbance. Safe. He shares his small table with three other Western diners, but scarcely registers them, doesn't engage in conversation. People like to ask him, once they hear his accent — where are you from? And he always answers, 'Fiji', not wanting to acknowledge that other place, even though it tugs so hard at his heart, and luckily most people don't recognise the New Zealand accent.

He takes the Metro home and crashes, deep and dreamless, waking with half an hour to get to Vasant Vihar for the party.

It's only as he gets out of the taxi outside the white, spreading house, set around with gardens, that he feels his appetite rise for company. It's a 180-degree spin from his previous mood of favoured isolation, leaping up at him over-excited and slathering, ecstatic at the prospect of treats, of communion, food and drink. A big wet pink tongue lapping at his solar plexus, a wagging tail propelling him up the path.

The party is mostly local, only a few foreigners — unless there are more like him, NRIs returned to Delhi from the Diaspora and wondering why they don't fit. They're all there to welcome the new CEO of the Asia Pacific Region. One of those men who slip around the world at a certain level of corporate enterprise, across the shining floors of glass towers the world over. Men in suits with slippery-soled shoes, men and some women who earn 200 per cent more than they did ten years ago. Those sort of people. While everyone else earns less.

Perhaps he should give away some of the enormous advance.

On the wide verandas in the winter sun the gathering is Christian, Muslim and Hindu, a percentage of Delhi intelligentsia milling together, some of the faces familiar now after two years here. Local writers, journalists, interested literary people. The publishers themselves number mostly from the business side, administrative and publicity staff. He looks around for his own publisher, and can't see him. He's usually easy to spot with his bright, dandy suits and mop of curly hair. Through a gap in the crowd, the outgoing CEO looms red-faced, balding. He'll be on his way back to London any day, post-monumental merger.

Adarsh accepts a glass of non-alcoholic punch, though the desire to drink bowls through him as rabidly as desire for society had. At his elbow is gathered a group of people, their backs to him. He looks over a shoulder, sees their attention taken by a Chinese man. Adarsh assumes he's Chinese. Speaking Cantonese. He sips the safe beverage, listens to the Indian woman who is translating into English. By its formality it could be a speech the man has given to interested strangers before. There is something of the showman about him, someone used to the rhythms and patterns of speech needed with a translator. He uses his hands expressively, a poi dance to accompany his Cantonese. Now and again he pauses, and by the aloof, almost bored expression on his face it's for the translator to catch up, not for a chance to think ahead. The man is about his height — which is to say not very tall at all — and towards the end of his address catches Adarsh's eye. He nods towards him in a friendly fashion, more life showing in his face than it had throughout the speech, and Adarsh's breath catches painfully in his throat. He feels himself darken, drops his gaze to the neckline of the man's red satin shirt, collarless, with a bright purple Indian scarf draped over his shoulders. A gift from his hosts. Glowing.

Then his publisher is beside him, with dust on his shoes from the garden and a faint scent of ganja hanging about his clothes under the spicy cologne — and he is leading Adarsh through the little audience to introduce him. Rahul seems to know the man well, or well enough to plant a kiss soundly on one cheek.

'Liu Wah, meet Adarsh Z. Kar.'

Mutual smiles. Adarsh recognises the name, he thinks. And perhaps Wah recognises his. He is catching hold of the translator's arm just as she is about to be drawn away by a friend or colleague, another impossibly clever and beautiful young Indian woman in her late twenties. There are more and more of them in these circles, which is at once comforting and alarming. Comforting because it's like home, a country overrun with clever women. Alarming because of the violence, the bus rapes, the barbaric dacoity defence, and the everyday groping and rubbing from men in crowds, the almost casual murders. Delhi is a violent city if you're a woman, clever or otherwise. He's glad he has little to do with them, it would be too worrying. He worries enough about himself. These ones are giggling and charming, and tease Wah a little before agreeing to go on.

He delivers a rapid message: 'The Ganesha book. You will forgive me for not having read it, but the subject matter makes me squirm.'

Adarsh sees the smile drop from Rahul's face as rapidly as he feels it fall from his own. A sense of dread. The translator listens, speaks again.

'I commend you for your bravery. You are a courageous man.'

'Two courageous men!' exclaims Rahul, bonhomie returned. He clamps a heavy hand on their proximitous shoulders. 'You have much in common.'

He smiles from one to the other and back again, while the men on either side register one another's modesty, and yes — embarrassment. Adarsh is further embarrassed because he cannot make a parallel speech. He could be honest and tell him that he hasn't read Liu's book but offer no excuse as to why not. He supposes it would be violent in parts — could he say that? 'The violence makes me squirm'? He remembers reading an interview now, about the poet's exile in Germany, about how he had been many times imprisoned and beaten in China, the first time after

Tiananmen Square in 1989. He writes non-fiction too, accounts of ordinary Chinese lives just as they are, with no authorial politics or criticism of the Party. Adarsh will read him. He wants to.

'I look forward to reading—' he starts, but Liu is speaking rapidly again and the translator is saying, 'You must not feel obliged. If you should find yourself reading my book one day, you do. If you don't, you don't. It is nothing to me.'

And he is moving on, Rahul proprietorial at his elbow, the young women following.

Adarsh takes himself around the house to the far end of a less crowded veranda, cooler and shadier, north-facing. Green parakeets cluster in a tree — an elm, is it? It's not an oak — he knows them, because the English colonists planted thousands at home. Maybe it's Indian, since it's hosting the birds. A native tree. He is completely at odds with the natural world here. No names for birds or trees or insects. Does it matter? Should he be making reference to flora and fauna? If he did it would be to celebrate it, not to mourn its imminent extinction. He hates it when writers do that. It's new bad manners. Yes, the world is fucked and what of it?

He stares glumly into the gathering gloom of the late-afternoon garden, the party still close enough that he can hear the clattering of glass and china, laughter, whole exchanges of conversation, the flick of cigarette lighters, murmurs of delectation over circulating plates of food. Shifting away a little, he leans out over the rail, concealing himself behind a white column, which he sees now bears a faint relief of a swastika, sanded down and painted over, misunderstood by some foreign resident since the war. It's smooth to the touch.

In the corner of his eye a mongoose flashes — a fleeting shadow among a planting of wide glossy leaves on the far side of the lawn, disappearing towards the pavilion and glinting swimming pool. A mongoose. A reminder, if he needed one, that he really has returned to the land of his forefathers, that life couldn't be in any way improved except by the addition of a partner. What does a mongoose need to do at this time of day, he wonders, does it have young to feed, eggs to steal, a mate to placate? Does it ever stand around and feel alone among a gathering of its own kind?

A servant is ringing a tiny, piercing bell and several of the publishing staff are moving through the crowd, asking them to adjourn through the French doors to the reception room for speeches. Whenever speeches are given informally in a room, in the round, Adarsh loves them, good or bad. He feels a little spark of excitement. Swiftly delivered, gracious and to the point, a joke or two — then that is an obvious pleasure. If the speech is slow, poorly delivered, long and excruciatingly dull, then much enjoyment can be had from watching the faces of surrounding fellow listeners and gauging the agony of their boredom. The trick is to light from one face to another quickly before they detect you staring, and imagine what they could be thinking about, what their lives are like. Very entertaining. He's met other writers who stare. It's an occupational habit.

The outgoing red-faced CEO doesn't speak for long. He seems fazed, a bit pissed, swaying on the thick carpet under the tinkling beaded chandelier. A breeze riffles in through the open French doors, lifting the hair of the assembled. There are tall vases of flowers, paintings, ornaments and ease, and Gilbraith could be slurring drunk. He's got one of those posh English accents that sound drunk to antipodean ears even when the speaker is sober. Such overgrown hedgerows of vowels in comparison to the close-clipped topiaries Adarsh grew up with. Has himself.

Poor bastard. Would there be another job for him, paunchy, bald, nearing sixty, the publishing industry at once exploding and imploding around him? Lay-offs, positions dissolved, restructuring, quailing in the face of social media, a giant corporation spread ever more precariously across the globe.

After only ten minutes, in which he gives a list of thanks from his device — locals and other firangi who have made him feel at home — the CEO hands over to the new guy, who is so anxious, nervous and ill-at-ease that it is obvious he is a man unused to public speaking. Possibly some South American heritage, or Italian, or Iranian. Adarsh considers himself a bad judge outside the Pacific. Whatever, the new guy isn't a big white man, but small and pale brown. His name — Mark Thompson — is instantly forgettable and gives no clue. Thirty-five. Straight. Boring. Wordless. Inarticulate.

Adarsh switches his attention to the guests, who line the room and spill out into the veranda behind him. Nearby, leaning against a swagged floor-length curtain in a dizzying magenta and yellow paisley, is Liu Wah. His red shirt and purple scarf blaze as pure blocks of colour against the pattern, his smooth profile intent on the speaker. Maybe his English is better than he lets on, thinks Adarsh. Once — or was it twice? — during their conversation he began talking to the translator while Adarsh was still speaking. Deciphering, absorbing, intent, Liu Wah is watching Thompson, who from a drearily large sheaf of paper is reading a speech he most likely hasn't written. It's as if he's seeing it for the very first time, stumbling a little over his attempt at a Tamil proverb. Trans-Atlantic accent. Possibly. It's unlike anything Adarsh has heard before. He needs a drink.

There are still knots of people on the far veranda, a group in the garden below the wide steps. A wine waiter holds a tray of scotch and soda in cut-crystal glasses. Softer conversations continue where people couldn't be expected to hear the speeches.

He slips away towards the servant, takes a glass from the tray and hears the whispered 'Pandit ji', the Brahmin honorific from moist lips, and rises to smiling seductive eyes. He feels the thrill spin through him, and knows that if he wanted to he could slip away with this pretty wallah, right now, to one of the many rooms in this vast house, and he sees that it's an inevitability, that it's going to happen, that the servant is making a gesture to follow him — when there is a loud resounding crash from the reception room.

Adarsh sees in an instant what has happened — the Chinese writer must have felt him slip from his side, concentration not as absolute as Adarsh had imagined. Wah had turned away too, perhaps to follow him, and caught his foot in the curtain, bringing the rail down on the many heads and glasses gathered inside the doors.

The crash, thud, screams and breaking glass are followed by an instant of total silence even from the new CEO, who shows a flash of mercy in waving off the remainder of his speech. Then there is moaning and consternation and blood from those who clocked the heavy carved finials at either end of the rod. Servants run to pick up glass, a doctor is called for and clusters of guests bend over prostrate forms.

Adarsh swallows his scotch and goes in search of the waiter.

The director

The meeting with the university had proved irksome and difficult to organise, with several postponements and cancellations, but now, at long last, it was going to happen. This morning. Not that Rae was looking forward to it, particularly, as she walked down to the carpark with Orla to take their separate cars into town and fuck the carbon. Their relationship had deteriorated to such an extent they could not bear to be in one another's company for any longer than necessary. Yesterday Orla had shouted at her — *shouted* — 'There are several names on this list I have never seen before! I have the power of veto!' and Rae had found herself shouting back, 'Since when? You don't read anything — you don't know the first thing about them!' To which Orla had shouted, 'I can google!' To which Rae had shouted, 'You're not my boss, Orla!' because she wasn't. They had an equal powershare in the administration, which was another irregular organisational aspect of which Cameron was continually scornful. Once he'd even said, 'You're mostly women, aren't you? Only women would come up with that idea.'

If only, thought Rae as she blipped her car lock, if only she could be one of those artistic directors for whom the *artistic* overwhelms the *director*, she could suddenly be seized by a passion to attend to something else entirely different from this annoying meeting. There was a guest festival director she met years ago in New York, crazy, always late, hair awry, losing things, dropping pens, books, forgetting appointments, a woman in her late sixties, a legend. Rae could cultivate that persona because it might make people — i.e. the board and maybe, eventually, even Orla — more tolerant of her failures. Instead of that, here she was in her usual neat skirt and jacket, two seasons old but Issey Miyake, still classy and expensive-looking. Hair in a French roll, 6 cm heels and the only ragged part of her invisible.

Out of the basement, head for the main road into town. If things were different she could have organised to meet Cameron for a late lunch. Would have, if she still enjoyed his company. Who would have thought separation could be so difficult to achieve? She'd asked him to go and he'd refused.

'I haven't got time to shift house,' he'd said. 'Haven't you noticed I'm never home?'

He was biding his time, waiting for something. What? She'll have to do it, happens all the time, more and more — the woman having to be the one to call it quits. Put her stuff in boxes. The man not man enough to do it himself.

Frowning again. Must not. End up with a monkey face. Funny how baby chimps and baby humans look completely different while lots of old humans look exactly like old chimps. Mick Jagger especially.

At the lights she smoothed the furrow with a fingertip and saw in the rear-vision mirror Orla queued two cars behind her, talking on her cell phone even though it was illegal, her bleached curls bouncing. She'd get away with it of course — any cop would falter before her Irish-smirish charm and rosebud lips, in exactly the way Rae had seen her massage relationships with all kinds of people — patrons, sponsors, publishers, publicists, reviewers and of course writers, about whom she had no clue. Curvy, blonde, small, quick, full of life. Rae, by contrast, tall, dark-haired, plain, thin. Gaunt, her mother had said the last time she'd seen her. Tired and gaunt.

Thanks, Mum.

But even-temperedish, wasn't she? Not like quotidian Orla, day-to-day-in-the-office unpredictable Orla — at her worst extremes either in full-bludgeoning furious flight or purring embarrassingly intimate confidences that came from nowhere. Last week a tale about how her current boyfriend had refused to have sex with her the night before, even though it was her birthday. Rae had struggled for a reply, and knew that Orla thought her cold because she couldn't find one, except for a possible gagging response.

Be nice. Move off at the lights, switch lanes and turn off earlier than is wise, just to lose her.

⌣

After driving around the clogged block, which took almost fifteen minutes, during which time a flash of Orla, striding head down towards Marketing and Communications on her shapely little legs, set off a further surge of paranoia — *She'll be there ages before me! What will she say that I won't hear?* — Rae found a park. Late morning and the public garden opposite the university thronged with students enjoying the last of the summer. Gaunt legs may not be attractive, she thought, but they're good for climbing hills fast. At the top she cut past the fountain and attendant statue of a colonial governor. In the late eighties, when she was a child, she'd seen it once without a head. Someone had knocked it clean off and stolen it, never to be recovered. The newish one was a little younger than her, then, thirty, a little weathered and seamlessly attached. More seamlessly than her own head, which burst with everything she had to get done today — the hundreds of — well, tens of — emails that waited for her back at the office to be got through before preparing for another meeting this afternoon; a phone call to return to the tiresome director of the Fringe; the plumber she had to get to fix the shower head at home; a doctor's appointment for Nellie, who has a rash; a lawyer to ring about the situation with Cameron; an American literary agent to negotiate with over a writer's outlandish fee. She wanted to scream, or at least retrieve her smartphone from her handbag to see if there was anything else, something she'd forgotten.

But the park she strode through was peaceful, happy, and she strove to pick up on the atmosphere, to chill out. See how the sun is shining. How the students lie about eating, reading, some of them social isolates fingerpicking at their phones, ears plugged. How at the foot of the governor's plinth a group of young Asian picnickers are convivial, sharing rice, meat, bread and vegetables, a lurid green and pink birthday cake set central.

Further on a couple of mutually enraptured young lesbians rolled on a blanket — and only after Rae had passed them did she realise one of them was familiar. The woman she met at Merle's. Jacinta, who wouldn't have recognised her, wouldn't have even seen her, since her eyes had been closed in rapture. Rae found herself smiling, something cute about it, young love in the summer sun. And then she remembered that Jacinta wasn't that young, it was just that English skin. They were about the same age, with similar responsibilities, kids the same age, no husband — and Jacinta was having an adventure, lucky cow. Unfair! Rae would have an adventure herself, but with a bloke, and why the hell not, you only live once. She's owed one. To have as much sex as she wanted. As most people had. Live life with a festive attitude, to delight in every moment, laugh, dance, be intimate with a lovely man, released from guilt for the first time in years.

Up ahead, beside the path that leads down to the Department of Marketing and Communications, Orla was waiting for her.

'I don't want you to push this too hard,' she said as soon as Rae was within earshot. 'Be sensitive to any resistance.'

Rae walked on ahead of her, up the narrow path fringed with glossy big leaves with prickly edges. Angelica. They snagged her stockings — she knew without looking they'd been scoured, marred, possibly laddered.

She'll push as hard as she has to.

Leave me alone, Orla.

Orla had. At the end of the path Rae turned to see where she'd got to. She called from the street, 'You can't get in this way — they've blocked it off.'

And so they had — a new construction behind orange wire and mounds of yellow clay, upturned soil of the old colonial barracks and parade grounds. They might've found bullets and bones, old shoes, whisky bottles — Rae couldn't remember what was there before, even though she'd been a student here. It wasn't that old, a late twentieth-century building already reaching its use-by date.

Back through the prickly leaves went Rae, sheers snagging, and followed Orla around the turn-of-the-century mansion — one of the oldest buildings left standing on campus. They passed under the ornate cast-iron lace, between the stone veranda posts and through the heavy door set with stained glass — all of which gave no hint of the interior, made bland over bland by successive renovations. There was no receptionist or front desk, just a faulty, finger-smeared interactive directory, which luckily they didn't have to struggle with again, since they knew where they were going, up to the second floor via a newish side staircase since the original central flight had long ago been removed to make room for more offices. A modern fire-door opened onto a luminous Edwardian panelled hall with many of the doors giving into sunny offices. Work stations, water coolers, ugly cheap desks. The first time she came here Rae wondered what had happened to all the original furniture, the heavy old kauri desks, the rolled-arm settees — it would have all looked so beautiful.

'Did you hear what I said before — about taking it easy? If there's any problems?'

Rae had a suspicion, belatedly.

'Do you know something I don't know, Orla? Has there been some correspondence?'

She stopped walking — Orla walked on — so Rae followed, keeping her voice low. 'I really want this meeting to go smoothly, you know that. But I also really want Liu Wah, as do many festivals around the world.'

Orla's silhouette flared and faded in the rectangles of light from the open doors, her face shadowed, expression hidden, silent.

'It's a coup to have got him. Comprendo?'

There was a man at NYBW who said that, several times a day: 'Comprendo.' Rae had hated him. Hated people who said comprendo. Hates herself now in her neat skirt and jacket and last season's shoes, and for saying comprendo. It's hard to follow her own judgement all the time, even with the millions of suggestions people make. And she genuinely likes Liu Wah's book. She's curious about him and is sure other readers will be too.

As they approached the office, without breaking her stride, Orla produced a clearfile from under her arm and from it a document. The agenda. In an edition Rae hadn't seen before. Just last week she'd sent out all the necessary documents to all participants, and Orla had gone red with rage: 'But that's my job!'

'I've amended the agenda and shifted things around a bit,' she said now.

Whatevs, Orla.

Rae scanned the list — sponsorship and venue-share for the city-wide event, naming rights for a series of ongoing lectures throughout the calendar year, change of personnel at Marketing and Communications, confirmation of guests and lifting of media embargo dates, her own Artistic Director's report — and saw at the very last, at number six, Liu Wah.

Orla's eyes were sparkly and challenging — there was no point in asking why she'd done it. Because she hoped they won't get around to it, or because she thought the matter would take ages to discuss?

'Shall we strike it from the agenda altogether?' asked Rae, saccharine. 'I really don't mind.' But Orla ignored her, the door was swinging open and the large figure of Malcolm Murchison was greeting them, introducing them to Lydia Lee from Asian Studies and Zhang Wei from the Consulate General. There were three other people in the room, two other men from the consulate and Murchison's P.A., whom they'd met before. Rae and Orla shook hands with them all, and they adjourned to a meeting room next door, which was overly warm, airless, the windows sealed. Rae felt her breath sitting motionless in her lungs, wondered if she could ask for the air-con to be turned up. But Malcolm wasn't wasting time, speaking as soon as he reached his chair at the head of the board table.

'I see the matter of Liu Wah's involvement in the festival has been moved to the last item.' To Rae's immense satisfaction he turned Orla's agenda face down. 'If it is not a problem for you, I'd like to return it to its previous place at the head? Mr Zhang, Mr Lin and Mr Huang are pressed for time.'

Orla had distanced herself from Rae by sitting on the other side of the table between two of the diplomats. They seemed embarrassed, almost, that she had slipped in. One of them shifted his notepad; the other had his body angled away from her.

Murchison's question was for Rae, but Orla beat her to it.

'Surely, surely. Of course. Whatever suits. It is the most important matter we have to discuss this morning.' She sent Rae a chastising look, as if it was Rae who'd made the adjustments and should have known better. Murchison's colleague — the minute-taker — pursed her lips disapprovingly while she noted the changes.

'Mr Zhang?' Murchison turned to the most senior of the consuls, who nodded and referred to his device lying on the table in front of him.

'We regard the decision to invite Liu Wah to the Writers' Festival with grave concern.' Zhang didn't lift his eyes from his screen. 'We urge the directors to reconsider. The festival may or may not be aware that this writer has gone into self-exile and his books are banned in China.'

There was a short silence, broken only by the sound of a group of students passing under the window. Girls. Laughing, high-pitched, speaking a language that was possibly the same one Lydia from Asian Studies was using as she leaned across the table. The three diplomats regarded her steadily, as did Orla from her position between them. Her tone was angry, chastising — and Malcolm Murchison made several attempts to interject before he succeeded.

'I wonder if we could agree to speak in English?'

After a pause Lydia sat back in her chair and assumed an immediate calm, an instant poise Rae couldn't help but admire.

'A visit from this writer will have repercussions at a very high level,' Mr Zhang said. 'It could be that there are downstream flow-on effects for the university.'

Downstream flow-on effects? Orla was doing a very good job of looking as though she dealt with issues like this all the time, nodding wisely, with a studied expression of informed contemplation.

'It could eventuate that it would be sensible for the university to reconsider its relationship with the festival,' said one of the other men from the consulate, who had been silent up until now. Mr Huang, was it? He had a slight American accent. Ex-Yale or Harvard, perhaps. Or a childhood in international schools. Frighteningly bright. Inscrutable. Unreadable. On orders. Rae supposed she was experiencing racial prejudice.

'Shame on you!' Lydia slapped her hand on the table, and Rae saw that the poise and calm of a moment ago was only an act. She was still furious. Hot and furious. A vanishing handprint showed white and steamy on the polished surface — the men were looking at one another — and then Orla laughed, that chortling, delighted laughter that everyone always loves. The atmosphere softened immediately.

'Oh, come now, come now,' Orla said. 'He's only a writer, after all, a poet. He's only a poet.'

She was half right — he is a poet, but not only a poet. 'Not my cup of tea,' she'd said, when had Rae tried to interest her in his work. 'Too depressing.'

'What is the worst that a visit from Mr Liu can do?' Orla was asking the diplomats, swivelling from one to the other and across to Mr Zhang. They didn't meet her eye.

'Protests by mainland Chinese students,' answered Zhang, 'on campus and possible further afield. Possibly they will protest at other venues around the city, outside the premises of affiliated parties.'

'But the number of students who know who he is is minimal,' Lydia said. 'Will you be disseminating him between now and his arrival? You see, Ms McKay, Mr Zhang will do your publicity for your festival — he will make sure the students know this apparently wicked man is coming. He will make sure that Mr Liu — actually a fine, brave, clever writer — is made unwelcome.'

Silence. Lydia's speech had been addressed to Rae and it seemed everyone was waiting for her response, Mr Zhang included.

'What is the university's position on his involvement?' she asked, finally. Piping up. Doing her job.

Get on with it.

Usually Malcolm was talkative at their meetings, excited about the programme and associated benefits for the university. The big man was leaning back in his chair, his hands clasped tightly together on the table. At first, it seemed as though he hadn't heard the question, so Rae began again, 'What is—'

'We have no blanket policy. We deal with each situation on a purely case-by-case basis.'

'Are you as concerned as Mr Zhang?' In the half-dozen times Rae had met him, she had never seen Malcolm so uncomfortable. He was a quiet, peaceful, old-fashioned sort of bloke, in his early sixties, his face set with laugh lines.

Laugh lines deeper than his frown mark. She rubbed hers again — *in company*! She dropped her hand.

'Yes, I do have concerns. This is a diplomatic matter, or could become one.'

'I don't understand.' Rae heard her words chime into the

room, ignorant and childish, and there was a shift in the air. An atmosphere of disbelief. Of course. The vast number of mainland Chinese paying foreign student fees to attend our universities, the benefits to the national economy. Our major trade partner in every respect. Of course Malcolm had to be careful.

How naïve not to have thought of it before. Orla looked at her pityingly.

'It would be preferable for us all to quietly bow out on this one,' Malcolm Murchison said to Rae, shaking his head at the minute-taking colleague. Her typing fingers stilled, and he went on. 'There are thousands of wonderful writers out there. I'm sure you and Orla could present us with someone just as interesting.'

'Are you suggesting I should withdraw the invitation? I've already invited him and he has accepted.'

'That is most irregular,' said Murchison, and Rae almost laughed. Irregular! He was a caricature, the over-institutionalised timid man, not long off early retirement, taking the path of least resistance, kowtowing to the authorities. Her blood was up, she felt more breathless than she had before.

Watch yourself.

'When?' asked one of the consulate men.

The consulate, or could Huang have come from the embassy in the capital? Was it really that bothersome, that important, they'd fly people up for the meeting? She forced a breath, told herself it was encouraging, in a way. Heartening. Reassuring that a writer could still be seen as so powerful, so dangerous, so able to bring about change.

'When was the invitation accepted?' Mr Zhang this time.

'A month ago. Orla, I thought you—'

Orla glared at her. And Rae was landing her in it, it couldn't be denied. But Orla had always been territorial about the relationship with the university — '*I am the prime interface!*' — insisting on responsibility for all communication with Marketing and Communications.

Rae smiled at the assembled, the stationary minute-taker, the embassy men. 'My apologies, I understood Orla was keeping you up with developments.'

Orla had had time to think. She threw her hands up, her initial pretty blush fading, her lively blue eyes wide with surprise. 'Oh, but I didn't realise. I thought he wasn't completely confirmed.'

'Barring war or natural disaster. Yes, he's confirmed.'

Vigorously, Orla shook her head — the gleaming, bottle-blonde curls — and addressed the room. 'I'm so sorry to have to have this conversation in front of you.'

Zhang had leaned back in his chair, another little smile pulling at his lips, the corners of his eyes, and was watching her. Even he was charmed by Orla, Rae could see.

'Nothing is confirmed completely until the sponsorship is in place. You know that, Rae, whether or not the writer accepts. Liu Wah's visit is dependent on sponsorship from the university and affiliated parties.'

One of the other men was checking the time on his device. For all she knew, the meeting was being recorded. Suddenly it was all very James Bond. She would not back down or respond to Orla's patronising lecture.

'This is not the time or place for this discussion. Suffice to say that Liu's presence is confirmed. There will be many willing sponsors, I'm sure, people who will want to help.'

Lydia was talking over the top of her: 'I understand that you previously worked for a literary festival in New York?'

She'd done her homework then, found out where Rae had come from.

'And did you ever have a dissident writer there?'

'Yes — Mo Yan.'

'Hardly a dissident. One book briefly banned, the rest of the time championed by the administration. After Tiananmen Square, while Liu Wah was in prison, Mo Yan was at liberty. And now he's won the Nobel Prize! You people know nothing.'

Who is 'you people', wondered Rae. Does she mean me?

'Why do you think it would be possible to do it here? Host a writer banned in China?'

'Because this is—' but before she could give her answer of geographical isolation, of this country's once proud championing of freedom of speech and of human rights, and how it is a literary festival's moral duty to freely propagate ideas, Lydia was talking again.

'You are enviably naïve. I wish I could join you in your fairyland.'

And I thought we were on the same side, lady, Rae thought, even as she quailed in the face of Lydia's fury.

'I have a lecture to give. My apologies.' The professor was standing, picking up an ornate silver and pink handbag at odds with her grey trousers, unadorned white shirt and suit jacket, and heading for the door.

'Doctor Lee.' Mr Zhang stood to detain her, and Lydia slowed her steps. 'We agree, it is not necessary to say, that this matter will be contained. Everything we have discussed in this room is confidential.'

There was the merest dip of Lydia's dark, silver-threaded head — then she was gone. Did she really nod? She can't have done. This will have to go public.

Zhang's colleagues were standing too, and they were all making their farewells with Orla in full flight, shaking and squeezing their hands, saying what a pleasure etc, etc, etc.

Go through the motions, sit again and try to think.

A fairyland, Lydia had said. Fairyland? Rae was adrift, bewildered. The earth had shifted on its axis. There were floaters at the corners of her vision. She thought about Liu Wah in Germany, about the people who had helped him, how in good faith she had invited him, how China's tentacles spread throughout the world. Her stomach felt cold, her mind dull. What a foolish mistake to have made, to even think that he could come.

If the head of Marketing and Communications noticed her silence it didn't seem to perturb him. Upbeat, energised by the intensity of the first part of the meeting, Malcolm and Orla moved swiftly on through the agenda until they got to the sixth and last item: the Artistic Director's report, which she had furnished last week as a document among their attachments. Unread, possibly. Otherwise they would have known already that Liu was confirmed.

'Rae?' Orla was waiting for her, the file she had been energetically adding to closed, the agenda once again gleaming on her screen.

Gathering herself, Rae brought up her report and talked to it, scanning the list of confirmed writers as she went. The elderly English crime doyenne, the South American magic realist, the handsome Ghanaian, the epic Norwegian, the charming Australian, Merle's Indian ex-student made good, scribes without number from up and down the islands. But no Liu Wah. She was sure she'd added him. She had. Where was he? What had happened — a gremlin? A digital dropout?

While Orla and Murchison read and enthused and digested the information, and the minute-taker brightened at the mention of Dame Roberta Cornish, whose whodunits make popular television, Rae checked the original sender. Had Orla sent another one that somehow cancelled hers out? But her own name sat at the top of the document.

'I see Mr Liu is not there, Rae.'

Either Orla was reading her mind or her eyesight was sharp enough to rake meaning from Rae's device, which lay flat on the table with hot camouflaging sunlight bright across the screen.

'No. I'm so sorry.'

Stop apologising.

'I thought I had — I was sure—'

'Not to worry!' Murchison was grinning and clapping his meaty hands together. 'I think we're done!'

After he called the meeting to a close, he walked them down the corridor to a small, scruffy lift hidden around a corner, a prematurely aging late twentieth-century renovation. The metal doors were scuffed, the blue wheelchair sticker was peeling off, the exterior doors hung on a wonk. Rae had never known it was here.

'We can take the stairs — it's only one floor,' said Orla, eyeing it nervously, and Rae remembered how in one of her confession sessions Orla had talked about being stuck in a department-store elevator as a child, how the resulting claustrophobia affected her so profoundly she could barely stand flying, even though planes are comparably bigger, and how she would probably never go home to Ireland unless it was by sea.

Rae loved planes and elevators. Especially this one, which would take her away from this meeting, this office, this university, this bewilderment. The loss of innocence. Is that all it was?

The door pinged open and Orla was following Rae inside, brave too.

'All in all a positive outcome, wouldn't you agree?' said Malcolm by way of farewell. 'Hear from you soon, Rae,' and the mustard-carpet-walled box was rattling and banging its way to the ground floor.

'See you at the office!' Out on the street Orla waved her fleshy little hand, pointy red fingernails flashing, and Rae managed a wave in return, noting that her middle finger had a blackened nail from peeling the potatoes last night, or was it from the Sunday hour yanking out weeds? Was it only an hour? She'd made the mistake of going inside and going online, and once she's hooked up it's hard to get off. Hours go by, plugged in, ignoring the kids and plagued by guilt.

A moment to herself. What she needed now. A garden.

She crossed the street to the park and took a seat on a bench near the fountain, stretching her legs in the warmth. A minute. A moment. An hour. The whole afternoon off. There was a hole in her stocking from those grabby plants. Her bun had slipped. The hot meeting room had left her with damp semi-circles in her synthetic armpits. Talk to Merle. What would Merle advise? And possibly Brendan, if he wasn't pissed?

When she was growing up, her much older cousin was a heroine. Now and again Merle's picture was in the paper, and her books were proudly bought by her aunt. They would be displayed on the table or kitchen bench, left lying about for visitors to see. Now and again Merle wrote letters and articles for the newspapers, criticising cuts to education and health, instances of idiotic greed or miscarriage of justice. She said unpopular things. Merle worked for the university in the days when a university would swim against the tide. And Brendan made all those honest documentaries, famous in their time.

She wants to tell them. What would they say?

Confidential, Mr Zhang had said. Contained.

The park had emptied, the students returned to campus. Jacinta and her girlfriend had moved off, disappeared, and the picnickers had disbanded. Governor Grey's thirty-year-old head hosted a seagull, and Queen Victoria had wizened, shrunken into her bronze robes.

She was afraid, Rae realised. Afraid of what was to come. Of what she might have to do. You have to believe in the good of humanity, she told herself. It is racist to be so afraid. You have to believe that people can safely tell the truth. You have to have hope.

Her phone was ringing. Orla. *Ignore it.* But no, she'd picked it up.

'Hey girl,' said Orla straight away, since caller recognition had done away with the human need for mutual salutation. 'Just wanted to congratulate you on getting through that meeting — you were fantastic — I could see you really weren't happy about it all, but you know it's the minnow and the whale and we really can't be seen to be—'

'Sorry, Orla, I'm driving,' said Rae. 'Talk soon.'

She texted the nanny — *I'll pick the kids up this afternoon. Will pay you tho* 😊 — and set off down the hill, soothed and settled at the prospect of spending some time with Ned and Nellie, of afternoon tea and story books, homework and cooking dinner. No screens for anyone for at least an hour.

Just the three of us.

A writer

Early in the evening Gareth turns his phones off, shuts down his computer and sits on his step-up stool at the kitchen window with Adarsh's book. Far rather would he be writing, but he has made a deal with himself, has gone so far as to write it in his Moleskine — 'Not another word until the reading is finished.'

Page 180. Four hundred to go. Some of *Gay Times with Ganesha* has small resonances. He remembers working with Adarsh on certain passages, remembers afternoons in the office and a single visit the student made to his old towerblock flat in the city. He remembers Adarsh's sensitive long hands, his ready smile, his quiet, soft eyes. Something assured about him, a trust in his unfolding story so absolute he had no prickly edges, no clanging ambition to get in the way of Gareth's mentoring. The student was cushioned by his considerable gift and the palpable sense, even then, that fate would smile benevolently on him.

But, oh my God, there's a sentence! A full half-page — colons, semi-colons, parentheses, commas galore. Pleonasms abound, one mixed metaphor, pronouns argue with nouns, but somehow the meaning stands clear, or does after two readings. Old-fashioned, elaborate — the antithesis of current literary cool. Lately it's all about paring down, opening out, subverting the genre, approximating it. A British novel published last year abandoned the letter e except for the title; another eschewed commas, inverted and standard.

The e-less novel lies in wait for him in a carton in his study. *'E' is punchy, direct, powerful*, said the critics.

Grat. Xciting. Can't wait.

A flare of orange from the sinking sun lies neatly captured in one long aluminium groove of the roof, a rectangular stripe of shifting, vanishing light. Gareth opens the window and cranes his head to the west — there are clouds rolling in and a chill in the air.

Late February, almost autumn. This afternoon a wind had risen. He'd heard it arrive, heard it suddenly banging around the building. A brown plastic bag that he'd thought at first was a bird had blown past his second-storey window. A bird flying backwards. Not beautiful like the much-imitated plastic bag in that film, *American Beauty*, the plastic bag leaping and twirling as an expression of joy. It was a bird blown backwards, wings stretched, useless. It's because he was half-blind, eyes blurry from the hours on the new novel, trying to get it to a point where he could happily leave it. Where he had a sense of a road map. Not too much of one — there still had to be an element of danger to what could appear on the page in front of him. Where would he arrive the next time he set off?

Be honest, he tells himself. You spent the last two hours on FB, reading posts by some of your 400 friends, many of them writers, ex-journalists, academics, students — people who constantly posted stuff. Interesting stuff, although Gareth rarely pauses long enough to read an entire article. Or poem. Or endure a three-minute clip. He finds that his brain goes into a kind of reverberating spin, like a car wheel dropped flat to the ground at a breakdown. A drumming wobble until it stops altogether and a strange rubbery numbness overcomes him so that the action of scrolling up and down feels almost mechanical. Overwhelmed to the point of boredom.

Concentrate.

Adarsh's baroque sentences curl and fold, twist and turn, bright and sparkly. There is a liberal garnish of Hindi words and expressions that necessitate turning to the glossary at the back and so break his stride. The other entries are too distracting.

Read them all. Forget them instantly. Gaze out the window.

When did he lose the ability to concentrate? No focus or self-discipline. Too much time alone; too much dependence on the lean media experience of social media.

Go out. Into the real world.

A great haste seizes him — no time to waste showering or shaving, though he pokes himself into a clean tee-shirt before he walks to the corner and hails a taxi. He'll be glad to move house — he doesn't like the streets they're driving through, commercial industrial, with no real heart and a funny chemical smell strong enough to sometimes sting your nostrils. Jacinta had liked the area. She'd even said, early on, 'We're the vanguard. People will follow us — musicians and poets and artists — it'll be a village. Like in New York.'

Hadn't happened yet. The other day a dog had rushed at him from a ground-floor premises, and when the owner called him back Gareth had looked inside — hundreds of paua piled on a high wet bench and a row of white-capped women with flashing knives. There was no signage to announce a fish-processing plant. The guy looked shifty and his dog was scary, and Gareth is convinced the whole outfit is clandestine, illegal, ripping the heart out of a stolen resource. He'd heard of these enterprises — the shellfish would be bleached and sold overseas as abalone.

Still, better to have molluscs for neighbours than party animals and Sunday lawnmowers. Jacinta got that part right at least.

The cab drops him off at the centre of town, not far from the pub he would sometimes drink at when he was teaching. He could have gone somewhere different, but it's the closest thing he has to a local. He walks up the cobbled lane which has gone through many guises since he was a kid — 1970s twee Victoriana, 1980s industrial chic, 1990s expensive minimalism, and in the last two decades native palms with koru-shaped inserts in the paving. The trees are scruffy, the lane scurfed with fag ends, and a tall thin white girl with a guitar is singing outside what used to be a shoe shop. Now it's another shop selling cheap Chinese shit, the containerloads shipped in at the port, everything in it shoddy and badly made and with a smell to rival his own neighbourhood. The shop next door is up for lease. Used to be, what . . . lingerie. He has a memory of a corset in the window, Jacinta pointing it out. She'd tried it on and he'd had to hang around while she did, and then she'd been mad because he stayed outside in the lane reading his Kindle instead of coming into the shop to admire her. She'd come out to the street in it to show him, red satin with black vertical stripes. Bones, are they? Lots of lace and a bra bit pushing her tits up. Outrageous. Laughing at her own audacity but an outraged sense of neglect directed at him.

Quash the memory.

Up the low flat stone steps, some of the few left in the city that bear the weight of a century, a shallow bowl in the middle of the tread — and he's inside. A dark interior. Booths. Like it's always been, the bottles and glasses gleaming, the high old bar — but empty. Pretty much. He's made a mistake — he needs to be among people. Monday night. Of course. He'd thought it was later in the week.

He orders a tasty sav and takes in a quartet of businessmen drinking further down the bar and, nearer to him, a couple. They're in their thirties, corporate types, lawyers perhaps. She's groomed bottle-red, attractive, bit dumb-looking, killer shoes, dressed by Trelise or Karen Whatsername or something expensive. The sort of thing a girlfriend would know. If he had one, he could ask her. The guy is thin, dark-haired, suit, receding hairline, intense-looking and slight American twang.

Not that they're talking much — they seem a bit ill at ease. First date?

The woman sees Gareth looking at them and smiles. She wears a wedding ring, so does he. Married, but not to each other? Or married swingers?

'Hi,' she says. 'I'm Chelsea. This is Cameron, my boss.'

She's pissed, Gareth realises. But holding it well — her head moves fluidly, slowly, as if she's pushing through water — she lifts a regal hand — a diamond. 'And you are?'

'Gareth Heap.' He can't help it. He likes to give his second name in case an interesting conversation about his work eventuates, but she doesn't recognise it. Laughs, in fact. 'Heap! You poor schmuck.'

He smiles good-naturedly, wonders if he should move off while he can, but she's too quick for him.

'Well, Gareth Heap — maybe you can solve a problem for us.'

'Chelsea—' warningly from the man. Cameron.

'Why not? We need mediation and we need it now!'

'Just ignore her,' says Cameron. 'Sorry about this, mate.'

'You see — Garth, was it? — I'm tired of sneaking around and he's all for sneaking around for ever. Not that I give a rat's arse.'

'Chelsea!' Louder this time.

'He keeps saying he's going to and I wouldn't mind if he did. Then we could get together when we felt like it, not when he can, which are two different things, you know? Sometimes I'm not in the mood.'

'Okay, Chelsea, that's enough.' Cameron looks up at Gareth, makes a subliminal nodding gesture for him to move away. Used to giving orders, perhaps. Gareth decides to ignore him. Fantastic. Live YouTube. Good material maybe, though he can't think what for. Adultery is so passé. Polyamory still has some gas in the tank — perhaps a short story where three people live together playing swapsies. Get down to detail.

'Different for me you see, Garth. No kids. You see, if he left her he'd have to look after them sometimes and I don't want that.'

'Gareth,' says Gareth.

'Shut up, Chelsea! You're pissed. You need to go home. I'm going to ring a taxi for you — get them to come to the door for you.' Cameron speed-dials a number and talks to the automated voice in the overly enunciated way everyone does.

Yes. Yes. Ready now.

Chelsea watches him for a second, then explodes into angry tears. At the other end of the bar the businessmen fall silent and stare. Gareth can tell that Cameron would like to just walk away. He should.

'This is so pathetic!' Chelsea sobs. 'Like you think I even care if you go home to her. Like you think you can order taxis and order me around! Fuck you.'

The barman catches Gareth's eye and shakes his head.

'Nothing to do with me, mate.' Gareth takes hold of his sav preparatory to retreating to a peaceful booth just as Chelsea picks up her half-full glass of red wine, the contents of which she tosses into Cameron's face.

One of the businessmen guffaws and leers at Gareth. 'Better than television! Three's a crowd, eh?' and Gareth resents him for it. His threesome idea out there in the ether. He intensely dislikes his unwritten thoughts being picked up by members of the public, no matter how banal. The guy is red-faced, possibly shaving rash, a splodge of dip on his tie with a fragment of chip, like a wafer in a vertical ice-cream sundae.

Cameron is halfway to the door, a puddle of red wine marking the spot where he had stood, and Chelsea makes a grab for Gareth's delicious sav to throw it after him as well, but he restrains her, his hand closing over hers, and Cameron, glancing back once before he disappears into the dark, could assume he is comforting her.

He isn't. He won't. He signals the barman for another glass of the same.

'Me too,' whispers Chelsea, 'the same as before.'

'Haven't you had enough, love?' asks the barman, who is fetching a damp cloth to wipe the floor.

'Give the lady a drink. My shout,' says Gareth, though his habitual parsimony rises and almost chokes him. Bugger it. He can afford it now. He could buy every weeping woman in the city a drink. Every smiling woman also.

They adjourn to a booth, Chelsea teetering on her killer heels and a strand of auburn hair escaping from her do.

'Thank you, Garth,' she says, sliding along the bench seat opposite him, 'you're a real gentleman.'

Jacinta would never have thought so, he thinks, and must have registered mild surprise because Chelsea goes on, slurring, 'Yes you are. Believe me. Unlike Cameron, leaving me here with you. You could be a rapist or a murderer.'

A lady of conflicting impulses, he thinks. She wants her lover to stay with her but she throws wine in his face. She thinks I'm a gentleman but also a possible rapist. He smiles, reassuringly.

'He's married,' Chelsea tells him.

'So I gathered.'

'To a bitch.'

'Have you met her?'

'Don't need to. She made him give up a promising career in New York to come back to this shit hole.'

Patriotism surges stronger than the previous parsimony. 'This country is not a shit hole!'

'Tell me what's good about it,' snarls Chelsea, leaning across the table. A sweet perfume rises from her lovely cleavage.

'Well . . . lifestyle, a thriving arts scene, improved relations with the indigenous, a clean, green environment sort of and—'

'She made him come home when he didn't want to and she made him have kids. Forced him to.'

'That happens,' says Gareth, glad it's never happened to him. 'Perhaps you should be grateful to her. If she hadn't brought him back, you would never have met him.'

'I wish I hadn't.'

Fresh tears. There's a paper-napkin dispenser on the table. He pulls one free and she blows her nose, smearing her red lipstick onto her chin. After a moment or two she calms, then sighs heavily.

'Anyway. Enough about me. What do you do?'

'I'm a writer.'

Sometimes Gareth says he's a builder or a butcher or an accountant in order to avoid the depressing rejoinder, 'Never heard of you,' but Chelsea is saying, delightfully, 'I thought your name was familiar.'

'Really?'

'You might know Cameron's wife. Rae. She runs the Writers' Festival.'

So she didn't recognise his name at all. Just fishing. He takes the safest option — a slight nod — and is startled by her incommensurate response. Her eyes, large anyway, too large for her narrow face, swell like booming green frogs. Her intake of breath is like graunching gears.

'Tell me what she's like. I looked on Google images and she's plain as. Ugly! And cruel-looking.'

'I, uh . . . I've actually never met her. Only talked on the phone. And emails. You know, not face to face.'

'So you've never been invited to the festival yourself then?'

Is she thinking he's a minor writer? Or maybe not a writer at all?

'Yes of course, but not since Rae came on board.'

'Even an ugly name. Rae McKay. If I'd married Cameron and I was called Rae I would have kept my maiden name.'

'What was that?'

'What?'

'Her maiden name.'

Chelsea curls her lip. 'How would I know?'

'Pillow talk.'

'What the fuck would I care?'

Tears threaten yet again, and he thinks he's really had enough of this and would like to go home. One swallow finishes his wine and he stands up — but from this perspective Chelsea seems so much smaller, childlike, little narrow shoulders and bony knees and kind of broken. She looks up at him with her luminous, make-up-smeared eyes, and he looks away, quickly, towards the door. Where is her taxi?

'The taxi didn't arrive,' he observes.

But she thinks he's a gentleman. Gentlemen don't abandon pissed, vulnerable ladies.

'Maybe you could give me a lift?'

'I don't drive.'

The barman is at their table.

'Sir — if you could settle the tab?'

It has been an expensive exercise, he thinks, as he follows Chelsea into the lobby of her eastern suburbs apartment block. First the tab, evidence that she and Cameron McKay had been drinking very good wine for some time before his arrival, and second the taxi fare. As they'd passed along the waterfront, she had lunged at him, pushing her tongue into his mouth and her hand under his shirt. Her hand had been cold but her mouth was warm, and on investigation so were her tits. Heavy and warm and inviting, as is her arse in the tight skirt going into the lift ahead of him.

Is this a good idea? She seems a little unstable, a bit damaged. But to hell with it — what woman isn't damaged or unstable these days and he hasn't had a root since Jacinta. At least Chelsea is independently wealthy if she can afford to live apparently alone in this swanky apartment with its harbour view, with the lights of North Head twinkling across the channel, and she's certainly up for it, leading him away into a white bedroom, pushing him onto the bed and straddling him while she undoes her blouse. Her high heels catch on an open-weave throw, so she kicks them off, rug and shoes together, and bends to remove her pantihose.

And pauses.

'What's wrong now?' he starts to ask, but doesn't get the whole question out because it's suddenly obvious. The hand clamped to the mouth, the frantic rush to the ensuite, the slamming door, and from behind it the unpleasant and unmistakable sound of retching.

Perhaps he should go. But he's comfortable on the bed, drowsy, and besides a gentleman abandons a vomiting lady even less than he abandons a drunk one. She could choke to death. He wonders what references there are in great literature to vomiting as a precursor to sex. James Baldwin's famous quote about art will not do, since it is lofty and more about survival. Something about vomiting anguish in order to tell the true story. In a way, he supposes, that's what Chelsea is doing. She doesn't have the look of the hardened drinker; her inebriation is all to do with Cameron. Drunk on a man. Drunk because she might love him but thinks Cameron doesn't love her in return. Jacinta was openly drunk on himself for a short while. High as a kite.

When Chelsea comes back, they can pick up where they left off. Maybe. As long as she's cleaned her teeth. He's very warm and drowsy, so sleepy . . . too sleepy. Would she be expecting it if she comes right? Surely the morning will be soon enough. He really doesn't want to disappoint her intentionally, though he supposes he will disappoint her in any case. Inevitable. How much does he really want her?

The question opens the door to unconsciousness so deep he barely stirs when she returns to the bed half an hour later and sleeps as far away from him as possible.

The director

As she walked up Merle's front path to collect the children, Rae tried to shake the week off, but it had gone from bad to worse. There was the meeting with the university on Monday, her mother hospitalised on Wednesday, and all the time Cameron either AWOL or impossible, the kids scratchy and the usual excesses from Orla at work — and then the phone call this morning. There was no way through it all. Couldn't breathe, felt burdened, overdressed. Sweaty. February heat renewed, redoubled.

She stopped for a moment, took off her cream jacket with its faint pink stain and took note of the plums lined up along the low wall in plastic bags, free to a good home. There were two bags of apples too, full of worms. The kids had come home with a bag last time, and Ned had dissected them, one after another, to find the tiny creature cosseted at the core and waggle it in their faces. Not all of the fruit had been bad. They had eaten a few. She picked out an apple now, examined it for holes and took a shallow bite. Delicious, sharp and tangy.

Deep breath. Go inside. Hang with the kids and chat to Merle. Calm down.

The seasons were changing, the days were drawing in — dusk already. Warm dusk. She ate some more of the apple, carefully inspecting it as she went. When the worm made himself known to her, she threw it into weeds growing tall in the overplanted front yard. Neither Brendan nor Merle liked gardening, which was just as well, since they lived in a forest of giant natives. Rae would have some of them culled, if it was her house. Knock some down. Let in the light. Save the pipes. Free the foundations.

Merle answered the door to her, the awful pink and yellow dog named after a prison leaping and showing its teeth, and the children galloping down the hall, happy and dirty and busy. When they saw who it was — 'It's only Mum!' — they turned tail and headed back out, a connecting door slamming after them in the northerly gale. Nell was in her socks, black from the garden, leaving marks on the grass mats.

'Hey!' Rae said, going after them, because she wanted to give Nell a cuddle and Ned a kiss. They were the best things in the world — the very best things — but they were gone and she was left with Merle, who gave her a searching look.

'What's wrong with you? You look terrible.'

'Nothing's wrong. Thanks for the compliment,' and she found herself irrationally irritated in the way that only relatives can annoy, and propelled away, down the hall towards the dining room, the dog leaping and licking at her hand and Merle's footsteps hurrying after her. No deep and meaningfuls. Just get the kids' stuff together — which could take ages since Merle let them drag it all over the house — and go.

'Rae?' asked Merle, coming up behind her and taking her arm as they went out onto the veranda. 'You really look awful.'

'I'm fine. Really.'

The new boarder, a Saudi student, was sitting on one of the dilapidated deckchairs, hair slick and gleaming skin, nostril-tingling aftershave. Good-looking in a babyish way, arrogant as hell. A petulant full mouth and knife-edged nose. Shirt neatly ironed, some nice chest hair inviting touch. In your dreams. He hadn't even noticed her arrival, being intent on his device, a green reflective glow in his lowered eyes.

In the back garden the kids were kicking a soccer ball through the weeds and long grass growing under the kauri, the rimu, the macrocarpa, the phoenix palm, the ancient grapefruit, the nikau and three cabbage trees. The dog barrelled out to join them, barking at the top of its voice.

'Ned!' called Rae, but Ned ignored her. 'Come on. Get your stuff. Nellie? We're going home.'

Ned booted the ball, and a thought passed with it between brother and sister, complicit, visible. *Pretend you didn't hear.*

'Ned. Come on. Hurry up.'

'It's not all about you, Rae.'

Gruff. A perfect imitation of his father. The same refrain in the same intonation, the identical profile, and now the back of the head as he ran away, though Ned had more hair. She crumpled, felt her face contort for a second, felt like an idiot.

Get it together.

Merle put her arm around her. 'Go and get your stuff, kids. Now!' But they ignored her too, reaching the tree hut, escaping, the dog hysterical with joy, running with them and leaping while they climbed the ladder.

Rae wept. Pathetic. Hormonal, it had to be. She coped with everything, usually.

The Saudi student had noticed her finally, a weeping, gaunt woman fifteen years his senior and half a metre taller, as was plain now he stood up. There was a gust of chemical musk as he passed them, the squeak of leather from his expensive shoes. He went down the steps, through the garden and out the back gate.

'Off to sit in his brand-new car,' said Merle, her arm still around Rae's waist. 'Bought it yesterday. No licence. Can't drive. Got a driving lesson booked for tonight with a friend from the language school.'

She gave Rae a little squeeze, real affection and concern. Rae loved her for it. There was some family dynamic that was good. There was, whether she liked it or not. Yes, Merle had the right idea. Talk about something else. The student. Rae didn't have to tell her any gruesome details.

'I'll give you a hand to find their things,' said Merle, and called out to the garden, 'You kids! Five-minute warning. Ned, did you hear me?'

'Yaaaaaas!' came a yell from Ned, with Nellie joining in, ululating 'YAAAAAAS!!' They helped up the puppy, which had inbred pain barriers high enough to withstand the scrape of his belly on the ladder. All three sat at the crooked window through the trees, grinning, defiant.

She followed Merle inside.

'You sure you don't want a glass of wine?'

Merle was rummaging in a low cupboard stuffed tight with plastic takeaway containers and jars, and coming up with half a bottle of merlot. Only half a bottle. One glass each. That would be all right.

'I thought I had some! With Brendan away the booze lasts longer! He finds all my hiding places.'

Old marriages. The old games. She wouldn't have any of it. Thank God.

'Trying to stay away from it at the moment.'

'Why's that?'

'Doesn't do me any favours.'

'Cup of tea, then?'

Rae didn't answer. Couldn't, suddenly. She wanted so much to tell her about the meeting, about the Chinese and the university. Confidential, they'd said.

There was a fuzz of dust on the naked luminous-blue lady painted onto black velvet in a cheap gold frame, a tasteless relic from last century. A rag rug from the century before that had lost all its colours, faded to various shades of brown like a chopping board loaded with sliced mushrooms. This room used to enthral her when she was a child, visiting with her mother from their germ-free open-plan house in a new subdivision on the distant North Shore. Now the clutter and grot annoyed her. Merle should have a cleaner. Everyone should have a cleaner. She and Cameron would have finished years ago if they hadn't had a cleaner. Tell her that, but not the other thing.

'Cameron is having an affair.'

'Oh no.'

Rae shrugged in an attempt at carelessness.

'Are you sure? How do you know? Lipstick on his collar?'

'What?'

'You know — the song —' Merle sang it — 'tells a tale on you—' in a high quavery voice.

Rae didn't.

'Did he confess? Oh, poor girl. This is very sad.'

'Wine down the front of his shirt. He said he got into a fight in a bar, but he's never done that in his life. And men don't do that, do they? Toss wine over each other? I think it's something women do. He wasn't marked other than that. No bruises or anything. I just know.'

'Well . . .' began Merle.

The children were chasing the puppy up the steps to the veranda and would be with them in a moment, ears flapping.

'I know he is. He's even more cold and distant than usual and some nights he doesn't come home at all. And then this morning—'

The children burst in, the dog barking so loudly that Rae felt her skull plates grate against one another — she already had a headache — and then they were gone again, down the hall, skittering on the layers of ancient, dusty grass mats set its full length.

'And then this morning he took a phone call from a woman who was screaming at him. Screaming! I could hear her while he walked outside. Something about how she'd gone home with a fuckwit and it was all his fault.'

'A workmate maybe?'

'Yes, she is. How did you guess? A colleague he's fucking.'

'Ummm!' Nellie was there, suddenly, at her elbow, eyes wide at the swear word, silent in her stained socks.

'Sorry Nellie.' She picked the child up, put her on her hip.

'Are you angry?' Nellie patted her reassuringly. 'It's okay to say eff when you're angry, Venice says.'

'Who's Venice?'

'The girl who was here before. She says fuck all the time and she says it's all right because she's angry all the time, fuckin' bugger.'

'Jacinta's daughter,' Merle told her, 'one of the twins. Remember?' She sighed. 'Nearly five years old.'

'That's appalling.'

'I can't be a hypocrite,' says Merle. 'Our lad was a potty mouth too, learned off us.'

'Do you see a lot of Jacinta? Is she here a lot, with my kids?'

Too crisp, but she really couldn't be having her children exposed to the moral and sanitary chaos that hung about those kids and their mother. A stricture of panic grabbed at her throat — with Cameron gone, there would be more and more of that unwilling exposure. It could become her own reality; she would find the job too much on her own, she would struggle for time, make the kids witness to grotty depths of human misery and depravity. She would join the ranks of women who climbed every night into an empty bed, mothers who had no loving co-parent to snuggle and chat with about the children, about plans for the future and moments from the past, about their friends, their jobs, about life, the future.

Oh, for Godsake. He isn't there for you now anyway. *Nothing will change.*

Merle was looking at her sympathetically as if she had some idea of what was going on in her mind. How could she, with Brendan the ever-faithful husband? Although there had been a story, something she vaguely remembered from her flappy-eared childhood hanging around in this very room, of Brendan straying with an aspiring young film-maker, or camera assistant or continuity girl. But he was still here after all these years, and he seemed to love his wife. Merle would have no idea, really, of what it was like to be standing at the brink of enormous change, at the end of a relationship that began when they were still in their teens. Rae and Cameron had travelled together, lived overseas, had children, bought a house, grieved for Rae's late father, done it all. What could Merle say? Only platitudes.

'Do you think you could forgive him?'

Rae hadn't thought of that possibility. She shook her head.

'People do, you know. Forgive each other. It's better, if you can.'

'No. It was over anyway. Was over for years.'

'You'll get on your feet again. At least you've got a good job.'

'That's the other thing. I'll have to let that go. The pay is no good, not enough, and it's too stressful.'

'Stressful?' Merle's tone had a streak of uncharacteristic sarcasm. Both women heard it, the dull, lifeless clang. Merle coloured, looked ashamed of herself but pressed on. 'It shouldn't be. It's a dream job. My friend Ripeka, the Fringe director, she really wanted—'

'It's just like any other job. You can't always do what you like,' interrupted Rae. Nellie was nuzzling her throat, her arms locked around her neck, and Rae glanced down at her — she was too heavy for this now, really — and saw how she'd closed her eyes and settled in for the long cuddle. Little darling who loved her dad. Who'd want him around.

'Very few people do what they like all the time and get paid for it,' Merle was saying. 'Not ordinary people. Maybe at some elevated, oxygenless, corporate level, where it's all about delegation and nothing that resembles actual work.'

'But not the likes of us,' Rae said, attempting an Irish accent that came out more New York, and made Nellie smile and wriggle in her arms. 'What happened to my glass of wine? And where are Ned and Parry? Ominously quiet.'

While Merle poured Rae's wine, Nellie scooted off in pursuit of her brother, reporting back within seconds that he was fast asleep with his arms around Parry on Merle's bed. The child sat herself at the kitchen table with her iPad, drawing with her fingertip, and Rae and Merle took chairs nearby. For a moment there was only the ticking of the clock on the mantelpiece and the soft scrape of Nellie's industry on the screen, and then Rae felt herself settle, and was able to tell Merle the story of Liu Wah and what had happened at the university and the assumption that the invitation would be withdrawn. Merle was thoughtful, and eventually gave a response Rae would never have predicted. 'It doesn't surprise me.'

'Why not? Why should the Chinese have any kind of editorial control over what happens in a university? Shouldn't a university champion free speech?'

'China is the major world power. Anyone who thinks it's still America is dreaming.'

'But it's wrong!'

'Of course it's wrong. But there's nothing you can do about it, Rae.'

'Why aren't you angry about it? You're more of a lefty than I am . . . Oh. I see. It's because you *are* a lefty.'

'No . . . it's because—'

'Don't tell me you're some sadfuck Maoist.'

At this insult, which was out of line — so out of line! — both Merle and Nellie lifted their heads and stared at her, and Rae saw for the first time a kind of family resemblance. The fine bones, the soft set of the mouth, the particular shade of blue in their eyes. Nell's lucky she looks more like her than me, thought Rae. I'm a grumpy bitch.

'No, I'm not a Maoist.' Merle put her glass down on the table in a gesture of finality, as if she wanted Rae to go, as if she was in need of some calm and silence. And she would be alone after they left, Rae thought, with Brendan away and the Saudi student driven off to God knows where, unlicensed, in his powerful car.

Nellie bent to her iPad again, her tongue flexed and protruding. An intricate multicoloured pattern lay across the screen. How much of it does the app do for her, Rae wondered. Was it as freeform as crayons and a sheet of paper? The pattern vanished and Nellie showed her dismay only by a soft tut-tutting, before she started again. In this new world it was normal for pictures to vanish under your gaze, for your mother to call Aunty Merle a swear word while they discussed world domination by a culture that has experienced the most brutal destruction of history ever known. A culture that underwent the greatest changes more quickly than any other, that went from feudal to post-industrial in a generation.

Rae has rehearsed all the arguments in her head, the reasons to be angry, to be apathetic, to be afraid. She has discovered that she is far less frightened for herself than she is for Nellie and Ned, who face a future of upheaval, a possible future of tenancy in their own country, should they choose to stay here. It is their generation that will experience incandescent rage when they realise their country and environment was sold out from under their infant feet so that an ever-diminishing middle class could continue enjoying the benefits it had had for nearly two centuries. If it's true that apathy and political passion usually alternate generations, then surely it was time for a new lot to come up fighting.

Will you fight, Nell? she wondered, but asked Merle instead, 'Don't you think people would be shocked by this? Okay, the university is supported by fee-paying students, but it's also supported by our taxes — it's supposed to be politically neutral.'

Merle snorted, picked up her empty glass and stood. 'Who says? You're living in the past. Some of the appointments to vice-chancellor have been very political. And of course the university is conservative. Name one large institution that isn't.'

Rae took the challenge seriously, thinking, one finger massaging her frown mark. She couldn't. The only radical organisations were small ones.

In the kitchen Merle was arranging cheese and olives on a plate, a bowl of homemade hummus, some crackers, some raw cauliflower.

'I love those,' said Nellie the moment the plate landed on the table, taking up two olives and putting them both in her mouth at once. The urban calf craving the saltlick purposefully omitted from her mother's cooking.

'Are you going to withdraw the invitation?' asked Merle.

Rae shook her head. 'I'll have to consult the Festival board. Another bunch of conservatives.'

'Wouldn't you say you are, though?' asked Merle gently. 'I remember Cameron donating his time and energy to update the systems at National Party office.'

'Cameron. Not me. I'm not anything. I don't vote . . . I used to,' Rae went on, seeing the dismay on Merle's face. 'Until we went to live in New York and I couldn't be arsed going in to the consulate. Got out of the habit.'

'Of voting for the Tories?'

'Doesn't matter who I voted for now, does it? We know that now. The two major parties are the same — pro-foreign ownership, free trade with anyone who asks.'

'Too glib. Too easy,' snapped Merle. 'Perhaps you will vote now? Now you've been politicised.'

'Have I?'

'Yes. You feel betrayed.'

Rae nodded. 'Betrayed on every front. Including by my husband.'

Nellie looked up from her fingerwork. The pattern had re-appeared, in monochrome this time.

'Daddy is your husband,' she announced. 'What means betrayed?'

After she helps Rae out to the car with the children, Rae carrying sleepy long-limbed Ned, his head bouncing on her shoulder, Merle goes into her study and flicks on her computer. She has been longing to do it for the last hour, now that it's morning in the Northern Hemisphere. Every evening at nine o'clock for seven months she has checked her emails, both addresses, and never found what she was looking for. Most nights she checks after a glass of wine, buoyed by alcohol and convinced that a response would have zapped from satellite to satellite and into her inbox. Tonight, tonight, tonight, she thinks. Tonight I'll know.

Other nights, like tonight, she has no real hope, being wearied by Rae's problems and the dull ache of missing Brendan, which surprises her because mostly she's been enjoying the peace and can see why the new social phenomenon of people separating as they stumble into late mid-life is popular. She's been sleeping like a baby, insomnia fled; and the spare tyre around her hips and tummy is reduced from lack of dinners, which she can't be bothered cooking. If Brendan was here, she'd feel guilty about not returning to his side, even if he was monosyllabic and hooked into his phone.

She types in her password, a reflex, a nine o'clock habit like an after-dinner cigarette.

And here is dear Brendan, checking in from Pram as he calls it, a place with a much longer original name, on the coast north of the capital not far from Paikok. He has collected some beauties. Not only what the culture would now regard as racially ignorant mispronunciations but some amusing re-inventions and simple contractions. Roto Vegas is the least of it, and how is Parry?

An email from Jacinta, for whom Merle seems to have morphed into not only an ongoing and unpaid mentor but also a patron. Or so FB has it, according to Brendan, who is her envoy into social media. If only Jacinta would regard her just as a friend, then the demands on her time might ease. With a profound sense of weariness, she opens the email, which carries an attachment. A poem? A short story?

An invitation to the twins' fifth birthday party at The Plough, which is an organic bakery and café. Venice reckoned they were going to McDonald's.

The rest is dross — Merle switches over to her new email address to see what's happening with Kyla.

It's there. A response from the agent. *Thank you!* in the subject line.

> Fascinated and keen to represent you. I would like to know a little more about this Kyla Mahon. How old are you, if you will forgive the question? Is this your first book? Could you please tell me a little about yourself?

She has to answer, to summon up Kyla, inhabit her.

```
Cheers for your msg.
```

Kyla's guileless, unsophisticated voice had only just sustained Merle through the novel. She has to be careful that it's not too much the same, the writer's voice and the correspondent's. The personae must be allowed a little artifice.

```
I am twenty-six years old and I don't
mind you asking at all since I find it
the most perfect age I've ever had.
```

Had or been? Or necessary? Kyla's grammar isn't perfect, but whose is? And it's important that she makes the most common mistakes that Merle has seen time and again over the years. Made herself. Kyla's egotism must be natural to her, not half-ashamed as it had been for generations passed. *Roadside Crosses* will require a heavy edit.

She deletes a few words, types on.

```
. . . asking at all and this is my
second book. My first was a pile of
crap. 'Roadside Crosses' is the first
one I'm happy for other eyes 2 c.
```

Careful. Backspace.

```
. . . to see. So chuffed you like it.
```

Or is chuffed too New Zealand? Maybe Kyla has picked up 'stoked', a piece of the argot of Merle's own youth, a word calling across the divide of three decades. Could it have made a return? She gets up from her desk to hunt for her phone to text Jack in Thailand, but then wonders if he'd be out of touch, he's been away so long. Chuffed or stoked? Chuffed is safer.

In her mind's eye Kyla is a little toughie, thin and wiry, dark-haired, vegetarian, irreverent, implacable. Her element is leathers and motorbikes, the open road, camping grounds all around

Australia while she wrote her book, which does not tell the truth about the roadside crosses she saw, who it was who was remembered there. The story is made up of musings on death and mortality, impressionistic, her journey undertaken after the sudden loss of the most significant people in her life. Kyla is one of those people surrounded by death — you meet them. She was orphaned early, burying siblings and two boyfriends, then losing her best friend in a car crash. No family for a journalist to go looking for further down the line. Merle has always wanted to write about it, the strange phenomenon that afflicts some families for no obvious reason, while in other families the only deaths are rare and elderly.

> We are surprised by how funny *Roadside Crosses* is, given its relatively bleak subject matter. There is some confusion in the office about its genre. Do you have images of your motorbike tour? I googled your name to see if you were posting or blogging and came up with nothing — no presence at all, not even tagged, which surprises us.

This was inevitable, of course. Merle has prepared a response to this.

> In the book I don't mention that I got married in my late teens. Didn't last no big drama but I'm using my married name. Sure I'm around under my born name but let's not complicate things. This is how I like it. Could be part of the marketing that I'm offline, off web?

The agent wants a JPEG and 'some more information about yourself other than what Merle Carbury wrote in her covering letter. Please give her our regards.'

So they remember her, across the twenty years since they represented her on her second novel.

```
Will get a headshot organised. Best,
Kyla.
```

As soon as the message flies away, Merle switches her computer off. What on earth is she doing? It's likely the agent will write to her to find out what she knows about Kyla Mahon.

On top of a pile on the desk lies her commonplace book, furred and much handled. She opens it at random — a quote from Samuel Johnson, copied years ago in her youthful hand: 'I know not any thing more pleasant, or more instructive, than to compare experience with expectation, or to register from time to time the difference between the idea and reality.'

Indeed. She had the idea, and now she must wait to see what reality will bring.

MARCH

A writer

Friday morning ritual. Take the twins to daycare, tidy their room and pack their stuff to put on the porch ready for their father to collect. Some weekends she'd delay the tidying until Saturday or Sunday because it assuaged the pain of missing them. And there was some pain, more than she'd experienced when Lila went off to England with her father for a whole year. She'd hardly felt that, being so in love with Gareth at the time. These days, the weekends when both children went were harder to bear. There were hours when she didn't know what to do with herself, wandering from room to room in an aimless miserable fug. It happened less since she'd got together with Jasmine. Jas believed in living in the moment, like a Buddhist or a dog, or a gardener, with no raking over the past, no daydreaming about the future.

This weekend, starting with tonight, Jacinta would devote entirely to Jas and being in the moment. As she tidied and mopped, threw away half-eaten sandwiches and went back and forth to the laundry, and looked forward to seeing Jas, she also — because she couldn't help it — thought back on yesterday's party, reflected on and relived it, which was not living in the moment at all. Nearly everyone she'd invited had come, some twenty adults and slightly fewer children, since children never went anywhere on their own now. Plus there were the hangers on, like Merle, who had mostly sat with Herman, which was traitorous of her, but then she supposed he would have known no one other than his daughters and Jacinta. He was old Blackbeard in the corner, the picture of slightly sinister doom, trying not to look in her direction. She even saw Merle pat his hand while they were singing 'Happy Birthday'. All choked up, and Jacinta's friend and patron comforting him. She'd had a moment of pure jealousy. Why didn't he just put himself in the circle and join in the party properly? Sing along? Had she ever heard him sing, come to think of it?

The people who run the organic fair-trade bakery seemed to be surprised so many customers had arrived at once, half an hour before closing time, and they were short-staffed, only two on with one making the coffee. Why did they want to close so early? Four o'clock! She supposed they had to get up early every morning to set the bread to rise or whatever they did, but here was an opportunity to make money and there was a recession on. It really was pathetic. Especially since the bakery had recently sold to Asians who are supposed to have the work ethic. After a bit of persuasion, the till had rung until a quarter to five. There were weighty bagels and date scones and lots of that Trade Aid coffee which had definitely improved. It used to be so ghastly.

The kids had got high on honey and raced around on the polished concrete floor, and Jas got there for half an hour but it wasn't her scene and fair enough. She wasn't that much into kids, and who could blame her, since she was only eighteen.

Dairy-frees and coeliacs were catered for, and at one point Rae had said she was surprised, she'd got it wrong, she never would have pegged Jacinta for a mother who was into organics.

'I don't believe in vaccination either,' Jacinta had boasted — yes, it had been a boast, though the twins had been vaccinated against her wishes and on the sly by Herman since they'd been in shared custody. He'd turned Lila into a pincushion before he took her away to England, and when he got back made Venice catch up. Hepatitis, tetanus, triple, MMR, diphtheria.

'I'll never forgive him,' she'd told Rae. 'He's compromised their immune systems in an already apocalyptic world.'

There were some mums from school and Natasha from the writing course who'd had a baby the following year, nearly one now. Cute as, but sickly-looking, a replica of Natasha and Darren, who looked so alike they could be related and probably were — maybe fertility babies out of the same test tube, who knew? Darren was working in a service station, and Natasha had been waiting a year and a half to hear back from a publisher about her kids' book and didn't know many people so she didn't stay long either.

Guilt took hold as Jacinta paired socks from yesterday's washing and stuffed them into drawers. Maybe she should have organised the party a bit better, speeches or something. Nobody here really did introductions, as if introducing oneself was almost rude, so you were left in a kind of vacuum.

She cheered herself up by remembering how Herman had seen her with her arm around Jas. If they had been introduced, he would have seen how she and Jas were destined for one another, having almost the same name with only one letter difference: Jass and Jas.

Toothbrushes from the bathroom, Venice's bubble bath, Lila's duck. Usually Jacinta made sure she was out on swap-over day, but today she'd stay in. Lie in wait for Herman. She wanted a word.

Venice's Venice tee-shirt, sent by Herman's mother, the Bridge of Sighs in a lurid relief of noxious plastic. Lila's blue denim cut-off shorts, their iPads, pyjamas. All in the same carry-all. A couple of times she'd tried to give them a bag each, but they always came back with most of their things jammed into one and the other one empty. How much were you supposed to encourage them to be separate? They even shared knickers, though Jacinta had fostered notions of ownership. It made her sad to do it. If everyone was a twin, the world would be a kinder place. It really would be.

She zipped up the bag and carried it down the hall to the porch, or the half that was hers, the other belonging to the old lady who shared the divided 1940s bungalow. Golden autumn, the light filtering through the shaggy branches of the macrocarpa that took up most of the front yard. Between two flax plants there was a white daisy bush that needed de-heading, and a raggy rose slumped by the letterbox. She may as well, even though she was only renting. She never went into the garden when she was married, but she was different now.

On a white wrought-iron stand on her neighbour's side of the porch was a fork and trowel. Jacinta helped herself — the old lady wouldn't mind if she borrowed them for a while. After she'd done the gardening, she would set up in the front room to work on her novel and keep an ear out — make that a whole eye out! — for Herman, which could interfere with her concentration, but sometimes she wondered if she really wanted to concentrate that deeply, because your mind could play tricks and instead of thinking about the characters in the novel you ended up thinking too much about your own life.

The gardening would keep her mind off things. Like what to do about Jas, for instance, who was a bit out of her depth, Jacinta could tell. Sometimes they'd be talking at four in the morning and it was obvious she just didn't have a clue what Jacinta was on about, she just hadn't had the life experience. Her little greeny-brown eyes would kind of blank out, go white on the tops like pistachio macaroons with white icing, like she just couldn't go there, to the blood-curdling delivery room or the execution of skilled fellatio or details of imminent environmental collapse, whatever it was Jacinta was colourfully describing. And what a relief that Gareth hadn't come to the party, even though Venice had invited him. She'd sent him the JPEG they'd made of the invitation but so far hadn't even noticed he was a no-show, as in 'Why didn't Gareth come, Mummy?' The question hadn't been asked. Out of sight, out of mind. Even for a five-year-old who hadn't known many humans of his gender.

He knew to stay away, knew that Jacinta couldn't stand the sight of him. What he didn't know, must never know, was how stupid she felt, how crass, how cruel. Cruel to Herman by busting it all up and leaving him for Mr Undesirable. Cruel to Gareth by punishing him for her own stupidity. She could see it now, weird sick shit going round and round, until she'd come right with Jas. It wasn't even as if she'd had to fight other women to get Gareth. Jesus, they were hardly standing in line. And now he's single again. The famous writer. She was probably in his next novel. He wouldn't have been able to resist it.

He was fascinated by her at first, and had even loved her for a few months. He said it once or twice. 'I love you, Jacinta.' He had definitely loved her — in a sad, stodgy, half-there kind of way. Kind of bewildered. She thought he'd be smarter, but he was more stupid than her, and that never worked in a het relationship. The man had to be smarter. Anyway, why was she thinking about him when she had Jas! Sweet loving Jas who was a gardener, and now she was a gardener too.

It was hard to tell which were weeds, though most of them looked like they could be. She pulled savagely at the plants clustered around the dusty daisy. Herman could arrive at any moment and she would have a meaningful discussion with him about Lila's health and coordination and general wellbeing. She would prise him open and suggest alternative therapies. He had to be open to her, he had to be. He was still single, as far as she knew, as single as Gareth, unless he was keeping someone a secret. Ex-husband and ex-lover washed-up and lonely, while she was a triumphant with a girlfriend, which neither of them had.

Ha ha, suck on that, fellas.

There were tons of snails in the flax, singly and in clusters, clinging together and a kind of foam exuding from them. She bent in, lifted a clump out on her trowel and examined it closely. Mass mating, maybe. Hermaphrodites doing it slowly. With slime. Or were the snails dying slowly, poisoned by some background toxicity, some battery fluid leaking into the soil, or old lurking pesticides, or were they freaking out with climate change, March as hot as midsummer? It was terrifying! She flung it away into the weeds by the steps.

Marigolds and forget-me-nots. She knew them from home — and there was a gerbera, spindly and sad. The soil was probably sour here, lying under the eave in a rain shadow in the summer and no sun through the winter. Only tough things could survive. Tough like me, she thought, tough like Jas, and tough like her girls would be when they grew up, even Lila. Roots tore like nerves in the dry clumpy soil, dry clouds scudded across the sun, and she counted three bees to tell Jas about later. Jas counted bees too.

After half an hour she sat back on her haunches, surveyed her handiwork and examined her hands, besmirched, aching slightly from the unaccustomed exertion. Peasant's hands. Hands across the centuries. A thin veneer of pale clay had dried across the ball of one thumb, tightening the skin, crazing and cracking when she wriggled it.

The dirt knocked off the trowel and fork, pretty much, she put them back on her front porch — old girl'd never notice — and went inside to wash her hands quickly, in case she missed Herman, leaving the front door open. While she made her coffee she checked for him three times, before she went to sit at her table in the window to write.

But she couldn't help going first to Facebook, where she saw to her astonishment that Adarsh wanted to be her friend. Less than a minute after she'd accepted him he messaged her.

```
Heading your way in June for the
Festival. Would be good to catch up.
```

Why would Adarsh want to see her? There hadn't been any connection between them when they were students. In fact, she'd caught him looking at her with acute distaste, even dislike. She messaged back, coolly, wondering if he'd got her mixed up with someone else. He was online still and replied graciously that no, he remembered her very clearly.

```
Where are you these days?

Delhi. Writing. You? Did you finish your
novel?

Same place. No.
```

There was a pause then, before he wrote back, which she spent scrolling through recipes, child-rearing advice and sickly moronic homilies — *Click if you've got a beautiful daughter* — posted by her mumsie friends; pictures of London friends on holiday in various European locales; and birthday wishes to the twins from Jacinta's sister, who hadn't bothered to send a proper card. How could a two-second missive to their mother's page replace an envelope with the aunt's handwriting and the wonderful truth that this actual thing has flown across the world in a mail sack in the belly of a jet? She felt like writing to her sister and giving her what for, but luckily for her Adarsh had written back.

```
Still with Gareth? Have emailed and
FB'd him to no reply. Is he still
around?

Split up months ago.
```

Felt like a decade ago.

```
Oh no. Sorry to hear.

Don't worry. It's all good.

Sorry to bother you Jacinta. Might see
you around in June.
```

And he had gone.

What's he up to? Jacinta prickled with the beginning of outrage. Why does he want to speak to Gareth? Maybe he wants to queer the pitch, no pun intended, to influence the decision. Would he do that? She wouldn't put it past him. Bloody old Adarsh. Who would have thought he'd be the one to do it. Finish his book. Sell it.

Get world-famous.

It was hard not to hate him. Gritting her teeth, she opened a file — pianistnovelc.docx, though it isn't really c, more like q. Some of the many books and blogs she'd read on writing advised not to slog it, but to work on the part of the novel each day that appealed the most. Go where your heart is. She liked that idea — it made it seem less like work and more like play even though it was actually work. Hardest work she'd ever done. Her life's work.

Really.

But what a mess. She needed to read the whole thing yet again from beginning to end because there so were so many gaps and holes, odd leaps in plot and shifts in character. But it was one thing to identify them and quite another to fix them. She took a breath, closed her eyes and summoned the elderly piano-playing sisters into the room. Tried to summon them. Address them directly.

'What do you want to tell me this morning?'

Nothing.

'Are you there?'

Footsteps in the hall — she really could hear them — and in they came, Annette first. She wore a Lurex cardigan. Following behind, Jacqueline was in her dressing gown, dabbing at her nose with a monogrammed handkerchief, R for Robert, the man both old sisters had loved and borne children to. It was night-time in their world, in

1954. Annette must be going out because her hair was set and she carried a silver evening bag. The sisters didn't seem to be on good terms, ignoring one another. Jacqueline drifted towards the shiny upright piano, which Jacinta used to play every day before Gareth happened to her.

'Come on, girls,' she said aloud, her eyes, still shut and listening hard. 'Which part of your lives together shall we revisit? Carnegie Hall? The Sydney Opera House? The first time you slept with Robert both together at the same time?'

Annette pressed her thin, lipstick-bleeding lips together and might have been about to say something — but a noise from the real world intruded. Footfall on the porch, the soft lifting scrape of the bag — and Jacinta flew out to come face to face with Herman.

Friday was a consulting day, so he was in a suit and tie and looked exhausted. As usual.

'Can we talk, Herman?'

'I'm on my lunch break. Twenty minutes. Ten here and ten back, and patients all afternoon, so no.'

He turned and began walking up the path, his head swivelling to take in her gardening efforts. He'd done the garden at their North Shore house, a strange metamorphosis from indoor man to outdoor guy in the new country. He wanted to grow things, dig in the dirt. He was always out there, like a gnome, two whole summers of watching him out the windows of various rooms and envying the calm that seemed to surround him, the brave disregard of the danger to his surgeon's hands. Spades, trowels, forks, abrasions and the occasional spike from a succulent. He'd found something he loved. She hadn't. How could you love cooking and housework in a brand-new hyper-sealed house that even when they moved out had a toxic chemical fug rising from the carpets and furnishings?

'Why did you do that? Pull out all the ground cover? Lobelia, wasn't it?' Without breaking his stride, he pointed at her gardening.

Now. Ask him.

'I need more money. I'm sorry but I do. It's not enough, what I get on the benefit and your contribution.'

'Get your lawyer to talk to my lawyer.'

He was almost at his car.

'Herman!' Screeching. A head turned on a neighbouring porch.

A dogwalker stared. Herman could turn her into a bitch so quickly.

'Jacinta.' He didn't turn around. 'If you are still short even with everything I give you — me and the poor New Zealand taxpayer — then perhaps you could get a job. Writing is not a career.'

And he drove off, but not before Jacinta picked up an empty takeaway coffee cup from the gutter and threw it at the driver's window. It made a hollow, ineffectual thump against the car and rolled into the middle of the road, where it was squashed almost immediately by a van.

She ran down the path and went inside, slamming the door, her chest heaving. Why was she so fucking useless? She felt like ringing up Jas and crying, but she'd done that already when she got back from daycare, since it was the twins' last time before they started school and she'd had a sudden panic that she'd wasted their babyhoods by not spending enough time with them. Jas doesn't need to listen to her crying. To all that shit!

Just breathe and get through it. Finish the novel and send it away to be published to great acclaim and then Herman will get off your case. Or self-publish on the cloud, from which it will be sucked into millions of devices and make squillions, surely.

The front room seemed more empty than ever, her elderly characters flown. She stood at the door, a beam of westerly sun slanting across the windows and catching, trembling in the mullioned panes of the leadlights. On the narrow mantelpiece over the electric fire — something Merle would love, all red and chrome and ineffectual from the fifties — was a photograph of the twins, side by side. Hair blowing wildly, chocolate ice cream on Venice's face, huge grin, squinting into the winter sun. Matariki. Maori New Year at a park with a memorial to a long-gone socialist prime minister piercing the sky behind them, the sky full of kites. That particular prime minister one of the prime creators of the myth that surrounded this country — egalitarianism, a concern for the common man and woman, the primacy of decent housing for everyone, the forty-hour week. Dragons and birds and boxes spiralled and twirled, a flock of seagulls negotiated a flight path. There was a thundery dark tinge in the light, an ominous chill. Lila looked cold. A day in mid-June, the year of the split.

She hadn't meant to talk to Herman about money. She'd wanted to talk to him about Lila. If they had still been together, she might have asked the question when they were cuddled up in bed: 'There's nothing wrong with Lila, is there?'

And Herman's voice would have resounded in his chest, tickling her ear, 'No. Nothing to worry about', and maybe there wouldn't have been if they hadn't split up. It was unfashionable to say it, but kids were really fucked by divorce. It was easier to blame too much daycare and screens and DVDs and the internet, vaccination and fluoride, pesticides, pseudo-oestrogens and missing trace elements.

At the birthday party in the bakery there were three autistic children, two not only with their parents but an extra carer as well. One of the mothers talked about how there was a cluster around here, how it came in clusters, more in one area than another. One in eighty-eight births, she said, the local school has a special unit. Why was that? How does that happen? It terrified her.

'Lila barely talks,' Jacinta would like to be able to say to Herman, her arms around him, around the other parent of the child, the only other person on earth who loves Lila as much as Jacinta does, 'and her coordination is bad. She's floppy. Chokes on things.' And he would say, 'She's all right. She had a slower start than Venice,' and he'd remind her of the incubator and jaundice and the tubes, as if she could have forgotten.

She had asked the wrong fucking question. She didn't give a shit about the money. What she'd meant to ask was: 'Lila's all right, isn't she?' She'd wanted to read him, doctor and father, to see if he was hiding something. She was sure he knew something that she didn't, was sure he'd had some tests done on the sly and not told her. She should have asked the question and waited quietly and non-threateningly for the response, and watched him carefully to see if he was lying, whatever he said. How do you co-parent apart?

She picked up the photograph and looked at it closely, and saw how Venice met her eyes. Jacinta had looked at the picture a thousand times and never noticed before that not both of them are looking at the camera. Smaller, anticipatory Lila is watching Venice, who is smiling for both of them, but Lila is in Venice's smile, beaming out of her sister's eyes. She's present there. They are about three years old. Herman took the picture. It was one of the last family outings.

How could he expect her to get a job? Doing what? Waiting

tables? Then she'd be here for Lila even less than she was now, though it was the kids who went out and Jacinta who stayed at home. The kids did office hours — school and after-school care — while she fucked about at home pretending to write. God she was useless! There was a novel of her mother's that Jacinta had read in her teens, by an English writer called Jill Paton Walsh, about a bad mother who sacrificed her relationship with her children for her art, only she was a bad artist. The daughter was full of rage about it and may not have been if her mother had been any good. Why did she remember that? It haunted her.

Sleep. It was the only thing to do when she felt like this. Otherwise she found herself going over and over all the things she'd done wrong, and the wrongs done to her, ever since she met and married her first husband at twenty-one. Ever since she met Herman at thirty-one and married him. Ever since the twins were born. Ever since they migrated to the other side of the world. Ever since she took her first fucking breath, face it.

Her mother had been ringing her lately to ask what she was going to do with the money from the settlement and was she going to buy another house. Jacinta had explained, patiently, that this backwater was fabulous for writing, and that when she had finished her novel, which her mother could be reassured was the hybrid fruit of both her expensive degrees — her BMus in Performance from London and her MCW from here — she would use the money to re-establish herself in the UK while she tried to sell it to a good publisher.

Jacinta lay down on her bed and closed her eyes for longer than she had done in the front room to summon the sisters, and thought about Jas. Sweet little Jas whom she would see later, who was small and dark, wiry and strong, and smelt of foliage and sunshine and sweet sweat after a day working in rich people's gardens. Jas with her ready smile and youth and astonished, listening ear. She would sleep, then bathe, get ready to go out to meet her at her flat, before they went to the girls' club. Jas finally was agreeing to take her there, even though she wasn't sure she'd earned her stripes as a fully fledged lesbian.

'You're just ticking the boxes,' Jas said to her one night after they'd made love, no pun intended.

Jacinta giggled at the memory, feeling excited again, anticipating the weekend. How could she not have known all this time that she was gay? If only Jas was here now.

No. Slow and deepen the breath. Sleep.

Midday silence so deep it roared in her ears.

A writer

This afternoon when he came in from his daily walk, the watchman emerged from his basement room to tell him a parcel had come and that he had taken it upstairs and handed it across to Adarsh's wallah. Adarsh suspected the watchman wouldn't need the excuse of the parcel to climb the narrow stairs to his flat to talk to his new servant, who inflamed the passions of almost every man in the square. She was a recent development. For much of his two years here he'd been away, touring with *Ganesha*, but the past few months he'd been at home. The pressure had never relented — men and women coming to the door and offering their services. He tried to tell them it was against his principles to have a servant, but it seemed it was immoral, unkind and mean-spirited not to accept. So finally he had taken Manjula, who was barely in her teens and had an invalid mother to support.

Or at least, that was her story and Adarsh had no way of knowing if it was true. He had never been a good judge of whether someone was telling him the truth, let alone if the person telling him came from a life so different from his own he could barely imagine it. If she was a character in his novel he could flesh her out with little trouble, but the reality of his servant's life was closed to him.

So far, at least, she was proving honest, reliable and respectful. He didn't like her talking too much and she seemed to understand that. And her youth was an advantage. An older woman might attempt to work her charms on him and offer a more intimate service for an extra charge, or go poking through his things looking for evidence of a lady friend.

As he made his way upstairs he wondered if it would have been better if he had got a manservant, perhaps even the alluring and elusive gintonic wallah from the publishing party. A *comprador*. Someone reliable to make small purchases for the household and keep the accounts. Little Manjula — and she was tiny, barely over a metre tall — was an unfortunate distraction from his solo life and broke the inevitability of unbroken concentration. And he felt so sorry for her.

It was his twenty-seventh birthday in a week, and the parcel had come all the way from his sisters at the bottom of the world. It sat on the small table just inside the unlatched door. He picked it up and weighed it in his hands. Something light and soft. Clothes perhaps. The sort of thing he used to wear, flashy shirts or retro tee-shirts emblazoned with retro rock bands, until he decided on a more writerly elegance, like David Malouf. Cashmere sweaters in the winter, his shirts always ironed. Well-cut jackets. A cravat sometimes. One of his sisters had written across the back of the parcel — Not to be opened until the 21st!

Obediently he put it down. There was no sign of Manjula, who might have gone to the bazaar. It was dispiriting how much the prices had dropped since she had started to buy the supplies, proof that he was still regarded as an outsider and possibly always would be. It was as if they smelt the difference on him, or saw it in the open stride of his walk. Here was a man used to empty pavements! Here was a foreigner! Sometimes, if he had got to talking, the stallholders knew of Fiji, the country of his birth. Those who had been to school or studied history knew about the indentured labourers of the early twentieth century, Indians press-ganged onto ships to work the South Pacific sugar plantations. Some of them had distant relations in Suva or Lautoka. Rarely they knew about the other country further south, closest to the South Pole, the islands he'd grown up in. The further away he drew in place and time, the more inconsequential that place became.

Flinging himself into his only armchair he noticed with some irritation that Manjula hadn't cleaned up the crumbs from his lunch. Neither was her bedroll tidied away.

Who cares? Grab the moment. Work while you are alone. *Carpe diem*. She'll be back any minute, hovering against one of the smeary walls. But he'd rather check to see if Gareth had written back while he was out.

No electricity. Again. And his laptop had run out of power. Fury rose, together with the thought that occurred more and more these days, which was that he should leave. Leave New Delhi. Leave India altogether. There was enough money to keep him for the rest of his life if he didn't live for too long. He could take up smoking to hasten the day, do a Scott Fitzgerald and go to the south of France, like Henry James and Edith Wharton and Graham Greene and countless other writers of past generations. Did it still happen? These days the Côte D'Azur would be overrun by thousands of tourists from Europe, Asia, Oceania, America, but perhaps more peaceful than Delhi. The nightmare fantasy filled him again, unpleasantly, of the whole world being a giant pyramid of rubbish and filth, and his adopted city only a scab on the top. It had come to him the day he'd arrived, jet-lagged and spinning out, and walked the early-morning streets. In north Delhi he'd come upon a rubbish heap the size of a three-storey building with a nonchalant cow perched on the apex, chewing. He'd gone back to his cheap hotel and quivered on the bed, filled with the conviction that he'd made a terrible mistake.

But the conviction hadn't lasted long. Bit by bit he'd come to love the city. Love the chaos and the stink and the brilliant hues of the sky, the scents of jasmine and madhumalati, the screech of parakeets, the stone ruins, the overwhelming colour and volume of the crowds. There were times his heart was so joyful and grateful for his decision to stay that an opposing flash of guilt and remorse would knife through — why does he have these yearnings to leave?

To the south of France.

Or the South Pacific, if he could find an island mountainous enough to keep above the rising seas, high enough to catch a cooling breeze. Some small islands in Fiji were already inundated, disappearing below the waves with scarcely a ripple in the media. Adarsh could write about that — climate change, the acidification of the oceans, the ever-expanding plastic gyres, the burden of overpopulation — but no one wants to read about it. Readers want entertainment. They want sex mixed with religion mixed with mythology. That's what he is good at. Escape. An Anglo-Indian reviewer in the *LRB* had called him a Punjabi Harry Potter for grown-ups. Maybe his sales figures would favourably compare.

On the arm of the chair rested a heavy tome: Andrew Solomon's *The Noonday Demon*, a book on depression. He'd thought it would help and it did in some ways, mainly through an early linking of depression to loneliness. If he was depressed it was because he was lonely. But then weren't all writers lonely? Much of the book made him furious, since it seemed to be about wealthy Americans suffering from neurosis who could afford weekly analysis and try out expensive crackpot cures.

So could he now, he remembered. Daily analysis. Spas. Massages. But he was chary of letting anyone that close, even someone he was paying. How could he be sure they wouldn't do him damage, stomp around inside his head and destroy what delicate balance remained to him?

He dredged up his usual consolations, conclusions he'd been lucky enough to come to while he was still in his twenties: mild depression is the human condition; depression and loneliness are occupational hazards. And longing. Inchoate longing.

He tried the power again and it was on. Laptop plugged, he scrolled through his messages. Nothing further from Jacinta. A new one from Rae McKay. She had him on a panel with Elizabeth Knox and Richard Dawkins, discussing an esoteric mixture of religion, horror and fantasy. And another panel with Tosh, the Rasta rap novelist whose book had sold only on home territory. It was insulting, and besides Adarsh hated panels. Wouldn't do them. Hadn't he told her that? He wanted a one-on-one session and he wanted Gareth Heap to be the one to talk to him. The fact that Gareth was his ex-tutor meant that he would know the book almost as well as he did himself. Better, in some ways. It had started to fade, intimacy with those characters dissipated by the characters in his new book, but wouldn't take much to draw close to them again, his old friends. He'd missed them. How strange it was that his fictional acquaintances outnumbered the flesh and blood.

```
Hi Rae,

Is there any way I can avoid the
panel? In all honesty I can't see
that my work has anything in common
with Knox's horror fantasies and
Dawkins's atheism. If at all possible
I would prefer to do a solo session,
as suggested in my earlier email,
with Gareth Heap. Apologies for any
inconvenience that may ensue. Also
— I have been receiving emails from
someone called Ripeka who directs the
Fringe. She wants to know if I can
do a reading as part of her festival.
Is that kosher? I'd rather not.

Regards,
Adarsh
```

He sent it away and wondered if he should have added a reason to encourage her sympathy. That he was a nervous public speaker, perhaps. That he disliked the free-ranging nature of panels, in particular the ever-present danger of being put on the spot with a question or discussion thread that he knew nothing about. It had happened in Boston on a panel with Anita Rau Badami and Kiran Desai, an assumption that he had read their latest novels when he had not. He was further embarrassed by their enthusiasm for *Gay Times with Ganesha*. 'I devoured it!' one of them had said, her eyes sparkling, and later, afterwards, had asked if he was anxious about his safety in Delhi, since there was little tolerance of homosexuality there. A number of responses had come to him, most of them graceless, and so he had said nothing. His expression must have registered his discomfort, because she had laid an unwelcome hand on his shoulder before hurrying away to the signing table.

Why hadn't he been able to read her intention of kindness and inclusion, of celebration of his own novel, in fact?

Another occupational hazard. Too much time to dwell on wrongs done by and done to.

He got up, took a turn around the small room, pausing at the window to look out on to the street. There was the usual tangle of vehicles blurred below a layer of fumes. An unseasonable wind had come up since he'd got in — the plastic roof of a roadside stall billowed and banged. As he watched, one corner came free and whipped in the air. Dust that had settled in its hummock flew in a red cloud, colouring the washed-out clothes of the stallholder's small skinny son as he leapt and reached to catch the frayed rope, his father yelling at him. Poor little kid. Yet again, Adarsh thought how lucky he was to have grown up where he did, and yet again quashed the thought the moment he had it. It was smug.

Smugness is loathsome and should be a sin. Perhaps he would take a break from the slow-growing novel and write a short story with a very smug character at its centre. Some complacent shit who gets his comeuppance.

He returned to his computer, checked his inbox again, and there it was. At last. A response from Gareth, winged in in the last few seconds.

> Adarsh old mate, good to hear from you.
> Hate to tell you this but you've been
> the cause of a total spinout. Can't say
> too much about it, but it's to do with
> the Opus.

Adarsh stopped reading for a moment and leaned back in his chair. From beyond the window, voices lifted in conflict. An argument. The unforeseen wind scattering possessions, perhaps. Or a set-to over poor-quality produce or short change or the appalling waste of money on the Indian space programme or a pickpocketed passer-by or groped woman or anything and everything in this crazy city.

A spinout about him and the Opus. The prize he was expected to win. His Indian agent had let him know there was even an illegal betting ring with substantial sums of money changing hands. An Indian winner of the Opus. For certain. What had happened? Was Gareth one of the judges?

In fact we probably shouldn't be
having any contact at all since we
could find ourselves embroiled in a
scandal. I have done some research on
that other prodigious, older prize
— the Booker — and discovered many
closer associations. Forty-odd years
ago Kingsley Amis was shortlisted
by a judge who happened to be his
current wife, Elizabeth Jane Howard.
Admittedly that was a long time ago
and you and I aren't married. There
have been countless scandals with
that prize, realised and potential.
I've been in touch with the peeps at
the top of the Opus and declared our
association as a possible conflict of
interest. They're not worried, so put
your mind at rest. It happens all the
time, they said, and shouldn't affect
your chances at all. All I have to do
is abstain from placing you and hope
that the other judges do. Looking
forward to seeing you again. Eat this
email. Cheers, Gareth

Adarsh read the message several times. *Peeps*. It struck him as
tragic that Gareth, who would be in his mid-forties by now, used
slang not only too young for him but slang that had already passed
from use. *A possible conflict of interest*. It's certainly a conflict of *his*
interest.

He knows suddenly, in his guts, in his bones, in his fucking
waters, that he won't win. Not that he was expecting to. But still,
the Opus was a reasonably new prize, only ten years old, and
already had a reputation for taking some risks, not going for the
safe option. He would have had a chance and Gareth had stuffed
it up for him. Adarsh could see it so clearly — how he would have
been invited to judge, how he would have wanted the kudos, the

attention. How he wouldn't have even noticed Adarsh's name on the list. It wouldn't have leapt out at him. Wanker. Swearing under his breath, he wrote:

```
Cheers Gareth. Thanks for letting me
know.
```

A writer

On the other side of the world Gareth is going offline and getting ready for bed. A new bed with legs, off the floor, bought online and delivered by truck, sheets and duvets and pillows included, as well as a tri-pillow, which he knows is old-mannish, but the best for reading, especially when your back is as fucked as his is.

He cleans his teeth, a habit still strong since it formed during Jacinta's era — she had a thing about fresh breath and dental health, had been brought up to it. Gareth's mother had left it out. Gareth's mother had left out a great deal of things. Oh, that's right, he snarled at himself in the mirror. Why don't you let your mind trundle along the same well-worn grooves as you do nearly every bloody night, snapping at the same tired old synapses: teeth, Jacinta, then your mother. Poor old bloody Mum, God rest her soul. Forty-six is young to have lost both parents, he thinks, as he thinks quite often but comforts himself always, as he does now, with the notion that we don't reach full maturity until we are orphaned. That's what they say. It's the final step. Denied him, actually, since there's still old Greg, his stepfather, sun-damaged face set in the horizontal lines of the geriatric stoner surfer. And then there's his real father's money, lots of it, which could delay maturity more profoundly than would the continued existence of his father, if he was still alive.

What a lucky man I am, Gareth thinks. Contentment, warmth, a tri-pillow and the cracking open of Adarsh's book, where the hero is leaving his family home in India to study at a South Pacific university. A rather bad university, and the reader is left wondering how it had been selected. If Navik was that clever, then he'd be off to an Ivy League or Oxbridge. Surely. It's a minor quibble, though, offset by the fun the author has skewering various local university characters, all fairly stereotypical in Gareth's sleepy opinion. The best is a co-student, English, good teeth, married to a doctor, working her way around the male members of staff to improve her grades. When one of them rejects her, she brings a case of sexual harassment against him. Could be Jacinta, except for that last bit. She doesn't come off the page as well as the autobiographical character, who is Navik's love interest, closely based on Adarsh himself. He calls himself Anil.

Gareth has never put himself in anything. He's proud of that. Not in his dozen short stories or two novels, not even a cameo appearance. His own concerns proliferate, of course, and characters based on women he's loved and lost, on men he's hated or would like to have known. A story for the great-grandfather killed in the First World War trenches. A poem for his first-settler ancestor. But never himself, not consciously. He isn't as interested in himself as Adarsh is in himself. He's a workman. He has printed out a line from Flaubert and stuck it to the wall above where his desk used to be.

Be regular and ordinary in your life, like a bourgeois, so that
you may be violent and original in your work.

You can't be violent and original if you write only about yourself, can you? He finds where he left off and reads on.

> I saw Anil the first time I went into the shop,
> my local. Brightly lit, musty smelling, open to
> the rainy, wet night. He served me (if you could
> call it serving). A glowering, hard-set face
> among the tins of beans and bags of sweets.
> My cigarettes slapped to the counter like
> dough. My milk and bread stuffed into a
> fracturing, splitting plastic bag. I had the sense

that his mother (a thin-lipped, prematurely
aged woman hunched on a stool) had been
arguing with him before I came in, and that the
quarrel would resume the moment I left. Anil
hardly noticed me in the few moments that
lapsed during our transaction, but I took his
measure. More, I knew in that instant what he
was and that a time would come when I knew
him intimately, as well as any man might know
another. Love at first sight? I wouldn't call it
that. Lust, curiosity; even envy. Envy because
he had a place in the world, working in a
superette surrounded by family, even though
it was not a happy place. Not at first glance.
I hadn't yet met his father and sisters, all of
whom I was to discover were as joyous and
pleasure loving as his mother was miserable,
overworked and embittered.

Someone is knocking on his door. Whoever it is has come up
the steps — the lower door on to the street must have been left
unlocked again. *Knock knock.* It comes again, more insistently,
pounding, until there is nothing for it but to get up and pull
on his trackie daks. As he goes towards the door the conviction
takes hold that it's Chelsea on the other side, the girl he hooked
up with the last time he went out. Since then he's been in quite a
lot, either entertaining Chelsea or reading the slowly diminishing
pile of prize entries, or writing something maybe destined for
another pile sometime in the future in some other judge's study.
Weeks of it, he thinks, as he trudges down the hallway, of reading
or writing or Chelsea, hence the bad back. She's the first girl he's
had, it occurs to him, of that generation. Sweet twenty-five. He
shouldn't go any younger than that. There are things he finds
moderately disturbing. The first is that she has shaved off all of
her little bush except for a narrow line that terminates in a tiny
curl above the pink lid of her inner labia like an ironic eyebrow.
And second is her predilection for pornography; she tells him
about some of the techniques and performances with a bemused

detachment, in much the same tone as he might attempt to discuss the style of a novel he admires but that failed to move him. The idea that sex could be a private act without external reference does not seem to occur to her. Was she like that with Cameron? Is like that, he should think. Cameron is still in the picture, which suits Gareth down to the ground, down to the very end of his little mate, which he can feel swelling happily against the soft cloth of his trackies as he turns the snib.

It's Jacinta.

He almost closes the door again but she's too quick for him, getting her foot inside, and in one swift movement coming right into the little hallway where her desk once stood. She is, as the Victorians said, begrutten, and the sight makes him look at his watch for some reason. What the hell does the time matter, whatever time it is? He doesn't want her here.

Go away.

But he doesn't say it because he can't help feeling sorry for her — she's completely out of it, reeking of booze and marijuana, saying sorry over and over again sorry, sorry, sorry. She's staring very hard about her while she sobs, especially at the spot where her little desk once stood —. nostalgia? — and refusing to meet his eye. Between sobs, he makes out that she has been dumped by her girlfriend, who is much her junior — her *girlfriend?* — who has gone off with someone else her own age and a real lesbian and so is Jacinta, but Jazz, or Jass is it — *another Jass?* — doesn't believe her.

'She thinks—'

Another heave, though less monumental, and an angry light enters those blue eyes, which settle on him fiercely all of a sudden, and he's grateful all tumescence has fled though it was scarcely more than a twitch, really.

'She thinks I'll go straight back to fucking men and if only she could see you, the last one — the fucking last one and there's been too fucking many — then she'd know — if she saw you, just saw you once she'd know I couldn't ever. Ever, ever again!'

An accusatory finger and a silence of some seconds, during which Gareth resolves not to speak at all. She's crazy. Always has been. He calculates the difference in age between her and Chelsea

— eleven years, which is exactly the accepted demographic generational divide. Is that what it is, a generational difference? He thinks of how hard Chelsea works, of how much cash she has, of how frighteningly independent she is of men or much of what could loosely be called a moral code. How he suspects she's only sleeping with him as a means of punishment for Cameron, who still hasn't left his wife, who happens to be Rae, the Artistic Director of the Writers' Festival.

Oh Jacinta, if only you knew how I've moved on.

Nobody knows. He certainly hasn't told anyone and they never go out into the world together, never will — unlike Jacinta, who was always wanting to go out and about and swan around and be public as if she imagined they were some kind of literary power couple. Chelsea just wants to stay in, as if she's ashamed of him. In between bouts in the bedroom, some of them really very hard on his back which was strong until recently, or strong enough, she's on her phone, communicating with hundreds of friends. She hardly talks to him really. What would they talk about? She's an alien. An executive for a private prison conglomerate, someone who draws her considerable salary from global misery and dysfunction. Someone who reads *New Idea*.

Jacinta is more familiar to him even though she's a lesbian now. Well, she would be more familiar. They were together for over a year. He even grew to love her kid in a way, he realises. Too late.

He raises his hand to the door again and turns the knob, but Jacinta is setting off for the kitchen.

'Give me a coffee and then I'll go.'

'It's too late for coffee.'

'Tea then.'

'Go home.'

'Home!' A snort, a rattle of phlegm. She has her back to him but he can tell from the angle of her head that her face will be contorting. She was always a great one for terrifying grimaces, even in the throes of love. He remembers thinking: from Scarlett Johansson to howler monkey in the blink of an eyelid, complete with sharp incisors.

He fills a mug with cold water, throws in a teabag and slams it in the microwave, and hears her pull out one of the new chairs from the new table and sit down. Kitset white rubberwood. He put them together himself. She should be impressed. When he puts the tea down in front of her, she's leafing through a glossy real-estate brochure that has come in the mail, and pausing at the properties he's circled. Mid-range, mostly distant suburbs.

'You come into some money?'

Post-hysterics, her voice is endearingly creaky.

'Just dreaming.'

Why has she cut all her hair off? She had beautiful hair. You see lesbians with beautiful hair. She didn't have to cut it off.

'New table?'

'Yep. Drink up, Jacinta, and get going.'

'Don't. Be nice.'

'Nice?'

'Does it ever occur to you that I don't have family here? You're the closest I've got to it. Like a brother.'

A brother? Has she completely forgotten what it was like for them in their early days? They were at it like rabbits. Sicko.

'Have you got anything to eat?'

He turns away to make her a cracker with cheese, and by the time he turns back she's got her head down on the table, her eyes are closed.

'I'm going to ring you a taxi.'

'Like a father. You're more like a father.'

'Don't, Jacinta.' He puts the saucer down beside her head, letting it clatter, but she doesn't move.

Nor does she respond when he rings a taxi.

'Yes. Yes. Ready now.'

'I'm not moving. If I move I'll throw up. You'll have to carry me down the stairs.'

'You can't stay here!'

She doesn't answer him and he can tell that she's not going to.

Flicking the kitchen light off, he leaves her there and goes back to bed, where the tri-pillow waits with open arms but with its head sagging, as if it feels as weighed and bowed as he is. What if she pukes all over the kitchen? He couldn't stand it. Gingerly he climbs in, getting his spine angled without too many pricks and stabs. If he and Jacinta were characters in a novel by someone like Flannery O'Connor or Richard Ford, maybe even Martin Amis, then something would come of this. There would be a revelation or a new understanding to make sense of the mess they made, the damage they did to each other and the twins. And to her husband — who'd probably be the main character. Clever, kind, decent, a genius surgeon with a broken hand. You would weep for him and no one else.

More fun if it was one of Chelsea's porn movies and Jacinta rocked in here now, ripping off her clothes and straddling him while he ran his fingers through her dykie hair and reacquainted himself with her thriving unlogged bush. It would be exciting. Dangerous.

Instead he feels stale and dull and wishes she'd go away.

He dozes, wakes, realises his lamp is still on and that she might take it as an invitation to come in, not to fuck him but to sleep off the booze and drugs.

Off. Right now.

The dark. How governing and soft it is, how desirable the deep rest it offers, the luxury of being able to sleep without a single disrupting glow. No phone in the room. No gleaming device. There's a faint roar of traffic from the Grafton flyover two blocks away; the closer halt and clap of a van pulling up outside the illegal fish-processing place or the drycleaner around the corner. No real neighbours to disturb the peace with televisions and loud domestics.

Blindness in the dark. Utter quiet. The delight of it. After this is all over, after he's made his decision and read the last word and written his last report and thought his last thought, he'll detex. Detox. No text in the old sense of the word, i.e. printed material, none at all for several days, on screen, paper, bound or unbound. He'll walk across the city, set off in a different direction each day, be in the world, be festive, respond directly to life. Occupy the commons, what's left of them. Whatever the weather. Live directly. He will not castigate himself with the thought that brilliant men in previous centuries never got tired of the printed word, but read their eyes out over candlelight, wrote weighty novels and sermons and entire newspapers and multiple-volume histories and thousands of letters; they didn't waste half the time he does.

He owes it to himself to have a break. On this vision of himself walking the city's sunny, windy ridges, through high-rise and sprawl, cutting through parks and dropping down to little coves, he is drifting, drifting to sleep — when he hears footsteps out of the kitchen and along the hall, steadyish.

Maybe a slight inebriated syncopation. They stop outside his room. Why doesn't he have a lock on his bedroom door?

He needs one. Once they decide they want you, there's no stopping them. The first time Chelsea tracked him down, visited him — he didn't think he'd given her his address — he wasn't too certain it was a good idea. But that was when his head was still in Jacinta-land and he wasn't up with the play, the modern way. There wasn't to be any bother about love.

'We're the loveless generation,' Chelsea had told him the first time they slept together. 'Too much daycare and material wealth.'

He'd quoted at her: '"Where affluence is the rule the chief threat is the loss of desire." John Gray, *Straw Dogs*. I get it now.'

Still, he wishes it was Chelsea standing at the door and not Jacinta, the points of whose hair are sparkling in hall light, whose really quite broad shoulders have the soft sheen of leather. She's whispering to him, 'Sorry, mate. Thanks,' and turning, clattering down the stairs, leaving the top door open, banging out into the street, and the following slam is ricocheting up the concrete stairwell.

Thank God.

In the morning he could think it was an uneasy dream, his conscience sent to plague him in the form of an unwanted visitor, but there are a drained cup and some cracker crumbs on the table and two faces drawn with ballpoint pen in the window of a grand old mansion in the Property Press. They both have spiky hair and wide grins. A heart with two interwoven Js decorates the front door. At another window are two smaller faces — he supposes the twins.

Oh, you silly old thing, Jacinta, he thinks, with tenderness. Almost. Sort of fatherly. Is that really what you want? Domestic life? You're not cut out for it.

He folds the supplement in half and goes downstairs to stick it in the recycling bin. It's going to be a warm day, the summer going on and on and on into a month past its expiry date, but he gave up angsting about that years ago. Beautiful weather, i.e. his luck continues. He'll take Adarsh's book, a Thermos and a rug, and go and read in the park. He'll feel as serene as he did last night, before he was disturbed.

The director

She would say in her defence that she tried and couldn't do it. She would not say that she was further spurred to inaction by the lasting conviction that her emails and messages had been hacked by Orla, only to find in early March the confirmation mistakenly filed by herself under *Writers 2015 Uncontacted*.

She has tried. She is trying again now, trying to think above Orla's braying laughter as she talks to a friend on the office phone. By the warmth and intimacy of Orla's tone, she supposes it's a friend. Could be anyone. Could be Ripeka.

When Rae had come into work this morning, she'd asked Orla to interface with the Fringe director. 'Orla, would you mind ringing Ripeka and telling her she has no access to our A list? And that Adarsh Z. Kar is distressed by her requests?'

'Surely!' Orla said. 'Isn't she great, though? Always thinking outside the square. Always pushing the envelope.'

Try again. The more pressing matter.

```
Dear Liu Wah,

I regret to inform you that after a
meeting with a major sponsor and on the
advice of the Board I am compelled to
withdraw my invitation to the festival.
```

Delete.

Dear Wah,

I am so sorry and very angry and
dismayed, but I must withdraw your
invitation since our government is
insistent on preserving our trade
position

Delete.

Dear Mr Liu,

I am as bewildered as you will likely
be on receipt of this letter. Against
my wishes and my better sense, our
organisation is forced to rescind our
invitation.

Delete.

Dear Liu Wah,

Firstly I must apologise for the lapse
of time between this and our last
communication. I have a crisis on my
hands the details of which I am not at
liberty to divulge.

Delete.

There are so many other things to be getting on with. Only three
months until the festival, and the festival programme, to go up online
next week, due at the printers on Wednesday. Two writers are still
not finalised — a Middle Eastern political analyst from Washington
and a Japanese poet who has written a novel in haiku. An event
with her and Tosh Hendrix would be a marriage made in heaven.
Novels in verse are becoming more and more fashionable — the
current Orange Prize-holder told a journalist she had one in her
bottom drawer too and wasn't sure if it should be allowed to see the

light of day. Perhaps, thinks Rae, they could have an event named for the late Australian Dorothy Porter, who refreshed and revitalised the genre. Brilliant. Get Anne Kennedy to chair. Or perhaps — Rae feels the heady excitement that is the sign an event is really coming together — we could put the haiku poet on one side of the stage and the rapper on the other and have a duel! Mai Hereniko's a fiery little chick by all accounts and writes only in Japanese, and Tosh could do some of his Maori ones, since he's been writing more in that language lately than the other one. A Poetry Duel. It could be spectacular. A few musicians on the side. Licensed. Late night. Off-site. Keep the board happy.

> Dear Liu Wah,
>
> You wouldn't believe how many times
> I've started this email.

'Rae?'

She startles — Orla is beside her suddenly. Usually Rae can hear her coming because of the racket her heels make on the polished concrete. This afternoon she is barefoot. A silver toe ring glitters beside the chair leg. A partial white footprint of condensation on the shiny floor. Late March and still steamy days, when the sun beats through the high windows, scary and hot, unwelcome.

'Hello dreamer — sorry to scare you,' Orla gurgles, bending to scan Rae's screen. 'What's that? Liu Wah!'

Rae closes the screen, risks multiple tabs.

'Don't worry about it, darling. I did that ages ago.'

'Did what?'

'Wrote to him. Told him we'd changed our minds.'

'What? When?'

'Straight after the meeting with the university. I could see the writing on the wall.'

'Why didn't you tell me?'

'It's on the hub. If you look for it you'll see it.'

'Did you cc me in?

'It goes on the hub. You know that. We don't cc any more. You're supposed to keep up with it — that's why we bought the program. It cuts out that waste of time keeping everyone informed. Look at the hub, Rae, look at the hub.'

'Excuse me.' Rae gets up from her desk, a tight squeeze since Orla isn't moving, hovering as if she hopes the screen will light up again.

'That was the printer on the phone, wondering when we'll have the final draft to him.' Orla examines a magenta fingernail, nibbles at its edge.

A book from the bookshelf. Move towards the sofa under the window. Move away. Why does she find Orla so annoying, no matter what? It's irrational. Chemical.

'Rae? What's happening with the programme?'

Rae kicks her sandals off, swings her legs up, opens the book. *Chinese Whispers* by Ben Chu.

'We need you to be finalising the programme.'

'I need to read this guy's book. I'm working even though I'm not sitting at my computer. There's a concept for you.'

'There's too much coming in the doors for you to do that.'

'Deal with it then. On your own like you always do. You cut me out of everything. Relationships I've fostered. They'll think I'm so rude not to have heard from me directly first.'

'Who?'

'Liu Wah and his friends. His English-language publishers.'

'Oh, get over it. He was never going to be a money-spinner anyway. No one's heard of him. Not one of your better ideas.'

Orla goes velcro-footed over to her desk, slips on her high-heels and picks up her bag as if she's going to go out — but the office door is opening and Martin Sponsorship and Marketing is coming in from a meeting on the other side of town. Doleful.

Arms out wide, Orla runs to him. 'Come to Mama. Didn't the meanies want to play?'

He side-steps Orla. 'In kind. Only more in kind. No hard cash,' and slumps on the sofa, narrowly missing Rae. He is all angles, his long legs and tattered leather boots bisecting a square of sunlight on the polished floor, thin arms bent to cradle his head. Twenty-eight, fresh from a paid position in a government organisation and until a year ago a salaried bureaucrat. Now he's on retainer and percentage commission and in a constant state of anxiety about how he's going to support his wife and two small children and pay off a crippling student loan.

Martin undoes his top button and accepts from Orla's maternal hands a cup of green tea with the teabag floating in it, a small puffy life-raft.

And then Orla is picking up her bag again and trip-tripping out the door to her lunch meeting — someone from the Art Gallery and a generous elderly patron — and mentioning casually that the team-building weekend with the English expert has been confirmed and could Martin please let everyone on the staff and board know, even though it is technically not his brief to have to deal with all that crap, and she's gone.

We can't have that weekend so close to the festival, Rae would like to say as she's already said a hundred times, most recently at the board meeting. But she doesn't, because she wants peace. And there is peace, because Orla has gone.

Go back to the book.

Cars come and go in the carpark below the window. A blackbird sings in the townhouse gardens on the other side of the fence. There's the faint clip of Orla's heels crossing to her expensive Mini Cooper. How could she afford that, Rae's wondered more than once. She has the odour of family money about her. But then lots of young women who work in the arts do.

Martin seems to understand that she doesn't want to talk. He's reading himself now, off his screen — she takes a look — no, not reading. A game. A warrior in fantasist Chinese armour is the baddy, evil and shadowy, and Martin's Celtic white-limbed avatar is the seeker, fighting him through a post-apocalyptic medieval world.

She turns her attention to the book in her hand, flicks through it, picking out a couple of random passages from the early pages: 'I've noticed a growing angst about China, perhaps we should call it Changst, injecting itself into ordinary conversations . . .'

So have I, thinks Rae. Injecting itself into my ordinary thoughts.

Further on, she reads, 'The English pulp novelist Sax Rohmer put sadistic infanticide at the heart of his Edwardian fictional super-villain Fu Manchu and, indeed, of all Chinese people. The thin moustachioed Fu was an "inhuman being who knew no mercy . . . whose very genius was inspired by the cool, calculated cruelty of his race, of that race which to this day disposes of hundreds, nay! thousands, of its unwanted girl children by the simple measure of throwing them down a well specially designed to the purpose.'"

She reads this piece aloud to Martin, since the enemy he combats seems to be a modern, digital version of Fu Manchu, but he's too busy to listen, so Rae turns the pages and reads on: 'If we treat China like an enemy it is liable to become one. The mentality of a zero-sum world will become a self-fulfilling prophecy. We need to accept the inevitability of greater international equality and messy multilateralism if the challenges facing the peoples of all nations are to be properly addressed, never mind solved. The world needs to be saved, not ruled.'

But how? wonders Rae, flicking to the end of the book to read the last paragraph. How are we going to save the world? The author might save his solution to the last.

'There really is no Chinese mystery waiting to be revealed. To understand, we need only to listen to our hearts.'

I can do that, she thinks. I can listen to my heart. She lays the book aside, opens the window to let in some cool air and goes to her computer.

```
Dear Liu Wah,

I understand that you have had some
communication from my colleague Orla
O'Connell. I'm so sorry but it seems
she is mistaken. The invitation still
stands!

My sincerest apologies for this error.
As you can imagine with so many writers
coming so far from every corner of
the globe there are the occasional
instances of misunderstanding.

I am a great admirer of your work and
hope to be able to offer you a platform
to encourage new readers. I don't know
```

how much you know about our city,
but we have a substantial immigrant
Chinese population as well as older
Chinese families whose ancestors
arrived in the earliest days of
colonisation. Your books will be of
particular interest to them, as well
as to the many other readers yet to
discover your work.

From now on until your arrival I
will be your sole point of contact
at the festival, so address all
communications to me. Sincerest
apologies once again for the mix-up
and wishing you all the best,

Rae McKay
Artistic Director

APRIL

Two writers

I

On April Fools' Day, Brendan toasts the glorious fools of the world and starts drinking at two o'clock. When Merle joins him at three she could be anxious, but so buoyed up is he by his recent travels about the land and his plans for the forthcoming project that his demons are nowhere in evidence.

'Tauwpoe. Ruapeyhoo. Owneehunga. Wangaray. Koikoiee. Taowrunga. Mangeree. Wakkawat. Paikok. Pram.'

The old placename pronunciations ring in her ears, bringing with them the sense of a passing era, a moment in history. You hear them less and less, especially in the city. And thank God. So ugly. The accent on its own isn't — it's all those things the nation prides itself on, friendly, decent, self-effacing — but so tonally orphaned that travellers are often asked, 'What's your first language?'

'Sometimes it is impossible not to notice the poverty of speech, the woodenness of expression among New Zealanders — unlike, for instance, the loquacious Australians just across the sea,' wrote Peter Walker in *The Fox Boy*, a book of the nineties. The statement had enraged her. It wasn't true. Or was it?

'Terrornakee. Wannanakee. Pieheeatooa. Woimattie,' says Brendan. 'Mackitoo.'

'Enough already.' Merle reaches for her own wine. She shouldn't so early, but what the hell.

They are out on the back deck, Parry sunning his pink belly, which is growing splotchy now he's almost through his house-destroying puppyhood and into teenage delinquency. She's had dogs all her life and never known anyone like him — loving but idiotic, off-beam. Visits from Rae's children have ceased since he bit Ned, who had been playing a rough game, grabbing Parry's snout, a game that resulted in stitches and an antibiotic shot. Just one nip, though, in and out, hyper-festive, the dog thinking, You're a dog, I'm a dog, let's play like dogs! That's all. But Rae was not empathetic with Parry's thought processes and made other arrangements for the children. Merle misses them — and Rae, though she's very brusque now she's almost single and under siege from the pressures of life and work.

'I wish Parry hadn't bitten Ned,' Merle tells her husband. This morning the dog had chewed a huge chunk out of the back doorstep, which was rotten, and she'd had to hose out his mouth, flecked with ancient, possibly, lead paint.

'I reckon he suffered substance exposure *in utero*. That's why he's such a fool. Born in a meth lab, then dumped at the SPCA.'

'Quite possibly. Parry P Lab. Might even have Labrador in him, don't you think? That's your name from now on, hound. Parry Peelab.' Brendan tops up his glass from the bottle in the ice bucket and Parry groans with the deliciousness of the sun, wriggling to scratch his back on the flaky boards.

The first day of April is weirdly hot all over the world, an early spring come to much of Europe as well. How could the sun burn so bright in both hemispheres? wonders Merle. Has the world tilted on its axis to face its star head on?

'Today it is twenty-three degrees Celsius in Berlin,' Jurgen had said when he rang last night.

Two secrets from Brendan. Kyla Mahon's fictitious existence and the ex-lodger's phone call. No, they're not secrets. They just don't belong in this world, this life, sitting on the late-afternoon deck with her old darling, who is extending a blackened big toe to rub Parry's chest. Summer and winter Brendan wears jandals, and so far Parry's destroyed five pairs, eating enough for rubbery lumps to show in his poo. The dog's paws hang limp-wristed on his long waving yellow legs, his tongue lolls, eyes rolled back in ecstasy.

'Do you know who I thought about a lot when I was away?' asks Brendan, opening a bag of chips. At the sound, Parry leaps to his feet and lays his head on Brendan's knee.

'Jurgen,' they both say at the same time, and Brendan doesn't look surprised because it is a comfort, mostly, to have a wife so in tune with his thinking.

'Yes, Jurgen. I was living his life, kind of, the life he led before he came to us.'

'He camped out. Minimally. Bedroll, tent and billy can. You stayed in cabins and pubs.'

Brendan is huffy. 'Sometimes I slept in my car. Bloody uncomfortable. More uncomfortable. At least he could stretch out in a tent. More than I could do, believe me.'

Merle nods, smiling, and he relaxes immediately, takes a sip and a crunch. It's a sign of the booze taking hold, this desire to make everything a competition, no matter how banal. He had a rougher time than Jurgen, more privation, more loneliness.

Okay, you did. Who cares?

Last night when they were getting ready for bed she had noticed he'd lost some weight. And now she sees how his face is leaner, how he looks younger and hungrier. It's a mad idea, this book, really, but Brendan's publisher is keen to take it after the success of his last one, which was not a bestseller but picked up some attention around the world — even reviewed in *Der Spiegel* and the *TLS*. Inspired by Jurgen and the torn books in his room. The memory of what we read through our lives. Creative non-fiction with a version of Jurgen as the main character. A much broader appeal than this one, which is local no matter how much he will try to widen it out.

She should tell him now that Jurgen rang, that he's read the book and what he thinks about it, that he was hurt and felt exposed, but Bren's on to his third drink at least. It would be touch and go. If the subject stays with them through the fourth glass and the fifth and beyond, then it could set him off. Door-slamming and shouting. She'll wait until morning.

'Dinner?' asks Brendan. 'What shall we do? Walk up the road?'

'Something. I'll have to cook for the student.'

'Bugger the student. Let's go out. The new Mexican place in the food hall.'

'I'll just . . .'

Merle is up, drifting towards the ranchsliders and passing into the house and down the hall to her study. If they go out to dinner

Bren will drink at least another bottle of wine and could go either way — fun and relaxed and amusing, or bitter and confrontational. He is calling after her: 'Merle?'

'Back in a tick.'

She's at her computer, looking for distraction, her mail, surfing the net for more guff on her current obsession — watertight pseudonyms. Most have been uncovered quickly, either by the writer herself or a journalist, especially in recent history. JKR's Robert Gilbraith. Dear lost Doris Lessing's Jane Somers. JCO's Rosamond Smith. But those women are giantesses. No one will come looking for Merle Carbury's Kyla Mahon. Surely.

In Kyla's inbox there is an email from Sandy at Scribblybark Publishers, with an attachment carrying advance publicity material. They've chosen the opening paragraph as an excerpt:

```
This is how I am when I ride into
Broken Hill. Aching from eighteen hours
in the saddle. Dusty like I was dead
and they dug me up for the ride. Mare
tail flying out the back of my helmet a
sieve for the living and dead of the
small-life world. Visor a graveyard as
much as the roads I've travelled and
I'm thinking that if bugs were of a
mind to commemorate their racing dead
as much as we do I'd be blinded by
tiny crosses. As it is, the wide brown
street blurs with the splattered lost
while I live on, longer than anyone
I've ever loved, riding high and proud
into the border town.
```

The photograph is one Merle took surreptitiously last summer in a carpark: a young woman dismounting from her Suzuki Boulevard beside a fortuitous gum tree. The white line on the road near her boot and dusky late-evening light could be anywhere; the helmeted figure in tight leathers anyone. There's a swaggering maleness to the stance, but the open visor shows a shadowy woman's face, the soft mound of her lips.

    Cheers. Looking good.

And she'd send it off straight away but for the publisher adding a note at the end of the attachment, asking again for a proper full-face photograph, please Kyla!!! with three exclamation marks, and as Merle heaves an anxious sigh she thinks again of the idea she had last time Jacinta was here. Bolt from the blue.

But how risky is it? It's a small publishing enterprise and the book is so parochial it's likely to have no market outside Australia, will quite possibly not even be reviewed. Jacinta might never know. The subject matter wouldn't appeal to her, death and motorbikes. And there are millions of books published every year — millions across the Atlantic, in Europe, across Asia, in America. Who's going to notice it?

She finds the filed images from the visit a few days ago — the twins side by side at the tree-house window; another close-up of Jacinta, head and shoulders in profile, smiling at them from the deck. Earlier she had been crying, having broken up with her girlfriend after only 'one blissful month!', but her tears had dried and she looks radiantly beautiful. Tired and emotional. The new toughness recent experiences have given her means you can almost believe she spent a year riding the crosses, taking up seasonal work on farms and punching the lights out of a redneck jerk in a Darwin pub.

Almost.

But her short-cropped hair is blonde and she's too beautiful. Merle has never imagined Kyla as attractive. A gorgeous woman cruising into town would attract too much attention. It would be a different journey, harder in some ways and easier in others. It would have made a different book. And Kyla's slow realisation as she comes down from the hyperactive, reckless state inflicted by her grief is that she must accept her own ordinariness, her own mortality, laugh as much as she can for the rest of her allotted span — will people believe it of that face? If Kyla looked like Jacinta, she would not have to accept ordinariness at all. Jacinta has money and beauty enough to afford tragedy and drama, to manufacture more of it to keep life interesting.

In the picture Jacinta's hair is unruly and sticking up all over her head. She wears a racer-back blue singlet and her shoulders are newly burnished by the sun. There are gentle crows' feet at the corner of her laughing eyes, her teeth are strong and white, the hand gripping the veranda rail is scratched from gardening. Or fixing a bike at the side of the road.

Send. Say a prayer.

And then Brendan is behind her, his quiet rubber tread. As she closes the screen, he drops a kiss on her head.

'C'mon. Kai.'

II

The student Farid is about to put his key in the lock as they go out. He's hungry, so he comes along too, though Brendan wishes he wouldn't. He just wants to be with Merle. It's less effort.

Farid isn't keen on the food hall, but after they've walked the length of the shopping strip, reading the menu boards and reeling away from the prices, they wind up at there as usual. Cheap and busy, and since it's only 6.30 full of rowdy kids. From the bar Brendan watches Merle watching them running about, her goofy smile — she should be careful, people could think she's weird. Too clucky, always has been. The familiar dark shadow crosses his mind — that it's his fault they only had Jack, that Merle should have had more, like she wanted. A daughter. A girl who hung around and didn't join the westward exodus. If they had a daughter, then Merle might not be compelled to fill the house up with foreign students, least of all young cocky specimens like Farid, who makes Brendan feel nervous, judged and inferior — old and soft and white. He can see Farid, waiting at the halal stand. He's a handsome young man. Full of himself.

Two glasses of red wine lapping at the bead, he returns through the crowds to the table.

'Here you go, darling.'

They clink glasses, carefully. 'To your new book, Bren,' says Merle. 'May it be as brilliant as it is eccentric.'

He's not sure he likes the eccentric part. But then Merle is probably a little jealous, since she hasn't written anything for years. Jealousy doesn't come easy to her and sometimes, when he's reading a fawning book review or watching a piece of formless self-mythologising shit on television, he wishes it did. The other day he'd asked her if anything had come of their trip to Australia last year. She'd taken thousands of notes and photographs of landscapes. He can't remember if she answered him or not. He opens his mouth to ask again, but Farid is here, bearing a tray, taking his seat.

'Why are you drinking? This is a family dinner. Merle didn't feel like cooking, that's all. Did you, Merle? There is no need to drink tonight unless we are celebrating. Is there something to celebrate?'

The boy takes too many liberties, he's too familiar. When Jack was growing up, he used to ask the same question. Brendan remembers him, his earnest freckly face, his crazy gappy eight-year-old's teeth. 'We're celebrating,' Brendan would tell him, and so the child got it into his head that that's all drink was. Celebrating. It has many uses, son, he didn't say. Good old alcohol.

'Yes, we're celebrating,' Brendan tells Farid. Merle should have told him to get his own dinner, leftovers from the fridge. Maybe there weren't any.

'Yes, we are.' Merle is backing him up. 'We're celebrating Bren's successful trip around the country and his safe return. There's lots to celebrate, one way and another.'

They clink glasses again and smile at one another, and Brendan thinks as he's thought more than once in the few day he's been home that there is a new reserve in his wife's eyes. If he didn't know her better he could wonder if she was having an affair, but at her stage of life he doesn't think she could be bothered. There is something different about her, an edge of excitement or secrecy or pride that he hasn't seen for a long time. She has turned away from his gaze and is involving Farid in a discussion about his course at the language school, about his family back home, about his father who is very religious and never takes a drink, which is illegal in Saudi Arabia in any case, so bully to him.

When the food comes, the conversation slows and halts and he dreams a little about his new book, which is all that occupies him these days. *Naming Rights* he will call it, with each place forming a short chapter, pre-European history and history since. It will come with recordings of each name pronounced twice — once correctly and once in the widespread twentieth-century usage. Older generations of listeners will be transported to a time and place that has almost disappeared. The accent is mum knitting by the fire, it's Weetbix, Dominion Breweries beer, scones and sheep dip, it's a trusting egalitarianism that few believe in anymore. It's watching the rugby with your mates, it's fish and chips on the beach, barbecues on the back deck and meeting pretty girls with chainsaw voices at the pub. It's the voice of brash business, braggarts and developers; the voice of writers, artists and intellectuals of the period. Of surfers, nurses, politicians and scientists. No one else will think to consciously preserve it. The South Island was gold.

Something, something, eh Brendan? Merle is saying, giving him a look, and he supposes he should make more of an effort. After all, the young man is living in their house, in their son's old room, which once held Jurgen the German overstayer, and a dozen girls from China, Korea or Japan before and since.

He nods, which is possibly not the most desired response, because Merle is momentarily nonplussed.

'I wonder what Jurgen's up to these days,' he says, changing the subject. 'Remember his story about Karitane and the lack of any tribute there to Doctor Truby King? Remember how he told us about walking around the long white building on the hill and not knowing it had been an infants' hospital? He was dead right — there's nothing with his name on it. I went looking myself. Not a plaque or any mention of the doctor who saved the lives of hundreds of babies.'

'Oh,' says Merle. 'We were talking about the war in Syria.'

There's a passive-aggressive tone in her voice, as if she thinks he's letting the side down. Too parochial. Too self-absorbed.

'Yes, yes, terrible.' He finishes his noodles.

'I would fight in a war,' says Farid, 'if I felt there was no choice. You wouldn't, would you? You would be a pacifist.'

He seems genuine enough, though Brendan doesn't want to meet his eyes in case he sees the condescending inquisitorial light he's seen shining there before. Farid wants to be a documentary-maker and doesn't appear to believe Brendan ever was.

Brendan sighs, formulating a reply that makes reference to his sailing to Muroroa, to his head injury protesting during the '81 Springbok tour, to his taking on a redneck in a Queensland pub in defence of his own country and getting decked for it. Oh yes, young man. I've fought in wars.

'Your book,' Farid is saying, 'shouldn't be a book. Why would you bother in these modern days? Put it online and push it out through your networks.'

Push it out my bloody arse, thinks Brendan. He's foggy with booze and indignation. His glass is empty.

'Make it interactive, why don't you? People can pick and choose what they want to read or listen to. Add some music to it. If you get enough hits you can start to monetise it. Test the market first, I think.'

It doesn't work like that, Brendan wants to tell him. There's no market for it, really, not in real global terms, but that doesn't mean he shouldn't write it for the few hundred readers — or a thousand or two — who might get a kick out of it, who would have fond half-ashamed memories, who would leave it on the table and leaf through it when the mood took them. And others who would perhaps be inspired to learn the original Maori pronunciation — that is, if it is the original pronunciation. Whole dialects have been lost. There is some dissension.

'I'll help you, Mr Carbury.' Farid has laid his hand on his arm. 'You'll make more returns on it that way than sitting round waiting for a royalty cheque. And it would look good on my CV if I will be your assistant.'

Since Jurgen, Brendan hasn't had much to do with the boarders. Jurgen got too close. They went out and about together for months, once to a gay beach where they met another German whom Brendan was sure thought he and Jurgen were a couple. His memory of that time isn't particularly clear due to entrenched depression. Lifting by then, slowly, with Jurgen's help. He's been good since. Pretty much. He's uncertain whether he wants to spend any more time with Farid than he's forced to already.

'That's a very kind offer,' Merle says on his behalf. 'Thank you, Farid.' She's picking up her bag from the floor as if they're going home.

'See you there,' says Brendan quickly. He wants a walk to clear his head. He wants another drink. He's out of the habit of fitting in with another person after six weeks on the road alone. He's remembered bachelorhood, which has many advantages, freedom being one of them. Freedom to do what you want.

As his wife shoulders her bag and heads off with Farid, Brendan thinks she might have looked a bit crestfallen, and he supposes she would have had some idea they were having a night out, even if it was only to the food court where in the current climate a man sitting alone among swags of kids could arouse suspicions.

Out on the street he takes the opposite direction to the one he assumes was taken by Merle, who may well have quickened her steps through this rising blustery wind from the west. She'll be rushing home to watch the long-running British soap she's watched all her life, first as child with her mother and grandmother. He can't bear watching her watch it. She's an intelligent woman! Hard to remember when she has a gormless expression on her face like a suckling infant. It makes him furious, especially if he's had too much to drink, like tonight, like most nights. It's a kind of ancestor worship, all those brainless bookless Poms. The theme music makes him want to scream the moment he hears it.

Irrational, possibly.

On the first block he meets up with two of the homeless blokes he often gives money to, one lucid and the other ranting. He gives the ranting one five bucks and has a cigarette with him, since somebody has given the guy a packet of Marlboro Red. He shouldn't. He hardly smokes any more. They stand out of the wind and the guy is basically nonsensical, walled off by his madness, though maybe he's comforted just by having another human stand beside him.

Across the roaring intersection Brendan goes, and down a street that lies against the slope of a gully, across a motorway bridge slung between the flanks of the hills. The steel railing is not so high that he couldn't jump it, if he wanted to — at a midpoint he stops and looks east to where another, older flyover shows its distant lights and the glitter of high perspex barricades. Why is that one proofed and not this one? You could do yourself just as much damage. He tips himself forward a little, breathes the fumes from the speeding cars and trucks on the motorway below, and feels the rail bite into the soft of his belly. Cold, an ice-pack where he doesn't want one. A thought where he doesn't want one, left over from his years of depression like a scar he can examine objectively: This is where I got sewn together. This jungle-gym behaviour is the only remaining symptom and it means nothing, a bad habit. *What if, what if . . .*

Upright now and looking at the moon ringed with tomorrow's rain. After dark the season is true to itself — there's a chill in the wind that strikes his kneecaps and buffets the baggy ends of his shorts — so he goes on, not so drunk that he can't put one jandal in front of the other, walk it off.

Flee from danger. The opposite direction, any direction, as long as it's not towards his study at home, i.e. the dining-room table, which is covered with his stuff. Escape.

He can't do it. The book. How did he ever think he could? The first one was an aberration, he knows that. So does Merle. He could swear she's exercising extreme forbearance every time he mentions it. *Eccentric.* Kiss of death. And Farid thinks it would be better off blogged. What would he know?

Everything, probably. Young, handsome, principled, rich. Ambitious.

He's turned into a narrow street, low on the rise of the hill, with a battered blue weatherboard building on the corner. This is one of the oldest parts of the city, mostly fallen prey to developers. Skinny, shonkily built apartment blocks rise among industrial and commercial architecture of the preceding century, some new since Brendan was last in the vicinity. Four years, possibly five. He has no call to come here. There is a basketball hoop on a lamp post outside one of them, and a group of young men, mostly Africans, are jostling and shooting. A white concrete building has Chinese writing above the roller door; a woman in full purdah walks past, towing a shopping trundler. The blue building is the most familiar to him, the most heartland. Colonial. Maybe it was once a blacksmith's, or a mechanic's, or an insurance office. Now it's covered over with signs, *The Flamingo Club* three times, and against the chimney a vast satellite dish; strings of fairground lights loop on the eaves. A man in a suit comes out of the door and down the steps to the street.

'Gidday,' says Brendan as he passes him, but the man doesn't answer, walking on and blipping his car. A Ferrari. New. The man is youngish, fair, squat, overweight, successful, with slicked hair that gleams yellow in the streetlight. He must be a man who is used to acknowledging his appetites and then answering them. In his square-jawed face there is dumb contentment — a glimpse of it through the windscreen as he drives away.

The door of the brothel is still ajar and a woman is standing there looking out, a security guard emerging from the shadows to talk to her. They light cigarettes and the woman, seeing Brendan on the other side of the road, waves. She's tiny, dwarfed by the bouncer.

Is she what he needs? He hasn't paid for it since his one experience when he was a young clapper-loader on a shoot in Thailand. Thirty years ago. Got dragged along by a pervy grip.

He could. Right now. Walk across the street, have one experience so out of line with everything else in his life it'll seem afterwards that he imagined it. A festive, fictional fuck. A dream. An adventure. Merle would never know. And he'd forget it happened too, soon enough. The quotidian would take over.

He'd never have the nerve. Walk on.

But the woman is beckoning to him, coming out into the porchlight so that he can see her properly. Filipino. Or Thai. In a short bare-shouldered dress with pink sequins. More of a tube. She has long black hair and thin brown arms. Like a child. Is she a child?

Fucking arseholes.

In three strides he's across the road to rescue her, coming to rest beside the security guard who is vast, tall and wide, and dwarfs Brendan as well. The girl is not so tiny close up, not so much smaller than Merle, and older than he'd thought. Gentle crows' feet and lines in her ivory skin.

'You looking for the company?'

Company? Well, yes, he is. Company he could do with, though perhaps not the other thing. The guilt would be distracting; it could slow down his thinking process, his book, his interactive website, whatever the bloody hell it is. That's if he even could manage to do it, get it up even. Have it off. No one says that any more. Have it off. Have it away.

Licensed Premises blinks a small red neon above the lintel. A drink and a look around. That's all. Research for a future project on the tidal wave of prostitution since legalisation, the life stories of the immigrant working girls and the girls who grew up in surrounding suburbs. He looks neither left nor right but straight ahead to the serried shining upturned bottles, the flaring gold beer taps, the red towel on the polished black surface of the bar.

The girl at his elbow is saying, 'I'm May. But you can have anyone,' and there's a group of women at a corner table — the only corner table, it's not a room they want men to settle into, not a real bar — and one of them, with long white legs and dyed red hair, is coming towards him and slipping behind the counter to serve him. She has soft sympathetic eyes and a loving understanding of how desperately he needs that drink.

Scotch on the rocks. He never drinks that, hasn't for years, but the situation calls for hard liquor. The day's chardies and cab savs and unaccustomed walk are catching up with him, spiralling into real time. He is returned to the back porch with Merle; he is in the food hall under Farid's scrutiny; he is flip-flopping in his jandals across the motorway bridge; he is coming in the door behind himself and hitting himself in the back, filling his own skin. One swallow, that's all it takes. A cube of ice bangs against his teeth and sets a nerve jumping.

'You okay?' asks the girl. She's Russian maybe, or Eastern European or something, and his eyes have suddenly rolled so far back in his head they ache and blur, settle in a series of throbs.

Too far gone to have a girl. Pay for the drink and leave.

She has her hand out. 'Eighteen dollars.'

The price makes his head thump but he digs in his shorts, pulls out his wallet and pays. May appears at his elbow again, guiding him not towards the front door but down a corridor with rooms leading off and he thinks there are men and women in the gloom coming in and going out some of them, but he can't be sure because he really is so deathly tired. His eyes are aching still, they feel wobbly. A rising panic would have him turn and run for the door if he were not so exhausted — the desire to escape is a flame that finds no fuel. Go on then, one foot reporting to his fuzzed brain the changing surfaces from sticky carpet to lino and back again, the other not — somehow he's lost a jandal. Shagpile now, in a room with a close human smell that makes him think of hot-day beachside changing sheds and stuffy long-haul plane cabins at the end of a flight. Human effluvia.

May is divesting herself of the pink glittery tube — and really she may as well be a child for her lack of breasts, and she really is very sweet, coming close now to cajole and croon, to untie the drawstring of his shorts and lift his tee-shirt away from his body. He's the child now, holding on to it, but she succeeds with the shorts and he's on his back on green satin sheets and she is doing her best to help him take advantage of the situation, murmuring phrases his ear that he can't decipher. Imprecations. Possibly curses, but sugar-coated.

It's no good. Almost bruising. He takes her hand away. Closes his eyes.

From a long way away a high sharp voice is calling, 'No sleep! No sleeping!' and he is shaken about, jostled. 'No sleeping.' And he wonders who on earth it can be, because he's on board a yacht, one of the protest vessels that sailed to Mururoa or out to sea to greet the American battleships or to set a flotilla around the first of the Anadarko robber rigs. He's not sure where exactly they're going, but there's salt air and sunshine and an aura of danger, the ever-shifting surface of the sea making it difficult for him to balance his laptop on his knee, to focus on the screen. He has to file his report, send his images by satellite, and he's already missed the deadline by some days.

'No sleeping.'

I'm not sleeping. I'm perfectly awake and so seasick I wish I was dead, he would tell this earnest crew member, whom he doesn't recall meeting before. While he's throwing up, he can see her little heart-shaped face, register the alarm in her eyes. China girl. No, she's Thai. He has the most tremendous pain in his chest, running through into his back, and he can barely breathe.

A ringing bell and running feet and other voices in the room and a woman swearing at him in broad New Zild — fulthy pug —

and the high Asian voice of his tiny crewmate saying sorry over and again, and he's wondering what she's sorry about while he's lifted off the satin sheets and onto something hard and narrow. A uniformed white back tows him down the hall and out the front door towards an ambulance on the street, its red light on slow rotate.

The director

It isn't ideal but then nothing is, given that the secret festival guest is preying on her mind. Also, Cameron has refused to budge from the house, so she has been forced to decamp to Merle's but only on condition that the dog stays outside. Even less satisfactory is the fact that her Saturday is to be given over to the team-building workshop with an overseas expert, and that Nell is crying at the sight of her mother in her work clothes on a Saturday morning. And the fact that Ned was taken to his soccer match by a team-mate's father, whom Rae had never met before but who seemed trustworthy enough on five minutes' acquaintance. The fact that Cameron was unable to take his own son to the match due to prior commitments. The fact that since Brendan spent a night in hospital, Merle is distant and preoccupied and is not forthcoming with any comfort or advice or details of her husband's illness, the treatment for which apparently dictates abstinence from alcohol.

They're all on the veranda, where Brendan has taken to spending long hours puffing on his rollies and writing by hand on the backs of old print-outs, surely a symptom of his mental illness. The pages are so chaotic and scrawled over no one could ever believe anything sensible could come of them. There are arrows and asterisks and circles — and just as it occurs to Rae that the turbulent page fairly accurately reflects her own mental state, Merle is swooping on weeping Nell, pulling her from Rae's arms and plonking her down at the table, purloining paper and a spare pen.

'Draw me a lovely picture,' she says, and then mouths at Rae, 'Off you go.'

Rae knows you're not supposed to do this. Everything she hears and reads advocates engaging in a moment of farewell with the child, teaching her to not make an occasion of saying goodbye, to give her mother a kiss and trust her to come back again. But Merle is of the antique persuasion that all kinds of children's behaviour can be nipped in the bud with a little forethought; that children can be psychologically manipulated for adult convenience. Only last night she'd interrupted a private conversation Rae was having with Ned about why they'd left Dad on his own in the house, and Rae was telling him it was because Mum and Dad don't love each other any more, and Merle had interjected, 'Don't burden him with all that.' As if it was any of her business. Some aspects of parenting are meant to be difficult. There are hard truths to teach them. How can you avoid it?

Down the hall strides Rae, the yellow dog suddenly inside and at her heels — she takes great joy in slamming the door in its horrible face.

Drive, radio on, pull out of Merle's street into the stream of traffic. The Saturday morning radio host is interviewing a writer of a book about alcoholic writers. Her subjects are all men, it seems, the writers past generations held as the giants of the time. Tennessee Williams, Raymond Carver, John Cheever, Fitzgerald. Every last one of them a tragic boozehound that generations of male writers sought to emulate. It takes off some of the lustre when you think of the masculine culture they promoted, the female suffering wrought by their mediocre imitators.

Forget it. My job is to help create the giants of the here and now, alcoholic or not, thinks Rae, and she would like to announce this at today's workshop session but suspects proceedings will be more prosaic than that. Usually they are — she's attended workshops before, in other jobs. This one is to be conducted by a man from the UK, his time and expertise paid for by the local arts funding body. Attendance, as Orla was vehement in pointing out to her when she pleaded for clemency due to her semi-disastrous living circumstances, is compulsory. It is conditional to their ongoing funding that they participate fully, and they will all be there — Orla, Martin, Rae and as many trustees from the board as can be summoned.

And that's not many, it seems. There are only four cars in the basement carpark. Orla's Mini Cooper is parked at a rakish angle, Martin's beaten-up Mazda beside it, and the other two — an Audi and a Citroën — must belong to board members.

She drags herself towards the lift. As it rises she gets stiff with herself: change your attitude. Get into the spirit of it. And yes, there can be a spiritual dimension to these things if you let the ethos take you over. They can be like revivalist meetings, with people weeping and pledging undying devotion to the organisation. People can laugh uncontrollably, flush with pleasure, join rousing singsongs, dance like no one is watching them, love like heaven is on earth or leave the room in tears. It can be intense.

Orla has bought flowers and tidied the office — including, Rae notices with some astonishment, Rae's desk and private corner. The board table has been tugged to the centre of the room and at every place is a glass of water, a yellow pad and ballpoint pen.

Ten minutes late — is that all she is? — and the coffee plungers are empty. A plate has two slumped slices of cake with surrounding crumbs, and they all seem well into the first exercise. A digital screen reads 'Our Mission Statement: To promote the love of books and reading' and a stocky, balding short man is adding to a list of words on a whiteboard beside it. At varying artful angles are Define and Re-define. Imagine. Dream. Inhabit. Strengthen. Support. Coalesce.

'Distil,' says Orla, glaring at Rae and gesturing to her empty seat.

'Expand,' says Martin.

'David' reads the leader's name badge when he turns to face her. Rae recognises him. Eight years ago. A similar exercise in New York, when she and her workmates went to a luxury upstate conference centre with everything laid on. She was newly pregnant with Ned and working for a wealthy arts patron who sent her entire staff away for the weekend. It was fab. The facilitator was thinner then, with hair, riding higher than he is now, slogging it out in this backwater.

Change your attitude: this is a thriving culture and David's reach is global.

'Hello,' she says. 'Sorry I'm late.'

'Half an hour late!' says Orla, injecting a fun and tolerant tone as if she often suffers Rae's unpunctuality, which she doesn't. Rae's problem is that she's usually early. She wants to say, 'Usually I'm early.'

Orla passes Rae her name badge.

'Rae,' reads David. 'Artistic Director. Very important!' He has one of those faux-South London accents fashionable among generations of upper-class Poms since Nigel Kennedy.

As she gazes at the board Rae remembers that he flirted a little with her in upstate NY over various dinners and lunches and that she would have been glowing then, not gaunt as she is now, and she supposes he won't flirt with her again, not that she wants him to. No thank you. Just as well he gives no indication of recognising her.

'Would you like to contribute?' he asks.

'To encourage the discussion of ideas and literature,' she says, and David laughs as if she's said something amusing.

One of the two board members, a retired literary-minded lawyer, gently corrects her.

'We're not up to that,' she says. 'Right now it's only verbs.'

'Yes,' says David. 'Let's just think about doing-words.'

Rae thinks she detects a raised lawyerly eyebrow, a degree of incredulity, as if Libby has never before encountered such foolishness. Maybe she retired from the profession before it became widespread and fashionable. Now it's the norm, all this meaningless babble, even in legal firms.

But Rae's had some good laughs at other motivational weekends; she's got into the groove of it. She can do it again. She can, only there has been such a cataclysmic shift in her own life that the only honest response is impatience. And then embarrassment that she feels impatient. It's not allowed. She is paid to engage, to accept the faith, to believe that the festival will benefit from this exercise. Be more functional. Enriched.

Participation has continued; the list is growing.

'Enrich,' says Orla, as if she's read Rae's mind, pre-empting her.

Pre-emptying her.

David adds the word with a flourish. 'All right.' He turns to face them. 'Let's see what emotions we have in response to those doing-words, how we will feel as we go about in the next few weeks actualising the festival. You'll see there are pieces of blue paper at various intervals around the walls. Have a wander around and see what's written on them. Take your pens with you and add your mark — just an anonymous mark — if you find a feeling-word that resonates with you.'

Libby the lawyer heaves a sigh — the gold chain at her throat and fine claret wool of her pashmina lift and fall. Her face is smooth, lifted, expensive. Rae would like a face-lift herself. Not yet, but in a few years. You would think Libby had never had a worry in her life, or a laugh, when she must have millions. She's nice though. Clever and warm.

'Emotions. Feeling-words. A secret ballot.' The facilitator is excited, encouraging, making pushing movements with his hand as if he's helping them jump from a moving train.

Hardly secret, thinks Rae, coming to stand beside the only other board member who managed to get here. Mostly the other six are busy professionals, younger than Libby and Gerard. Gerard is retired from a shrinking publishing company. If shrinking is the right description. More like partially digested, a gob of local history slipping down the great intestine of the biggest publishing company in the world. Microscopic and giant at the same time. Gerard in weekend garb of chinos and brown leather boat shoes, and wafts of flowery aftershave.

'So pleased Richard Ford is coming,' he tells her. 'Congratulations. He's my pick.'

'Lots of men love him,' Rae says. 'Funny he doesn't appeal to women in the same way.'

'Why do you think that is?'

'Well — a lot of his books are sort of discursive — they take one point of view and elaborate from—'

'Stay on task!' calls David. 'Please, people!'

Happy says the piece of blue paper.

Rae makes a mark and so does Gerard.

Sad has no takers and neither does *Anxious*.

'The last time I did this,' Rae says, 'it was all onscreen digital.

192

Games and flashing lights. More fun.'

'Stay on task, people!' calls David again.

The next piece of paper is *Excited* and Orla is inscribing a row of exclamation marks. 'Got carried away! Read them as one, Davy!'

Davy.

Rae makes a single mark a distance below Orla's picket fence and heads back to her chair. Bored. Self-castigating. The thing is, if you don't engage properly in these sessions they're even more interminable.

Be a sport. Enjoy it.

'Did you get all around, Rae?' Davy asks after a long indulgent gaze, his tone that of an encouraging primary school teacher.

Shaking her head, she absorbs herself in her phone. Merle might have texted to say Nellie had calmed down, though she wasn't crying when Rae left. She was grinning at the prospect of sitting up with Brendan and doing a picture. Now she will be in the tree hut perhaps, with a biscuit and a drink for her morning tea. But there is no point in wondering how she is.

Compartmentalise, like they did in the eighties. She remembers her mother talking about it. It was how a whole generation of middle-class women learned emotional dishonesty, how they drove away from daycare centres with their hearts breaking. Try not to think about them during the day, her mother had advised her when she went back to work in New York. Out of sight, out of mind.

Rae gazes into her screen, and thinks about how much more she enjoys these sessions if they're digital. No eye contact. Private. Maybe Davy's old-fashioned, hasn't moved with the times, got left behind, grown dependent on gigs in the Antipodes.

Orla is writing actual words on one of the closer pieces of paper and Libby is reading them aloud.

'"Anxious only that the festival will not be a success." Oh Orla, you're a card!'

This time David is less tolerant. 'No qualifiers. Come back to your seats now, if you don't mind.'

Martin returns looking thoughtful, clicking his pen. He's seems to be taking it the most seriously of anyone really, letting it speak to him, to put him in the zone. David hurries around the room, pulling the pieces of paper down and returning with them sheafed in his hand. At the table he glances through them and Rae thinks she detects some disappointment, as if they have somehow failed him.

But he will already have categorised us, she thinks, confronters and mismatchers, the active listeners and the catalysts, the supporters and guides.

'Interesting, interesting,' he murmurs.

Orla and Libby are talking about Orla's new Italian handbag, Martin and Gerard have embarked on a subdued discussion of current interest rates, and David is pulling his laptop closer to brush a key and wake it up. An image comes up on the standing screen beside the whiteboard: a pink lump on a black background, amorphous, gleaming, like a pink turd or piece of gut. He's on his feet now, reaching for a box of yellow plastic pottles — individual servings of Play-doh — opening and upending them before each participant.

'Now for some fun!'

Music swells from his laptop, tinny and thin. It sounds like cartoon music, electronic and frenetic. Rae pokes her chemical muck with a disapproving finger — the preservatives, the additives, the colouring, the danger to toddlers not old enough to know not to eat it. When she raises her eyes again to the facilitator, he has undergone a metamorphosis. A red foam clown nose.

Oh please.

'I want you to think about trust and openness. Close your eyes and lay your hands on the Play-doh. Imagine a shape that suggests a working environment that has trust in the water. A culture of trust, where everyone believes the others to be doing the best job possible. Openness. Trust. Responsiveness. Creativity.'

In the last winter before she went back to work, Rae made play-dough when they came home from the freezing park. Flour, oil, salt and water, cooked up in a pot and tipped out on the table while it was still warm. The kids had buried their chilly hands in it, and then made a paradisiacal landscape of hills and valleys and farmhouse. The simple luxuries of being a stay-at-home mum. Ned and Nellie would love this game. She should have brought them with her.

'Open your eyes and get busy!'

The music swells again and Rae wonders if Davy has his programme on a timer, if he knows exactly how long it takes to get through each preamble. Gerard gazes perplexedly at his Play-doh, which is green like Rae's. The others have blue.

A green hill. Quickly. She pats the mixture into a mound, makes a valley, another hill, smaller. It looks like two uneven breasts. She mows one down and pinches the dough up into little blades, fashioning them as best as she can into a group of people. Mountain climbers.

'A shape,' says David, materialising behind her, 'more than a representation. A suggestion. An abstract. Have some fun. Take some risks!'

'Give us a laugh!' adds Orla, who is making a starburst, a radiating happy sun. Martin's is a long squiggle, a curling Pasifika river scored with currents and waves; Libby's a square box with a rounded roof. A cottage. A loaf of bread. An old-fashioned TV. A bunker. Anything.

Rae squishes her little people flat and re-forms their flesh into two little spherical mounds. She shaves off the top of her mountain, makes it a narrower column with a kind of turret on the top.

'Only a few more seconds. Try and respond more to your feelings, rather than your thoughts.'

The tinny music concludes abruptly and the red foam nose is returned to his pocket. 'Okay . . . STOP! Hands off!'

The shiny, fleshy spheres of his face take on a serious cast — the analyst replaces the clown. 'Interesting, interesting,' he says again, slowly circling the table to regard their creations from all angles.

Rae takes another glance at hers and feels her stomach drop. Surely she hasn't made a big fat . . . But she has. She puts out a hand to squash it flat, to return it to an inoffensive, inchoate blob — and withdraws it. Squashing would be against the rules.

'Bit risqué, isn't it?' says Libby.

'Oh my God, Rae,' says Orla beside her, before she drops her voice to a whisper. 'So fucking childish.'

'Very interesting,' says David, his thin English skin flushing as if he'd only just noticed the resemblance.

'She was channelling D.H. Lawrence,' says Libby, smiling, 'giving us all a phallic symbol.'

Under her summer tan Rae feels cool as a phallic cucumber, since embarrassment in these situations is facile, and wonders why people of a certain age associate Lawrence with phallic symbols. Maybe he invented them. She picks up her phone and Googles *DH Lawrence phallic symbols*.

'Everyone look at Martin's Play-doh,' David is saying. 'What is the first word that comes into your head?'

'River,' says Libby.

'Snake,' says Gerard.

'Tongue!' says Orla. 'Ooo! Who knew we be so sexy!'

In 0.31 of a second Rae's device finds a list of 895,000 results. While the workshop goes on around her — more interpretations, and then a kind of dance to get them in the mood for lunch — she reads in one of Lawrence's letters, 'People should have phallic symbol branded on their foreheads.' As her colleagues prance around to Edvard Grieg's 'In the Hall of the Mountain King' in the manner of a bird of their choice, she reads how he saw sexual intercourse as the moment of union with our primitive selves and the natural world, how the man returns to his daily life among other men revived and refreshed by his evenings and nights of congress with a woman, how he emerges from the 'tide of dark blood' that is sex. She reads how he thought sex and all that went with it was the province of the night and not the day, and how lucky he thought the Etruscans to be, surrounded by phallic symbols, how the decorative phalluses gave their tombs a 'quick ripple of life'. There is a pdf called 'D.H. Lawrence in 90 Minutes'. She gives him five and wonders why it is she's never read his novels, and meanwhile the Play-doh is being tidied away and a caterer appears with wide, flat brown cartons of baked goods for lunch.

At least she's learned something, thinks Rae, taking a quiche over to her tidy, alien corner and pulling a book from the shelf, not that she can concentrate on it. How would DHL respond to a workshop like this, where adults are returned to a pre-sexual, infantile state? In America these workshops are part of the culture, they fit with the self-examining, self-aggrandising ethos. Theatre meets therapy, she'd heard an older New York colleague describe it as. Grotowsky's exercises for actors co-opted to the corporate world, where the fiction exists that everyone is capable of such stripping away of instincts for privacy and basic human dignity. All for a happy workplace. A productive business. A team in tune.

Fuck! When would it be finished?

'Knock, knock!' David, behind her, knocking on air. Pastry flecks gild his upper lip and the arc of his tummy in its checked shirt. He's holding two cups of coffee.

'They tell me this is how you have it,' he says, putting one cup down on her desk. 'How are you, these days?'

And Rae realises from the 'these days' that he's remembered her now but hadn't before. He nods, working hard, glistening a little in the sunlight glancing through the high factory windows, his round lips slightly parted. Earnest. Fishlike. More guppy than puppy.

'You worked for the Borrie Foundation in New York, didn't you? About . . . eight years ago.'

Rae nods, and David looks relieved, as if he hadn't been one hundred per cent sure. 'This is a step up!' He seems as proud as a father or a husband. Or a fondly remembered lover, which he never was.

'I worked for New York Book Week after that.'

'I wasn't sure when I saw your name, but it is you. You've hardly changed at all. Physically.'

'Oh, I think I have,' Rae begins. 'I've had two chil—'

'I'm worried for you, Rae. There's resistance everywhere. In your eyes. In your posture, the tone of your voice. Even now, when you could relax and eat with your colleagues, you've taken yourself off alone to a corner. Is this not a good time for you?'

He's speaking very quietly but the room has no soft furnishings to soak up sound. Martin and Gerard are talking over their plates, Orla is at her desk on the phone and Libby is on the sofa, leafing through the *LRB*. No one is listening, but even so Rae is filled with outrage at his presumption of intimacy. She doesn't want to open up to him or anyone.

'I have to go soon, actually,' she tells him. 'It's been great. Fascinating. But I've got a festival in five weeks, a little girl at home and a son who needs picking up from a soccer match.'

He is recoiling, leaning back in his chair. Careful. Temper your tone.

'But I'll be here tomorrow. Bright and early. Don't you worry!'

'Oh, I'm not —' begins David, and as she pushes past him — 'not for me — for you — I think you need—'

Her bag is under her chair at the board table and the coast is clear: Orla has swivelled her chair to put her back to the room, talking intently to someone called darling. David doesn't leave his place in her sterilised and sanitised workspace, no doubt drawing some mistaken conclusions.

'Family crisis,' Rae tells Martin as she passes him, and it is of course, just not the immediate, urgent kind. This one's been unfolding for months. Years. Thank God, she thinks as she hurries down the hall, thank God I never slept with David — but then I never slept with other men when I was pregnant. It wasn't a conscious thing, she just didn't feel like it. And she realises she can hardly blame Cameron for having an affair and staking out the family home. It's been a long time coming.

She drives out of the carpark, planning her afternoon. Two hours' uninterrupted festival work in a quiet café, an email to her lawyer about the ongoing battle over division of assets, then head home to collect Nellie. They'll go to the library for new books for bedtime stories, and Rae can take the opportunity to check to see if the festival posters are up yet, to see if a shiny pile of programmes is prominently displayed.

the judge

On the Wednesday afternoon he sent off his shortlist, Gareth's part-time-employed half-brother came to pick him up and drive him out to one of the city's western beaches. As they made their way through streets of intensified housing, past malls, car yards, warehouses, supermarkets and filling stations towards the forested hills, they came to an arrangement for Gareth to reimburse for petrol and a generous cost-estimate of running the car and also thirty bucks for Danyon's time. Since the inheritance, their relationship had chilled. Danyon was jealous and didn't deny it. Gareth would have been able to tell anyway, since the ability to spot jealousy in others at a hundred paces was part of being a writer — experiencing it in yourself for other writers' successes and weathering it when it came your way in the shape of envious stares or tall-poppy cutters with acid pens. It wasn't Gareth's fault he'd inherited cash and brains from his father and Danyon never would from his.

He kept his gaze away from Danyon's sour-mouthed profile and made a note in his notebook of the total sum owed. His brother seemed more jealous than even those associates of ten years ago when *Root* won the Opus 2005. First novel. Instant fame. That wasn't his fault either.

Closer to their destination, as Danyon's old car rattled and banged its way around the twisting coastal road, Gareth said, 'If you weren't such a tight-arse I would have given you some cash anyway, you know. I was going to. When the baby comes. Something to keep you going.'

'Yeah sure, whatever. I'm not celebrating,' said his half-brother, strangled by regret and over-active sperm, about to be a father for the fourth time to the third different mother. Disgruntled. Jealous. So heartbreakingly disappointed with his lot that for a moment Gareth could see how his own wealth and freedom might seem obscene. For a brief moment. But he would not feel guilty about it. Why should he? Nothing was his fault. At all. Enjoy life.

At the carpark he chucked forty bucks' deposit on the dash and got out without inviting his brother along. They could have gone for a walk or a coffee at the little café, before he made his way along the beach. That's what he'd thought would happen — had hoped for, even — and now he was striding away alone through the gap in the low wooden fence to the foot of the sand dunes while Danyon spun the wheel behind him and flung the car into reverse. A ricochet of gravel sprayed a panel of the only other waiting car — Gareth turned to see — an old Holden stationwagon that would cost a bomb to keep on the road.

Tight-arse. Why would you think of that first? Wouldn't that be the second or third thing you thought while you looked at the fine old six-cylinder beast? It was a beautiful old car. Caramel and cream. Gleaming chrome. Red upholstery with matching steering wheel. 1960s. Revel in the spectacle.

Don't watch Danyon's rusty piece of Jap shit take the first deep corner and disappear.

Walk on.

⁓

At the peak of the dunes he was buffeted by a strong westerly tugging at the roots of his hair and puffing out the sleeves of his hoodie. Rain clouds boiled on the sea's horizon, the weather from Australia blowing in. There had been floods in Sydney, a cyclone strong enough to have had its own name ten years ago, if they'd known it was coming. A huge, sudden, cataclysmic storm that was supposed to rain itself out as it came across the Tasman.

According to Metservice. He had checked. Not a complete idiot. A tight-arse, yes he supposed he was, from too many years of his life spent without a decent income or girlfriend to spend money on. Impractical, no. All fatherless boys have the capacity to be more forward-thinking than they'd otherwise be. To triumph in their unguided attempts to think like a man. To carry out their own plan. Women's protective instincts crushed them. He'd seen it, time and time again; he'd seen it in his friends when he was growing up, saw it in friend's children these days, and knew he'd passed the test only because his mother hooked up with his stepfather and had Danyon in time to take the pressure off him. And because a beloved teacher at Intermediate had introduced him to Jack London, to Conrad and Henry James and Hemingway, and from them radiated out all the other writers that came after, the ones that had sustained him all his life, spinning tales of adventure imbued with dignified liberal compassion and human decency. Cormac McCarthy, Steinbeck, García Márquez, James McNeish. His fathers. He'd learned how to be a man from reading books written in an era when men had real autonomy. When men ruled the world, when the masculine principle was honoured. When an elderly man was a repository of knowledge and wisdom much like the internet is now.

The horror, the horror.

The storm clouds weren't moving. They'd stalled. Maybe there was no wind that far out to shift them along. They lay low on the horizon edge to edge like a dark bandage, static, the rest of the sky a bruised stomach pressed above it purple and grey. It reminded him of the one line of poetry his stepfather knew, from 'Prufrock', the sky like a patient out cold on the operating table. Of all the images for the sky, that was the one he knew.

On the downward slide of the dunes Gareth's running shoes filled, so he stopped at a silvery tall-necked piece of driftwood resting above the strandline, as big as a waka, a high tide receding before it leaving the black expanse of sand glistening, reflective. As he sat on the driftwood to empty his stinkers, he thought of how Danyon had not asked him a single question about his book, about his forthcoming trip to the UK, or how much he had enjoyed being the honoured only local judge on the Opus Book Prize. Not a word. Or a query. Just a suffocating silence. Jealous, ignorant shit.

And in the next instant he was filled with remorse that he could think that about his brother. His own brother whom he remembered being born, and how he'd adored him. He'd fed him his bottle and held his podgy little hands when he was learning to walk. Remembered things he'd said. *Gaff. My big bruvver Gaff.* Why should Danyon be interested in his brother's inflated sense of self-importance?

Half a kilometre along the beach the diagonal bag strap bit into his right shoulder. He'd be more comfortable with a backpack but he'd never been the tramping kind; always thought it was moronic to want to endure that kind of discomfort and exhaustion when you didn't have to. Four solid walls and a bed with legs any day.

But that could change now. Through the long hours reading reading reading in the last months, through all that over-indulgence in verbiage and resulting bad case of word-sickness, he had felt it stir more and more. A longing for silence and primary experience. For doing primary experience well. Succeeding at it. And here he was, giving it a go. The fact that Danyon had been two and a half hours late to pick him up could be a problem. Four o'clock already and the days getting shorter.

The only thing was to head north as fast as he could to the track that led up through the trees, a three-hour walk that led in one direction to the cliff path to the next beach around, but he would climb the steep, bush-clad bluff until he found a way to head inland. He'd drop down on the other side of the next west-facing ridge, get out of the wind. Make camp. There were tracks everywhere, he'd find one.

In the weighty sports bag was a new tent, a shiny billy, a tin of beans, a small salami, an apple, a bottle of water, a cigarette lighter, a bogroll. A sleeping bag tied to the side. No cell phone, no book, no Kindle. A notebook and pen, but only for emergencies. Only when he couldn't resist it — a line, an idea, an improvement to the novel-in-progress. There was to be no picking up the pen, waiting for inspiration to strike. Warming a pen in your hand, soppy to say, can be like sitting with an old friend.

He had three teabags, a mug, a packet of biscuits. And a skinny joint, which had taken some procuring. All his old contacts had fallen away, and he'd had to wrack his brains for the last time he'd smelt it, let alone seen it. Jacinta. The night she'd invited herself in and gone to sleep at his table. Yesterday he'd had to get a forty-dollar cab fare to her place and she'd charged fifty bucks for one small roll-up, but at least he had it. He hadn't hung around, in and out like a robber's dog, but long enough to learn she was back with Jas. At first he'd thought she was talking about herself, which freaked him out until he realised she was talking about her girlfriend. Out the window there had been a short, olive-skinned girl in a red singlet and straw hat digging in the garden.

'How old is she?' he'd asked.

'Eighteen,' Jacinta had replied, 'and don't say a word. If I was a man you wouldn't bat a fucking eyelid, would you? She's exactly half my age.'

And now, as he tramped along, he thought, Good on you, you silly bitch. The drawing you did on the real-estate supplement of the smiling women at the window. It's what you want. A woman. You must be insane.

He didn't want one. Chelsea had moved on to fresh pastures and he'd willingly opened the gate for her, seen her cross the paddock with her defined biceps and hairless pussy and killer heels, and wished her well. A relief, really. And his back was much better now.

Just up ahead was a crowd of people, a big family group, with the boys and men throwing a rugby ball around. Pairs of dogwalkers passed with their slathering hounds. There were always people here now, with the growth of the city. Who were these morons who called for a bigger population, pushing for an extra two million immigrants? More people, more cars, more plastic, more poos, less wilderness. Crazy. Keep it for ourselves. The zinging air surged in his lungs and he tried not to fret about the colour of the foam scurfing the dark sand, scattered spongy brown boomerangs with an oily glint. What was that about? Surely the sea was cleaner here now, must be, since they'd moved the treatment ponds from this side of the isthmus.

Yes. It was still paradise, for sure. The swells arched clear and blue, the chop frothing the surf glittered pure white. Gulls wheeled past in the cold wind and so did a sandyacht, a homemade wooden trolley with bicycle wheels and patched sail. Gareth watched it go by, two young fathers at the helm grinning, a swag of yelling kids running after it. You still saw it sometimes. Number 8 fencing wire. Not everyone had a plastic kayak or a Chinese surfboard. He felt a swelling of national pride.

It was cold enough to want to wrap his sleeping bag around him, but the track — who knew, he'd never been here before — could be overgrown. He might have to climb. Hand over hand. Adventure. Danger. The possibility of injury from something other than falling off your desk chair, catatonic with boredom. Or going blind by reading the shortlist, some of them twice. Adarsh only once. Once was enough. No. Exercise mental discipline. Don't think about that. One foot in front of the other, deep lungfuls of ozone. Shift the bag so that it doesn't aggravate your sore back. Less sore than it was.

It was a relief he had to abstain from making a decision on Adarsh's book. It rankled more each day, what the younger man had done. When Rae had rung to try to charm him into chairing Adarsh's session at the festival, he'd refused outright, so vehemently she had seemed taken aback. He wasn't going to tell her that in the novel there was a certain minor character. A writer, just like him, who hadn't published for years, who lived in squalor, just like him, but who unlike him depended on the state for his income. Who spoke out against white privilege but enjoyed it every day, who took advantage of the grants and fellowships offered by a wealthy democratic system, who unlike Gareth didn't need to teach, being a proud exponent of the theory that writing couldn't be taught. Who had, like Gareth, a square Celtic head, and carried too much weight, who had a disastrously sparse love life with mutually disrespectful women. Who couldn't drive. Who drank too much.

There were too many similarities for it to be accidental. You had to start from there, Gareth thought, and not be distracted by some sentimental hope you were mistaken. And once it was accepted that Brendan (a strange choice of name — wasn't that Merle's husband?) was in fact himself, then all that was left was the question: why? Why had Adarsh been so cruel? Brendan was superfluous. He wasn't necessary to the plot. He could easily have been excised or conflated with one of the other useless fat fucks the hero meets during his time as a foreign student. That was the book's great weakness — the enormous number of characters, all given names and histories, and most of them so irrelevant they hardly justified the reader's commitment to memory. *Gay Times with Ganesha* would not have made the shortlist of any of the judges, Gareth was sure. It had other flaws: being exuberant and vast and at the same time struggling for oxygen because of its deadening articulation of insignificant minutiae; and it was emotionally unreliable, being by turns generous and big-hearted, then mean-spirited and breathtakingly cruel. Humane and barbaric. A novel of enormous contrast, which was why people liked it, quite apart from the revolutionary Hindu homosexual angle, which possibly wasn't revolutionary at all. Wikipedia's Gandhi apparently had homosexual tendencies that he denied, at the same time as destroying many homoerotic friezes and carvings. The internet had also given up an article from an Indian newspaper that claimed Adarsh was following in the footsteps of one or two others, and that the sales of these others had been disappointing. And what about Isherwood and Forster, who had written about homosexuality and India without being Indian themselves? They couldn't be counted as antecedents but still they were there, they'd been outspoken in their own ways and Adarsh may well have read them. He was a big reader, Gareth remembered, of Indian fiction. Not only the greats — Anita Desai, Salman Rushdie, Rohinton Mistry, V.S. Naipaul and Hanif Kureishi — but he talked about others before and since, risen from the Diaspora and the subcontinent. As he strode along the beach, Gareth remembered how he had found himself envying Adarsh his voyage of discovery. Discovering his identity through his literature. Gareth hadn't had that experience, he didn't think. There wasn't one relevant particularly to him, a strictly urban writer of strictly European descent living strictly in the South Pacific.

Not so urban now though, he thought, as he crossed the shallow delta of a creek that flowed out of the bush and across the beach to the sea, keeping his shoes dry by leaping from low strand to strand. When he lifted his sights again, the sign and arrow pointing to the track was just ahead and there was more moisture in the air, weighing the salt spray that had dampened him all the way along the beach. Rain was on its way, it really was coming, bugger it, so he hurried to the foot of the hill, plunged into the mouth of the track and felt the temperature drop under the trees by several degrees. Freezing. Clean. Salty and green.

A selfie. That was what was required at this moment, to com-memorate the occasion. He dug in his pockets. Remembered. No phone.

A trickle of moisture from an overhanging branch ran down the back of his neck, so he pulled up his hoodie and went on. Steps had been cut into the first part of the incline and after that the track was mulch and leaf mould and tree roots. It was steeper than he'd wanted to anticipate and the sports bag kept swinging around to bang against his stomach. As soon as he found a spot where he could haul himself upright by bracing his feet between two wind-bent kanuka, he took the bag off and tried to figure out a way to carry it more comfortably, but there really was only one way. Not far ahead the track levelled off and the going would be easier. He hoped.

There were voices and group of five Maori fishermen lugging rods and a huge chilly-bin came in to view. They smiled and waved and the more senior of them asked Gareth if he was all right, which Gareth resented. They would be the ones in trouble soon, trying to get the outsize bin down that steep hill without going arse over tit. It was the size of a small fridge.

'Perfectly fine,' Gareth answered.

'Severe weather warning, bro. Came over the radio.'

Gareth shook his head, refused to believe him. 'Thanks. But I only just got here.'

'Reckon it'll hit just after dark. You camping out?'

'Might.'

'It's going to be rough.'

The younger members of the group had gone on, the pair carrying the chilly-bin between them slipping and sliding and laughing, so the harbinger of doom bade farewell and went on too, unhurried.

Harbinger. Hard bringer. Harp binger. What was the etymology? If he had his phone he could find out. It was odd, not being able to sate his curiosity immediately. It felt healthy, disciplined, like refusing a beer or a meat pie.

It was less windy up here than it had been on the beach, and there were places on the track where Gareth could see that the fishermen had skidded with the weight of their catch. He fell himself at one of these markers, his foot sliding back and putting him off balance so that he came down hard on one knee.

Onward, despite the fact that it was throbbing and bleeding. First-aid kit. He supposed he should have packed one. Hadn't even thought of it.

He turned at the first fork the track offered and went along for half an hour or so, his knee pinging and back straining with the unevenly distributed load in his bag, around the shoulder of the hill before the track narrowed and dropped again to a small clearing. Perfect. The trees were taller here, not so wind-bent, and there was a stream and a blackened fire spot, evidence of other wild campers, who may not have had tents like his brand-new two-man dome, bright yellow and green, compactly packed, a cylindrical marvel with tiny instructions written in pale ink. He opened the bag.

> Insert male push rod inside of female rud. Bend for make arching. Raise high the tent roop up by sliding rud flaps.

The best Chinglish for months folded up and put in his pocket. The rods and slots were colour coded, the tent pegs and guy ropes less complicated than the tents he'd erected at surf beaches with his stepfather. The tent took shape quickly, sitting on the ground like an igloo, a child's playhouse. Clever design. Any fool could put it up.

There were enough twigs lying about for a small fire, which he could have if the lighter held out. *Rugby World Cup 2011* found under the sofa in his flat. Ancient. He sat on the ground, pulled the joint from his pocket and took a deep drag. And another, until he felt the warmth seep into his brain. Night was falling bit by bit and so was the rain, he realised, heavy drops plinking and plunking on leaves high and low in the bush around him like music, the higher tones above and the bass pattering on the clearing floor. On the humus. Hummus. Hubris. Gusts of wind higher in the canopy sent scatters of rain falling in a rush, like a kettledrum on the tent roof and dead leaf litter.

One last drag took the last of it — Jacinta was hardly very generous. It had belonged to Jas, who'd said it was okay as long as it was a skinny.

'Fifty bucks for that?'

'I'm taking a commission,' Jacinta had said. 'Then I won't feel used.'

A torch. He'd forgotten to bring one. Or even a candle, and it was the hour for candles, as they used to say in the long centuries before electricity. He stood up, his legs stiff from the two-hour walk — was his knee actually swollen? — and felt his head spin as if he was going to topple forward. Might have been a skinny, but it was strong and he was tired and unaccustomed. Gave it up when he gave up tobacco in his mid-thirties. Crazy idea to do it now after all this time. And alone? What was he thinking? He felt anxious suddenly, panicked. No torch. The night coming. Just him and a cigarette lighter.

Just him and his thoughts, his chance to do what he'd come here to do. Think about his relationship with the written word. If he even liked it any more. If he really wanted to go on writing after this next book. Deprive himself of any access to it for forty-eight hours. Go through it. See what was addictive and what wasn't. Live each moment in his own head. Shift the glut. Just be.

It was a mistake. What a wanker. What a lofty ambition, when most people on the planet are worrying about how to get hold of clean drinking water and where the next meal is coming from. And to think he'd had this dream of escape in the back of his head all through the reading of the shortlist. He'd never really relaxed into it. If he was ever asked to judge anything again he'd make more of a game of it. Not take it so seriously. Read festively. With joy and forgiveness. He'd wasted the opportunity.

Mea culpa . . .

But then he realised he was stoned, the self-abasing alter-ego haranguing the paranoid ego for suddenly perceived failure or under-achievement or an instance of bad behaviour. He would have to try to shut it off. There was a bird nearby calling out mournfully, a single downward cry, as if it resented the rain. The bush was quiet apart from the wet and that one bird. Too quiet. He'd heard nothing other than gulls as he'd made his way up the bluff, and on the dusky ridge path only insects. The single bird called on and on with little variation. *Coo-woo. Coo-woo.* The wind was strengthening, playing in the treetops, swirling the rain. The bird went on and on.

He went into the tent, spread out his sleeping bag on the lumpy groundsheet and lay down. Almost immediately, as if it suffered sudden death, the bird stopped mid-cry and the rain drummed more steadily on the roof, still pale sunshiny yellow in the gathering gloom, the nylon rustling gently in the wind. He would go over his list of finalists. Once. He would only do it once and then go on to other things. Promise. What's done is done.

E because it was extraordinary. Really. Literary social science fiction, rich with references to the great Aldous Huxley, to H.G. Wells and Mary Doria Russell and the ancient Egyptians. A long time since a book of that genre had made the list, a book that put the novel back in novel, as a judge said when Eleanor Catton won the Booker with *The Luminaries*. Gareth would borrow it if *E* won. At first, the eschewing of the letter e had been a gimmick, but as she'd gone on the writer had made it so integral to the work that it really was as if the letter e had never evolved among the upper class and remained the scorned province of the Epsilon Semi-Morons, who also claimed the number 5. It was because of their ownership of e and the corresponding number 5 that they threw off oppression and gained control of their apocalyptic world. E was code, culture and faith. Brilliant.

And the others. Oh, the others. He hadn't played it safe. Javier Flores, the elderly South American moustachioed magic realist with his weighty 800-page pale imitation of his earlier works. If he wins people will say it was a lifetime achievement rather than a prize for the book itself. Cruel and inevitable but it rankled that the man had never once won any major prize. He should have, before now. Shouldn't he have?

The Sudanese tale of bitter woe, of internecine war and starvation and brutal rape, with a disturbing underlying authorial misogyny. There was only one woman on the judging panel, a senior English crime writer known for her witty, acerbic feminism. Dame Roberta Cornish wouldn't have a bar of it — but Gareth had found himself thinking about the story and the characters even when he was onto the next one, or trailing around the supermarket or surfing the net. It was adhesive, atomising of any belief in human kindness. Bleak as. A triumph that the deeply flawed autobiographical protagonist had even survived to write it.

And the fourth, with the title *Wellfed Urban Malcontents* but in the end a rather bloodless British middle-class postmodernist tale about clever, articulate, distrustful people with low libidos, who had the time and money for endless self-examination and sessions with psychiatrists, who attended gallery openings and writers' festivals and—

There was a scuffle in the leaf mould outside; the impact of flesh on feather, a low growl, and the tent wall bulged suddenly against

212

his head — solid, animal, alive — and gone again. He was up and out of his tent and into the clearing, working the cigarette lighter to a flame, shielding it from the wind and rain. A flash showed him two reflective eyes the size of golf balls and a dark, muscled shape hunched over a feathered mess. He flashed the lighter again, held it cupped towards the animal who was nonchalant, jaws working, eating the catch where it fell, pricked ears gleaming, a flash of white incisors.

A fucking huge wild cat. A supercat. He'd read about them. How feral cats were evolving after nearly two hundred years of going wild in the bush, breeding ever stronger and larger offspring, how they feasted on flightless birds and nestlings and more recently on introduced mustelids and rabbits. It was easily twice the size of a domestic, uncaring of the rain and the increasing chill of night, a small tiger, brindled and strong, fearless. It must have known Gareth was standing there, but it chomped on, implacable. What kind of bird was it? He hardly knew the names of the city birds, the starlings and mynahs, the wax-eyes and sparrows. It wasn't a kiwi, thank God, not the national icon. This one had a short beak, tossed to one side, the head eaten. Horrible, horrible. A tui, was it? He wouldn't go any closer.

The flame died in the same instant he realised his finger was burnt from holding down the flint. He put it in his mouth and waited for his eyes to adjust to the gloom. The cat's eyes reflected dully but with more of a challenging air than they had before. And moving, coming nearer to stand between him and the tent.

And vanished. Into the tent. He was sure of it. He'd heard the sweep of its fur against nylon as it passed through the opening. Or had it just brushed against it on the way back into the forest?

His hair was dripping into his eyes, his hoodie was soaked and he was paralysed with indecision. If he could get the lighter going again, he could bend into the tent and see what it was doing — but it could fly at him, blind him with its poisonous claws. It was big enough to knock him flat, rip his throat out, eat his eyes. There had been blind writers in the past and there would be in the future, but he hoped not to be an entry on their page. Groping in the dark, he patted the tent roof once, twice — and a third time harder, against the wall lower down, to scare it — then listened.

There was the sound of packaging being ripped open, like an eager child on Christmas morning. Through his alarm came a memory of Jacinta's daughter Venice, of how she had woken early on their only Christmas together and opened all her presents on her own, chattering away eerily to the vanished twin. He had lain there listening, unnerved but not computing, while the child's mother snored gently beside him. Later, it was all his fault. He'd ruined Christmas. He'd let Venice open her presents on her own.

More ripping. It must be the salami. Or the small slab of cheese. The cat was quieter now, difficult to hear over the wind and rain. When he held his ear to the wall, he could hear another sound, a low rumble, and it took him a moment to realise it was purring. It hadn't purred when it ate the bird. Obviously it preferred his meagre supplies. Nitrates and garlic. Processed pork *sans* feathers. Genetic memories of ancestors' lives spent eating human food and sleeping on soft beds. Happy to enter their habitats and steal their kai.

'Puss, puss!' he called, in the way his mother had summoned the family moggie. 'Puss, puss, puss!' Falsetto.

The purring went on, as did the chomping and tearing, while outside the rain beat down and the wind picked up.

It's going to be rough.

Ridiculous. 'Be a man!' Jacinta would say to him in the dying throes of their relationship when he backed away from yet another pointless argument; when he refused to beard the lioness in her den.

'Right!' he said aloud to the listening forest. 'I'm coming in!'

The cigarette lighter gave one last wavering flame, enough to see the way to his bed and observe the scavenger hunched in a corner. He climbed into his sleeping bag and pulled it tight over his head, should the animal decide to spring for him. There was a short silence, then the cat let out a low growl and went back to its meal, crunching, purring, the liquid mastication of cheese and sausage. Gareth would be left with the tin of beans, that's all. If he'd stayed in town in his own bed he would have had a quieter night and a good breakfast to look forward to. No intruders — not since Chelsea had gone her own way and Jacinta had been reunited with her lady-love. The universe had conspired against him, as usual. On the days he'd dedicated to reading the shortlist, the phone never rang, the downstairs door onto the street remained sealed, nobody posted interesting stuff on

FB, his inbox was static. Should he devote a day to his own writing, all hell broke loose. Phones, emails, door-knockers, road machines, proximitous demolition sites and outraged women.

Peace evaded him.

Uninterrupted time. He could buy it for himself now. After this weekend. He had the money. A couple of weeks in a remote hideaway with all the creature comforts. The last novel he'd read for pleasure, David Lodge's *A Man of Parts*, showed how H.G. Wells had led a life crowded over with wives and mistresses and children but always wrote steadfastly on. He had writing rooms everywhere — the garden, the house, flats in London and country cottages. Quiet domains for writing and lots of sex. You could guarantee he never spent a night in a wet tent alone with an apex predator that had a sharp, gut-wrenching stink. Gareth could smell it even from the confines of his sleeping bag. Tomcat. Had it crapped or sprayed? Both?

Don't even think about it.

Eventually he closed his eyes — it was no darker — and slept.

In the morning, when he woke, the cat was curled up against him and the tent floor was a wasteland of greasy paper and plastic wrappings. The cat woke too and for one long moment met his sleepy gaze. Tooth and claw. Brute nature. His first waking thought was a projection into its primitive mind: it was wondering what was next on the menu. Can I eat you?

Rapidly, so fast, with no warning, it extended a long hairy arm and scratched a long deep incision into Gareth's brow and cheek, narrowly missing his eye. Then it was gone, a swift tumbling backwards movement and leap through the flaps. He heard the drumming of its paws, the shift and fold of the enclosing bush.

At the bus stop he endured curious stares from the locals and knew he must look a sight. In the public loos he'd bathed the scratch as best he could, wishing again for a first-aid kit with antiseptic cream.

It throbbed and so did his knee. His foul-smelling tent had refused to pack as neatly into the cylindrical bag as it had in the factory of its manufacture. Gagging from the stink and half-blind with pain, he'd stuffed it in and carried the segmented rods loose in one hand. After the night's rain parts of the track had been washed away. He'd fallen, slipped, skidded, scraped his arms, knocked his head on a low branch. His clothes were thick with mud, drying now but still likely to besmirch the seats of the bus when it finally arrived.

'Rough night, mate?' was all the driver said as he took his fare. They wound up over the hills until the city spread below, midday, mid-working week, everybody going about their business as normal. There was the distant sheen of the busy harbour, grey under the moody sky and the arched girders of the bridge, the sea below criss-crossed with white wake of boats and ferries. It was the most welcome sight in the world. When the road dropped away from the view again, he concentrated on the autumn leaves blowing along the edges of the road, the gutters running with stormwater and the fitful attempts of the sun to pierce the clouds and set the rush gleaming. A deep contentment welled, satisfaction as unheralded as the sudden claw of the cat. He'd confronted the wilderness, he'd not once taken up his pen, he'd been alone with himself and the elements, and survived. He was ready for anything now, to defend his decisions on the Opus, to return refreshed to the world of letters, to appear at the Writers' Festival and speak eloquently and wisely.

Best of all would be getting back to his flat, to his lovely bed, his tri-pillow, his books, his Mac, his phone. He was going home. He would have a bath and bandage his knee.

MAY

A writer

Show me a child of seven and I'll show you the man, said the Jesuits and millions of people after them, and Merle has the axiom running through her head as she presses a five-dollar note into seven-year-old Ned's hand, urging him and his sister and Parry on his lead out the front door.

'To the dairy and back,' she says, 'and keep Parry close if another dog passes you on the street.'

'Why for?' asks Nellie, still wrestling with the laces on her shoes.

'Because he's unsocial.' Ned puts up his hoodie. 'Eh, Merle?'

'Just on his lead. He's only like that when he feels he wouldn't be able to fight back if a dog fought him.'

When he finds himself compromised, leashed, frustrated. Children can be the same, she thinks. They have to be allowed to go to the corner and back by themselves. Rae has never let them do this before, Ned had informed her, and they hardly ever have ice cream because it's bad for you.

'You won't be able to get the really expensive ones,' she tells him. 'You won't have enough.'

'I can see that, can't I? It'll only be ice blocks, not ice creams,' says Ned, waving the five dollars in her face. 'Thanks though.'

'I'll show you the man . . .' thinks Merle. He'll be like his father, another Cameron. Clever, careful with money, dictatorial. 'Hold tight to Nellie's hand and Parry's leash and remember about crossing the road.'

'Do you want me to go with them?' calls Brendan from the bed, where he's recuperating from the flu. Or a cold. Caught off Nellie. A virus that made his dicky heart race and sent him yet again to the doctor. 'It's having bringers of disease and vermin in the house,' Brendan had said after he started coughing. 'No-neck plague-bearers.'

Merle thought it was nostalgic in a way; it made her remember Jack's early school days of endless dripping noses and earache. Mostly she'd stayed healthy then and she stayed healthy now — she could afford to be nostalgic. Brendan had always got everything, ringworm and scabies, flu and tummy bugs, even though he was so often away on shoots.

'Merle? I could do with a walk.'

He could and he should. He's pasty, grey-faced, Paul Cleave propped on his tummy, a wealth of pillows, tissues, a glass of water, the plate with the crumbs from the toast and cheese she brought him earlier balanced precariously on his bedside table. But expedience is necessary. She needs to go into her study, she needs that piece of ice in her heart. She will not wait for him to get ready and faff about, even if it would be good for him. She wants the house quiet. She needs to think straight right now.

'No, no. Ned knows. Don't you, Ned?' She's walked with them to the shop a few times, watched him pause at the kerb and check. Left. Right. Gauge the speed of the oncoming. 'Off you go.'

'Yay!' says Nellie, skipping. Parry is barking and leaping, and Ned is assuming a very adult expression of forbearance as he goes down the steps and into the autumn afternoon.

Twenty minutes. Half an hour, tops. Merle closes the door and heads down the hall, calling 'No phone calls', not that the house phone rings much these days and not supposing Brendan will get up to answer it if it did. Her stomach roils with anxiety. Guilt, actually, she realises, wishing she could recapture the elation that had first captured her when Kyla's book first elated Scribblybark. Now it seems as though she's done a foolish, amoral and dangerous thing, not so far removed from Brendan's visit to the knocking shop. The stupid arguments they've had since then, about the levels of his deceit.

'It was spur of the moment,' he's told her over and over. It occurs to her as she goes online that he says most things over and over except the things she wants to hear, like 'I love you, my darling, you're still my only girl.'

'When I first saw her I thought she was a child.'

'So?'

'So I went to rescue her.'

'A child in a brothel?'

'Yes. What's so hard to understand? You would have done the same.'

'I would have called the police.'

'No time.'

'Why not? Did you have an appointment somewhere?'

'No.'

'Which doesn't change the fact you were in bed when the ambulance came. In the nude.'

'You don't know that.'

'Then where were your clothes? Where are they now, your jandals and shorts and tee-shirt?'

'I don't know.'

'Did you actually have sex with her?'

'I don't think so.'

'You don't think so!'

On and on. Round and round. She'd told no one. Not her friends, her mother, or Rae, who is soon to move out. And certainly not Jacinta . . . oh my God, Jacinta. She has to get hold of her. Now. Tell her what she's done. Used her image. There's a law against it, probably, borrowing a person's face without her permission.

Her computer is playing up, won't go online. Or maybe the server's down. She feels overwhelmed, nostalgic for the time before this all started, this great deception, a time of seeming ease and inno-cence. Pre-Flamingo Club, not that the two things are connected. A good idea. An experiment to see what would happen. She should have fessed up by now. But surely they suspect? No social media presence at all is a dead giveaway, isn't it, instant proof Kyla's a fake? Or perhaps social media really is on the wane and Kyla will ride in on the next cutting edge. That is, to be anonymous is cool. To be nomadic. Hard to trace. Off network. Like all of us would like to be really, at heart, even Brendan who daily finds himself paralysed for hours in front of Twitter and Facebook and the hundred or so websites he trusts to stay in touch with the world and not think about the mess he's in.

How sad it all can be, that question of trust.

But how lucky you are, really, she tells herself, to have lived so long trusting him body and soul, wrapping yourself in him, your hopes for the future for so many years. Just be glad it was good for as long as it was. Only one other betrayal, early on, thirty years ago. Just after Jack was born and Brendan was away on a shoot. No one since then, and here we are pushing sixty, dealing with all these adolescent feelings of heartache and disappointment. So idiotic. She straightens her spine.

Oh, come on. It was a prostitute. Get over the foulness of that and there's no reason to doubt his love for you. You're indulging yourself, staging some kind of test to see if you're still capable of those feelings. And he's embarrassed, ashamed of himself. And now there's the pact made last night not to discuss it any more. The subject of Brendan's naked cardiac arrest in a brothel is closed. Dropped from the narrative of your marriage.

Merle wants that to be possible.

Ah. Success. The connecting whirl in the right-hand corner flicks off. She types in Kyla's name and password.

There is an attachment to an email from Scribblybark, an early mock-up of the book jacket. They've used the photo Merle sent them, the half-profile of Jacinta on the back veranda. 'Wow!' a publicist had written a few weeks back. 'I had no idea you photographed so well.'

Too beautiful, though. It still doesn't feel right. It's so not her own rough diamond Kyla, the little desiccated Aussie chick, wiry, olive-skinned, Italian-Irish three generations back. More Catholic-looking. If there is such a thing. A smoker. Drinks too much. Funny as. Of dubious sexuality but ultimately likes the boys better. On her motorbike all over Australia. The ghost of Kyla past reincarnated with Jacinta's fair Anglo-Saxon Proddy-dog beauty. The new reality. Different appeal, entirely. Merle reads the caption and the text beneath that.

```
Kyla Mahon is of no fixed abode. She
makes the open road her home.
```

Roadside Crosses is a eulogy for the
lost travellers of Australia. It is
also the story of a courageous young
woman's journey through the stages of
grief. Tough, lyrical, laugh-aloud
funny and seven-tissue sad, this is a
travel book like no other.

The back cover is effusive, enough to make her blush.

Disconnecting from the cyberworld as a
means of healing herself after multiple
bereavements, Kyla Mahon connects
with real life at its most poignant.
Phoneless, addressless, off-network,
enviably free, she takes us riding the
crosses. In the cool, clear light of
solitude she examines our very human
longing for intimacy and everlasting
life. Kyla Mahon is a young Australian
writer to follow, wherever she leads us.

But how will anyone ever believe Jacinta is Australian? She launches
into damage control.

Dear Sandy,

I know I've played my cards pretty
close to my chest, but perhaps you
do need to know more about me. Now
that I've seen the mock-up of the
artwork, etc, I realise you were
right, the author note needs to be
more than two sentences. I was born
in England but lived most of my life
in Australia. As you know from my
book my father moved around a lot,
hence the eleven different schools.

```
I trained as a motorbike mechanic in
2001 and mostly in work since then,
or I was until everyone died on me
and I took to the road.
```

There's someone knocking at the front door at the other end of the house and enthusiastically trying the doorbell, which has never worked on the Carburys' watch, and probably hadn't for fifty years before that. It whirrs, clicks, burrs, sheds ancient paint. The last person to try the doorbell was Farid, who managed to lose three keys in the six weeks he was staying. But Farid has finished his course and left the country.

'Brendan!' Merle yells.

```
Cheers,
Kyla.
```

Send.

'Brendan! Answer the door!'

———⌣———

Silence. He must have gone back to sleep. She gets up, irritated, and then in the next instant knows without any doubt that it's the police, that they are reporting an injured or dead child or a witnessed abduction, that she has taken an appalling, selfish risk in sending Ned and Nellie to the shop alone. Feet barely touching the ground, she flies down the hall, the fastest she's moved for decades, and flings the door open, her throat closing with panic.

Gareth. Gareth scrubbed up, recently showered, hair still wet and a taxi pulling away from the kerb.

'Mate!' He kisses her on the cheek. 'Did you get my text?' He looks well, rested, except for a deep scratch down his face that narrowly misses one eye.

'What's happened?' Some of the unbridled terror is still with her. She peers past him into the street, searching for the children, glancing at her watch. 'Why are you here?'

Gareth's eyes widen defensively. He's taken aback — and who could blame him. She registers her own tone as anxious, almost aggressive.

'Sorry — I've got these kids staying here and I'm . . .' She steps past him on to the veranda.

'Didn't you get my text? The announcement is tonight and I thought I'd give you a heads-up.'

'What announcement?'

'The list of finalists. The Opus.'

'But why would I—' begins Merle, then remembers. 'Oh. Adarsh. Is he on it?'

Gareth looks over each shoulder, covertly, like a spy, making a joke of it. 'Can I come in? I didn't want to leave a trace of it anywhere, didn't want to message you the results. Better face to face.'

'I'm waiting for—' Merle cranes her neck again between the trees and lamp posts and sees, far away at the end of the road, too far away to be returning from the dairy without a significant detour, three small figures: two children and a dog. They would have to have crossed at least two streets to get to that point — she's hurrying down the steps to the footpath.

'Come with me for a minute? Got these kids staying, you see.'

'Fine,' he says. 'Could do with the exercise. Looking good, though, don't you think?'

Before he joins her, he turns to give his side view and demonstrate his slimmer profile, but Merle hasn't seen him for so long she can't remember how slim or fat he was the last time and also, she considers with a slight pang, she's only seen him twice since the department was dissolved, re-formed and recently renamed *Creative Theory*. Since she lost her job. And each time she saw him it was only because they bumped into each other, once at a bookshop and once at a Saturday market. They were hardly close enough for Merle to be commenting on his relative fitness, like a mother or a girlfriend.

'What happened to your face?' she asks instead as they hurry along past old picket fences and new security gates with code locks, past edible gardens and displays of succulents, berms mowed and wild, past the last old cottage in the street that's as scruffy as theirs. 'And why are you limping?'

'Long story.' Gareth shrugs. 'Tell you sometime.' *Tell you sometime*. It's something Gareth says, she remembers, a writerly promise of a story, rarely fulfilled.

The children are close enough now to call out to, and she can see that Nellie is crying. Bloody hell. She should never have let them go off alone. She hurries across the road, picks the little girl up.

'Parry ate her ice block, he just jumped up and ate the whole thing even the stick,' Ned says, 'and we didn't have enough money to buy another one.' He regards her sternly as if it's all her fault, which she supposes it is.

She performs perfunctory introductions and shushes Parry, who is growling at Gareth. On the way home Gareth and Ned walk behind and she can hear Gareth making an effort to talk to him: 'So you're staying with Merle?'

'Yes,' comes Ned's serious little voice, 'but we're moving out just before the festival.'

'The festival?'

'Yes. The writers' festival,' says Ned firmly. 'We're moving in next door to Jacinta.'

'Jacinta?' His limping footsteps are slowed.

'The old lady in the flat next door has gone into care,' Merle tells him over her shoulder. 'It's quite nice. Half of an old bungalow.'

In his rejoining silence Merle thinks she detects remorse, or regret, or even familiarity, as if he has visited Jacinta there and is picturing it. She could detect a whole lot more, especially when she turns to look at his glum face, but they're home now and the children are running inside to tell Brendan of Parry's latest crime.

'Anyway,' she says briskly as they go towards her study, 'you didn't come here to talk about Jacinta, did you?' She doesn't normally entertain in her study but they are less likely to be disturbed here.

Gareth stands awkwardly in the middle of the small book-lined room. His earlier composure has left him, perhaps because of the mention of Jacinta, perhaps not.

'Well then,' she says, 'out with it. What did you want to tell me?'

'The finalists. Burn after reading,' he says, smiling now, digging in his pocket. 'You'll be pleased.' He produces four pieces of paper, each with a name on it, and hands her the first one. 'Not in any particular order.'

'*Breakfast with Butterflies* by Javier Flores, Argentina.' The name resounds with Merle as a writer she's loved for years.

'Old magic realist,' says Gareth helpfully. 'Published last year. You read it?'

Merle shakes her head. 'It had bad reviews.'

'I thought you took no notice of reviews.'

'I don't. But I thought the book before that was . . .' She sighs, feels disloyal. She so deeply responded to his first books that it's almost as if she took a vow of lifelong fidelity and can't bear to criticise his later ones. The three first are battered copies on the shelf of favourite books in the living room. And it's a frightening idea, that writers *go off*.

Very frightening.

'He's back. He really is. Right on song,' Gareth assures her, handing her the second name.

It's one she doesn't recognise. *E* by Sophie Salter, England.

'Bizarre,' says Gareth. 'No letter e for nine-tenths of it, not until the Epsilon Semi-Morons are victorious, just before the end. Weirdly poetic. Pretty amazing.'

'Sounds gimmicky,' says Merle.

Masaad Deng is the next name. '*Blood Desert Womb.*'

'Horrifying,' Gareth tells her. 'But amazing. Really depressing though. The most depressing thing I've ever read.'

'That's not a good recommendation.'

'Never read anything like it before. The violence. Horrendous. And see! We can relax.' His square-tipped forefinger jabs at the name on the last piece of paper. *Gay Times with Ganesha* by Adarsh Z. Kar, Fiji/India.

'Relax?'

'He's there. I had to abstain, you see. Because of our association. But the other judges loved it enough to finalise it. I read it, though. And to be honest I wouldn't have anyway. Placed it, I mean. There was another one that was better.'

'Oh.'

They are standing close together with the list between them and Gareth is examining her. 'What's wrong, Merle? I thought you'd be pleased.'

'I'm allergic to book prizes. Writing is not a competitive sport.'

She moves away from him. Should she offer him a cup of tea? There are still things she needs to get on with. She should fetch some antiseptic cream for the scratch on his face, which is puckered at one end, a slick of infection.

'Have you had that looked at?'

Gareth makes an impatient gesture. He's not interested in talking about his mysterious injury. 'It'll be good for us if he wins.'

'Us?'

'Yes. All the attention. He was our student, after all. We helped him get to where he is.'

'So people could believe — but you and I know that isn't true, don't we? Adarsh had the winning combination of prodigious talent and burning ambition. He would have done it without us.'

'You're wrong. I was his mentor, as you recall, and I did endless work with him, cutting down on over-writing, editing, refining. You weren't part of that process. I've never agreed with you, when you say that writing can't be taught.'

'I've never stated that as an absolute. You know my argument: that to teach a student with no instinct for writing is as impossible as teaching a tone-deaf child the violin. You can't teach the ability to hear the difference between—'

Gareth finishes the sentence for her: '—semi-tones and full tones. Yes. I know. That you can't instil a gift for writing. I do think, Merle — well, I wonder if that isn't part of the reason you lost your job. You've got to sell the dream.'

'I know. I did try to, Gareth. I thought I had.' She sees him glance towards her computer screen, the saver showing a lioness on a rock, and in the same instant wonders how long Kyla's inbox has been hidden by it. Did it flick off before they came into the room? Would Gareth have noticed, registered the name? His eyesight is still good, he doesn't wear glasses.

You've got to sell the dream.

'Not everybody on earth can write well,' Merle says quietly. 'And I do agree with you that a competent novel can be written with a lot of help.'

'There are passages in Adarsh's novel I remember from two years ago.' Gareth goes to the window and looks out at her inspirational view of the clothesline and rusting barbecue.

Watching him, Merle remembers how the historian Michael King once talked of the 'operatic view' from his study window in the Coromandel. He'd had to draw the curtain sometimes, he said; it was too distracting. It had made Merle feel better to hear it as she toiled away in her dark room.

'Passages I helped him refine and intensify,' says Gareth. 'It all came back to me.'

'Memorable, then. That's some achievement.'

In the next room the television springs to life with the old theme music to *Doctor Who. Oo-oo oo, oo oh o oo* — Ned must have discovered Brendan's boxed set, and who knows if Rae would approve of them watching it. She should go and check.

'What I remember,' Gareth says with barely suppressed irritation, 'what I distinctly remember is suggesting that he cut adjectives and simplify sentence structure, and mostly it's been put back the way he wrote it in the first place.'

'Galling,' Merle agrees and heads towards the door.

'It would have been a better book if he'd listened to me.'

'Give me the mote Ned my turn you always have the mote,' little Nellie is yelling over the top of booming dialogue and frenzied strings.

'It really pissed me off!' Gareth is following her out into the hallway.

Merle takes his hand, gives it a squeeze. 'Don't let it worry you. Let it go. You must have also helped him to trust his instincts so he could write a novel that's not only controversial but also a bestseller. A coup, don't you think?'

He doesn't look convinced.

'Gareth, old son!' Brendan, wrapped in his new red dressing gown, is coming towards them down the hall. 'Turn that down!' he commands the children as he passes the living-room door.

It's taking Gareth a second or two to recognise him, an interval Merle finds curious. Has her husband changed so much? The last time they saw one another was at the party she gave for her students at the end of her last semester teaching. Admittedly, what little hair Brendan has left is standing up on end and he's slimmer since the rigours of his road trip. He's slapping Gareth on the back. 'You'll stay for a cuppa?'

How lonely he is. Merle sees it suddenly. That's what's changed. A loss of confidence, a new, forced conviviality with his fellow man. Has she been too hard on him? He's already hard enough on himself. Guilt and love rise in equal proportions. She gives him a kiss, lets her lips brush his dear face, his dear familiar old beloved face, and says, 'Good idea. You put the jug on while I check on the children.'

By the time she emerges from the living room — yes Mum lets us, yes she won't mind, give me the mote right now Ned! — Gareth and her husband are sitting out on the back deck in earnest conversation. As she settles cups on the tray she hears Jacinta's name, and also Rae's, and wonders what Bren is telling him. She doesn't really want Gareth to know about her making the present of the laptop or how regular a visitor Jacinta has become.

'Not too good for the old ego, is it, mate,' he's saying as she brings out the tea, 'when an ex decides she likes the old tongue and groove better?'

A corner of Gareth's mouth lifts in a half-smile and he glances in Merle's direction, but with her fresh resolve not to undermine her husband she pretends she didn't hear it. She pours out, changes the subject.

'How's your own writing going?'

'Oh it's—' begins Gareth, but Brendan interrupts him.

'Nightmare, I bet.'

Gareth gives him a curious look — he's not old enough to subscribe to the once-national malaise of looking on the dark side of creative endeavour, of wallowing in the pain. He'd rather talk about his successes.

'Pretty good. Book due out for the summer market in the UK. They're rushing it through for June. Started another one. Steaming ahead. My third. Third novel.'

Brendan laughs. 'I meant having your girlfriend go lezzy.'

'Never happened to you personally, has it, mate?' Gareth has decided to engage, which so alarms Merle that she chokes on her first mouthful of tea. Her colleague was sympathetic, she remembers, when Brendan was at his worst after his breakdown. Sympathetic to what little he knew about it. He's not sympathetic to her coughing and neither is Brendan. Their conversation goes on.

'You haven't lived, old man. I get them coming back the other way too. That's even better,' says Gareth, and Merle wonders if he's lying.

'Feminism and porn.' Brendan is rolling a cigarette. 'Powerful bedmates. Female sexuality gone bonkers. They all exfoliate their pussies now. You know that?'

'Yeah — yeah — you could say that's been brought to my attention. Very interesting, especially the shaving rashes.'

'Jacinta's got a shaving rash?'

'Well, no, actually. She hasn't.'

Merle finds herself unable to meet either man's eyes or to contribute to the discussion. There's a huge dockweed growing up against the grapefruit tree that demands to be uprooted right now while the soil is still soft from the rain. She picks up her cup and goes down into the garden, leaving the men who are laughing now at some further dirty crack of Brendan's. He's behaving like a child. His adventure even has something childish about it, the impulse to follow the girl into the club. His slip. Women shaving their bushes to look like children, her childish husband, the children inhabiting the living room with two distracted parents who want to play endlessly in the world and never at home. What a foul temper she's in.

The dock comes up with one yank. From here she can't hear what Gareth and Brendan are talking about, but it's something that's got them both excited, their voices running over each other, competing. She's glad she can't hear.

Perfectly positioned for a moment's peace is the seat Brendan scrounged from the last inorganic collection, a wrought-iron ladies' patio chair, peeling white paint and fiendishly uncomfortable even with the thin old mildewed squab. It stands behind a screen formed by the trunk of a thirty-year-old kauri, an agapanthus and a tall flax. She settles into it, closes her eyes. Just for a minute. To gather herself together, to breathe the chill winter smell of rain and snails and dormancy. To absorb the enveloping, comforting sense of the garden waiting out the hard weather, the ever shorter hiatus before the hot weather starts again.

The rumble of the men's voices is quieter, more considered, familiar. After a moment they go inside and she hears the clink of a wine bottle. A kingfisher comes to land in the lower branch of the kauri, with his bright green feathers and his comical, curious, beaky face taking a long look at her and then away again to peer below him at the ground. There was a creek here once, a century or so ago — the land must bear a pattern strong enough to tell him that the creek still exists, running along the bottom of the garden and out across the street.

Slim pickings now, bird, she would like to say — just as he dives for the sodden upheaval of soil that once held the dockweed. He retrieves a long, wriggling worm and returns to his branch to slip it down his throat.

'Merle?' Gareth is back on the veranda. 'Where have you got to? Come and join us.'

'Yes, come on, love.' Brendan beside him. 'We'll behave ourselves. Promise.'

The director

She is at a bowling alley with Ned, Nellie, Merle and Brendan, her mother and a shadowy distant figure she knows without seeing clearly is her ex-husband. There are bright lights and shiny floors, rowdy families and the noisome smell of fried food, and everyone except her is dressed for the activity. She is naked but for a pair of stilettos, which she never wears in real life and which make her tower over the other players and slip and slide as she takes her breast-jiggling run up. It's just as she lets go of the ball that she glances towards the end of the channel and sees that all the pins have human faces. There is the moustachioed South American magic realist regarding her lustfully, the stern British ex-MI5 crime writer with one perfectly raised eyebrow, the handsome Australian Lothario whose expression says he's seen better, and the pale Norwegian epic mythic poet in a state of shock. Wreathed in smiles are bestselling Adarsh, Tosh the rap novelist and the Canadian lesbian comic poet laughing uproariously. There is Orla, Martin and Malcolm from the university, Gareth Heap the local Opus judge, Liu Wah the exiled poet and social historian, Ripeka the Fringe director, volunteers with swinging lanyards, and loyal supporters and many others she doesn't recognise: little heads on plastic bodies like the murder suspects in Cluedo. The crowd grows and grows until it fills the channel, so many that she could brush them aside with one foot. It doesn't concern her. What is uppermost in her mind is fury with Merle that she has let her come to the bowling alley in the nude.

The dream breaks as she hurries from the carpark across acres of wet pavers towards the main festival venue, the slippery, reflective surface casting her back to her restless, dream-ridden night. How facile dreams can be, she thinks, and how lucky she hadn't recollected it in the middle of a conversation. Orla could draw from her confidences of that nature, of the mythic side of life: not even Rae is immune to her charm, in the final analysis. They've been getting on better lately, the pressure of the festival lifting a little now that it is so close. Yes — the great machine is in action, it is rolling on, bringing fifty writers from all over the world and over a hundred local scribes and thousands of punters. Bring it on! Rae heads for a side entrance, lecturing herself: let your subconscious take care of anxiety. You don't have time for it in real life.

There are countless meetings scheduled throughout the day, the kind of meetings that spawn other meetings, with venue executives, lighting and sound technicians, floor staff, caterers and the director of the Fringe. With the volunteer in charge of the volunteers, with the bookseller.

At the main entrance to the auditorium Orla is waiting, turning at Rae's approach to lead them in. The doors swing shut behind them, engulfing them in a darkness so complete they may as well have dropped down a well.

'Oh,' comes Orla's voice. 'I thought we were meeting in here.'

'Obviously not,' says Rae as lightly as she can. She thought she was late. She needn't have rushed so much.

Outside again in the lobby that more resembles an airport departure lounge than the anteroom of a theatre complex, the aroma from the coffee bar mingles with carpet damp from wet shoes and dripping umbrellas. Heavy rain — more heavy rain — is the long-range forecast as far as the festival weekend in a fortnight, which could have disastrous effects on sales. Or not. Sometimes the wet weather keeps people here, buying ticket after ticket in a kind of frenzy, marvellous and validating to observe.

'I swear it rains more in this country than it does in Ireland,' says Orla, gazing towards the glass wall at the far side. A leak must have sprung in the cantilevered concrete awning above — a torrent of freakish yellowish water gushes against the pane. In the square beyond blows a blur of dark-clad figures and bright umbrellas. Small blue backpacks bounce against the backs of a flock of kids being ushered towards a nearby cinema.

That's what she should have done with Ned and Nellie, instead of leaving them with Merle, enlisted them in a programme of activities rather than leaving them to Parry and the tree house and their own devices, the gleaming screens that take their cyberselves travelling out into the wider world whenever the mood takes them. Which is most of the time. The teachers' strike has left her off guard — at this time of year the kids are normally safely corralled at school. The strike shows no sign of abating. But really it's the least of her worries.

Orla is on her cell phone, trying to locate the first meeting. Listening to her always-enthusiastic chatter, Rae feels a sharp pang of something very like guilt. None of her correspondence with Liu Wah is on the hub, nor is her correspondence with Xu Wang, a local journalist. He had rung her one day at the office, luckily at a time when Orla was out, and explained that he was a blacklisted Chinese national who emigrated after Tiananmen Square. Now he works for the only one of four Chinese-language newspapers in the city not controlled by the Communist Party. He had heard from Liu Wah himself that he was invited to the festival and wanted to help in any way he could, so he and Rae had met at a teashop in a distant south-western suburb. 'How will you recognise me?' she'd asked, about to launch into a physical description. Tall. Brunette. Gaunt. 'Don't worry,' he'd said. 'I will.' At the teashop he'd chosen, Rae was the only non-Asian customer.

'Upstairs!' Orla clicks off her phone and sets off on her teetering heels across the carpeted expanse towards the stairs. As they climb to the third floor Rae retrieves her own phone, checks the time and frets that the delay will make her late for her meeting with Wang later in the afternoon to keep the lid on everything as far as she can. He understands the need for secrecy: Liu Wah will not technically be a guest of the festival. 'A sideshow?' he'd asked her at their first meeting, and cracked up laughing, though Rae had not seen the joke. That was when the terror first set in. What on earth had she done? It was hardly a schoolgirl prank, a harmless exercise in independence. She could lose her job.

This is the sideshow, she thinks, watching Orla greet the centre management, telling the story of going into the dark theatre as more entertaining than it was. The small assembly laughs politely and draws the women to sit down at a round table set with coffee and biscuits. There have been some staff changes since last year. A new Director of Marketing, introduced as Wally Lim. A new Head of Catering, introduced as Naleem Shah.

The circulated agenda is summoned onto their devices and Rae sees she's really required only for the first item: the finalised programme. She talks them through it, noting that the British crime writer is the one name that really floats their boat. The Opus Award Ceremony also rouses some curiosity.

'Adarsh Z. Kar,' says Naleem. 'I read his book — very risky. Does he live under a fake name?'

'Javier Flores!' from the Box Office Manager, a woman in her fifties. 'I read his first book about thirty years ago and loved it.'

'I understood,' says Wally Lim, 'that there is a writer from China coming to the festival? I don't see his name on the other list.'

Rae feels her ears grow hot and a weight shifts in her stomach. Orla is answering for her. 'Liu Wah? Is that who you mean?'

'I think so,' he answers carefully, looking at Rae. 'I think that was the name I heard.'

Who from? Rae wants to ask, but doesn't.

'Oh yes,' Orla is telling him, 'you're quite right. There was talk of inviting him, a long time ago.' She is topping up Wally's coffee cup as though she is hosting the meeting. 'But we decided he wouldn't pull an audience big enough to justify the expense of bringing him such a long way.'

'That is a shame, Mrs McKay,' Wally says. He is a middle-aged man, his dull grey suit leavened by a pink shirt and clashing tie of swirling browns and greens, thin hair clipped close to his skull.

'Yes, it is. The festival will not be bringing him.' Rae meets his eye and detects an ironic disbelief, or even a challenge. He knows something of the situation. She's sure of it.

'In China there is a saying that culture is a platform for business,' he says, 'but the platform must be strong and solidly built with no uneven planks or unforeseen obstacles.'

Orla is at a loss, Rae can see, from the way she is smiling hopefully across the table. A flurry of rain strikes the window behind Wally with the sound of thrown gravel, and the treetops in the park across the square wave and tremble against a racing sky.

'Excellent sentiment,' Rae says, with more steel than she truly musters. 'Is it Confucian?'

Wally shakes his head. 'Modern Chinese.'

'Culture is a platform for business,' repeats Orla, smiling. 'I like it. Who knows what deals and bargains have come about at the bookstall or the festival bar?'

'Indeed,' says Wally, disbelievingly.

'Who is Frans de Waal?' asks the catering manager, changing the subject, and Rae with some relief tells them about the primatologist, re-telling an anecdote from the book that supports his theory about hardwired primate empathy and kindness.

'He watched a younger female care for a sick old man chimp — she tucked straw and grass behind his back, just like a nurse would with pillows in a hospital.'

It amuses all of them except perhaps Wally, who remains unsmiling. Rae remembers the last sentence from Chu's book, *Chinese Whispers*: 'There really is no Chinese mystery waiting to be revealed. To understand, we need only to listen to our hearts.'

She is listening to her heart. That is why she is taking this tremendous risk. Why should a writer as gifted and humane as Liu Wah remain locked away from the world? He should be free to go wherever he pleases. He has committed no crime, caused no harm, brought no shame.

The meeting moves on through the agenda, with Orla doing most of the talking. Rae feels less and less involved, only half listening. Lunch comes and goes, delivered by the catering staff — filled rolls, sushi and pastries, none of which appeals to her queasy stomach. Early in the afternoon she and Orla return downstairs to brief the ushers, and after that the volunteers who are mostly women and all keen readers. Many of them have been helping out at the festival since its inception fifteen years ago. Rae's predecessor, now retired, had spoken of the volunteers as if they were an honourable army deserving of medals and accolades, and their enthusiasm and good cheer is certainly infectious enough for Rae to banish some of the anxieties of the morning. They are familiar with most of the writers on the programme, even the most obscure. A smiling Scandinavian says of the epic Norwegian, 'I am in love with him! Those eyes, those eyes! I want only to touch the hem of his garment!' A delighted lesbian asks if she can bring all her existing copies of the Canadian comic's books for the writer to sign and also if she could take her out to dinner. There are only two men among them, and the most senior announces that the happiest day of his life was when he discovered Javier Flores and he never thought he'd actually be able to sit in the same room and breathe the same air.

As she feared, she is late to her last meeting, by half an hour. The bar has tables on the cobbled lane, one of the oldest parts of the city and now closed to road traffic. Xu Wang is waiting for her there under the canvas awning, rising from his seat as she hurries towards him.

'I got your text,' he says. 'Don't worry!'

'But I am worried!' Rae tells him about her exchange with Wally Lim, and he is alarmed by it too, immediately lighting a cigarette and inhaling sharply.

'How did he know Wah was on the list? Do you make your wish list public?'

'Never. Only the staff and board.'

'Is there anyone on the board who would have leaked it?'

'No. They will have forgotten about him.'

Uneasily, Wang glances up and down the narrow lane. The pub has few customers sitting outside, because of the weather, but the thoroughfare is busy with pedestrians and commuters heading to the nearby bus station.

'I would like to make the announcement soon,' he says. 'Tomorrow. It will be in the paper.'

'Good.' Rae hails a passing waiter and orders a glass of wine. One glass, that's all she'll have. She has to stay clear-headed. 'Have you contacted Ripeka at the Fringe?' she asks Wang. That's the plan. A Fringe event in Cantonese to draw a mostly Chinese audience. Ripeka's consolation prize, since she'd missed out on Adarsh. And for it to remain a secret that Liu had ever been invited to the main festival.

Wang nods, the visor of his baseball cap eclipsing his face. He would have to be in his forties at least, Rae calculates, to have been involved in Tiananmen Square, but he dresses like an American teenager. College jackets, gothic tee-shirts — today the head of a slathering Rottweiler — and baggy jeans, the only discordant note struck by suede moccasins, recreational shoe of senior professionals.

'Very keen to have him. Crazy, really crazy lady, though.' He twirls a finger by his ear. 'She told me about a spiritualist who is getting in touch with dead writers, so you can go along and call for Charles Dickens. Or Shakespeare! What if we call for Li Bo or Lu Xun, et cetera? Someone she has never heard of!'

'There's a hunger for that kind of thing,' Rae says vaguely, 'but I'd be surprised if she gets much of an audience.'

Wang leans across the small table that separates them. 'Last night I spoke to Liu Wah in Berlin. He is perplexed — upset — not to be in the main festival.'

'Did you explain to him the situation? The point is he will still be a guest in our city and people will—'

'Of course I did,' Wang interrupts. 'Unhappy sponsors, et cetera. I explained that our government is happy for him to come here. It is just the festival that is unable to host him. That is correct? The government is happy for him to come here?'

'I arranged his visitor's visa months ago, just as I do for all the writers who need them. It's an enormous job — it takes months.'

Wang nods, appeased. 'And his airfare is paid?'

'Out of my own pocket.'

'Ah. We can reimburse you perhaps. From the ticket price. Although . . .' He trails off, watches with a suspicious eye a young Asian couple passing hand in hand. What must it be like to suspect everyone of watching you, Rae wonders. Even here, thousands of miles away from any threat. The young couple are completely engrossed in one another and pay no attention to them. A cool westerly finds the mouth of the laneway and drops the temperature, blowing litter along under the awnings.

She feels chilled, suddenly. Actually frightened. The whole

situation is of her own making. And what for? She can scarcely recall now what motivated her. An adolescent desire to challenge authority perhaps, a desire she hadn't even had when she was an adolescent. By the time she'd gone to university in the late nineties, aspirational greed had displaced the long-reigning pinko sentiments evident in student politics since the sixties. Rae was just one of their number, voting for the conservatives. 'You were always such a good girl,' her mother liked to say.

'Although I wonder if the event should be free,' Wang is saying. 'You have never before done this. Perhaps a . . . what is that Maori word you use? For donation?'

'Koha.'

'Koha. He will stay with me. I will employ some security. You know in Germany he has been picked up off the street a few times and taken to drink tea.'

Rae hadn't known that. She supposes that 'to drink tea' is a metaphor for something unpleasant. Interrogation. Intimidation.

Wang is finishing his beer, putting his cigarettes in his pocket. 'So. The ad will be in the paper tomorrow, and soon on Chinese-language radio and television if they agree to run it. And do not worry, dear Rae, from now on you need have nothing to do with him. I do it all! Meet at the airport, et cetera!'

Rae smiles at him — first the endearment, then yet another et cetera.

'I'm moving house tomorrow,' she tells him. 'My husband and I have separated — the children and I have been staying with relatives.'

Wang makes no reply. Despite his zany clothes he is perhaps old-fashioned and disapproves. Does he have a wife? He has never mentioned her.

'I only mention it because—' Why did she mention it? 'Because I will have a housewarming party after the festival and I would like you to come. With your wife and children, if you like . . .'

He rescues her. 'I am divorced also. My wife did not like it here and went back to Shanghai. But I have a son. He is grown-up and owns a chain of menswear stores.' He pulls at his youthful jacket and indicates the baggy jeans.

'Oh, I see.' She has the sense, just for a second, that he is lonely.

Lonelier than she is, since for now she has the madly accelerating distraction of the festival, the sole responsibility of the children and hardly any time to see the friends she'd like to see.

'Thank you,' says Wang. 'I would like to come. And Liu Wah, if he is still here.'

'Yes, do. That would be great.'

'He would like to explore as much of the country as he can while he's here. He had an idea to write a book about the Chinese Diaspora in the South Pacific, old families and new.'

'That's a good idea,' agrees Rae, though she's sure it's been written before. It's the way of things in the parallel universe that exists at the bottom of the world: books bloom onto the local market and disappear without a trace. A few years later the same topic is addressed by a different writer, either far-flung or local, and presented to the public as if it has no forebears or antecedents.

They make their farewells and she sets off, wondering, as she pushes along the crowded street, if the shit will truly hit the fan tomorrow when Wang sends out his press releases. Her arms and the back of her neck feel colder than the rest of her body — there is the first real sting of winter in the air — but the deeper icy chill against her skin is different. It's a physical expression of fear. Is she being watched? Are they on to her? Who are *they*, anyway?

It's ridiculous. She would like to scream out in the street — Liu Wah is just a writer. A wordsmith. Nowhere in his work, as far as she can tell, does he incite revolution or rebellion or the taking up of arms. He is a gentle poet, one of thousands, really, in the final analysis. She hurries towards her waiting car, head down, jumping at shadows.

the judges

His flat is beginning to resemble a furniture display set up in a shabby showroom. All of it was ordered online and none of it measured in advance. To get into his tiny living room, he has to vault over the big brown faux-leather couch which can only stand against the door. The other wall is almost entirely taken up by a giant 3D-capable television for which he'd had to buy special glasses that he can never find when he wants them. There are an oversized pouf, half-assembled bookshelves and a La-Z-Boy rocking chair. A glass-topped coffee table is covered over with Opus books and dirty crockery and DVDs from the local rental. The furniture might all be new but it's certainly lived in — the flat, these days, is the one place Gareth feels entirely at home, which is why, though he has barely admitted it to himself, he hasn't spent any of his new money on a new place. He has decided, finally, that he likes it here. This little flat answers all his needs — warm, secure, on all major transport routes, quiet and, best of all, bathed in a careless air of transience. If he does go overseas, and he will, for the next book — he's already fielding inquiries as to his availability for festivals and far-flung conferences — he will buy a one-way ticket and hock off all this stuff on TradeMe. Furniture is like cars, though, he reminds himself as he looks around at it all: it loses its value the moment it's delivered into your hands, especially this kind of furniture, bought from a franchised knock-down chain, manufactured in the East and steaming into the country by the containerload. The sofa retains a vague, unpleasant chemical smell which at its most noisome required the windows of his flat to be kept open at all times no matter the hour or the weather. Gareth doesn't mind it now. It smells like home. He positions his head on the tri-pillow brought from his bed, having climbed over the sofa again to fetch it, settles his laptop on his chest and readies himself for the Skyping session with the other two judges and a facilitator from the Opus people.

R.P. Cornish, Dame, the very famous senior British crime writer, is first to pop up on his screen.

'Hello Gareth Heap,' she says, her short silver hair catching what must be early morning English light from the window behind her. Here it's dusk, a soft golden glow surrounding his image at the bottom of the screen. R.P. Cornish must be in her study, where she writes all her popular bloody but moral tales. It's what Gareth would have imagined for her — a wall of books, a wingchair, a gloomy oil painting, a deep sill at the window, greenery tapping on the glass. R.P. Cornish wears a pale blue sweater and a string of pearls, a touch of pale lipstick. She looks tired, but it might be just that she's old.

'Good morning Dame Roberta.'

'Good evening to you. What . . .' She leans closer to the screen, peers at him. 'What is that behind you, if you don't mind me asking? It looks like a dead body — a pair of fat, mottled legs on either side of your head.'

What kind of mind do you have, Gareth wonders. He supposes the tri-pillow is rather stained, possibly because he sleeps most nights gripping it in his arms as if it were his wife, as if it would save him.

'My tri-pillow.'

'Your what?'

Another pop — and the facilitator has come on line, Eric Kimboi, a thin, serious-looking African man who turns out to have a strong African accent that Gareth struggles to understand. The way they talk in Nairobi. He is Kenyan, Gareth remembers from the brief biographies sent with the agenda for the meeting. Professor of African Literature at Berkeley.

'Now we are waiting for Wilbur only,' he says. 'He is having technical problems somewhere in the dead heart of Australia. Sometimes I wonder if it would be easier to all meet physically somewhere like we used to in the old days.'

'Some of us will meet at the festival in the South Pacific!' Roberta says. 'Very soon!' She is jotting something on a piece of paper. 'Extraordinary. It really looks like a pair of decaying legs. Interesting. You look well, Eric dear! How is your family?'

They must know one another personally. Gareth listens to them talk about Eric's children and somebody significant in Roberta's life called Muriel, until he feels as though he's eavesdropping on a personal conversation. He puts his laptop down and goes to pull the stiff new curtains to halt the glare on his screen, and by the time he gets back to his machine the connection has been broken. He must have bumped a button when he got up, or maybe it just severed — whatever — he reconnects eventually and they're pleased to see him since all are present now, including the third judge whose elderly, weatherbeaten visage comes and goes through a storm of interference.

An apt metaphor, thinks Gareth, since the writer was once famous enough to have a book in every language in every library of the world and has now all but faded away. When he'd seen Wilbur's name on the list of judges, his first response was 'Is he still alive?' But there he is, the author of the first grown-up novel Gareth ever read. The adventure writer Wilbur Dart. It's like seeing the face of God, or at the very least the face of someone who helped to shape his twelve-year-old world. Wilbur's face is bearded, with a beaky nose and heavily lidded eyes.

'Right,' says Eric. 'Not the best reception for some of us but let us press on. We'll begin with the third place-getter.'

'Oh,' says Roberta. 'Really? I think the winner is obvious and we can argue about second and third after that.'

Wilbur laughs, wheezily, his segment of screen a sandstorm.

'Good on you, Robbie!' he says. 'I agree entirely or I think I do.'

'Gareth? Do you have an obvious winner?' asks Eric.

'Well, no,' begins Gareth, 'and I think it would be a mistake not to debate the pros and—'

But Roberta is speaking over the top of him, 'One two three — go!' and then she and Wilbur pronounce in perfect unison, 'Adarsh Z. Kar.'

'But—' starts Gareth.

'We know your situation,' says Roberta, 'that he was your student and so on. That's already been properly dealt with.'

'Happens all the time,' assures Wilbur. 'It's a small world.'

'It's a very large world!' Gareth says. 'And what about Javier Flores? Don't you think he's more deserving than Kar?'

'Second,' say R.P. Cornish and Wilbur Dart, once more in unison.

'And third?' asks Eric smoothly, as if they have already reached that stage of proceedings.

'Well . . .' Roberta is looking at papers on her desk. She must have notes. I should have notes, thinks Gareth. 'That leaves either the English novel *E* or the Sudanese horror story.'

'I found Masaad Deng's novel very powerful,' says Wilbur. 'Credible, affecting and . . . yes, bloody powerful. In fact, I would place it second, on second thoughts.'

'How can you be having second thoughts at this late stage?' Gareth asks, but it's as if he hasn't spoken because R.P. Cornish is saying, 'There are aspects of *Blood Desert Womb* I find absolutely repellent, I must say. The rapes and so on. And the protagonist doesn't seem remorseful.'

'Ah, but there is authorial remorse, wouldn't you say, Eric?' from Wilbur, lost in white mist.

'My opinion on that matter is neither here nor there,' replies Eric as smoothly as before, while Gareth wonders why Wilbur doesn't seek his opinion, since he is in fact one of the judges whereas Eric is not.

'I think—' Gareth starts.

'Have you ever before judged a major competition?' asks Roberta.

'Well no, but I won the Opus in 2005 and—'

'Yes, yes. We're all aware of that.'

Gareth remembers from the bios that R.P. Cornish is a previous winner several times over of the Gold and Silver Dagger awards, the Agatha, the Theakstons Old Peculier, the Orange and several others he can't recall.

'But this game is new to you, dear, so listen and learn.'

For a second Gareth's finger hovers over the Esc button and he quells a desire to say something he would regret later. If she was a character, he'd delete her. Pretend it was a game. Roberta as shape-shifting avatar morphing into a gun-bristling automaton, weapons styled circa World War Two bursting out of her pale blue sweater and fangs curling over her lower lip. By the time he returns his attention to Skype, Wilbur is saying, 'For all that, I think it's the most powerful anti-war novel I've read since *Good-bye To All That*.'

'That's going back a bit,' remarks Gareth, groping for more recent anti-war novels. 'What about *Catch 22* or *The Fox in the Attic* or *For Whom the Bell Tolls* or *Legion of the Damned* or even *The Cellist of Sarajevo*?' but the conversation has gone on without him.

'Do you really?' Roberta sounds incredulous.

'Absolutely,' says Wilbur. 'Without question.'

'Am I miked?' asks Gareth, since it occurs to him that he might not be.

'Yes, perfectly,' answers Roberta. 'Tell us what you think, Gary. You've been very quiet.'

'It's Gareth.'

'I beg your pardon?'

'You know, I think his volume might be down—' begins Eric.

'I can hear him perfectly well,' says Roberta loudly. 'Give us your thoughts, Mr Heap.'

'I would put Javier Flores's novel first, *E* second and Adarsh third.'

Roberta snorts and Wilbur disappears again in a cloud of static, fine white points whirling around him like a bad case of dandruff.

'While excellent,' comes his voice, '*Breakfast with Butterflies* is not Flores's best.'

'He's never won the Opus before and should have done,' says Gareth. 'It's a scandal.'

'We are not here to mop up after previous judges.' R.P. Cornish is reaching for something. A floral teacup comes into view, steaming. Gareth is glad his tasty evening savvy is out of shot.

'Quite true,' ventures Eric, 'and may I remind you that your decision must be unanimous.'

'Oh, yes and no.' Roberta is smiling, showing a row of small brown teeth. 'Yes and no. We'll certainly come to an agreement, Eric. You don't need to stay with us, you know. You could go away and join us later. We're quite capable of doing this ourselves. We're all grown-ups!'

'I'm happy. Carry on.' Eric has picked up a gold fountain pen. He writes something down, his right arm making an emphatic sweeping motion low down, as if he's underlining something or striking it out.

'Where were we?' asks Wilbur, static cleared all at once, a late-afternoon blue sky and worm-eaten veranda post behind him. There's a gum tree, half burned away, and a dust-covered four-wheel-drive. All that's missing is a kangaroo.

'You haven't actually decided anything yet,' Eric says. 'May I ask if you are all absolutely sure that this is not in the running?' He waves in front of the screen a copy of *Wellfed Urban Malcontents*, which Gareth had all but forgotten.

'Absolutely,' says Roberta. 'Aren't we?'

'Yes,' say Gareth and Wilbur together.

'Although . . .' says Wilbur.

'No. We're sure. It's not as . . . well, I do think that for some readers the other novels could be life-changing. All very different and quite startling,' announces Roberta, 'whereas I do feel as if I have read this story about middle-class metropolitan neurotics in a hundred other guises.'

It could be the half-bottle he drank before the Skype, or the chemical smell lifting from his sofa, or the close proximity of his tri-pillow, but Gareth is beginning to feel sleepy. The room is darkening slowly, the one still-uncurtained window showing a single streetlamp on the other side of the road. It clicks on just as he glances at it. When he was a boy, he'd thought it was a moment of magic to see that flicker and coming to life stringing throughout the streets of his hometown. As a teenager pulling all-nighters it was just as magic to see them switching off just after dawn. Better. Secret, illicit, a spectacle for the wicked, the privilege of an exclusive club. The streetlamp casts a soft light into Gareth's living room so that his murky image at the bottom of the screen glows with a lopsided penumbra.

'Shall we take a vote?' Roberta is saying. 'Irregular to the usual procedure, but useful. I think we face a deadlock.'

'As long as the result is only a discussion point and not definitive,' cautions Eric.

'*Gay Times with Ganesha* is the winner. Wilbur?'

'Do you know,' says Wilbur, 'I'm beginning to agree with Gareth. I think it's unfortunate that Flores has never won. And who knows, he might never write another book. He's pretty old — at least as old as me—'

'But in excellent health, from what I hear,' says Roberta dryly, as if she wishes he wasn't. There's a history there, Gareth realises. Perhaps she was one of his long-ago conquests. Or a recent one. Who knows? The old dog's affairs are almost as famous as his novels.

'Gareth, old son,' says Wilbur, 'you've almost disappeared.'

'Don't you have electricity where you are?' Roberta sounds exasperated. 'Turn a light on, for goodness' sake.'

'Perhaps we should consider possible repercussions of giving the prize to a gay novel with limited appeal,' says Gareth from out of the dark.

'Hardly limited appeal. It's selling well, I understand,' snaps Roberta.

There's a small silence while she glares at him. She thinks I'm homophobic, thinks Gareth. I'm not. I'm really not.

'I don't classify it as a *gay novel*. It has such a large cast. The whole world is in *Gay Times*,' says Wilbur.

'You know, don't you, that he lives under an assumed name in Delhi. That his publishers have received death threats,' persists Gareth, feeling increasingly desperate. That awful character based on himself. The arrogance likely to breed in Adarsh's own character if he wins.

'And your point is?' from Roberta.

'My point is that giving him first prize may compromise his personal safety,' Gareth persists. 'Some crackpot could track him down and shoot him.'

Roberta snorts and slams her teacup down hard enough to chip it. Another silence, longer this time. An Australian bird screams from the burnt tree behind Wilbur. In London a wind springs up and rattles the shrubbery against Roberta's window.

'Perhaps we could reconvene at our earliest convenience,' says Eric. 'We don't seem to be making any progress and I have a lecture to give in twenty minutes.'

'Listen to me for a moment!' Roberta says as if they haven't already. A lot. 'Here's what I think. Adarsh Kar is a young writer of enormous potential and I think we should give him first prize, Javier Flores second and Masaad Deng third. That's my final judgment.'

'They're all men,' Eric observes.

'Oh, so what? That's hardly a consideration,' says Roberta.

'I thought you were a feminist,' says Gareth, unadvisedly.

'I am. But I would never promote a woman's book over a man's simply because it was written by a woman. *E* will not survive. It's a party trick. Clever, I grant you. But a difficult read.'

'Aren't most literary awards won by difficult reads?' asks Gareth. His spirits are lifting. It feels as though they're coming to the end of the road.

'If you're talking about your own experience, then that's true,' Roberta responds. 'I had several attempts at *Root* and never triumphed.'

'But you reviewed it!' Gareth remembers suddenly. He knew he had a connection with her, aside from knowing of her books, none of which he'd ever read. How could he have forgotten? 'In the *Guardian.*' *Almost six hundred pages of culturally apologetic drivel*, she'd written, but he doesn't want to quote her because he has no wish to give it new life. Instead he feels himself close off to her, to her opinions, to her face. He turns off her screen image so that he can only hear her voice.

'I rarely review anything, actually. I think you're mistaken.' So posh.

Is he mistaken? It was a long time ago. Maybe it was another dame. He turns her image on again.

'You know,' says Wilbur, after a pause, 'I'm happy with that line-up. Gareth?'

'No. I'm not. I would put *E* ahead of *Blood Womb Desert*. By miles.'

'So you're suggesting replacing Masaad with Sophie Salter,' says Roberta.

'Yes,' says Gareth. He has to have some influence.

'So,' says Eric. 'Are we all happy with *Gay Times with Ganesha* first, Javier Flores's book second and Sophie Salter third?'

'All right,' says Roberta.

'Okay,' says Wilbur.

'That's good,' says Gareth. He wants it over with.

Eric brightens. 'We have a decision?'

'We do.'

'Adarsh is the winner?'

'Yes,' the judges say in unison and unanimously.

JUNE

A writer

Three hours into the five-and-a-half-hour flight to Hong Kong, Adarsh considers himself one of the luckiest men on the planet for the simple reason that he fits perfectly into 78B. It's as if the Economy Class seat has been designed to accommodate him above all others, to fit the line of his back, to cushion his head and provide elevated and elegant rest for his arms. He can tell that to watch films on his individual screen he will not have to move his head either up or down but stare straight ahead, which is what he's doing now as the stewards make their slow progression with the dinner trolley, beginning in what they call Pacific Class. If he'd paid the extra, Adarsh could be among their number, answering the questions, 'Fish or chicken? Something to drink with that, sir?' instead of having to wait.

But waiting is character-building, he reminds himself, and expenditure on a Pacific Class seat would have been wasteful. As he watches the attendants bending to slide the trays from the narrow drawers, he muses on how there was an idea when he was growing up that the world was becoming more egalitarian, that class distinctions were being broken down. He reaches for his breast-pocket notebook and makes an entry in his tiny, neat handwriting: 'By cabin class distinctions, we are just as divided as we ever were', and realises he is already slipping back into his Western mindset to make such a banal observation when he's barely left behind the multiple, enduring social divisions of India. Divisions he's never come to terms with and never will.

The woman beside him doesn't fit her seat nearly as neatly as he does. She is a tall American, over six foot, her knees pressed uncomfortably against the seat in front. When they first boarded she had tried to engage him in conversation but he had engrossed himself quickly in his book to put her off, that book now face down in his lap: Liu Wah's *Wan Ma Ben Teng: The Lives of Chinese Workers*, published last year in Germany and posted to him by the author himself.

So far, only ten pages in, Adarsh considers it empathetic but didactic and supposes it could not have been anything else. Despite his uncomfortable discussion with Wah at the February publishers' party, he can't help but acknowledge the writer's big heart, his concern for the oppressed masses of his country. Jung Chang, the London-based Chinese author, has said that after so many years away from her homeland her heart is no longer in China. Wah's is and ever will be, despite what is doubtless a bewildering exile, and Adarsh, perversely, envies him. To be in exile you had to have had a home first. Where is his home? The vast country he speeds away from as the jet flies through the night into tomorrow, or the Pacific islands he was born in just before the coup forced his family to leave, or those other cooler wealthier islands he grew up in and that he journeys towards, or more precisely the open-all-hours dairy that sent his mother raving mad — were any of those places home? And does home matter? In his first book it did, it was all about home. In the new one, no one even thinks about it.

An inadvertent sigh, and the American beside him shifts, looks at him — 'You okay?' — and he nods, avoiding her gaze, and flicks on his entertainment centre. Headphones in place, he selects a music clip. Kylie Minogue's latest, which he's already watched many times for research purposes. His current hero loves her above all others, and so does Adarsh.

> As my father switched his fealty from Krishna
> to Shiva to Ganesha to Rama and back again,
> so I keep my pantheon of Western divas —
> old goddesses and new — Billie Holiday,
> Judy Garland, Barbra Streisand, Carole King,
> Kylie Minogue, even Beyoncé and Lorde,

who have only one name apiece as if they are
indeed true divinities.

On the screen, Kylie sings and dances first in an old European street
and then a glamorous apartment, weaving herself around a young
actor moony-eyed and adoring. Everything is white and clean — the
billowing curtains, the bed, their clothes, her teeth. They writhe on
the bed fully clothed and kiss as chastely as Bollywood stars, and for a
second, as the diva hangs above the spreadeagled young man, there
is an astonished look in his eyes as if he can't believe he is cavorting
on camera with the pop pixie, beloved of millions, especially gay
men. How Adarsh envies him. He would swap places with him in a
flash. He freeze-frames on a close-up of the actor and is certain he's
gay. And how astonishing it is that this eternally young goddess is
the same age as his mother would be if she was still alive, not worn
out and vanished by her own hand.

He settles his glasses on his nose — a new and unwelcome
necessity — and peers at a close-up of the singer herself. Flawless
skin, perfect make-up, blonded hair, pure blissful joy. He feels a
pulse of hatred for the critics who pick holes in her, write about her
'jerky' dancing and 'thin, overproduced' voice, call her the singing
budgie. He can find no fault. How would it be to inhabit a character
that hated her? That would be a challenge, and one he could never
accept. Is he less of a writer because of it? Or more?

The food arrives and Adarsh chooses chicken, the first meat
he has eaten for months, but one mouthful is all he takes before
spooning up the soggy tomatoes and zucchini and tucking the foil
around the plate. He's lost his taste for the meat, and the vegetables
are tasteless. Who knows where the food was sourced? Did they load
it in Delhi or elsewhere? The flabby white flesh tasted deathy and
chemical, and continues to convey from tongue to brain an image
of thousands of beakless battery fowls enduring short, crowded lives
before mass slaughter. He drinks his plastic cup of Pure Spring,
chews the chill white roll, and counts down the minutes before he
can recline his seatback and sleep more comfortably than most. He
dreams vividly of Kylie in thigh-high boots kicking down the door of
a chicken farm and liberating the tortured thousands.

In Hong Kong he has a stopover. It had taken some organising with Rae McKay. 'I'll pay for it,' he had said, 'any extra costs.' It's a mid-range hotel with an infinity pool on the roof, which he avails himself of soon after arriving. Then he will ring the closeted Chinese writer he had the affair with at the Adelaide Festival. Why not? Invite him for an evening away from his wife.

But in the pool he doesn't think about him at all, but how it was when he first fell in love with swimming, how he'd learned in the pool of a boy from school whose mother taught them both to swim. Adarsh's parents were proud of the friendship — a wealthy white boy from a large house in a nearby leafy suburb — and his friend's parents were proud of their son's association with Adarsh. It was proof of the humanitarian, non-racist side of their right-wing small 'l' politics. The family had taken him with them on holidays to their beach house in a new coastal subdivision where there was further swimming, but in big surf and where everybody was white except for himself and the Pacific Island lady who came to vacuum the floors and sanitise the toilets.

As he swims up and down the hotel pool, catching glimpses of the surrounding towers lit up in the murky dusk, he thinks about this childhood friend and wonders what became of him. His destiny was professional — they had lost contact when he went on to a private secondary school and Adarsh to the local co-ed — but perhaps that innocent boy had gone into business with the motivation of making a lot of money, pure and simple, and perhaps he is here in Hong Kong, even now looking down from one of the million windows. Perhaps, as he regards the slender Indian man doing his laps a thousand feet below, he is recalling his childhood friend and how they could dissolve into fits of laughter that kept them convulsed for hours, how they had planned twin careers as intergalactic explorers, a destiny that at eight years old seemed not only possible but as inevitable as school on Monday morning.

Back to your room and ring your Hong Kong writer friend. May as well.

Held to his face, the striped hotel towel smells baked and meaty, oddly similar in fact to his airline chicken, and he wonders why it is that as he matured and made new friends he never had another of such mutual delight as that childhood mate. Then his eye falls on the cover of the book read by the only other pool user.

It is his own.

The man hadn't been there when Adarsh stepped into the tepid water but he is now, in a short yellow silk robe, his hairless legs extended along the sunchair, his face obscured by the book's cover — the UK edition with Ganesha pink and pot-bellied and carrying a furled black umbrella. Adarsh can tell from the top of the man's head, visible now as he passes by with a sense of panic, of evading capture, that he is artificially blond with a dark grow-out, and that he hasn't looked at him since he got out of the water.

In the lift down to his room he gives thanks that he wasn't recognised, that the man had been reading so avidly he hadn't lifted his eyes from the text. Protected by the pen, Adarsh thinks, mixing himself a gin and tonic. The pen is mightier than the sword.

It occurs to him then that if he wins the Opus he will be recognised more often. In the author photograph for all editions he has a beard. Right now he has no beard. The beginnings of one, certainly, as he rubs his hand around his chin, one that has a few days to grow for the post-award photographs. As he stands at the high filmy window, Victoria Peak a dark looming mound to his right, the busy harbour below and a heavy brown smog lifting from the mainland across the strait, he has a second realisation connected with the first, and that is that he doesn't want to win. He couldn't care less. He doesn't need the prize money. It's enough to be shortlisted, to be riding into his hometown trailing clouds of glory.

Besides. And in addition. Wouldn't he have been told by now, if he'd won? They must let the winner know so that he — or possibly she — has time to write a gracious victory speech. The awards are less than a week away. From the pocket of his suit jacket he retrieves his phone and goes online, though he'd checked before his swim.

Nothing.

A knock on the door.

Without thinking, without even looking through the spyhole, Adarsh opens it. His book again, held open at the author photograph on the inside cover, and the blond man in the yellow silk robe announcing from behind it, 'This is you, isn't it,' without a rising, questioning inflection.

———⁓———

There was nothing for it but to invite him in and let one thing lead to another, which took his mind away from his previous concerns and meant that when he took his flight the following morning on to his final destination he was more relaxed and happy than he had been for a long time. His companion for the night was not only a swimmer — he had removed a pair of skimpy bathers — but also had the most ridiculous schoolboy sense of humour. He was well-off, well travelled, in Hong Kong on a buyer's trip for a famous men's fashion label based in Milan, which he said he owned. Adarsh decided to believe him. If this was being recognised, then it wasn't so bad. It was a great pleasure, especially since they agreed to arrange to see one another again. In the near future.

When the airline food came it was magically delicious and sat easily on his stomach sore from laughing, and his lack of rest the night before meant he slept nearly all the way through changing time zones and across oceans to the small islands at the bottom of the world, entirely restored to himself.

The director

It was Merle's idea for Rae to take the next-door flat to Jacinta's, since she still believed in a mythological feminist utopia where women looked out for each other. 'You'll be able to help one another,' she'd said when the flat became available. 'It's worth a look, even if you stay there just until the lawyers sort things out.' Of the two flats in the bisected bungalow, the available one was the best — reasonable rent, bigger, in good order. And Ned and Nellie liked the climbable macrocarpa in the front yard, the swing Jacinta had slung from it for the twins, and the rising green hill of a park only two blocks away.

Almost 10 p.m. said the little clock on the dash of her car as she parked it on a filthy winter night under the macrocarpa and sloshed her way towards the shared front porch. The rain had kept up, as predicted, as far as the festival weekend, the tails of two tropical cyclones tangling in the close Pacific and pummelling the islands. There were flooding and road slips, and some of the local writers were stuck in southern cities. Thank God the internationals were starting to stream into the country — the wind was blowing them in.

The television was on inside — Rae could hear a sharp soundtrack with canned laughter and see the blue glow through the glass panel in the door. So far, though it mostly wasn't in Jacinta's nature to do so and also not very fair, Jacinta had been doing all the helping. It was the difference between being unemployed (Jacinta) and working more than full-time hours (Rae), and Rae supposed she should once again offer financial recompense despite Jacinta saying it would interfere with her benefit.

There was no sound of children's voices, and when Jacinta finally came to the door she seemed half-asleep, her hair tousled and clothes rumpled.

'Sorry,' said Rae, slipping inside.

'The kids are asleep.' Jacinta led her into the front room. 'We went next door and got the mattresses off their beds and put them on the twins' floor. Hey. Look!'

On top of the piano was a bottle wearing one of those instant chill jackets and beside it a plate of cheese and crackers. Mumm champagne. How could she afford that? Rae wondered again, though she shouldn't since it was none of her business whether it was the ex-husband or wealthy parents helping her out.

'To celebrate! Day one today, wasn't it?'

'The schools' programme. Big opening night tomorrow, Jacinta, and I really need to get some—'

Sleep. But Jacinta was enthusiastically twisting the wire clasp on the cork.

'Don't — it'll be a waste—'

Pop! The two glasses filled to the brim and Jacinta raised a toast. 'To the festival. May it be the best yet!'

The least she can do is spend half an hour with her neighbour. Her neighbour and child minder, and she less of a friend than Jacinta would like her to be.

'How did it go?' Jacinta sat down on the sofa and patted the place beside her. 'Tell me. Have a cracker.'

'Great. Busloads of enthusiastic kids. Elizabeth Knox and J.K. Rowling kept them transfixed.'

'J.K. Rowling. That's such a coup! I love Harry Potter — I had the grown-up editions when I was in my twenties.' Jacinta's eyes were shining, genuinely pleased for her, Rae realised as she watched her down her champagne and pour another.

'Sorry,' Jacinta said, 'been hanging out for it. Just before Jas and I broke up I promised her I wouldn't drink alone any more.'

'You've broken up again?'

Jacinta nodded, unusually dry-eyed. 'Oh yeah. For good this time. We're so unsuited. She's not interested in books and writing like I am.'

Rae had a bad feeling, a premonition, a sense growing daily

271

more finely honed that a request was coming. A plea to be included.

'You didn't move on my suggestion? A panel on self-published writers? I suggested it to you weeks ago. Remember? Did you even think about it?'

'Please don't, Jass.'

'Don't what?'

'Put the pressure on. It's too late. I suggested you contact Ripeka at the Fringe. She could well be looking at self—'

'Self-publishing is the way of the future and should be in the main programme! Come on. Drink up.' Jacinta held the bottle out but Rae shook her head.

'There are all sorts of interesting things in the Fringe.' Rae was thinking of Liu Wah in particular.

Jacinta was glaring at her. 'Like what? B-list shit?'

'No. There are some very accomplished writers on the list.'

'Like who? That psychic woman who contacts dead authors? I'm sorry, but I'm actually quite offended.'

The phone started ringing in the flat next door, only just audible over the heavy rain. Rae stood up to go to answer it.

'You can't go yet. I have to tell you — I'm going to put my novel *Heart of Ice* on the web. Any day now.'

The phone rang on.

'Rae? I expect it to have wide appeal — at least five hundred hits in the first few days. Jesus, some of those poets of yours have smaller print runs.'

The phone was still ringing.

'Don't worry about it,' said Jacinta. 'It's been ringing all night.'

'All night? Oh no, Jacinta!' Rae headed for the door. It could be anything — a writer stuck at Customs, her mother in hospital with a heart attack.

'I'm not your bloody secretary!' Jacinta was standing up as if she was going to follow her, a full glass wavering. 'Do I have to answer the frigging phone on top of everything else?'

The phone stopped, but Rae stayed at the door, her head pushed forward, shoulders slumped. She felt paralysed. A fly in a web.

'We'd better shift the kids,' she said, after a moment.

'It's pissing down. They can stay here. I'll send them home for breakfast.'

'You sure?'

'I wouldn't offer if I wasn't sure.' Jacinta sat down again and took a deep draught of her champagne, the wide blue eyes over the rim of the glass sending Rae a message of wounded pride. More — betrayal.

'Thank you. I really appreciate it.'

'Well. It would be nice if there was something coming back the other way. You could have put me in the festival. Me and the other self-published novelists. There must be hundreds of us.'

Rae nodded. There were.

'We deserve more respect. It isn't easy, what we do.'

'I can see there would be lots of ground to cover,' Rae said, carefully. 'Maybe next year when we know how your novel was received. We'll talk about it. Can I look in on the kids?'

'Whatever,' said Jacinta, flapping her hand towards the bedroom. 'It's a bit of a mess. Don't turn the light on. You'll wake them up.'

'Of course I won't.'

How quickly mythologies spring up in women's friendships, Rae thought, as she picked her way between discarded toys down the hall. In this one Jacinta was a good, devoted mother and Rae was a bad, distracted one. Jacinta was forever offering advice on diet and alternative treatments for common childhood ailments, and counselling Rae on how to deal with Ned's new post-separation behavioural issues when she didn't have a son of her own and so had no idea.

Barking her shin on a toppled pink tricycle just outside the bedroom door, she went in, bent over double, rubbing the smarting bone. The light from the hallway showed the twins' beds, each with a small body humped under the duvets. On the floor was one mattress — she was sure Jacinta had used the plural — and in it Ned and Nellie were asleep in one another's arms. It was a picture of innocence and peace, and through Rae's exhaustion came a warm, energising shaft of love. Ned's profile, so like his father's with his sharp nose and full, clever mouth, lay against the pillow. All that could be seen of Nellie was a flushed little ear and her ruffled hair, her face pressed against her brother's chest. If her phone wasn't on the blink, Rae would take a photo and put it on FB. It was cute enough to go viral. No, she wouldn't. It was private. Her children asleep. For her eyes only.

'Sleep well, my darlings,' she murmured, turning away, longing for the morning to come quickly so that she could kiss them and hold them and hear about their lives and how school was since the teachers had returned from the strike.

The front room was empty of Jacinta and the door onto the porch stood open. She was out there smoking a joint and drinking the last of the champagne straight from the bottle.

'Helps me pass out,' she said, as soon as she was aware that Rae was behind her. 'Otherwise I lie awake all night pissed off with everything. You?'

She held out the joint, a tiny glow bright against the rushing dark of the stormy garden. The swing in the macrocarpa banged and flapped against the trunk.

Rae shook her head, pulling her key from her bag. 'I'll knock on the door around six-thirty. Have to be at the venue by eight. The kids are going to Merle's after school tomorrow.'

'Oh, right,' said Jacinta. 'You'll regret it, you know.'

Regret not spending enough time with her children, is that what she meant? The key was in the lock.

'Rae? Ignoring my book. It's going to be huge.'

'I hope so, Jacinta. I really do.'

Inside, the flat was cold and empty. There had been no time to unpack properly. Boxes and bulging rubbish bags stuffed with clothes and linen loomed out of the dark, and the light, when she switched it on, was still a naked bulb. Heart aching for her kids and consoling herself with the thought that they were just next door through a wall thin enough to hear a phone ringing in heavy rain, and doing her best to quell rising anxiety that they were in the care of a stoner, Rae went to the phone. Five messages. The first three were silent, only the click of a phone being replaced and the caller's long number not one she recognised.

'Hello, Rae,' began the fourth message. A man, a German. 'I hope it is all right for me to be ringing you at home. I thought I might catch you there with the time difference and your mobile doesn't seem to be working.' There was a pause while the caller spoke to someone else, presumably in the same room, in another language. Chinese? Chinese with a strong German accent. 'I am Gert Richter.' He was back. 'I have been corresponding with you on behalf of Liu Wah and his invitation to the Oceania Festival. We have a problem. His visa has been revoked at the last minute — his transit visa through the United States. As you know he was booked to travel through Los Angeles since the other way could have been difficult for him but it seems the Americans had a problem with it too. Ring me when you receive this message, should you wish. I am sorry to be the bearer of bad news. I will be in touch with Wang.'

Click.

Rae put the phone down. The empty flat swam around her and she had suddenly, from nowhere, a bad case of hiccups. Why would the Americans refuse him a transit visa? The nearest carton offered a seat and she sank down onto it until she felt something break under her weight and scrambled up again, catching one foot under the other and finding herself sprawled on the floor, hiccuping.

China — kitchen read the label, perfectly visible from here. It was the dinner service, one that had been her grandmother's. She raised one hand, ruffled the newspaper under the lid and pulled out the gravy boat, white with yellow and gold flowers, broken clean in half. She never used it anyway. Who gives a shit? Her back hurt. She stood up slowly, feeling for any other injuries. Elbow. Knee. Wrist.

She wished she could sob like other women. Too dry, too dry-eyed, too gaunt. What had seemed only a local power play between the university and the Chinese Embassy and the festival now was global. Terrifying. Even the Americans accepted the need to limit this writer's exposure. Was there something in Liu Wah's background that alarmed them too, something Rae didn't know, or was it simply that by writing his courageous, big-hearted accounts of ordinary Chinese people he had come too close to challenging Party shibboleths? It was nearly thirty years since Tiananmen Square and the poems he had written as an angry young man in response, the poems that kept him in prison for so long and the source of so much of his trouble since. His recent books made no judgement directly of the Party except by depicting the poor quality of life for so many of his subjects, the often-appalling pollution and work conditions and family-destroying displacement. She'd read both of the books, which was excessive, because she couldn't get through everyone's — a hundred and fifty writers a year, a few with terrifyingly long backlists. You did have to google google google until you were blind.

Stop hiccuping!

In the kitchen she ran the tap for a while before she filled a glass — old pipes here, which worried her as much as it worried Jacinta. The lead. The toxic sediments.

What had happened to her? In New York she had had two children, she had dealt with the pressures of family and work and Cameron and lovers galore in a big city, and life had been pretty much a breeze, a constant high, no obsessing about peril and danger. Now everything seemed to offer the same potential for disaster — from tainted pipes to the possibility of a terrorist attack wiping out a planeload of international literary treasures; from the kids breathing Brendan's toxic sidestream smoke to the fact they'd be exposed to Chelsea, who had moved in with Cameron and was proudly embarking on a career as a porn star; from the tsunami of writers even now pouring into the country, in and out over the next four days, to the imperative that none went AWOL just before an event, or got horribly sick or went dangerously insane; from the fear of sound-system failure or inconvenient fire alarms to this irrefutable evidence of the global influence of the Chinese administration.

She lay her aching body down on the sofa with the phone on her tummy, drank her tinny water and thought about how Merle would tell her to let it go. Had already. 'Sometimes we have to sacrifice a minnow to keep the peace,' she'd said about the first change, from main festival to Fringe. Rae had tried to accept that advice, but Liu Wah was hardly a minnow. And what peace, exactly? The dark, anxious peace got from walking around with your eyes shut?

The phone began ringing again, vibrating with the bell, relaxing her stomach muscles sore from hiccupping — quite a pleasant physical sensation and there weren't many of those on offer these days.

'Hello Rae, it is Xu Wang. I left you a message.'

'Wang — oh, thank you for calling.' She struggled upright, tried to focus.

'The man in Germany with Liu Wah. You've had the news?'

'Yes.'

'You know I am not at all surprised. I am surprised that we got this far.'

'I'm um . . .' Rae said, a lump rising in her throat, not a hiccup this time. She pictured Wang at the other end of the line, his anxious face and sad eyes. His little wispy beard, his fine-boned slim hand holding the phone. It had been a mistake to get him involved, to think for a moment she could do this brave foolish thing.

There was a silence before his gentle voice said her name again, asked if she was there, if she was all right, before he began to talk about what he would do now: he would re-publish the ad in the newspaper, but this time stamped with 'Cancelled', and then he would set to work on an article on why the writer's visit was prevented.

'But that would be speculative,' said Rae. 'How will you know? How can you find out the facts?'

'The facts are staring us in the face.'

'But we don't know what went on, who said what to who, who made the phone call.'

'No. If there *was* a phone call. I think his name is on the list, that's all. Part of a bargain, a deal. Diplomatic immunity, et cetera, but only to a point.'

'What can we do about it?'

'Nothing. You know that. I had a long talk with Liu Wah. He is philosophical. His books still travel. That is the main thing. It's not necessary for the writer to follow along, not at all.'

It was too late at night to be questioning the necessity for writers' festivals, the whole ethos that supported her life. The writer on show. The performing pony.

'Try not to worry, dear Rae. We can't all be guns blazing, et cetera. There is much we have to accept in the world. We are lucky to live in this beautiful country where it is possible to speak your mind and stay out of trouble.'

'Yes.'

Rae didn't want him to ring off — she searched for something to say — but he was talking again, telling her that he was coming in to the festival venue tomorrow evening to hear a scientist expound on new advances in the big bang theory. 'A particular interest of mine.

The formation of the universe puts everything in perspective.' He said he would come to find her afterwards, and if she was not too busy they could have a drink together.

It was past midnight. Half a sleeping tablet and into bed. Turn it all off.

A writer

Merle and Brendan had tickets to the opening night of the festival, which this year was to take the form of the Opus Award presentation.

'You look nice, love,' he said, as they walked up to the bus stop. 'Not too foul at all.' And Merle laughed, as she was expected to, at another one of Bren's discoveries of idiomatic argot. All over the nation for around a century men had said, 'You don't look too foul at all, love,' and their women had gone pink at their chivalry.

Once we were famous for understatement, thought Merle. One of our national characteristics. Now we indulge in hyperbole like everyone else.

She would like to return the compliment, but Brendan really did look foul, if you were going to be critical. He was in his usual uniform — shorts, a tee-shirt with a few small stains, and a pair of jandals as yet unchewed by Parry. Merle forbore to comment. He would fit into that small dwindling sector of the bohemian crowd, mostly men, who regarded clothes as something you hauled on to cover your bits and give no hint of your bank balance. One or two of their acquaintances had been worth millions and she'd never known. Well, she did know about one of them, eventually, after he died and bequeathed what amounted to a fortune to various children from various wives. It was a peculiar inverted snobbery.

No such luck for their son Jack. Brendan dressed the way he did because he had to. Almost.

Fortune smiled gently because they got all the way to the bus stop in a break in the rain, the umbrella still furled in Brendan's back pocket. Up on the strip, Friday-night traffic was thick and the footpath jammed with pedestrians. It was dark already, six o'clock, mid-winter. Freezing out here and doubtless steamy inside the venue — had she overdressed in long black skirt and fur jacket? Fake fur, from a second-hand shop a decade ago. Not even a label. Oh wait. Target. She'd end up carrying it, exposing her glittery sweater that had moth holes so tiny she couldn't see them without glasses, which was comforting. She and Brendan were better matched sartorially than she liked to think, then. Different expressions of down-at-heel scruffy.

Sparkling from the last deluge, passing cars streamed water and the trees in Western Park danced in a strong nor-easterly pluming up the ridge from the harbour. Passers-by shrugged into their coats and quickened their steps — the chill wind stirred Brendan's hair and made him shiver.

'You've got the right idea, Merle. Furry. Beware of girls in furry jackets. You'll only want to cuddle them.'

He put his arms around her, and Merle let herself meld into him, against his chest and under his encompassing arm, even though she suspected he was reaching out for animal warmth rather than in affection. She felt him soften against her and kiss her brow — it was affection then, and also a kind of returning trust. She had been too hard on him and he had recoiled from her, and now he was returning. Through all that shame and fury, in spite of it, she had missed him. Turning her face into his neck, she held him tight, breathing him in and kissing him, and his arms tightened around her. Why didn't they cuddle like this more often? Because it made life worth living — one of the things, a good cuddle. This is as close as we can be, she thought, as close as we are. We still love each other and that's all that matters.

When she opened her eyes again, a car was pulling into the kerb, indicator flashing, the front-seat passenger getting out and running until she was upon them — a woman, whom Merle vaguely remembered from a long-ago writing workshop, gesturing wildly towards them, 'Merle! Come on. I'll give you a lift' — and she and Brendan were hurrying in her wake to be driven in style to the Tizard Centre doors, where the aspiring writer bade farewell to her obliging husband driver and sped off into the milling foyer crowd.

Merle was assayed by an attack of claustrophobia. It was as if she had needed the trundling journey of the bus, the walk through town — the slower entry to the night — to be in the right frame of mind. And it was embarrassing that a virtual stranger had interrupted her and Brendan mid-embrace like a pair of teenagers. The claustrophobia gave way to nerves — though why would I feel nervous when I've got nothing at stake, she wondered, and knew the answer immediately.

Because I don't really want to be here. Not really. I wouldn't be if it wasn't for Rae giving me the tickets as a thank-you present for all my minding of Ned and Nell, but surely I've told Rae of my antipathy for prizes, how I hate them. Rather tickets to any other event but this. Even the marine biologist talking despairingly about the vast, multiplying dead zones in the ocean full of jellyfish. Or the astronomer giving a perspective-inducing view of the birth of the universe. Or Javier Flores presenting his regal profile while he composes his lengthy, ponderous responses to questions. Or Adarsh holding the floor in his solo session. Or the revitalised Australian doing the programmed joint reading with his young wife, who had of course turned out to be a very talented poet. Or Tosh and his crew belting out their latest rap novel with head-splitting drum accompaniment over the course of the whole weekend.

The queue to a glass of wine was fifty long at least, but Brendan needed one and calculated the service was fast enough for him to have one down before the summoning bell. She went with him, passing through clouds of perfume and chat and buzz, mostly over-forties with rarer clusters of younger people. A man with his head down pushed past her, his hair slicked with rainwater — or was it an over-application of gloop — and it took her a second to recognise him. Gareth. She put out a hand to detain him.

'I'm in a hurry,' he said, before he even looked at her. 'Oh. Merle. I'm supposed to be at drinks with the other judge.' The cut on his face was not quite healed, still livid against his pale face, and he seemed harried and anxious.

'Is there something wrong?'

It was the wrong question — he shook his head, his expression bordering on alarm or distaste, and moved off as fast as he could for the door that led backstage. He had a suit on. Very nice. It was well cut, expensive, an emerald-green lining flashing at the placket. His departure left her wafting in a suspension of heady cologne.

Brendan was already five or six deep down the line. She went to stand beside him, recognising faces from previous festivals and other occasions in the city's cultural life, and from her lost job at the university and her dimly remembered experiences as a published author. She had grown to enjoy the anonymity bought by her long silence — or, more exactly, had returned to enjoying it. When her books were well known, she had not liked being recognised by people she'd never met, endured it when it happened to her, and then perversely mourned it when it dwindled and stopped altogether. Now, she supposed, she was turning into one of those older, eccentric bookish women on the fringes of the literary scene. Quiet, sincere, ageing without a fight, half a dozen books on an ancient backlist and observing peaceably enough from the sidelines.

Fuck that. She should shout it from the rooftops — writing is not a career. Quit while you're ahead. Think of it as an occupation that lasts only as long as it takes to write each book. It's the truth for most of us.

Brendan had ordered her a glass of wine as well — bubbles to cheer her up — and brought it to her already decanted into a foaming plastic cup to take into the auditorium. They filed in, took their seats and gazed at the wide, warmly lit stage with its oversized pot plant, the podium, the row of chairs for the speakers with a low table and water jugs, and endlessly rotating screen of sponsor and patron names above it.

'Well done, Rae, eh?' said Brendan. 'Don't you reckon? All this. Clever girl.'

'She has quite a team of helpers.' She knew she sounded snippy.

'Even so. And Adarsh one of the finalists. Well done you too.'

'None of it has anything to do with me.'

But Brendan didn't hear her. He had turned to the man next to him and was telling him about how the director of the festival was his wife's cousin, and how one of his wife's ex-students was up for the Opus. Merle could only hear part of it, but registered his pride. She should feel proud of the connections. Of course she should. What was the matter with her? She hated this meanness of spirit in other writers and loathed it in herself. She took a sip of wine and settled back in her seat, waiting for the show to begin.

A writer

Adarsh was hoping to run into Gareth, who would be bound to give the game away by some subliminal clue, but he was nowhere to be seen. As he was ushered along the backstage corridor he saw a hand-written sign taped to an open dressing-room door: OPUS JUDGES. The passing profile of Roberta Cornish moved across a mirror inside, her upraised chin just like it was in her much younger author photographs. He had the sudden impulse to burst in and ask, 'So? Have I won?', and it took some effort to redirect his gaze to the wobbling black polyester buttocks of his guide disappearing around a corner. Why did they have to wobble, and why did they have to be in black polyester?

In the contestants' room there were mirrors set with light bulbs and two small blue sofas, and only two other people waiting. Breathlessly the festival volunteer introduced Javier Flores and Sophie Salter and offered them tea or coffee.

'Glass of wine?' asked Sophie, who had possibly dispensed with her manners along with the letter e.

'Sorry. We try and keep everyone sober before events.'

'Jesus. One measly glass would steady the nerves.'

She had an attractive, croaky late-night party voice and posh accent, which reminded him of Jacinta. The rudeness, too. Sophie Salter didn't look like Jacinta, though, not at all. She was freckled and small, as tiny as his servant Manjula on whom he'd pressed a wad of cash on the day he gave up the flat, the day he departed Delhi. Now he was on the move again and he wouldn't be coming home, that's for sure. How irksome it was to come from a land so small that every move you made seemed to send out ripples of effect. So far it had not been much of a homecoming, his sisters envious and resentful of his freedom, his father resentful of his absence and imminent re-departure. He needed to be in a big city where it was possible to move between large groups of people with no crossover. Crowded but peaceful. Thronging but connectionless.

He accepted a cup of tea and sat beside Javier, unnerved by the mirrored walls bouncing their reflections across the room and out into infinity.

'It's quite a performance, isn't it?' said Javier gently. 'You know I have been twice shortlisted for the Premios Ignotus, three times for the Miguel de Cervantes, once for the Rómulo Gallegos.'

Adarsh had never heard of those prizes.

'And once for the Booker,' went on Javier Flores. He sighed heavily.

The volunteer offered them biscuits. A quarter to the hour.

Time ticked by. Sophie regaled them with the guts of an essay she'd read by the Australian writer Helen Garner, who had a great antipathy for prizes and how they lined writers up against one another, how loathsome they were, but even so had accepted a place as judge in an international competition. It really all was pretty fucked, and further so when it appeared that Masaad had gone missing. Just after eight the volunteer relented and went off to get them all a glass of wine.

At twenty past the judges walked by the open door and Adarsh bent his ear to the conversation but heard nothing. Gareth was walking along at the end and looked different — but of course he did, it was two years since he'd seen him — his hair was thinner, touched with grey, and he'd put on weight. He looked wired, pale and wide-eyed, which Adarsh took as comfort, that you could still look wired at his age. Forty at least, striding along in his suit. A pair of nicely tooled brogues was an improvement on the cheap battered runners of yore. Gareth passed from view and Adarsh thought about how true it is that writers reach an age where wiredness isn't attractive. Gareth was pushing it. He could do with some dignity and containment.

Javier Flores maintained his dignity even though he was leaning back in the blue sofa, sucking on his moustache and looking worried as he entered that stage of post-writerly grizzle that is the realisation that it would have been wiser to keep one's own counsel. Adarsh admired him for his outburst though. It wasn't that the old man was wired; it was more that he wore his heart on his sleeve — which Adarsh found himself brushing lightly with his fingertips. The sleeve of a velvet maroon sportscoat. Good-quality velvet with a deep pile. He wanted to comfort him.

'We should boycott all the prizes. Send out a petition to every writer in the world to write to their publishers and ask for exemption.'

'Oh wise up!' said Sophie Salter. 'You know as well as I do that the book trade would collapse without them. A certain British writer sold sixteen copies of one of his before it was shortlisted for the Man Booker. That's one-six. Sixteen.'

'Julian Barnes,' guessed Javier. 'Ian McEwan.'

'Hanif Kureishi,' said Adarsh.

Sophie shook her head and zipped her mouth.

'Surely it's public knowledge,' said Javier, but Sophie wouldn't be drawn.

'I'm serious,' said Adarsh. 'It would be a good experiment. Bow out. See what happens.'

Javier laughed. 'Every man needs a mountain peak to aspire to. This is ours and only one of us will get there.'

'I couldn't care less either way,' said Adarsh. 'I really couldn't.'

As soon as the words were out of his mouth he realised that Javier cared very much. Seventy-five years old at least and time running out. The older man sighed again.

'You are still young. You are a good writer. I read your book.'

'Thank you,' Adarsh said, and wanted to tell him he'd read his even though he hadn't, none of them, not a single sausage. He should have. He was remiss.

There was movement in the corridor again and finally the missing writer was coming in with his minder, a plump young woman. Another plump young woman! Adarsh had forgotten how many there were in this country, brown and white, well-nourished, open-faced, always with a sheen of moisture to their glowing skins. This one was agog at Masaad Deng, and didn't she have every reason to? He was simply the most beautiful man Adarsh had ever seen in the flesh, tall and thin, with quiet all-seeing eyes and serene mouth, a wide clear brow. Gracefully, his thin cool hands took his and Javier's in turn as he murmured greeting. In Sophie Salter's direction he only nodded, perhaps because of her position at the back of the room — she had been on her way to the adjoining convenience — or perhaps because she was a woman and might barely exist for him. His novel, Adarsh remembered, was full of men. It was as if the hero never knew a woman better than he knew a distant neighbour's dog. When Sophie came towards him to shake his hand, he seemed impervious to her, and a curious expression of embarrassment and fury crossed her funny little English monkey face. Adarsh tried to go to her rescue, 'This is Sophie S—' but Javier interrupted him, 'Masaad! What a pleasure to meet you,' struggling to his aged feet with the help of the gleaming minder.

The returning angle of the minder's body to Masaad's and her expression as she looked up at him seemed proof that he had gone further than shaking hands with her at least. It was after all a time-old source of hanky-panky, the writer and his publisher, the writer and his agent, the writer and the arts bureaucrat. She could have been the one to pick him up at the airport and things could have raced on very quickly from there. Ah, romance. Fast and fleeting. He wondered how his Hong Kong lover was, back in Milan, awaiting his arrival.

Then they were on the move again, backstage, to be miked up with the sound of the audience restless from out in the auditorium. Almost 8.45. Three-quarters of an hour late to kick-off, as they said here in reference to the ever-diminishing national sport. The delay must have been because of Masaad's late arrival, Masaad who was now kissing the young woman farewell and murmuring to Adarsh as she departed on teetering heels, 'My wife.'

What idiocy, thought Adarsh as a technician asked him to pass a wire between his shirt and skin, for him to assume some tardy affair when they were married. It was more than passing titillation. A marriage. He was as racist as anyone, never once assuming that the well-fed creamy-skinned lovely was the writer's wife. What if he'd persuaded his new friend to come with him, instead of arranging to meet in Milan as they had? They could have gone about his hometown as a couple, the bottle-blond white older fan and young

Indian literary miracle. It would have caused a sensation. Or not. It was difficult to cause a sensation these days.

There was a frightening swelling of applause at his own appearance as they walked on — he was the local boy, after all — and Adarsh found himself holding shakily to the thought that Masaad must be the winner, which was why they had waited so long for him to show up from the airport or bar or hotel room or wherever he was. Masaad was the obvious winner. Too late for Javier, too soon for Salter, and Adarsh couldn't give a fig. The gods would know that. If Masaad won, then it would change his life for ever, for the better. He deserved it. No one should have had to live through the trauma and violence he had. Boy soldier, witness to the most terrifying cruelties mankind was capable of, rape, massacre, poisonings, beatings. He would win. His book was hell on earth. It was the only one he'd read.

Head down, he was on his way to a row of chairs on the stage when he was stopped by whispering Rae McKay, who smelt of Issey Miyake and was head to foot in white, like a bride or a midwife.

'You didn't read your notes. You don't have to be on display for the whole thing.'

She pointed towards the other finalists, who had taken a quick bow as their names were announced before going down the stage stairs to sit in the front row.

He followed Javier to the last seat, feeling an immense sense of relief. It was over for him now, he was sure. Masaad would be the winner; he would be the one to climb the stairs, cross to the podium and make an acceptance speech. Happily, Adarsh crushed his own bit of grateful yabber in his hip pocket.

the judge

In a wavering beam of light, Rae brought the judges on from the other side of the stage, Gareth falling behind Dame Cornish who went at a clip in her sensible shoes and pearls and pencil skirt. She had been very entertaining over a glass of wine backstage, he thought, much dirtier and drier than her uppity Lady Pom schtick would suggest, and he supposed she had spent most of her working life among men. She had a military background, a quick wit and a wicked sense of humour. Tory as, of course, but refreshing in an odd way. He liked her despite the bad review she'd given his first book.

He followed her towards the three chairs set beside the podium, his shoes pinching and collar digging into his Adam's apple. Thank God he'd dispensed at the last moment with the tie, though he berated himself that on the one night he'd had to scrub up in almost a full calendar year he'd made the mistake of spending money on poncy clothes that made him uncomfortable. He could have just worn his old jacket and black pants and had a better time. He would feel more like himself.

Beside Roberta stood the chair set for the Australian judge. At the last moment Wilbur had not been able to fly across the Tasman due to heart issues. Word mustn't have got through to the stage manager — the chair sat empty, as if this was an Amnesty International event. The imprisoned writer. Poor old Wilbur, imprisoned by his dicky heart.

Rae stood at the podium.

'Welcome to the opening night of the Oceania Writers' Festival!

Tena koe to every kaitito, author, escritor, ecrivain, literato, skrywer, schrijver, qoraa, chosha, penulis, onkqwe, udar and pengarang among us, writers from all over the world—'

Excellent googling, though 'penulis' is risky, thought Gareth, wishing he could undo his belt by a notch. If only the same courtesy had been extended to the judges as to the contestants. After their slightly eggy catwalk, they had retreated safely to the front row. He had to chill. Maybe giving up teaching had affected his ability to relax in front of an audience.

'—and I haven't even begun on the readers. This festival can only go ahead because of your ongoing curiosity, excitement and support, for which the Oceania is very grateful. If you could just bear with me for a few minutes, I would like to name some of the sponsors and patrons whose icons and logos you've been watching come up on the screen—'

'—for over an hour!' yelled a wag with an Australian accent, and Gareth caught him in the crowd, up in the circle — a novelist, one of the invited guests, here with a wife barely out of high school. Rude bastard, thought Gareth.

Rae looked momentarily flustered before she began with her list of publishers and media concerns and vintners and importers and manufacturers, and Gareth tried to concentrate but tuned out, looking along the row of authors to find Adarsh — who was as fate would have it looking directly at him and smiling broadly and shrugging his shoulders, infinitesimally, but Gareth didn't get his meaning. He was sure he'd won? Or was it that he knew he hadn't and didn't care?

He lifted his gaze to a safer level, well above the audience's heads. Rae eventually drew to the end of her speech and a lighting technician lowered the house lights, plunging the crowd into darkness and the stage into hot tropical sunshine so blinding that Dame Cornish, crossing to the podium to rapturous applause, drew a pair of aviator sunglasses from her top pocket and slid them on. Laughter.

'Well,' she said, 'I knew I was coming to the Pacific but this ridiculous! And apt, don't you think, that such bright lights should surround a prize as strongly contested and well regarded as the Opus. Our finalists this year could not have come from more different backgrounds or have produced more startlingly different, rich, exuberant work.'

An airbrushed and freckle-less black and white photograph of Sophie Salter appeared on the giant screen backstage — Gareth twisted in his seat to take a glimpse — a bleak denuded bluff hovering in the background over a grey smooth sea, a scarf tied around her head in an old-fashioned style, like Queen Elizabeth or Jackie Onassis. She really is no great beauty, thought Gareth, but it's a pity she didn't make the cut. It would have been a vote for innovation, for inventive language, for recklessness.

The stage lights cooled further and the front row once more loomed out of the gloom. All four faces were intent on the screen, which now showed a picture of Masaad and the cover of *Blood Desert Womb* and Dame Roberta's RP tones were chiming, 'challenging . . . frightening . . . violent . . . confronting . . .'

Head and shoulders above the others, Masaad sat listening quietly, his gaze drifting now and then to Gareth as if he was wondering what he was doing there, what his exact function was. Perhaps due to nerves or exhaustion, Rae had not introduced either Gareth or Roberta Cornish by name. Roberta needed no introduction. He did.

Javier Flores was next, his photograph displayed briefly before rapid-fire book covers, fifteen or twenty of them, dealt out onto the screen like a round of cards. If Gareth was Javier Flores he wouldn't have risked making the journey all the way to the bottom of the world, further south than Tierra del Fuego, almost to the South Pole, to further endure humiliation. He wished he'd written to him, broken the confidentiality clause and saved him the agony. The writer's face was lowered now, unreadable, avoiding the view of his own books and visage, but Gareth imagined he must feel a certain amount of excitement and anticipation and hope, which would be dashed once more. If only he'd been able to persuade Cornish and Wilbur that Flores's time had finally come. Fury at the injustice pinged in his veins, though he'd vowed before he left home that he wouldn't allow himself to think about it. For a blind second he entertained the notion of shoving Roberta out of the way, interrupting her '. . . if not the father of magic realism then Javier Flores is certainly one of the great-uncles,' which got a titter, shutting off the '. . . shaped a nation . . . distinctive, much emulated voice,' and carrying out a guerrilla ceremony. It would be like something that would occur in one of Javier's novels, a bloodless revolution.

'And the prize goes to Javier Flores for *Breakfast with Butterflies*,' he would say, 'vintage bliss from a senior writer beloved by millions all over the world.' And Javier would rise from his seat and the award would mean everything to him, vindication, respect, gratitude, absolution, gold watch. It would be the bravest course of action, the biggest literary scandal of the year. Roberta would stagger backwards, open-mouthed as if she'd been shot and the cheque would have to be rewritten.

Adarsh's picture was on the screen now, the amused eyes, the alluring one-cornered smile. The dame invited Gareth to stand beside her, and the Opus Trophy, a carved opal and pounamu naked muse, was handed to him by a glamorous assistant, whom he vaguely recognised as an ex-student. Then Adarsh was bounding across the stage, his vigour and health and general state of excitement winging him through the air, kissing the dame and shaking Gareth's hand before he took the podium to wild clapping and cheering. He uncrumpled a squashed speech from his pocket, glanced at it and put it away to a small ripple of admiration.

Took a breath, let his shoulders go.

'I'd um . . . I'd decided I wasn't going to win this. I suppose I thought . . . well, yes I did, that there were more deserving winners than my own book, writers overdue for acknowledge-ment and—' There was a quiet click of the tongue from Roberta, which Adarsh must have heard too. An admonishment. He seemed to regroup his thoughts and gather himself before he went on. '—And so I am honoured to be among such illustrious company. If you haven't yet read my competitors' books, you must. They are all . . . ah, wonderful. *Gay Times with Ganesha* is my first novel — which was a complete joy to write and a roller coaster of an adventure afterwards, most of it fantastic, much of it confronting, some of it scary. I began the book here in this city, under the guidance of Gareth Heap and Merle Carbury.'

This was perhaps ill-advised information, thought Gareth. So far the media, in their general lack of interest in things literary, had not recorded their connection. There had been a flutter on Twitter and postings on other portals between disgruntled ungenerous green-eyed monsters all clutching unpublished novels and poems and stories and journals and blogs and narrative non-fiction or whatever. But nothing had stuck and there had been enough said in his defence — that the process was rigorous enough to withstand the relationship, Gareth had abstained from voting for him, et cetera — that no interest had been widely sustained.

The audience remained silent. Nepotism, if that was how they saw it, was now so much an everyday phenomenon that any lingering sense of illegality or immorality was fast being eroded. Nepotism was ubercool, unquestioned by anyone under thirty. Shit, thought Gareth. I've done something cool without even trying to.

As the thanks and tributes went on — to the author's departed mother, various friends and relations in Delhi, including agent and publisher — Gareth felt the world open around him. He felt forgiven for a crime he wasn't sure he'd committed, his shoes were wearing in — they really were! — and his Adam's apple balanced precariously but painlessly on the top of his collar. The auditorium ceiling was somehow lifting higher and the air growing warmer and the night suddenly promising greater hilarity and celebration than he had anticipated. He thought about his own novel soon to be published in London and New York, about his imminent departure for half a dozen festivals in Europe, and about how exhilarating was this moment in the sun. From now on he was going to love every moment of it.

The three of them, judges and victor, acknowledged the final applause and Gareth found himself bowing extravagantly, flourishing like an actor and ending with his hand on his heart.

THE
FESTIVAL

the directors

Another sleepless night even though she'd abstained, mostly, from the Opus party booze. Two chards, that's all. When she'd finally got home and fallen asleep, it was well after three and here she was in the shower after two and a half hours' sleep with the conviction that she and Wang had last night exchanged a long kiss in a doorway and, not only that, she had felt him up, sliding her tongue between his lips and her hand between his legs and hadn't she for some reason already shared this information with Jacinta, who had immediately asked, 'How big is his wang?' So childish.

The water drummed on her head, helping her to think straight and realise that the kiss was a dream, that Wang had not been in touch at all, or shown up to take her for a drink as he'd said he would. Or maybe he'd gone straight to the venue bar to wait for her without making a firm arrangement first. If he had waited, then she'd stood him up, because she'd been called away to deal with a Tuhoe poet displeased with his hotel room, which didn't have a view but faced out into an airshaft. He had decided this was a racist decision when it was just the way the rooms had been allotted. The princeling had been overheated and shouting, and Rae had wanted to yell at him 'Pull your horns in!' which would have been idiotic and inevitably interpreted as further discrimination. Least said soonest mended — a festival mantra — and easy enough to switch with the room of a late arrival, one of the raft of writers yet to check in. The poet was appeased and wanted to involve her in a conversation about his genius and burgeoning fame — he was a poet in his own right as well as a member of Tosh's Rapnovel Crew — until it had seemed the only polite way to curtail him was to invite him along with her, back to the crowded Opus drinks.

It had been an evening of chat, of diplomacy and people behaving nicely. Her new friend from the hotel had held court to a group of fascinated women; Adarsh and Gareth had avoided one another, which was politic, but both seemed happy and pleased with themselves. The losers were gracious enough, although Masaad absented himself early with his new wife, and Sophie Salter had got hold of Merle to ascertain that Gareth was indeed Adarsh's ex-tutor, which fact had somehow escaped her.

'It's a small world,' Merle had said.

'Bullshit. It's a fucking big world!' was Sophie's riposte, and Rae had thought it the right time to move away. Almost immediately she was waylaid by a bookseller who wanted to congratulate her on the exciting and interesting programme. Sales were up already. In the distance, Orla had circulated among sponsors and shareholders in a glittering sexy good-humoured bubble until two hours before the end, so that she didn't have to pack up or drive guests back to the hotel or make endless farewells. Rae wouldn't have minded if it hadn't been for the ridiculous management structure of paralleling the two roles. How many times had they each been asked what they actually did, to define their functions? Maddening. The Director and the Artistic Director. Orla took too much credit and wasn't there when it counted. Her favourite author was Dan Brown.

Back in the bedroom now for knickers, bra, trousers, blouse. Smear of lipstick. Last night she'd worn a powder Jacinta had lent her to take the yellow tones out, as she'd instructed at six in the morning when Rae had collected her kids. It had reflectors in it, like a mudguard.

Away from the house and into the car, pull out from under the macrocarpa where Jacinta had lashed the swing to the trunk to save it from the storms. A flash of the children at Cameron's, at this hour of the morning sitting up at the breakfast bar. The deal was that Chelsea wouldn't be around. Was she? Was she there pouring milk onto their cereal before heading off to a porn shoot?

Don't think about it.

Down the street to the intersection, remembering what it was like to be able to leave the house unencumbered, without having to consider the needs of two other small beings. Maybe it's easier to live without the father of your kids, to have him elsewhere to give you a complete break from parenting. Maybe our connected lives are too clamorous and noisy to maintain long marriages, so that moments of relative peace become more valuable, more longed for, than another body in the bed week after week, year after year. Maybe that's why so many women leave. A man has to be pretty special to be worth all that exhausting selflessness.

At the lights she turned her phone on, though she'd hoped she wouldn't until she had a coffee in the other hand. Eight voice messages, all from yesterday. Her phone was playing up again — she'd checked at 2 a.m. and there was nothing. She listened as she drove on, making illegal stabs at the keyboard on the passenger seat. The first one Nellie, a plaintive plea for her iPad charger which she thought was under the couch; the second from Equinox the outraged poet, apologising for his bad temper but he had been tired from the long journey; and the next four from Orla about a crisis at the ticket office. A glitch in the system had resulted in the event with J.K. Rowling being rabidly oversubscribed, which was curious because she'd been worried at the last minute that the vast auditorium wouldn't fill. Harry Potter was old news now and her subsequent books for adults had not caught on. Not really. Or had they? The problem wasn't insurmountable — digital feeds onto screens in the biggest conference room. The seventh message from Orla to say that she'd organised exactly that, got it sorted. Forgiveness, then, for her absconding last night.

The last message was from Wang. His hesitant voice, the one he used for more personal conversations, brought the fantasy kiss back again as she turned on to the motorway. In the outside lane she put her foot down and was frightened of herself — she had to get over this one, it was never going to happen — but it had been so nice to kiss him — and had to play the message again because she hadn't really been listening the first time.

'Rae. I want to invite you. I am thinking of going to Berlin to visit Liu Wah. He has invited me to come. It will soothe my pain at not meeting him this time for the festival. Rae — would you come with me? I will ask you tonight in the bar if you do not get this message. As my friend, I mean. To come to Berlin as my friend.'

A welter of responses — disappointment that she'd missed his call, delight that he had rung with his invitation, dismay at his insistence that they remain only friends, mild indignation that he could entertain the idea that it would be possible for her get away from the kids and a job for a jaunt to Europe. Impossible, of course, but all the way into town she dreamed about it, what it would be like to travel in Wang's company and finally meet Liu Wah and the people who had helped him get out.

A pale watery sun, the first for weeks, set the myriad windows of the Tizard Centre shining. Inside it was the calm before the storm. 8 a.m. Wide expanses of untrammelled carpet, venue staff setting up for the day, festival volunteers arriving at the hospitality desk, a few early queuers for the first event, the coffee machine luring her to the first fix of the day. Orla was at her elbow, surprising her with a quick squeeze.

'All going well so far, young Rae. All set for J.K. tonight. You got my messages about the digital feed.'

'Yes, thanks, I did.'

Orla seemed ridiculously happy, the cat that got the cream, almost purring, 'You'll never guess who I went home with last night.'

The chick is rapacious. Far worse than I ever was, thought Rae. During one of their fights Cameron had said to her, 'You'll wear your thing out,' which was a line from a Joe Orton play she was pretty sure, and if it wasn't it should be. But then Orla wasn't married or in a relationship, so why shouldn't she have who she wanted? Next year they would invite some writers on monogamy — there were enough of them about, leading, popular writers — Alain de Botton! — who recognised it as soul-destroying, self-dividing, energy-depleting. No one wants a divided self any more. It's too hard.

'Who?' she asked Orla.

Lucky bitch.

'A finalist.'

'Oh for Godsake.'

Uncharacteristically Orla had a moment of discretion, realising that the barista would overhear. After they were handed their coffees, she drew Rae towards two empty workstations that would later hold two writers working on two chain stories, swapping back and forth, the old children's game forming on screens above their heads. Sport and entertainment. Rae had stolen the idea from last year's Fringe — a pulse of guilt which intensified as Orla took a seat on one of the desks. No one sat on tables any more. It was rude in the extreme — a cultural norm that had strengthened during the years away in New York.

'Get off, Orla.'

'Well?' She stayed put.

Lightning equation. It can't have been newly married Masaad or the local gay hero, or Ms Salter, since Orla was strictly heterosexual.

'Oh no. Flores.'

'So sweet. We just held each other. He couldn't . . . you know. Too tired. I tried everything.' She made an obscene pumping gesture.

'You could have given him a heart attack!' Quite suddenly there was pressing work at her desk. A sip of hot coffee and she was heading off, Orla beside her.

'Then we just — it was amazing. To hold one of the greatest writers of the twentieth century in your arms. I'll never forget it. Amazing experience.'

Wouldn't you rather have one of the greatest of the twenty-first for that purpose? Rae almost asked, but concentrated instead on getting through the double fire doors and down to the bowels of the building to her office for the weekend. The dressing-room mirrors were covered over with pieces of A4 and pages from the *Herald* to hide her gaunt reflection.

'Oh, so this is where you are,' Orla said, having not come down here before. And it was Day Three, really, after the two days of kids' events. Orla had spent her time circulating upstairs, chatting and laughing, the Festival Director. Once or twice, when she hadn't answered her phone, Rae had had to go in search of her.

'Yes,' she answered, tersely. She sat down and rang through to the hotel to be put through to Frans de Waal's room. Orla sat down on the small blue sofa, sipped her coffee and looked around.

Frans wasn't answering his phone.

'I wonder if that sale's still on.' Orla pointed at a full-page ad taped to the nearest mirror.

'Have you seen Frans de Waal? He has arrived, hasn't he?'

'Who's Frans de Waal?' asked Orla, and when Rae didn't answer, busy making another phone call to the publisher's assistant detailed to pick him up from the airport, she realised she wasn't wanted and got up to leave the room, first flapping a hand in Rae's face to draw her attention.

'Got to split,' she mouthed. 'Breakfast meeting.'

It was true. Orla did have a breakfast date, with a couple of keen young woman bloggers and poet Equinox Te Tutara, who had got in last night from a mountainous forest somewhere down the line and gathered quite a crowd in the hotel foyer when he had a meltdown about his room. As she hurried upstairs she couldn't help but wonder why her colleague gave herself such a hard time. Of course Frans du Wawa or whatever he was called had arrived. If he hadn't they would have heard. Everything was rosy. No typhoons or terrorist attacks or fogbound airports or sudden deaths. Everyone was here, or nearly.

Upstairs the crowd was thickening for the first event, some guy talking about how monkeys can be as kind to one another as humans, which Orla knows is very very kind, and also can be just as extremely cruel. Orla had thought she might like to hear him but it would be more interesting to eat a salmon bagel with a Maori prince. She had half an hour to spend with him before she legged it up to Albert Park to massage the festival relationship with the Fringe.

A writer

J ust as well she booked, thinks Jacinta. The Fringe has completely underestimated the interest in Margaret Boon, literary psychic. From a half-floor of one of the many half-empty proliferating office blocks in the city the event has been moved at the last minute to a tent in a central park, the marquee hired especially for a vast crowd, mostly women. Hand in hand Jacinta and Jas, who are back together again as of yesterday afternoon, walk under the high canvas roof down the slippery plank designed to protect the audience's shoes from the boggy ground. Muddy water poaches the edges and smears the surface.

On the stage are a single chair and a screen rigged up at the back — is the psychic concealed behind it? Margaret Boon, internet sensation? Jas is a huge fan, live-streaming her shows in Perth (to contact dead surfers), in Alice Springs (pub brawls and knifings), Sydney (drug overdoses and suicides) and the west coast of the South Island (miners). It seems Margaret has quite a business going with special-interest groups. One of the dead surfers from the Perth show was called Siobhan and the psychic had pronounced it with a b. Jacinta and Jas had almost had an argument over Jacinta's opinion that if the dead surfie had really been in Margaret's ear then she would have pronounced it correctly.

Only three rows from the front. They sit and wait, still holding hands. Jacinta would rather have seen the primate expert, but one of the conditions of the resumption of their relationship is to allow Jas to make more of the decisions. She is only eighteen after all and needs to be allowed to mature. Jacinta has to remember that she isn't her mother, though sometimes she feels as though she is. She slips a sideways glance at her lover, so pretty and young, her little pointy face intent on the empty stage while the tent fills around them.

'Don't diss my religion,' Jas had said at 4.30 this morning.

Jacinta bites her lip and waits. Then they yawn, almost at exactly the same time.

The psychic, when she emerges from behind the curtain, looks just like Janet Frame in later life, a resemblance that wouldn't be noted by Jas since by her own admission she hasn't read a book since school. At least a year. Margaret has the same cloud of sparkling grey hair, the same mischievous blue light in her eyes. Possibly less sartorial, with lime-green polyfleece over an unseasonable summer frock, her very white legs flecked with long dark hairs and her wide feet shoved into Crocs. Shyly she acknowledges the quietening crowd with a gentle nod and takes to her chair.

'Looks like Su Bo before they jushed her,' whispers Jas.

Subo — Jacinta has to think — who is Subo? Popular culture spins around so fast for people not interested in it, like herself. Oh. Susan Boyle. Susan or Janet? Janet or Susan?

Neither. Margaret is just a big lady in her sixties or maybe even older, and how she thinks she's going to pull the wool Jacinta has no idea. It isn't exactly visually stimulating. The psychic is closing her eyes, breathing deeply, and Jacinta's attention wanders to the exits, in case it is really so lowbrow she has to beat a hasty retreat.

Right up near the back, mid-row, sit Merle and a tall thin older lady who looks very like Rae, although plumper, less gaunt. She must be Rae's mother. Is this Merle's thing? She always says she's an atheist. And a few rows ahead is Gareth, settling a stoned-looking weatherbeaten old surfie dude in his seat — his stepfather. Jacinta met him once or twice. Total loser. The first time he'd asked for her star sign. 'Leo, and what of it?' she'd said.

Good on you, Gareth, for taking Pop out even though you can't stand the thought of sitting through it yourself, she thinks, watching him hotfoot it out of the marquee.

And there are aspiring writers — Natalie and her husband from the writing class, Equinox Te Tutara the angry poet, a collection of wimpier poets and emerging novelists she recognises from pub readings. And isn't that man across the aisle a deeply cynical columnist with a long and varied career behind him, someone the chattering classes love to hate? He'll no doubt write something cruel and amusing. 'Cynicism is easy,' remarked Colum McCann in one of his novels, one of the few men Jacinta reads these days. 'The optimist is the braver cynic.'

Is that what this crowd is, then? Braver cynics? They're not your usual festival-goers, she thinks. There are some sad faces — the newly bereaved or terminally ill, people wanting comfort and proof. Did they all have writers in the family? Had they all personally loved a writer? What is a writer anyway? Everyone who has an FB page is a writer. Anyone who goes blab blab blab anywhere on the blabosphere. Can Margaret Boon contact all of those that have died since its invention?

More silence. The capacious shelf of the psychic's bosom rises and falls, rises and falls, and Jacinta feels herself growing drowsier and drowsier — she's only had three hours' sleep after all — until another woman walks out on to the stage as quietly as she can in her high heels and tight skirt, motioning to the audience to hold any applause.

'You know her?' whispers Jas, rubbing a blackened gardener's fingernail under the name in the programme: ORLA O'CONNELL Festival Director.

Jacinta shakes her head. It's so sweet that Jas thinks she knows everyone, that she's part of the writing world when she isn't. It reminds her of Venice the year they lived with Gareth, how she would ask of anyone that caught her attention in the street or park or supermarket, 'Do you know that man, Mummy? Do you know that lady?' When you're three years old the world is small enough to know everyone.

Orla pauses beside Margaret and asks, hushed, 'Are you right?' She has an Irish accent, which seems to win so many more friends in this country than Jacinta's English one does. Under Jas's tutelage she's trying to get rid of it. They agree it's something she'll have to do consciously.

The psychic gives an infinitesimal, closed-eyed nod, smaller than the one she gave the audience. She is at work.

The Irish woman in the high heels whispers into her handheld microphone. 'For those of you who don't know me, I'm Orla O'Connell, the Oceania Writers' Festival Director. It's a sign of the friendly relationship between the main programme and the Fringe that I was asked to present this very exciting hour with Margaret Boon.' She gestures again for no applause. 'If you have a question for her, kindly line up behind the microphone.'

Stage right is a stand that Jacinta hasn't noticed before, on the far side of the tent from where she's sitting. Couldn't be further away. There will be a stampede, surely, and she'll never get a turn. She feels cheated even though actually, be honest, she wouldn't ask a question if she was paid to. Jas's hand has somehow slipped from her grasp. She takes it up, remembering Jas telling her this morning at 4 a.m., 'You look for problems when there aren't any.' The little sunbrowned hand is damp with anticipation and some of it sings through her skin to Jacinta. This could be incredible. You never know. In the modern sense, as in amazing, not unbelievable. She is at long last caught up in the moment and wants this to be fabulous. Really something fabulous to tell other people about.

If she were to get up and go across to the microphone, she would ask for Dorothy Parker or the Australian verse novelist Dorothy Porter, both of whom she loves. Or Belinda Starling who sadly passed away after her only gothic, erotic and completely brilliant novel, *The Journal of Dora Damage*. What if she wants to contact Anaïs Nin or the Marquis de Sade or Norman Mailer or John Updike or Dominique Aury, or any of the dead writers she'd discovered who could write about sex and wickedness as well as she can?

Already, people are moving towards the microphone and the first voice echoes through the speakers, though the speaker herself is concealed by other hopefuls rising from their seats. Jacinta finds she cannot move. She'd look a dick.

'Hone? Is Hone there?' The questioner sounds young, tentative, though not so tentative that she couldn't have got to the front of the queue.

'Honey?' asks Orla, who must be a more recent immigrant than I am, thinks Jacinta. At any rate she hasn't bothered to acquaint herself with the nation's poets.

Margaret Boon is shaking her silver curls and working her mouth.

'Hone Tuwhare?' comes the plaintive voice again, from a thin young Maori woman.

Margaret's shaking head speed-blurs and Orla says, 'I'm sorry. As you know from the programme notes, not every writer will come when called. Next please.'

A distinguished-looking gentleman with a thick moustache and a strong accent asks for Pablo Neruda. 'Have you written anything since you died?'

'Of course,' answers Margaret gravely, with a matching accent that could be Chilean. 'I never stop. Everyone is a poet in the afterlife.'

'Can we hear a new poem, then?'

Margaret seems to listen carefully to the spirit, and then begins:

> Cómo hablar del Amor,
> si tu Reino tan lejano?
> Y quien es tu soberano,
> sin piedad por los humanos?
>
> Oh! Paraíso Celeste!
> Tu mar inconmensurable!
> La barca de los terrestres,
> se hunde en promesas vanas . . .
>
> Oh! Paraíso Celeste!
> reliquias azules vibran,
> en el corazón de los hombres,
> y en él, germen del Amor.
>
> Pocos son los jardineros,
> que cultivan esa Flor.
> Pero cuando nace uno,
> sentido tiene el sol!
>
> Que la inocencia renazca,
> iluminando misterios!
> A cuando una caricia,
> de lo Eterno al humano!

Jacinta is impressed. What does it mean? She wishes she could speak Spanish. Pulling her hand free again, Jas leans forward, transfixed.

But the man's face, as he returns to his place, is disbelieving. A woman reaches out from an aisle seat as he passes.

'What did it mean, Mr Flores?' she asks, loudly enough for everyone to hear. Orla is gesturing frantically at the next in line to step up to the microphone.

'Love,' says the man. 'Heaven. Claptrap. If Neruda was watching the mess the planet is in, he'd have more to say than that. He'd be worried. And he was an atheist.'

'I would like to ask William Shakespeare a question,' comes an emphatic female voice. 'Did you really write those sonnets for a male lover? And did you really write the sonnet found in an attic in Switzerland?'

'That's two questions —' begins Orla, but Margaret is telling us in a deep voice, 'We all loved him, every poet in London wrote for my fair lover. And no, dear lady — the poem is a fake.'

'And can I ask—'

But she is moved aside by the next in line who wants Angela Carter, and as she asks the question Jas rises from her seat and goes behind the chairs on squelching grass. So anxious about what Jas is doing, Jacinta barely listens to Angela's answer, the ominous words 'cancer', 'loss', 'too soon', but the contact alone must have been cheering enough, because the woman returns to her chair with a smile. Jas moves steadily up the queue — the dead writers are far less prolix in their afterlife communications than they were in their writing lives. Coleridge makes an appearance to counsel a scruffy poet on drug addiction, though Margaret could surely have taken her pick of hundreds, possibly thousands, of others. Hunter S. Thompson tells him, 'If I hadn't used drugs I'd have had the mind of a forty-year-old accountant' and Jacinta is sure she's not alone in marvelling at the incongruous means of transmission.

J.D. Salinger mentions the existence of yet another posthumous manuscript, buried in the forest near his house. Frank Sargeson gives advice on growing capsicums. Evelyn Waugh mocks the audience for believing such rubbish. Edgar Allan Poe corrects the balance by assuring them that every word Mrs Boon utters is clear and true. Elizabeth Gaskell envies contemporary women their freedom and

Katherine Mansfield takes offence at a query as to whether or not she bore an illegitimate child. Basho composes some sparkling lines for an indoor water feature. Sometimes Margaret takes on the qualities of their voices and periods, other times she answers in her own voice.

'She's here,' she says briskly for Doris Lessing, 'but she isn't in the mood for talking.'

Jas is next in line. What could she possibly want to ask? Perhaps she was a bookworm when she was a kid, which isn't that long ago. Who were the popular children's writers of ten years ago, eleven? Jacinta wasn't interested in children then; she knew nothing about them.

'Can you tell the future?' Jas's question rings out in the tent. 'My girlfriend is an incredibly talented writer and I want to know if she's going to be famous.'

'I don't think that—' Orla begins, but Margaret is laughing, a delighted childlike giggle.

'Oh yes! Lights, cameras, pursuit. A marvellous trick. Well done her!'

Jacinta's face is burning. How could Jas do this to her? In public? At least she didn't mention her name. With a grin from ear to ear Jas is returning and heads are swivelling to see if the incredibly talented writer is among them. Jacinta covers her face with her hands.

'Time for three more questions,' comes Orla's voice. 'And please, if you could only ask about writers who have passed.'

Whoever were the last three poor scribes to be roused from their eternal rest Jacinta couldn't care less. She just wants to hurry away from the scene of her humiliation. As they race towards the carpark, Jas tries to take her hand again but she can't do it. That would be saying to anyone watching them, 'It's me.' And she would want to explain, 'And I didn't set her up to ask the question on my behalf, I really didn't.'

'No one's looking at you, Jass,' Herman used to say when she was overcome by panicked embarrassment — a broken heel, a vomiting twin, a cause far less directly personal than this one.

'Babe?' Jas is hurrying after her, taking hold of the back of her jacket and pulling her up short. 'No one's looking at you. They're not. You don't need to worry.'

They're under a spreading tree, a Morton Bay fig. It's cool and damp and smells of leaf mould and death and possibly faeces. Look for the positive, her psychologist told her in the last session.

Resist catastrophising.

Under the tree it's cool and damp and smells of incubating life.

'Why did you do that?' she asks Jas, close to tears.

'So that we know. And now we do.' What do you think she meant by "marvellous trick"?'

Jacinta shrugs, heaves a sigh. The emotion is subsiding, leaving her weak-kneed. She shouldn't get so worked about things. It's because she's so tired. Maybe Jas and she should have an early night tonight. Herman's got the twins. She heaves a shuddery tearful sigh. She wants to say, From now on you will make more decisions and we'll have more early nights, but Jas is talking, gently, sweetly, 'It's only 'cause I'm so proud of you, honey — that's why I asked the question. That poem you wrote just before dawn this morning was amazing,' and she gives her a kiss.

Sometimes it's as if their age difference is the other way around. How did Jas get to be so wise when she's had half the life experience that Jacinta has? Never travelled, never married, never had a baby. She's so calm. It's like sitting beside a still pool in a forest glade, which Jacinta has never done in her life but still the image speaks to her. She remembers how Gareth used to tell her to dig deep, to discard the first image and metaphor that occurred, to look for the subtle and complex. But she likes to think of Jas as a peaceful, fern-ringed pool, especially while they're under the lovely trees. They put their arms around each other.

'You're going to be famous,' whispers Jas, 'famous for a marvellous trick.'

the judge

Gareth has the full day booked, one event after the other beginning with primatologist Frans de Waal then on to Richard Dawkins, then Richard Ford, Richard Powers and Richard Wolfe. As he files out of the Richard Dawkins event, it occurs to him that you could have a whole festival of Richards and he wonders why no one has done it yet. Richard Kramer, Richard Calder, Richard Gwyn, Richard Flanagan.

He is entirely at peace with the world, which is an unusual state of mind for him, and it's all to do with the inspiring words he's been listening to. Frans de Waal's account of primate altruism, of the fact that our closest cousins have nothing to gain from acts of kindness to their fellows but perform them anyway, was the greatest comfort he could have asked for. It seems kindness is hardwired into our natures. All the centuries of religion, the polarities of God as love and Satan as evil preached to increase human altruism, have been needless. All the millions of mothers past and present who exhorted their children to be kind and share needn't have bothered, because a child will behave empathetically anyway. Who would have guessed? Gareth had never been remotely interested in religion except as something to rail against in long-forgotten adolescent verse — he'd barely been inside a church in his life — but still, it was satisfying to see it dealt a double death-blow, first by the primatologist and second by the famous atheist. It had seemed to him that Dawkins argued his case as passionately as any priest.

At question time a woman had risen from the audience and

said, 'Professor Dawkins, you are an educated man and you have plenty of time to think about these things. I wonder if you've ever considered the possibility that atheism is a position of privilege, and that the notion of an all-powerful God of love is comforting to the uneducated and the oppressed?'

The over-enthusiastic interviewer had intervened yet again and answered for the author. A ripple had run through the audience — they hadn't come here to listen to him.

'Isn't the question itself elitist? Are you suggesting a two-tiered belief system — atheism for the rich and religion for the poor?'

'Oh, we have that already,' the woman had responded before she turned to take her seat, and it was only then that Gareth recognised the back view as Merle's. She'd stopped dying her hair.

Ahead of him now, her motley red and silver head is moving towards a coffee van parked by the children's play park on the far side of the square. Gareth hurries to fall into step with her.

'Good question, mate.'

'Oh, I'm sure he gets that asked that a lot.' Merle turns to him. 'Don't you reckon? Probably relieved the other guy answered for him.'

Feeling magnanimous, Gareth orders and pays for two flat whites.

'And another one.' Merle digs in her purse. 'I'm meeting Brendan here.' She holds out some coins but Gareth is too quick for her. He pays for that one too. Empathy and kindness.

'What did you think of the primate guy?'

Merle looks a little embarrassed. 'I um·. . . . I missed him. I went to the psychic instead with my cousin. In the Fringe. Mad. Huge audience and atmosphere of belief.'

'Atmosphere of belief here too, don't you think? Dawkins's atheism is endearing and old-fashioned. Most of us don't even think about it any more, the existence of God. God is a non-issue. Dawkins comes along and gives us a chance to do just that, reconnect with ancestral concerns.'

Merle is stirring sugar into Brendan's coffee and Gareth wonders if she's even been listening. She's about the same age his mother was when she popped her clogs, and he remembers her doing just that, gently stonewalling him. Downcast eyes and impressive expression, and slight air of desperation as she waits for him to stop monologuing.

'It's nostalgic,' he finishes lamely, following her to a nearby bench. It's steaming in the sun after weeks of rain — but dry enough. They park themselves.

'I wonder where Brendan is,' she's saying quietly, before running straight on as if the two things are connected, 'do you think moral questions have also become an ancestral concern? For example, if a God-fearing forebear told a lie, then his religion might have made him feel guilty and seek absolution. Lying was a sin. If we lie now and that lie improves our own lives or that of someone close to us and does no damage to anyone else, then we have no reason to examine our consciences or feel at all guilty.'

'Maybe lying always damages someone,' Gareth is surprised to find himself saying. 'Maybe it's a rule of the universe.'

Merle snorts into her coffee, which is lidless to minimise the burden on the waste-stream. 'Rule of the universe. You sound like a hippy, a child of the sixties.'

'I wasn't even born until 1969,' he says tersely. He can't stand it when her generation take all the credit for cod philosophy. Or anything else. The whole world has had enough of them. Time they shuffled off. Besides, that 'child of the sixties' is a misnomer. Children of the sixties were born in the forties, or early fifties, like Merle. He wonders again how old she is exactly — is she sixty yet? — and almost asks, but remembers his manners in time. We might be able to lie like flatfish, but it's still unseemly to ask a woman her age.

Instead he launches into an unrequested update on the happy reviews his own novel has been receiving in London, in case she hasn't kept up with them. 'Rae's talking about an event with me next year. Book won't be released here for another two months.'

'Looking forward to reading it, Gareth.'

'How is your . . .' he begins, and trails off. That would be uncivilised too, to ask a writer whom you know has been blocked for years how her work is going. Strangely, Merle has put her hand over her face. Did she guess what his question was and is distressed by it?

'You all right?' he asks.

'Merle?' A tall, thin woman all in shades of green is walking across the pavers towards them, dodging puddles. Short-cropped hair, thirtyish. Rae? No Rae's hair is darker, her complexion sallower than this woman's, which is redder, sun-damaged. She's older too, closer to forty.

'Merle? It is you!' Australian accent.

Merle has taken her hand away, which is a relief. Hiding your face with your hand is primal. Monkey see. Monkey don't. Her behaviour is odd today. Brittle, thin-skinned, but somehow harder than he remembers. Less confident. What was all that hackneyed stuff about lying?

'Sandy! What are you doing here?'

The women squeeze hands and Sandy, whoever she is, launches into an explanation of how a group of Australian independent publishers has come across the ditch for the festival, and how she was hoping to meet up with Merle to discuss Kyla's book.

'Who's Kyla?' he asks, but Sandy is motormouthing on about the buzz surrounding the publication of *Roadside Crosses*, which must be this new literary marvel's tome, and how she's sure it's going to be huge. He doesn't remember a Kyla among the students, but you don't remember all of them. How can you? He gives Merle a nudge because she's forgotten her manners, staring up at Sandy with a slightly panicked expression. She must have temporarily lost his name. A senior moment. He comes to her rescue.

'Hi. I'm Gareth. Gareth Heap.'

'Oh, I know you!' Sandy has big yellow teeth and a curly smile. She's all right, he can see. One of the decent people in the world. One of the trusters. One of the blokes. 'I know your book, I mean. And you've got another one on the way, I hear?'

'He has.' Merle has recovered herself. 'Sorry, Gareth. I should have introduced you. This is Sandy, Australian publisher. Oh look. There's Brendan.'

She's standing up hurriedly with Brendan's lidless coffee, which sloshes at the toes of her clunky winter boots. The women check their clothes for splashback, when it's Gareth who has clocked the worst of it, but his trousers are brown and so neither woman notices. He stands up too, pulling the cloth away from his skin.

'Hello there!' It's Brendan joining them, rumpled as ever, as if he's just got out of bed. He smells of bacon.

Immm. Bacon.

Gareth is reminded he's hungry and so he takes his leave to find some lunch, passing beside the perpetual construction zone running down one side of the square. Since the row of sturdy stone Edwardian buildings was demolished during his childhood, it's as if licence has been given to develop one cheap, temporary structure after another. He can't remember what stood there before, or the one before that. Shielded scaffolding covers the three steel storeys and it's alive with power tools, the men inside working on a Saturday. Some of them are on harnesses, scaling the unfinished sides, primate agility lost to them. Gareth thinks vaguely of that, and also of the demise of the unions and the lost assurity of time-and-a-half, which makes him ponder injustice, which leads him on to Brendan and how, should he read Adarsh's prize-winning novel, he could take umbrage at the use of his name. He might not even recognise the Brendan character as Gareth but think it is based on himself, name and all. In a moment of unsettling clarity, Gareth sees that he and Brendan are really very similar, the older and younger versions of a certain archetype. Scruffy, disorganised, competitive, prone to long bouts of depression.

Thank you Adarsh for another insight I don't need, he thinks. In fact the novel is full of insights he doesn't appreciate. None of it — the poofters, the religion, the writhing masses — has any bearing on his life. It doesn't touch him. He is a successful writer, whereas both Brendans are not.

He turns into the underground food court next door to the construction site and orders butter chicken and roti.

A writer

All day as Adarsh passed in and out of various events, listening to many writers familiar and newly discovered, he was aware of a thumping bass line muted under the floor of the thronging foyer. 'What is that noise?' people asked one another. 'Can you hear that sound?' Finally, though he could have found it in the programme, he overheard someone say it was Rapnovel Crew and that it was a free event that would run all weekend.

He has to have a look, even though his head is swimming with words and ideas in a sort of soupy exhaustion. He feels almost deaf, a kind of deafness that isn't physical but more from an inability to absorb any more meaning through his ears. The conduit between ear and brain feels blocked. Last night he hadn't got away from the Opus Awards until late, then his local publishers had wanted to take him for a nightcap at a city bar. This morning he'd got up early to have breakfast with his father, and because straight afterwards he'd had 'media', as the Opus publicist called it, he'd missed the Richard Dawkins and Frans de Waal events. Through his interviews he'd found himself repeating the same statements — yes I'm delighted, no I don't live here any more, yes thank you my income is pleasing, no the book is not autobiographical, although it was, of course, in parts, but so far he hasn't had to get down to details. The journalist from the queer newspaper wanted to discuss his queerness in more detail than the others did, and remarked how quaint Adarsh was when he told him it was off-limits and suggested he didn't bother writing the article at all.

It is quaint, Adarsh supposes, as he pushes through the crowds and down the stairs towards the pumping sound. It's also safer. The faithless mouse-haired silver-spooner asking the questions couldn't understand why Adarsh didn't want any more exposure than his father was only just able to cope with, his father who hadn't read the book and never would. Over breakfast the old man had been silent and sad and his sisters standoffish. One of them had asked why he hadn't invited his family along to the awards; the other said that they hadn't understood quite how important the Opus was. Adarsh had shrugged — it wouldn't have been difficult for them to find out. They would have found out, if they'd been that interested.

On the stairs the noise is louder, a man's voice percussive, a driving beat-box, screeching brakes and beeps and bops and sirens laid in. A woman passes him, saying to her friend, 'What *is* that? It should be in the Fringe. Ghastly.'

The stairs leads him down to an open terrace slick with the afternoon's rain. Crowds of young people, mostly men, mostly in black puffer jackets and baggy pants, gather in clouds of cigarette smoke and something more pungent. Synth, he supposes, since this country was foolish enough to keep it legal for long enough for massive stockpiles to be laid up. How fucked was the government with its rule of thumb that nothing should stand in the way of commerce, even if it could destroy whole communities? One night in Delhi, feeling homesick, he'd live-streamed a news report that showed a queue of people outside a synth outlet in a provincial town wracked with unemployment and violence, every shop window roller-doored. Should he write about that? Write to change the world? Is that what you were supposed to do; was that the ideal, if you were as lucky as he was to be able to afford to write? To illuminate the human spirit more than express your inner self? To give hope even when you see none? To give the voiceless a voice . . . only everyone has a voice now. Don't they?

And this one is bloody loud.

He passes through the groups, avoiding the challenging stare of various dudes. The only Indian in sight. 'Curry,' says one as he goes by, eyes down.

But he's here now, run the gauntlet, pressed up against the wall not by the crowds but the volume. On the stage a caramel youth wrapped in electrical cords, the plugs swinging wildly around him, writhes in a red light, howling into the microphone. The rest of the crew are dimly lit in the background, hissing and thumping, stamping their feet, all of them tied up in leads like the soloist. The howling gives way to words, urgent, quieter, less distorted. Adarsh can't make them out — they're in Maori and he never garnered any more than he learned in primary school.

The crew are more in the gloom than the audience: skylights are set into the low roof of what is really, he sees, just a temporarily closed-in carpark. A canvas wall flaps like a sail and the less populated far end is open to the elements, concrete floor puddled, skirls of rain blowing in over the painted lines.

It's not a huge crowd — about the same number as are gathered outside. A hundred? The first two rows are full and in the middle gather a group of girls attempting conversation, yelling into one another's ears, having rearranged the chairs to make it more convivial. There's a bunch of dancers at the corner of the stage, a woman amongst them dancing with a boy of about ten, who is all in black leathers. A huge PI guy stands with his arm around a tiny ginge, who looks like Sophie Salter but isn't. And there are some other 'curries' in a group of tattooed mates of every colour, covertly passing a silver hip flask.

Maybe he should take up drinking, Adarsh thinks. He never has. It could break the monotony. If that's what this is. He heaves a sigh. There's a cultivated air of boredom. Infectious.

Up on stage the screaming djin gives it away, stepping backwards into the gloom — another rapper steps forward into the light. Tosh, breaking free of his electrical wires. Whom he hasn't seen since the end of the writing course. Since that party at Merle's. Who would have known then that he was onto something that had legs, that would generate so much attention? A hundred or so is a healthy enough audience for such a long event. He realises that the youthful crowd he'd seen spilling out into the square on return from his interviews would have been overflow for this, for wild-haired Tosh, who is pointing into the crowd directly at Adarsh and then giving him the thumbs-up and a grin.

He's pleased he's here.

'All hail the King of the Book,' Tosh says. 'All hail the King of the Book. Rangatira pukapuka. Tena koe Adarsh Z. Kar!'

Heads turn and Tosh leads the applause. It's not what Adarsh wants, even though he knows Tosh has welcomed him with the kindest of intentions. A guy standing close to him shakes his hand — or rather his arm, taking hold of him above the wrist and pulling him nose to nose. Adarsh's face burns and his stomach roils. He wants to get out now, as soon as possible. Two of the girls sitting in the convivial arrangement are standing up and walking towards him. Is this what celebrity is? Why does everyone want it? He wants to be anonymous. It's important for a writer to be anonymous. The girls look freezing, in small clothes.

On stage Tosh executes a vigorous pirouette and returns to his mic to begin what is presumably the next chapter of *Rapnovel*, in English this time, writhing and gesticulating while his crew in the semi-circle behind him fall in and out of the narration, drumming and stamping.

> Godman says: Jesus save our souls
> every nigga that falls
> every gangster in the mall.
> Call the pigs!
> Got no business with dem,
> got no shelter from the rain, unleash the pain
> Here it come burning bright,
> singe da wings, fly into light.
> Fire. Flame.
> Here's the pigs — hey,
> youse know my name!
> Family connection.
> Old man's in correction—

The girls are almost upon him.

> —famous for his crime, crystal sublime,
> cooked it sold it fucked in the head from it—

'Hey. Did you win the thing? That big prize for writing a book?' shouts one of the girls.

He nods, taking a step to one side and glancing towards the exit. On cue, two cops have appeared in the doorway. He supposes they're cops — they look genuine enough. Or maybe they're members of Tosh's cast in costume.

'Did you win it?' shouts the other girl. She's gazing at him appreciatively, and Adarsh can see that she sees a handsome famous man and nothing of what he really is. He's a fish out of water. Again. 'What did you get for it?'

> They've stolen our land, imprisoned our men,
> Rise up, rise up and fight, says Tosh-man
> Lie down, lie down and die, says Godman
> Pigman say oink
> say oink
> say oink—

Tosh holds the mic out to the crowd and they join him, 'Oink oink oink!'

> — steal your freedom, fuck your ambition
> die from drugs, die from religion, fast cars and women —
> die young gantsta, like your brothers on the road,
> in the jails, E.D. and custody,
> violence and corpulence,
> viruses and vagrance.
> Rise up rise up —
> Pigman say oink
> Say oink
> Say oink
> Say oink oink oink —

No, they are real cops. Too straight-looking, too neat and tidy, moving now towards the stage. The crowd is clearing around them — four more are coming in at the open end, where a chill wind blows fresh rain.

The voices rise with the chorus, 'Oink oink oink!' There are snorts and thumps and the cops are being jostled. One loses his cap.

As fast as he can without breaking into a run, Adarsh heads towards the exit — there's a blur of fists, a collapsing of bodies, eddies of movement swirling in the wider room — and squeezes through the incoming crowd pushing to see the action. At his back Tosh abandons the microphone, and a high, keening woman's voice rises eerie and strong in karanga new or borrowed over frenetic drumbeat. Outside, a patrol car and police van sit in the square, and Rae is flying down the exterior stairs, a stricken expression on her face.

'What's going on?' she asks as she passes him.

Adarsh shrugs — she can find out for herself. He doesn't want to be the one to tell her.

Hard on Rae's heels is an older Asian gentleman, who looks as anxious as she does, as if the festival is also his personal concern. He lays a hand in the small of Rae's back.

Upstairs Adarsh glances through his programme. He's arrived just in time to hear Sophie Salter in conversation about the process of writing *E* and why she did it, what difficulties plagued her and how she persisted, the reading she had to do and what joy there was in her headiest moments of creation, what she hopes people will take from it and how she must acknowledge with deepest gratitude Ernest Vincent Wright's 1939 novel *Gadsby — A Story of Over 50,000 Words Without Using the Letter 'E'*, but he passes up the opportunity to witness any possible confession to plagiarism and goes out into the dusk, pulling his iPhone from his pocket. There are a couple of old school friends he might still have contacts for, downloaded from device to device over the years he's been away. One happily married in the suburbs with small children and working in IT. The other a courier as gay as a robin, still firmly in the closet and fending off wives suggested by his mother. Both of them funny, sensible, down-to-earth, wise-cracking. They used to have some good times, the three of them, didn't they? Wouldn't it be blissful to abandon his writer-self for a while, to be in their world where books never mattered much and would only matter less? With luck they've never heard of the Opus and have no idea what a writers' festival is.

He tries their numbers, one after another.

A writer

'**B**it of a scuffle at the writers' fest yesterday,' says Brendan as he brings in her morning cup of tea.

Merle hears the word 'scuffle' and imagines a verbal discussion got out of hand — two drunken poets, or an atheist and a Muslim, or a feminist and the much-married Australian. Who knows? Festivals bring together diametrically opposed thinkers of every persuasion. She makes no response, being occupied in trying to extract Parry, who has seized the absence offered by Brendan's tea-making to burrow between the sheets to the foot of the bed.

'D'ya hear me, love? A scuffle. Fisticuffs. Came over the radio on the morning news.'

Merle gives up. Parry is weighty and recalcitrant and, besides, her feet are cold and he's lovely and warm. She takes her tea, still not properly awake. Her heart is racing, she supposes because she went from a comatose state to wrestling a large dog in the space of about two seconds.

'Who hit who?'

'Wasn't much. Over in a flash. At Tosh's thing. Sounds like he incited it and then a young woman sang to calm it all down.'

'Our Tosh?'

'There's only one Tosh these days, isn't there?' Brendan climbs back into bed and Merle makes way for his feet on Parry's warm body. 'Bloody famous in New Zealand.'

'Anyone hurt?'

'Don't know. But Tosh could be in trouble, couldn't he? Inciting a riot?'

'Don't believe he did. I saw some of his stuff earlier in the afternoon. He was preaching love and tolerance then — how we all have to love and help one another while the planet implodes around us. "Plastic sand, plastic sand, per square metre a hundred thousand grains." That was the chorus. He was saving the world.'

'Cheers to that then,' says Brendan. 'And that's a fact. Plastic sand. They studied one of our beaches and came up with that figure. The triumph of pseudo-oestrogens in the biosphere.'

It's too early in the morning for such misery. Merle's stomach drops, her heart twists. Poor old world.

'Do you remember . . .' she starts. But he won't. He remembers so little of what's gone on between them over the years. She could remind him of how they made a pact one evening during their forties that they would no longer terrify one another with deathy depressing facts; that together they'd occupy a sensibility where the parlous state of the environment and the global reach of corporate capitalism was acknowledged but as background. In the foreground would be curiosity and quests and adventures and being good parents to Jack, who was a teenager then. Love and laughter, good food and merriment. Merle sighs.

'Maybe you should ring Rae?' Brendan says. The edge of his foot is icy against hers. She shifts further up the dog.

'What for?'

'Well, you know. The police came and everything. She'll be upset.' Brendan yawns, finishes his tea and opens the Sunday paper.

She won't ring Rae. Not today anyway. She'll be flat out even without having to deal with Tosh and whatever happened at his event. Surely not a riot. Merle reaches for her phone and texts 'Heard the news. Hope you're ok.'

'I'm going to see Jacinta this morning,' she tells Brendan, who gives no indication of having heard her.

Merle slips out of bed, showers, dresses, deals with the morning chores and sets off in her car — hardly out of the garage these days for reasons personal and political — and drives over to Jacinta's place. On the passenger seat are the page proofs of *Roadside Crosses*, and scarcely formed in her head is a plan of how to approach her proposal.

Park under the tree beside my car, Jacinta had told her, so she does, drawing up by the lolling swing. A motley teddy bear the size of a three-year-old child is tethered to the seat, rainlashed on his western side, gently steaming in the sun. The sky showing above Jacinta's roof is streaked with blue. Jacinta and Rae's roof, she supposes it is. Jacinta and Rae's garden. Who would have thought? Rae's part of the house is closed up — she will be at the venue already.

Jacinta's door stands open and Jas is coming down the hall with a bag over her shoulder, woolly hat and battered old trousers, as fresh as the cool winter day outside.

'I'm just off. Said I'd help my pop in his garden.'

Merle nods — hello — and wonders if she should offer her congratulations on the rapprochement. She hadn't known they were back together until she saw them at the psychic event.

'She's through there.' Jas points up the hall to the bedroom.

Merle hadn't thought that there could be anyone else here other than Venice and Lila, but the children are nowhere in evidence, and Jas is taking her leave. The flat is tidy and calm. A hopeful sign that this will go smoothly. In the night she had woken to the sudden alarming possibility that Jacinta and Sandy from Scribblybark could come face to face over the weekend, or that they already had; she got back to sleep only by assuring herself that there were literally thousands of people passing in and out all day and that a chance introduction was unlikely.

This idea is completely crazy, thinks Merle. What on earth am I doing?

'Bye, darling!' calls Jas, slamming the door after her.

In the dimly lit bedroom Jacinta lies limpid and languid, tousled among her pillows. The room is scented, warm, a sandalwood candle burning on the mantelpiece.

'Hi, Merle. Sorry I'm not up. You don't need anything, do you? Coffee or tea?'

Nothing would be nicer than a coffee, but she demurs since that would mean Jacinta would have to rise and plainly she doesn't want to. She's stretching her bare arms luxuriously, her elbows bendy enough to be almost double-jointed, Merle notices for the first time. Aren't double-jointed people supposed to be very amenable?

'I'm fine.'

'What's this all about? Your text last night was very mysterious.'

'Where are the kids?' Merle sits down on the bed with the proofs on her knee, face down. Like a child about to be spanked. A very naughty child it is.

'With Herman. It's his weekend. Luckily, since it's the festival.'

What if Jacinta says no? She's obviously back with Jas, she's got the twins and a tricky custody deal with her ex, who could take them off her if she stays away too long or too often.

A flash in the pan, she reminds herself. That's all Kyla's book will be. So many thousands are published every year; it'll be swamped by the tidal wave. Sandy's excitement and support are infectious but have to be kept in perspective.

'What's that?' Jacinta asks, tapping *Roadside Crosses*.

The moment has come. Merle takes a deep breath and begins, not with the invention of Kyla Mahon but with what came before that. 'You know — or perhaps you don't — the year after you did the writing course, I finished my sixth novel and sent it away to the company that published my earlier books.'

Already Jacinta looks bored.

Merle hurries on. 'But they rejected it. They said they would have rejected it even if they'd liked it, that I had fallen off their lists because my others didn't sell enough.'

'Oh,' says Jacinta. 'Poor you.'

'Yes, poor me. So . . . a little while after that, Brendan and I went for a holiday in Australia and while I was there I was struck with inspiration — not so much for a book but a character, a character who would write the book.'

'A pseudonym,' says Jacinta, helpfully.

'Exactly. And then—'

On the bedside table Jacinta's phone croaks like a frog. Herman, presumably, because she's making arrangements to collect the twins at five o'clock. 'I'm going to an event at the writers' festival,' she tells him quickly, 'a panel of publishers from overseas.'

Merle does not want Jacinta to go to that event. She must not. So far, so lucky. It seems Herman isn't interested in his ex-wife's plans for the afternoon and why she'll be late for the kids. The conversation ends abruptly, Jacinta not even bothering to say goodbye.

The phone is tossed on to the pillows and Jacinta looks at Merle, a little resentfully perhaps. It is Sunday morning after all. Merle wouldn't have felt anything like the urgency for this meeting if she hadn't seen Sandy yesterday.

'I hope Jas didn't leave on my account,' Merle says.

'No, no. She was . . . oh, you know. She's always got something else more important to do than hang around with me. Hurry up. What do you want?' Jacinta throws off the covers and gets out of bed, starkers, beautiful, and pulls on a red dressing gown. 'I'm making coffee.'

Meekly, Merle follows her down to the tiny kitchen where wholemeal bread is set to rise on the counter and a piece of paper taped to the fridge has in pink felt-tip a handwritten aphorism: 'Your Thoughts of Today Create Your Tomorrow! Be Happy!' Jacinta bangs about with the coffee pot and cups.

'And yes,' Merle goes on, trying to keep out of her way, 'so I came back home and wrote a book called *Roadside Crosses* by Kyla Mahon. Then I sent it to a publisher and they accepted it. There is a . . . um . . .' Her natural modesty prevents her from going on. Yes, that is what it is, she supposes. Natural modesty. And fear.

'What?' Jacinta is running the tap, the column of water sparkling in the easterly light from the window.

'There's a buzz. So I'm told. Now, the thing is . . .' She steps aside so that milk can be removed from the fridge, and loses her impetus.

'Cold milk okay?'

'Yes, of course.'

'Merle, I really can't see how any of this has anything to do with me.'

'The thing is, they asked me for an author photo so I sent them one of you.' There. It's out. Merle feels nauseous with the effort.

'You did what?' Jacinta's face is suddenly almost the same colour as her dressing gown.

'I'm sorry. I shouldn't have. I should have asked you.'

'Yes. You're bloody right you should have asked me.'

There's a pause while Merle tries to gather the courage to go on, but then Jacinta is asking, 'Is it obviously me? The photo?'

'I should say so.' But not obviously Kyla, she would like to say. Jacinta shakes her head in disbelief.

'What will happen when I publish my own book? Won't it be

really odd that two writers look exactly the same?'

Merle hadn't anticipated this line of questioning.

'Has your book been accepted?'

'No. As it happens. Not yet. But I'm thinking of putting it up in the cloud.'

'By the time it is published, Kyla Mahon will be long forgotten.'

'Is that it?' Jacinta points at the folder in Merle's arms. 'The book?'

'What I'm proposing is . . . you see, the publisher would like to meet you.'

'Me?'

'Kyla.'

'Meet me where? Her, I mean.'

'Melbourne. Kyla doesn't live in Melbourne — so you could go there at my expense and for a liberal fee — and be her. Be Kyla.'

'This is nutbar, Merle.' Jacinta turns her back on her, pours the coffee.

'No, it's not.' More urgency. 'The book has sold into the American and European markets. Germaine Greer wrote an endorsement. You could have the trip of a lifetime.'

'Pretending all the time I'm someone else? For a book I didn't even write?'

'Yes. You would have to travel under your own name of course. We would insist that Kyla does all her own bookings. She's very secretive. Nomadic. Independent. Refuses to give a physical address. She has an email account and post office box.'

'I would have to read the book.'

'You would.'

'Know it backwards.'

'And inside out.'

'And you'd pay me?'

'Yes. A lot. The advance is generous, amazingly. It goes to show — when they want a book they really want it.'

'I used to want to be an actor,' says Jacinta, dreamily, 'but I did music. And then writing.'

'You see. You're a performer. A natural.' Encouragement, flattery.

'What's she like, this Kyla? Don't tell me you based her on me!'

'Nothing could be further from the truth,' Merle tells her. 'Although you do have similarities. Grew up in England. Tough.

Smart. Likeable. Capable. Brave.'

Jacinta smiles then, for the first time since Merle arrived.

'How long have I got to think about it?'

Merle shrugs. 'Not long.'

'What if I won't do it? What will you do then?'

'Kyla will have to disappear. Go bush. I don't know.' Merle holds out the folder and Jacinta opens it to look at the front page and a copy of the press release from the American publisher.

'The next *Eat Pray Love*. Wow.'

'Don't believe it. It's all bullshit.'

'Might not be.' Jacinta is reading the first paragraph intently.

'You can't tell anyone, Jacinta. You have to keep it to yourself. Not even Jas, or anyone.'

'Have you told Brendan?'

'No.' The guilt. 'No, I haven't.'

'Not about the money, or anything?'

Merle sips her coffee, changes the subject. 'You're making bread.'

'Jas did that. She's a cook and a gardener and a total darling. You should get yourself a girlfriend, Merle. Give old fatguts the shove.'

'I love Brendan,' Merle says, quelling outrage. If she didn't want this thing from Jacinta, this risk and pretence and experiment, she'd slam her coffee down and march out.

The perfect arches of Jacinta's eyebrows are raised in disbelief and her cheeks have coloured a little as if she knows she's gone too far.

'Well, I've never been happier, that's for sure.' She sounds less English, as if she's made a concerted effort to ditch the accent. There's the upward inflexion, the dulling of vowels.

'Good. I'm pleased.' Merle puts her cup down very gently.

'Have you ever? Gone with a girl?' The English accent is back again.

Merle doesn't want to talk about sexuality right now. She wants an answer. If it's a no, she'll have to meet with Sandy, she'll have to tell her the truth: the book was written by a woman whom no one has any cause to be interested in. She knows that because years ago she overheard a conversation between her publisher and a publicist from the same firm. They were supposed to be discussing publicity for Merle's third novel but the subject had switched for a moment to a Canadian writer who was married and lived a quiet middle-class life in a small town with her healthy, normal family. The publisher wanted to tour her, the publicist said, 'But she has no hook. She has no story!' and Merle had said, butting in because she knew this writer's work, 'But she's written lots of beautiful stories!' and the two women had cut the conversation short to return to the book at hand. For Merle it had been a loss of innocence and a wake-up call. In those days she was young, adventurous and causing a stir, writing a lot about sexuality and sex with relish and verve. And here she is all these years later, without a story, without a hook.

'You know, Jacinta, if you say yes you could have a fabulous time. If you read the book and think about it, and you and I talk more, and you really consider whether or not you want to do this, or whether you actually *can* do it — then we'll make a decision. Who knows — there could be a book in it for you later. *My Life as Kyla Mahon*.'

Jacinta nods. 'Yes. I already thought of that.'

Good girl, thinks Merle. You do that. Lay claim. 'In the meantime . . . would you mind not going to the event this afternoon. The publisher will be there. If you somehow come face to face, then it's all over.'

'But I've paid for my ticket! And it's in the main auditorium so there'll be hundreds there. I'm going, Merle.'

'What if she sees you?'

'She won't.'

'She might. You do draw the eye, Jass. You must know that about yourself.'

Jacinta smiles again, delighted. 'Do I? Really? Still? I mean, when I was younger, but I'm thirty-seven now. Getting old.'

'Hardly,' says Merle, fifty-eight in October.

'I could go in disguise. That's what I could do! I'm going on my own, so I don't need to explain to anyone, and if I meet up with someone I know then I can just make a joke of it. The wig and whatever.'

'Where are you going to get a wig from today?'

'Umm . . .' Jacinta thinks. 'Friend. Woman about your age having chemo. She only came out a year ago, Merle. It's not too late. She's got a lovely girlfriend. You could too.' Jacinta downs her coffee and turns to the tap to fill her cup with water, which she drinks noisily.

The fervour of the newly converted. 'I think I'll be with Brendan forever now, love.'

'How do you know? You could be as happy as me. You should try it. Have you ever? You can't die without trying it.'

She really wants to know, so Merle says, 'I thought I might have been a lesbian, years ago. A political lesbian. That's what we called them in the late seventies, women who had sworn off men for political reasons only. But one day I heard a man singing with a guitar in the street and the way his voice went through me . . . I knew then.'

Jacinta is looking at her as if she's insane. 'His voice?'

'It was one of those moments when you learn something about yourself by the simplest of means.'

'Huh. Is Kyla queer?'

'Could be,' says Merle, carefully. 'She's had one or two relationships with men in the past. You could present her that way. Up to you. You have to own her in the present tense.'

Jacinta walks past her, carrying the folder. 'I'll get reading then, shall I?' She lays it on the table.

'When—' begins Merle, and Jacinta interrupts, 'Tomorrow. Or the day after. I might have to tell Jas, Merle. I really will. It's a big thing to keep all to myself.'

'It might not be big. It might be just one trip to Australia and then all over. The book could fade and die.'

'All right. If I do it, big if, and if it's more than that, if it takes off, then I'll have to tell her.'

'Not till then. But yes, I can see that you might have to.'

Jacinta has found the page with the author photograph. 'Oh! I remember you taking that. That day I came round all upset and cried and cried . . . I don't look as though I've been bawling though, do I?' Something occurs to her. 'Have you had this planned since then?'

'No. Look — I know this is bizarre. It was something I did without thinking it through.'

Jacinta is suddenly sympathetic. 'Don't worry, Merle. I am interested. Fascinated, in fact. It could be a lark.' Very English. Then she says in her new, tougher voice, 'And you and me, baby, we could ride this horse till it falls over.' Almost Kyla-ish. 'I'll be in touch.'

She leaves Jacinta opening the folder at the table, and drives home with her heart racing again. She and Bren could have a competition to see whose heart is the dickiest, whose is the most deceitful. She will have to tell him what she's done, she will, but only if the book takes off. Only then.

The house is empty, the new lodger out and a note from Brendan on the table — 'Taken P to the park.' Merle goes through to the living room and lies on the saggy sofa, closing her eyes and seeing only Jacinta bent over the table reading Kyla's book.

If she has to come clean with Sandy, it will be too late to pull it. Sandy will have to be in on it, willingly or not, and *Roadside Crosses* will go out on its truncated journey to terminate in a minor literary scandal. Then I could write a piece for the *Listener* or *Metro* on why I did it, thinks Merle, a piece on the dropping of older women writers from the lists, on the celebrity culture in publishing, on the pursuit of a younger demographic — if, that is, she could be bothered.

One day at a time. There is no telling what is going to happen next week, the week after. For a minute or two she feels completely overwhelmed and has to concentrate on breathing, on staying calm, and on how peaceful it is here on the couch with the old house creaking around her and the sound of children playing in a nearby garden. She breathes, tries to remember half-forgotten meditation techniques learned in yoga classes thirty years ago. The rose. A red dot in the solar plexus that slowly slowly with each breath grows into a rose bud and then blooms to its full scarlet beauty. Finally she falls deeply and gratefully asleep, waking only when Parry, covered in mud, comes back from the park and leaps joyously on top of her.

The director

Rae had hoped, this year, to be so well organised that she would be free to wander in and out of events, to stand quietly at the back for long enough to see what worked and what didn't, to scribble notes about the proficiency of chairpersons and the relative success of presentations, especially the digital ones. There was a five-minute loss of connection when George R.R. Martin was beamed in for two thousand impatient Thronies; the marine biologist illustrated his doleful hour with murky clips of giant jellyfish billowing through dead ocean zones. The Norwegian mythic poet entertained a tiny but appreciative audience with blurry animations of Nordic gods major and minor cut with music to accompany his verse.

They were the only fault reports she'd had so far, though she'd seen nothing of the actual events. Since the Rapnovel Crew brawl happened yesterday afternoon, her phone had rung hot with patrons and sponsors and the festival lawyer and journalists and board members and her mother. She was tempted after the twentieth call to leave a message, 'Please be reassured that the festival is doing all it can to ease the situation,' so that she didn't have to repeat herself over and over again.

And now, escaping wickedly — for half an hour tops — hurrying across the square away from the venue, she turns her phone off altogether. Wang will be waiting for her as arranged, at an outside table at the café on the far side. Half an hour, sorry, she'd told him, which would be just long enough for her to give him an answer on his proposed pilgrimage to Berlin. How could she possibly say yes? The kids, the job, the fact she hardly knows him. But what if he's offering to pay for her to go with him? That part hadn't been clear. And if he was offering, then he could be doubly offended by her refusal. It could be the end of their association.

At the mouth of subterranean stairs to an underground carpark she passes Jacinta wearing a wig and dark glasses. If she wasn't in such a hurry, Rae would stop and ask her, What's with the wig? but Jacinta doesn't seem to have seen her, her eyesight presumably impeded by the sunglasses in the wintry light. She only just avoids the strut of a steel sculpture set in her direct path.

Rae strides on — now she can see Xu Wang waiting, a teapot and two cups on the table, and he's smoking. It's the only thing she doesn't like about him. She doesn't mind that he dresses like an American teenager or the disparity in their heights. And why would she mind that, since they're only friends — not even that, acquaintances. The dream kiss comes back to her as she greets him — they were about the same height, lip to lip, and he didn't smell of cigarettes. How embarrassing.

'I meant to ask you ages ago if you had any response to your article about Liu Wah,' she finds herself saying because she can't say, straight away, that she won't come with him to Germany.

Wang nods, vigorously, setting the crockery rattling. 'Yes, I did. Emails and phone calls, et cetera. One woman all in tears — she said that for her to have met him would have been the culmination of her youthful hopes and ambition.'

Perhaps she's the one you should be taking to Europe, Rae thinks but doesn't say.

'But best of all was hearing from Liu Wah himself after he saw it online. That's when he invited me.' He is grinning so delightedly that Rae can't help smiling too, and when their eyes meet she sees there not only his good humour and optimism but also his regard for her. And desire. Is it desire? Why would he want her, exactly?

A little tremor runs through her, delicious, anticipatory, unwelcome. Too complicated.

He leans across the table and takes her hand. 'You see, we are about to embark together on an exciting adventure. Who knows where it takes us?'

'Wang . . . I'm not sure that I can—' Rae starts, but he is going on.

'There are other exiles in Germany, not all of them from China of course, but I am thinking that for you it will be a business trip. You will gather inspiration. You will meet other writers.'

Rae can't think of a reply. Instead, she looks at her watch, which Wang sees her do — and removes his hand.

'I haven't decided yet,' she blurts. 'I'm so sorry. When were you thinking of going?'

'Soon. August.'

'August is high season. It'll be expensive.'

'I have some money. Enough for both of us.' He maintains his cooler tone.

'I don't expect you to pay for me. The problem is I have the children to think of and I'm not sure if I'll get leave — and yes of course it does worry me, the money thing. And the carbon.'

'Lots of problems, then,' says Wang, nodding but smiling now, 'and all of them to dismiss, one by one.'

'I don't know.' She should be heading back. She shouldn't even be here. She turns her phone on. Four messages.

'Do you want to come?' he asks softly. 'Only three weeks, not long.' He tips his baseball cap back on his head and lifts her hand and kisses it. There is a long, faded scar at his hairline, something she hadn't noticed before. One day she might learn how he got it, whether it dates from that long-ago uprising when he and Liu Wah were cellmates. 'Please decide to come on the journey with me. I would like to share it with you.'

She so wants to say yes, but lifts her gaze away from him and sees at a nearby table, all by herself, Sophie Salter, who is filming the surrounding scene on her phone. Sophie pans across the outdoor café, across Rae and Wang sitting at the table, and returns its orbiting arc to herself, talking earnestly all the time. Not filming then, just showing a friend where in the world she is. In a square, in a city at the bottom of the world, at a writers' festival. Wang hasn't noticed what she's doing — which is a good thing. He would be alarmed by her surveillance. Or would he be? How can we be concerned about that now, when everyone has that extra recording eye? It's pointless to worry. Or is that an opinion born of naïveté and privilege, of spending all of her life in constitutional democracies?

'Can your husband take care of the children?' Wang is asking. 'What are their names, by the way? You have never told me!'

'Ned and Nellie,' she says. 'Seven and five. Only little.'

'But they have a father still?'

Rae nods. They do, with a girlfriend she could never approve of. But if she asks Merle to take them sometimes, and her mother, and keeps the children to their normal routine of every second weekend with Cameron — which after all is all he wants — then maybe it would not be too disruptive.

'Then you can't say no. The festival boss would like you to go. What do they call it? Professional development.'

I am the boss, she would like to say. Me and the board. And Orla. She'd forgotten about Orla, who might not approve of Rae vanishing for three weeks.

Wang is standing and moving his chair around the table, closer to Rae. He sits down and puts his arm around her waist, kissing her on the cheek. She turns to him and kisses him properly on the mouth, quickly.

'Okay, you're on. I'll do my best to be with you. I'll try.'

She would get up then, and hurry back to the last hour of the festival for the year, but Wang is kissing her again and she's thinking about how they are the same height when they're sitting down and that he does taste a little like cigarettes but it doesn't bother her as much as she would have thought.

AFTER THE FESTIVAL

The writers

I

Adarsh, waiting at an airport for yet another plane, is reading the novel he bought at a second-hand bookshop, *The Hamilton Case* by Michelle de Kretser. 'Life is bearable only if it can be understood as a set of narrative strategies,' she writes, and Adarsh realises, as he commits the statement to memory, that it will be one of those ideas that helps him to survive. All of this, before, later, now — all of it could be narrative, no more no less, with strategies come about from perspective and time.

He feels inspired to write, though what about right at this moment? The book put away, he sets himself the exercise of describing a transit lounge — the wide windows onto the tarmac, the crush of bodies, the atolls of carpet set in seas of shining floors, the uniformed attendants, the low furniture, the annoying repetitive warnings and announcements . . . but after a few sentences wonders why any writer would bother. Every contemporary reader knows what an international airport looks like; even if he or she hasn't personally been inside one they've seen it on television and in films. There's no need to draw on his powers of descriptive language. A character may venture to the check-in and through Customs with no call for the writer to employ a single adjective other than those required to describe his mood. Apply a narrative strategy.

He turns off his battered Notebook and gazes at the lumbering airbus loading beyond the gate, the means of his next stage of escape. On his last morning at home his father had asked him when he would return and how soon, and his younger sister had wept as he'd climbed into the taxi. He'd left them a copy of his novel, since they had not yet bought one, and he hopes they will read it, that they will come to know him by it. Perhaps one of them is reading it right now while he makes the long journey to Europe, to meet his new lover in Italy, a country he has never before visited. He will stay in his lover's apartment in Milan, he will enter a new world of glamour and privilege, he will be alert to all of it. At his solo session at the festival, which had sold out the morning after he won the Opus, a man had risen from the floor and asked him if he had been concerned for his safety in Delhi.

'I don't understand the question,' he'd replied, though he had of course. Delhi had woken him up out of complacence. It had given him an edge. It had brought survival skills to the surface, skills he didn't know he had, useful for ever.

Another question, from a woman, was about how much he had drawn on his own life to write his novel. In answer he'd quoted the Canadian writer Robertson Davies: 'Asking a writer if his work is autobiographical is like asking a spider where he buys his thread.' A third query came from someone else curious about what he was writing now, which he refused to answer. His earnest interlocutor spoke for him, saying it was common for writers to dislike talking about works in progress.

He had been fairly graceless, he thought now, bad-tempered, because he was stung by Gareth's refusal to chair the session and his later avoidance of him not only at the party but throughout the whole weekend. It had made him perplexed and irritable. Gareth should have been proud of him. He should have offered his congratulations.

The airline staff was calling now for row numbers that included his. Before joining the queue, he went close to the window that gave a view of Victoria Peak at the centre of Hong Kong Island and thought he could just make out, through the murky air among the towers, the hotel he'd stayed in when he was last here, where he'd swum in the roof pool and fallen into limerence.

Limerence is all it is now, he thinks, clutching his boarding pass and joining the line. One day it might be love.

II

'Don't expect me to be giving you progress reports every five minutes,' Jacinta had told Merle, as a parting shot. Merle didn't, but wishes now that she had made an arrangement for Jacinta to contact her after today's meeting with Sandy, one o'clock local time, 11 a.m. in Melbourne. She is fretting about it, imagining the worst: Sandy suspecting and asking difficult questions, Jacinta losing it and blowing the gaff. Surely the hours she'd spent with her going over and over the book would pay off, the quizzing, the coaching. In the end Merle had almost begun to believe that Jacinta had written *Roadside Crosses* herself, so convincing were her pronouncements on the work, on Kyla's life before she wrote the book, on what she was doing now. Living in an isolated outback location, Jacinta had decided, alone with her dog and horse, no phone, no internet, the nearest wifi eighty kilometres away.

There is no time to be fretting, anyway. Merle has ended up with all four children — Ned and Nellie, Venice and Lila — a day of crossover before their fathers take over. Yesterday Rae had left on her mysterious overseas trip, ostensibly talent-scouting for the next festival. There was nothing mysterious about where she is actually going, Merle has the itinerary — Berlin, London, home via New York to see old friends — but she suspects Rae isn't travelling alone. There is a new glow to her, a softness, a happiness that wasn't there before.

'Has Mum got a new boyfriend?' she would like to ask Ned or Nellie, but abstains. It really is none of her business.

'My God, what's going on?' Brendan had said this morning, when the twins arrived. 'Are you running a blimmin' children's home?'

Soon after, he had gone out to the local library, in search of peace, so that he could put the finishing touches to his book due out early next year, with an accompanying CD.

Lunchtime and the children sit at the table, working their way through an enormous mound of cheese on toast. Merle sits with them, listening to their chatter and laughter, and trying not to dwell on Kyla's distant fate. Ned feeds Parry his crusts, Lila gets the giggles and sprays crumbs all over the table, Nellie and Venice continue with an imaginary game where both are princesses in a magical land and Parry is a handsome prince changed into a smelly dog by a vindictive witch. Merle tries to enter the game too, offering even to take the role of the witch, but Venice tells her firmly that grown-ups don't play games.

Little do you know, thinks Merle.

III

In London, Gareth finds himself now and again thinking about Jacinta, how during their time together he had sometimes imagined her life here; how he had envied her for coming from the land of his presumed forefathers, from a bigger population base, where he might have had more of a chance of making it earlier, bigger, brighter. Where he might have not endured his twenties wracked with guilt about being a member of the land-grabbing colonisers and the privileges bestowed by his gender and race. Where it was easy to get on a plane and fly in the space of an hour to countries where different languages were spoken, where known histories were thousands of years old.

But he is in London for the first time in his life and until a few seconds ago he was loving every minute of it, breathing the gritty air and listening to the voices raised around him that echo with every accent on the globe. He has walked everywhere, avoiding the tube. He has rested up in parks if the weather was fine, or cafés and bars if it's not, and filled notebooks with observations. He has indulged in tourist activities — a boat on the Thames, a tour of the Tower, a spin on the London Eye. He drank one night in a pub that Oscar Wilde frequented, and one morning visited Dickens's house, gazing with a religious kind of fervour at the great man's desk, going so far as to lay a reverential hand on it when the guide wasn't looking. He has seen how the city has been a hotbed for literary imaginations from Shakespeare through to Martin Amis, from Keats to Hari Kunzru, and he has wondered if he could set a novel here. He has wanted so much to belong. Sometimes, in the grip of homesickness, his own city seems to rest just behind his eyes, glittering and fresh, so that this new old place is removed, out of reach. He experiences then the phenomenon shared by his countrymen where the land of his birth shifts perspective, where it seems he views all its idiosyncrasies and beauties and irritations clearly, but minutely, as if he is peering around the curve of the globe through the wrong end of a telescope.

It'll take time, he has often told himself, to feel at home here. And as long as that period doesn't exceed the time it takes him to work through his advance and his inheritance from his father, then the experiment will have been worth it. The experiment to see if, after five generations passing on the other side of the world, he belongs. He has wanted so much to belong.

At least, that was true until today, when as usual he returned from his wanderings through the long, light summer evening to his flat. A garden flat, the rental agency had called it — which meant ground floor, with an asphalt square for his rubbish bin. Mostly he has spent his evenings alone here, trying to finish his third novel, just as he intended to tonight, but he won't now. He won't be able to concentrate. At home, he had told friends and family how he was subsumed by the book, how it had a life of its own, how he often had the eerie feeling when he sat down to write that it had gone on without him. That sense fled on arrival in England. If he were to talk about the book now with anyone — his agent, say, as he'd intended to this afternoon — he'd liken it to a machine he was building. Labour, pure and simple. He has to search for the right tools, the right bolts, pulleys and springs, the steam-punk parts. But his agent does not inquire as to its progress.

Until a few seconds ago he was able to blame this sense of dislocation, of loneliness, on the fact he made the shift too late in life. He should have come years ago, like previous generations of writers did, when they were young. In an email to his half-brother yesterday he had said as much, and Danyon had written back overnight, 'Get over yourself. Make some friends.' 'I've tried,' Gareth wrote back, because soon after he arrived he contacted Sophie Salter. He had assumed, erroneously, that she lived in this city, and might like to meet up again. But she lives in Bristol and did not extend an invitation to him to visit her. Even his agent seems too distracted and busy to make any attempt to welcome him, to settle him in. When Gareth persuaded him to meet for a drink in Russell Square this afternoon, it was only the second time they'd met up. The first time was on Gareth's first day, when he had appeared with no warning in the office and introduced himself. The agent had seemed taken aback.

'Why are you here?' he'd asked, and Gareth had replied, 'To enjoy the fruits of my labours.'

The agent had seen fit to remind him that the second novel had not sold as well as everyone had hoped, though few novels do these days, after all. Later, Gareth had comforted himself by re-reading the reviews, which, as he'd told Merle during the festival, had all been positive.

This afternoon, the hottest day ever recorded in London, he had wanted to talk the third novel up, to tell the agent it was nearly finished, but the conversation had centred on the hoopla surrounding a daft Australian narrative non-fiction by someone called Kyla Mahon, on its wisdom and humour and acceptance of death, and how the literary world was mad for it.

Now Gareth sits at his table in his tiny flat, his laptop open on the table. The sun is going down behind the chimney pots, the couple next door are having a row, a crazed London dog is barking behind a gate. Because Kyla's name had resonated with him, though he couldn't remember where he'd heard it, he is googling her. She will be young, he expects, and good-looking. She will be a writer of great promise and daring.

Her image flies on to the screen, and for a moment or two Gareth can scarcely breathe.

The bitch. It changes everything.

IV

Swinging down Brunswick Street, Melbourne — yes, this is the way Kyla would walk, with almost a swagger — Jacinta is triumphant. She remembers, years ago, explaining to Gareth that she was a born liar, that without any effort at all she could make shit up, and that's why she thought she'd be a good writer. But actually, she realises, she was wrong. She's better at this, at acting. There was not a moment this morning, she could tell, when Sandy suspected she was not the real deal. The *pièce de résistance* was showing her a photograph of a slumpy-roofed outback cottage, complete with a blue heeler on the porch and dusty trail bike in the shade of a gum. 'This is where I live,' she'd told her, and pointed out a window. 'That's where I write.'

'Oh, so you are you writing another book!' Sandy had said. 'I'm so pleased!'

'Yep,' Kyla had answered. 'Early days yet. But it's a sequel to *Roadside Crosses*. Not so deathy this time. More about birth and renewal.'

That was the riskiest thing she'd said for sure, but she supposes that if Merle isn't writing another one then she can do it herself.

'We've had some invitations for you to attend festivals. Would you go? I mean . . . I know you value your solitude and anonymity, but look — Byron Bay, Sydney, Hay-on-Wye. People are very interested in what you've got to say.'

A pub stands with its doors open onto the dusky street and there's a sign, 'The Greyhounds'. Inside two tall skinny dudes in grey suits are setting up with their guitars. Kyla goes in and orders a beer. Jacinta would prefer a red wine, but this is part of her discipline, part of her art. She's been Kyla all day — bought a pair of RM Williams boots and a riding whip with some of the money Merle gave her — and she'll stay as Kyla all night, no matter who she talks to. She'll tell them, even if she has to shout over the top of the skinny dudes, that she's written a bestselling book and that she lives all alone with her horse and her dog in northern Victoria.

'Email's the best way to get hold of me,' she'd told Sandy. 'You know I don't like those phone things. I like to be unconnected, off network.'

And Sandy had murmured, 'So refreshing. Even though it makes life difficult for me. How about getting an Australian agent, and then I can deal with them?'

'Nah,' Kyla had said, 'only adds another complication. Gets like Chinese whispers.'

And Sandy had looked a little uncomfortable because, as Jacinta could tell, she was pretty PC and didn't approve of those kinds of similes.

When it gets crowded at the bar, she takes her beer to a seat up the back and thinks that if she was still straight she could possibly fancy one or other of the tall musicians. Greyhounds like the American bus line, like travel and adventure, which she's having. In spades. Later, when she gets back to the hotel, she'll ring Jas and tell her the truth, not the bullshit tale she'd told her about her mother being sick and having to race back to London to look after her. Maybe Jas could come along to some of those festivals, be in on the game. Why not? It's a free world and getting freer all the time. The twins are happy staying with Merle and they love their dad. Jacinta will hardly be missed. Besides, what did her life amount to, really, if you were going to analyse her achievements? This is the best thing that's ever happened to her.

V

Carrying flowers from the florist on the corner of the Strasse and a box of kiwifruit liqueur chocolates brought all the way from New Zealand, Xu Wang and Rae climb the three flights of stairs to Liu Wah's home. On the U-Bahn from their hotel, Wang had been quiet, holding her hand and shaking his head now and again, as if he could hardly believe they really were about to see his old friend. After Tiananmen Square he and Liu Wah had been kept in the same cell with thirty others, jammed into the airless, stinking space for weeks. When Wang was beaten to within an inch of his life, Wah had helped him as best he could, bathing his cuts and tearing his own shirt to make a bandage. Last night Wang told Rae this for the first time. Told her how after he'd got out he'd encouraged Wah to do the same, but he wouldn't. He loved China. China was his heart and inspiration. He had wanted never to leave.

They are admitted by a helpful young German and taken through to a small, sunny sitting room where Liu Wah himself is rising to greet them, taking Wang's hands and smiling. The friends do their best to include Rae in their conversation, but since it is mostly in Cantonese she understands very little of it. She is not bothered, though, sitting close to Wang through the afternoon and absorbing from him his great happiness and relief. Here is a writer he has loved since they were students, a writer whose fate he has followed closely and championed, despite all opposition. And the writer is healthy and as happy as he could be, living in a land where language and customs are alien to him. When his German friend brings through a tray of tea things, Wah turns to Rae and says, through Wang's interpretation, 'I was so happy to be invited to your festival and very sad that it could not happen this time. Perhaps you will invite me again and I will be able to come.'

For a moment they fall silent, imagining a world where that might be possible. A soft, yielding mood comes upon them all, as if they are children who have just finished listening to a fairy tale with a happy ending. Then Wah laughs, as if he has made a joke, and Wang laughs too, and they slap each other on the back.

Acknowledgements

Thanks to The Orion Group, London, for permission to use the extracts from *Chinese Whispers: Why Everything You've Heard About China is Wrong* by Ben Chu, (London: Weidenfield & Nicolson, 2013) ISBN 9780297868446.

To Creative New Zealand — thank you. I could not have written this novel without your necessary and much appreciated assistance.

Although *The Writers' Festival* is a work of fiction, I would like to acknowledge all those responsible for the establishment of a certain real festival as well as the many others who ensure its continued health and vitality. I hope you will enjoy this entirely imaginary literary knees-up.

Many thanks also to Michael Moynahan, who gave me the benefit of his insight.

Thank you to Graciela Grau for the beautiful 'Neruda' poem and to her son Maximiliano Pierret for helping us to connect.

Thank you to my publisher, Harriet B. Allan, for fighting down the demons and keeping the faith.

Thank you Jane Parkin for your sensitivity, boundless enthusiasm and laughter through the editing process.

And to my darling Tim — thanks for everything else and more. Coo-weh?

ENGLISH TRANSLATION OF THE 'NERUDA' POEM ON PAGE 318

How to speak of love
when your reign is so far away?
And who rules this love
without pity for humans?

Oh celestial heaven!
Your infinite sea!
Where the terrestrial barque,
Filled with vain promises, sinks . . .

Oh celestial heaven!
Your blue relics vibrate,
in the heart of mankind,
and in the germ of love.

Few are the gardeners,
who cultivate that flower.
But when one is born,
It gives the sun its very meaning!

May innocence rise again,
giving light to mysteries!
When will there be a caress,
from the eternal to the mortals?

ALSO BY STEPHANIE JOHNSON

Novels

Crimes of Neglect (1992)

The Heart's Wild Surf (1996, published in the United States
in 2003 as *The Sailmaker's Daughter*)

The Whistler (1998)

Belief (2000)

The Shag Incident (2002)

Music From a Distant Room (2004)

John Tomb's Head (2006)

Swimmers' Rope (2008)

The Open World (2012)

The Writing Class (2013)

Short story collections

The Glass Whittler (1989)

All the Tenderness Left in the World (1993)

Drowned Sprat and Other Stories (2005)

Poetry collections

The Bleeding Ballerina (1986)

Moody Bitch (2003)

THE
WRITING
CLASS

STEPHANIE
JOHNSON

This unique novel is both a compelling love story and an insightful writing manual.

'Writers take what we learn of human nature and, fuelled by our longings for other existences and other times, forge new identities that can be as real as she is, sitting with her dog on the weathered step of the old house, stories that move us to tears or laughter.'

Merle Carbury, an author in her own right, also teaches Creative Writing. Amid the tension of the final semester of the year, her many and varied students prepare to submit their manuscripts. As Merle mentors their assorted ambitions, observes the romantic entanglements of her colleague, worries about her husband and is intrigued by their mysterious German lodger, she both imparts and embodies how to write a novel.

Written by a prize-winning author, who is also an experienced teacher, the overarching intelligence, compassion and wicked humour in this inventive book make it a joy to read.

'Above all, this is a book fuelled and inspired by the act of writing, as lives and minds engage in a highly choreographed human tango.'
— **DOMINION POST, YOUR WEEKEND**

'Stephanie Johnson is a New Zealand author who has an award-winning career. This book should certainly add another accolade to that illustrious line-up.'
— **OAMARU MAIL**

'Beneath it all, shining through, there is the compulsive writer's transparent affection for and bafflement at the craft and business of writing. Also noteworthy is her collegiality: the names of writers are salted throughout, and they are drawn from the canon of the novel, from the ranks of contemporary luminaries and from among Johnson's New Zealand peers with a generous lack of discrimination. If you want to learn about writing, whether by rote or by example, then *The Writing Class* is for you.'
— **WEEKEND HERALD**

'It is a compelling literary work and, since it stems from Johnson's experiences mentoring and teaching creative writing, it is a particularly valuable read for those with creative-writing ambitions . . . richly descriptive with a cast of intricately constructed characters.'
— **SUNDAY STAR-TIMES**

'There are lessons to be learned — about life as well as writing — and Johnson teaches them pithily and well . . . *The Writing Class* would be an informative and entertaining read for anyone interested in the craft; from beginners to published authors, and firmly cements Johnson into place as one of our most accomplished.'
— **HERALD ON SUNDAY**

'For the reader, *The Writing Class* is a delectable novel that needs time and attention to fully appreciate its complexity. For writers, it is a reminder that "some of us are not satisfied with one life — [we] take what we learn of human nature and, fuelled by our longings for other existences and other times, forge new identities".'
— NEW ZEALAND WOMAN'S WEEKLY

'Intelligent, tender and funny, *The Writing Class* is evidence of that quality control.'
— NEW ZEALAND LISTENER

'Stephanie Johnson explores whether writers are born or made in this engaging novel . . . Woven through *The Writing Class* is a lesson on writing that is informative and illuminating; well worth a read.'
— AUSTRALIAN WOMEN'S WEEKLY (NZ)

'I loved the book. Merle is an immensely appealing main character, whose observations of people and life in general made me smile with recognition. The pupils' work examples are cleverly done and a neat fit with their personalities. And I enjoyed the way that, in spite of serious issues, Johnson's humour poked through the novel at often unexpected times.'
— OTAGO DAILY TIMES

'. . . a book that's sophisticated, witty and — best of all — generous in its attitudes to its characters. It's a love letter to reading and writing and things readers and writers share, especially the mutual effort to understand the world and the people in it.'
— NORTH & SOUTH

'*The Writing Class* is not only entertaining, but also refreshing.'
— TIMARU HERALD

For more information about our titles, go to
www.penguinrandomhouse.co.nz